REVENIRE

HUNTER'S MOON (VOLUME 4)

RAMÓN TERRELL

ISBN: 978-1-9990903-7-1 (Paperback)
Tal Publishing
Published by Tal Publishing Vancouver BC
ebook Edition: September 2020
First Edition: January 2013
Printed in the USA

DEDICATIONS

Tanya, my loving wife, Terrel, my big bro, Fandy and Leonard Paisley, the best parents-in-law I could have prayed for, and Moms and Pops, parents beyond measure. Every work I have done and every work I will ever do is for you.

CHAPTER 1

Three remained. Three of the seven who had been captured. Alicia had not exaggerated. Not that Mariska thought she would. From the moment Mariska had seen the look in her eyes, she knew that Alicia was dangerous. Perhaps more dangerous than Massius.

She settled in a corner and surrendered to her thoughts. Across the room, Reed paced back and forth between her and Akin. Aside from the twins, Mariska had five allies who served as her eyes and ears in Castle Peles. She'd thought herself clever in keeping her interactions with them infrequent and restricted to the day. Apparently her adversary was more crafty.

Either Mariska had made a mistake, or the Elder had suspected her from the start. Either way, she had patiently waited. Instead of dispatching Mariska's spies as she'd discovered them, the Elder had waited until she was sure she had discovered them all, and moved on them at once.

"We could just talk," Reed suggested. "Tell her just enough to skirt the truth, but not enough to do any real damage. Maybe she might believe we fear death enough to tell her everything."

Mariska narrowed her eyes at him. The younger vampire's lips tightened and he sat on the floor and leaned his head against the wall.

"That idea is not only a bad one," Akin said, "but an irritating one as well. We weren't able to fool Alicia with our best efforts. Do you really think a half-conceived story skirting the truth would fool her?" The dark haired vampire shook his head. "A better question. Do you believe she would not syphon the truth out of our idiotic attempts to misdirect her?"

"If you've got anything better to offer," Reed said, staring at the ceiling, "I'm listening."

"What good we could do from in here, I have no idea," Akin admitted. "If we must die, then better to die without taking the chance of failing Eldest Hunter."

"But if we were able to convince her that we decided to side with her and betray Eldest-"

"We would die anyway," Mariska interrupted him.

"Why so?" Reed asked, lowering his gaze from the ceiling to stare at her.

Mariska returned his stare until he looked away. "A chameleon can shift its color more than once," she said.

Reed frowned. "What?"

She continued to stare at Reed, wondering if it was a mistake to keep him with her. "Are you truly this dull-witted, or do you simply enjoy having the obvious detailed out for you?"

"You're saying she wouldn't trust us if we would be so willing to betray the trust of Eldest?"

"I wouldn't," Mariska answered. "I would kill you the moment you imparted all your information and pledged your new allegiance to me."

"That's it, then," Reed said. "We just wait to die."

"Or wait until an opportunity presents itself," Akin said.

"I don't know what opportunity that would be," Reed replied. "Every time Alicia sends for one of our number, two Reapers come. I've no doubt that they go before Alicia and say whatever it

2

is they have to say, and then she kills them. I don't see any opportunities lying in the path between this room and her chambers."

Akin gave him a look. "Do not worry so much, boy. We will find an opportunity or we will die. This is simple. Try not to fret so much, it is annoying and cowardly."

"I didn't know you were giving orders as well," Reed snapped.

"I didn't know we had a cravenly Hunter in our midst," Akin replied. He looked over at Reed with a bored expression. "I thought only Remy occupied that station."

Reed leapt to his feet.

"Be silent," Mariska ordered.

Both males turned to regard her, then Akin lowered himself to the floor and sat cross-legged. Reed looked from one to the other. Mariska watched the indecision on Reed's face as he looked from her to Akin. The fool was about to speak again. Must she kill him?

"What about Barakus and Lydia?" he asked.

Akin sucked air through his teeth and Mariska shot Reed a warning glare. "Never speak your ally's name, fool," Akin hissed at him.

Mariska continued to glare at the young vampire. Massius had made him a Hunter prematurely in an attempt to discredit Yako, hoping the inexperienced Reed would die under the Eldest Hunter's command. The plan had failed and now Yako was back in Vancouver, hopefully due to return soon.

Mariska's eyes never left Reed's, and the look that crossed his face when he averted his eyes told that he'd read the threat in her expression. If he spoke another word, Mariska would see to his uncreation before Alicia ever got the chance to interrogate him.

She watched him until he went and leaned against the far wall and slid down to the floor. Once she returned to her thoughts, she had to admit that it was a good question, if a stupid one to voice aloud.

Lydia and Barakus had not been among their number when they were captured, and without any intelligence outside the door to their room, there was no way to know whether the two had been captured or killed. If they had somehow managed to avoid Alicia's attention, there was still hope. Mariska closed her eyes. There was a reason Yako had chosen her as his Second. Like himself, she was not given to concepts such as hope, or luck. She would make her own luck, and didn't concern herself with hoping about anything.

Time passed indeterminably in their windowless holding room. As if in a mockery of comfort, Alicia had seen them detained in a spacious room with warm half-wood half-stonework decor, but devoid of any furnishings. It was a beautiful room with smoothly polished hardwood floors, but it was nothing more than four walls.

"I wonder how long she's going to keep us here," Reed said.

"You just can't stand it, can you?" Akin asked. "You just can't stand to be quiet. The laws state that only purebloods can be Hunters, but I'm beginning to think they made an exception. You burble like a fledgling *shaquora* who just can't be still."

Reed bristled at the reproach. A sure way to instigate a fight with a pureblooded vampire was to liken them to a *shaquora*; a vampire who had previously been a human and had been turned to the night. "Are we at that level now? Insults?"

Akin shrugged. "Observation."

"Go to hell," Reed said through clenched teeth.

Akin laughed at him. "I'll send you there first, kid."

"Try it."

"Be … *silent*." Mariska leveled her gaze at the other two Hunters. Yako might very well have ended both their lives for this foolishness. "I will not say it again. Speak if you must, but only if it is something that will aid our situation. If you have no such information or revelation to share, do not speak."

Akin bowed his head in deference, and Reed did the same, if stiffly. Mariska would need to work with that one if he was to survive at Yako's side. She was beginning to see what the Eldest Hunter saw in the boy. He was possessed of an occasional cunning that was useful, and he was quick on his feet. But he was also impetuous and impatient, qualities that led to fatal mistakes.

The sound of heavy bolts being released pulled Mariska from her thoughts. The thick iron door swung open and a somewhat short woman stepped into the room followed by three males. They each bore a struggling captive.

The female looked at Mariska. It was amazing how identical she was to her twin sister. The same black hair, green eyes, and diminutive five foot three inch frame. They could even mimic each other's personalities if the situation required it. Mariska always knew, however. It was their eyes. Where Meilana's eyes were strong and sure, Tara's eyes were cold and remorseless. It was the main trait that separated the twins, and was why Tara was a Reaper and Meilana was a Hunter.

"You've gotten careless," the small woman said.

Mariska bowed her head in respect to one of a higher rank. "You suggest our foe unworthy?"

Tara conceded the point with a nod. "And so it's time for another four of our species to die."

She nodded to the three males who one by one dispatched their captives with a silver knife through the throat. The lifeless bodies fell to the floor where they began to rapidly decay, death rushing to claim its prey.

"The Lady Alicia may be crafty, but her servants have not been blessed with such guile." She shook her head in mock regret. "Only one left."

One of the male vampires put away his knife and drew a sword. The pure silver blade glimmered in the light of the room. Mariska thought it ironic that death could be so beautiful.

"It will be as you command," the male said as he stepped forward, gleaming sword at his side. "But are they not to die before Elder Alicia?"

"Normally, yes," Tara said. "But it seems they had a stroke of courage and killed you before we were forced to kill them." The

Reaper's voice was so casual she might have been speaking over a mug of tea.

The male turned a questioning expression on her. As soon as he'd turned his back, one of the other males sent his silver knife spinning end over end to imbed itself in the back of his neck. The stricken man's eyes bulged and he reached back, trying in vain to pull the weapon free. In seconds the strength drained from his body and he fell to his knees, decaying.

They watched until it was over. Four piles of clothes and ash were the only evidence the dead vampires had ever been there.

"You brought one with you who was loyal to Alicia?" Akin asked.

"Because you needed to show that there was a struggle," Reed reasoned. "And it would have been too neat if you had just killed us without any casualty."

Tara glanced at him and then at Mariska. "Obviously I would not sacrifice one of my own men, and those three," she indicated the ashy clothes on the floor, "were annoying anyway."

"We don't have much time," one of the other males said.

Tara pointed at a pile of clothes. "Dust it off and get dressed. You have the ill luck of being the only woman here, and will need to leave clothes with what is, of course, your remains." She looked at the other two. "You as well."

While the three prisoners changed, Tara and her two remaining escorts carefully stabbed through their old clothes and rolled them in the ash. Afterward, they slipped out of the room and through the corridors. They came to the same huge steel door that Braggus had taken Yako through. So much had happened since then that it seemed long ago since they'd first spoken with the giant Reaper.

"I trust you understand I cannot accompany you any further," Tara said. There are no guards present at the moment, and no one is searching Sinaia for you, since you are detained. I'm sure I need not stress the importance of timing when making your resurrection?"

"No need at all," Mariska replied, bowing her head respectively. The Reaper had put herself and her sister at considerable risk in aiding them. "Thank you."

Tara waved her away. "Just keep away from here at least until that gruff Eldest Hunter of yours returns. I'm sure he's tailing that chicken-hearted cretin all the way back here."

Mariska couldn't help a half smile at the truth of it. "I'm confident he is."

"And hopefully he won't be long behind Remy," Tara continued. "This situation is coming to a head rapidly. Vicken suspects something and is keeping an eye on Massius, which leaves Alicia more room to move."

"Can you not warn him?" Mariska asked, stepping through the door behind Akin and Reed.

"No," Tara answered. "And not for lack of desire. I cannot discuss this matter openly, but when the time is right and the proper threat arises, I can act."

Mariska nodded. As the elite guard of the Elders, Reapers underwent a process that made them unable to strike against those they protected, and unable to discuss the inner details of their ranks. Her unusual mind bond with her sister was a way around it, and a secret known only to Mariska and Yako.

She turned away as one of Tara's men closed the door. The night was quiet and still, the normally rainy weather cold and breezy.

"What now, Second?" Akin asked, coming to stand beside her.

Mariska stared out into the starless night and beyond, where her thoughts resided. The weather may be calm this night, but a storm of a different nature was surely coming. "We go to Sinaia tonight. Tomorrow I will speak with the lycans."

CHAPTER 2

They sat on the couch talking, sipping two steaming mugs of tea—chamomile, no doubt—and sharing little fresh baked cookies. It was just another night for them. Another night of gossiping and awful television and giggling.

Jelani sighed. Even from his position on the roof of a building across the street, he could still read their lips. They had no recollection of the night's events. No memory of the many vampires that had converged upon his and Daniel's apartment in an almost successful effort to kill them both. The stray thought of his friend sent an icy lump into the pit of Jelani's stomach.

He shook his head in regret. Wen and Alisha had no memory of any of it, and no memory of him or Daniel either. He supposed it was for the best. Whatever vampire had wiped their minds of this whole mess had done them a favor. Still, it hurt. And that they knew nothing of Daniel's death made it worse, though a small, selfish part of him envied Wen the pain she was spared.

"I'm sorry, man. I tried and failed. I failed you, and I failed the girls. But I promise you I'll make it right." The voice that answered him from behind chilled his blood.

"You gonna do that all by yourself?"

Jelani froze. The voice he'd just heard had to have been his imagination, which meant he was likely going insane.

"Cat got your tongue?" the voice asked. "You not going to turn around and greet your dear old friend?"

Daniel? How was that possible? He saw his best friend dead, that huge guy looming over his lifeless body while his lifeblood pooled underneath him. Slowly, Jelani turned around. Standing a dozen feet behind him was indeed Daniel. Questions assaulted Jelani, not the least of which was the fact that Daniel had managed to get so close without Jelani hearing him. Since he'd been turned, Jelani's hearing was many times more acute than when he'd been human. He opened his mouth, but could think of nothing to say.

Daniel leaned to the side, looking around Jelani at the girls across the street. When he straightened and looked back at him, Jelani saw no friendliness there. Those brown eyes were not that of a friend. "You gonna stand there with your mouth gaping like that until you catch a bug or a bird or something?"

Jelani struggled for something, anything, to say. "How—"

"How do you think?" Daniel snapped.

Jelani blinked. "I saw you, man. You were dead. That big son of a bitch killed you. I tried to get there in time, but I didn't. How are you alive?"

Daniel rolled his eyes. "Has lack of sun slowed your brain?"

Jelani flinched as if he'd been slapped. Daniel had never spoken to him with such venom. "Dude, I understand if you're mad at me, but just try—"

Daniel came at him, punching and kicking a flurry of combinations that were both familiar and surprisingly fast. He avoided every attack, trying not to hurt his friend. He ducked a roundhouse kick at his head, came in close, and shoved Daniel away.

"C'mon man, stop!" Despite his enhanced abilities since being turned, Jelani found Daniel to be the same challenge to him he'd always been when they used to spar. This wasn't sparring, though.

It felt like his best friend was trying to do real damage. "Daniel, what the hell is wrong with you?"

"You still don't get it," Daniel said, snickering.

Jelani narrowed his eyes. "I'm trying not to hurt you—"

Daniel laughed and came at him again, this time with even more ferocity. Jelani found himself hard pressed to avoid his friend's attacks. They had always been somewhat equally matched, but Daniel was slightly stronger while Jelani had always been quicker. After another round, Jelani realized he was avoiding Daniel's attacks for no good reason. *Not like he can hurt me. Why not let him hit me and get it out of his system?*

Jelani let his guard down and Daniel, smirking, punched him square in the chest. Jelani's surprise was complete when he found that not only did the blow hurt like hell, but it knocked him back at least a dozen feet. He landed hard on his back, but rolled to his feet, staring in shock at the slowly approaching Daniel. *What the hell?*

Daniel lunged with a series of kick combinations, then straight punches. Finally, he came in with a roundhouse punch that Jelani caught with his hand. His eyes widened when, despite his best effort, Daniel resisted him. A thin smile crept across his friend's face and he yanked his fist away.

Both men retreated a few steps and regarded each other, Daniel with amusement, Jelani with undisguised shock.

Seeing the look on his face, Daniel laughed at him again. "Okay. Maybe I didn't give you time to think."

"About what …" Jelani started to ask when he remembered. Daniel lying motionless in a pool of what was no doubt his own blood, the big man with the thick goatee leaning over him. Jelani remembered the strength of the guy, and how he had referred to Jelani as something apart from what he was. A blood, he'd called him. Jelani's eyes widened when he remembered the blood all over the man's mouth. "No. No way, man."

Daniel's smirk deepened. "And the lumbering wheels in your mind begin to turn."

Jelani took a step back. "That guy was ... was a ..."

Once again Daniel rolled his eyes. "He was a lycan, Jelani. A *lycanthrope* if you prefer to use all the syllables."

"A lycan?" Jelani whispered.

"That's the term I prefer. It has a sort of catchy ring to it, don't you think?" Daniel looked to the sky. "Lycan. That does have a really cool ring." He noticed Jelani still staring at him and lifted his hands and let them drop at his sides. "How long is it gonna take for you to get over the shock? It was funny at first but now it's getting annoying."

"Dude I'm ... I'm sorry. I'm so sorry. Between trying to hunt down Remy, and all these other Hunters slinking around everywhere—"

"You can drop the violin, Jelani," Daniel said. His voice dipped dangerously low with each word. "I don't need it."

They stared at each other for a while. Burning guilt seared Jelani's mind so that he couldn't think of anything to say. "So, what now? It seems like you hate me, and I can't say I blame you. Maybe you want to kill me, I don't know. I do know that werewolves and vampires seem to be predisposed to dislike each other, so I guess I've got a lot of chips stacked against me on this."

"Seeing you makes my world go red," Daniel said. "I don't know if it's because of what I am now, or the fact that Wen's lost to me. All I know is that I'm a monster, my fiancée has no memory of me, and I apparently belong to some pack. I feel a rage that makes me want to tear you apart and I'm not sure if it's because you're a vampire or you're just *you*."

"I'm sorry—"

Daniel was suddenly right in his face. He grabbed Jelani by his jacket and lifted him off the ground. "WILL YOU FUCKING STOP SAYING THAT!" He hurled Jelani away with such force, he flew over the roof and across the street, slammed into the neighboring building and fell sixty feet to the ground.

"That hurt," Jelani groaned, picking himself off the ground. He heard a gasp and looked further down the sidewalk to see a wide-eyed girl staring at him. She had her fists over her mouth and her eyes so wide they looked like they would fall out of their sockets.

Jelani held up a hand as he climbed to his feet. "S'all right," he rasped. By the time he had fully straightened, the pain was gone as if it were never there. "Just slipped and had a little fall, that's all."

The girl said nothing, just looked up the side of the building—where there were no low balconies or ladders or stairs—then back at him. There was nothing he could say, so he simply smiled, waved, and turned the other way.

Once he'd rounded the corner of the building, he leaned against the wall and looked up at the sky. A tiny droplet of water spattered on his forehead. Then another. A minute later, the rain came on in full and he was soaked through his clothes. He closed his eyes and let out a long sigh. "Fitting."

CHAPTER 3

Remy stared out the window, his self-satisfied smile hadn't left his face since escaping Yako and boarding his private jet. Those months living in that dive of a motel room had paid off —at least to a small degree—in that he now commanded the Northwest Coven and was afforded the coven's private jet. Yako would follow, but let the lowly Hunter squat in the back of a plane, hoping no one opens a window shade and drenches him in sunlight.

Remy smirked at the thought. Wouldn't that be the grandest of ironies? The former Eldest Hunter, sitting in coach and killed by a clueless human passenger who opened a window shade to get some sun. As much as he hated Yako, he knew the man wouldn't be so careless. Still, it was a pleasant thought.

"What will you do once we reach Peles, Eldest?" It was Marcos De La Vega, one of the few Hunters that remained at Remy's disposal. The Northwest Coven had taken a sizable loss under Remy's leadership and he was forced to grudgingly leave all but two Hunters and a Reaper behind. He'd had to think quickly to avoid being thrown into the sun's deadly embrace by what was left of the coven's leadership. Massius's hand in his ascension could only stretch so far, and if Remy hadn't so effectively villainized Yako and made him the focus of the losses, Remy was sure he would be no more than dust, charring under the hateful gaze of the sun.

"Prepare," was all he said, not bothering to look away from the window. After a lingering moment, he heard De La Vega's retreating footsteps. The man didn't like him, but he was obedient, and that was all that mattered. His thoughts turned from Yako to Melinda. He had been loath to depart Vancouver without her, but there had been no time. He'd thought her killed in the conflict when he couldn't feel her mind, but later learned the truth when he felt her awareness return. She'd likely been unconscious. Remy found it convenient that she'd regained full awareness once his plane was about to take off and his influence over her would be weakened by the distance.

Thoughts of his now wayward fledgling brought Jelani to his mind, and the smile left Remy's face. What was it about that one that placed him out of Remy's control? It was like his mind was closed off. Death should have been the only thing that could sever his connection with one of his creations, but there he was, not only resistant to compulsion, but by all appearances coming after him beside Yako. That thought grated on Remy's ego more than he wanted to admit.

"You're thinking about your new creation, running loose without a leash."

This time Remy did look over his shoulder. Scarlene stood behind him, leaning with most of her weight on her right foot, hand on her hip, as was typical. She winked at him. Remy would have liked nothing more than to take her in the back room of the jet, but he couldn't be sure what she thought of him. Even when the coven was under the old rule before Remy had taken over, Scarlene had never been one he could easily read. Dealing with her was like dealing with a particularly lethal cat. One minute you're stroking its head, then it bites you without warning.

"The situation is a mystery to me," he admitted.

"Maybe you were a little too excited when you fed on him."

Remy frowned. "Explain."

Scarlene shrugged. "Maybe the foolish human lore about us is grounded in a tiny morsel of truth. Maybe you created your own little revenire."

Remy rolled his eyes. "Why, Scarlene. Must you be so poetic about everything? Revenire?" He smirked at her. "I hardly think that I killed him and he simply came back from death." In response, Scarlene winked at him again.

He sighed and turned back to the window. She knew just how far to push him without crossing a line. He had to tolerate it for now, but once Massius took control of the High Council, and Remy was firmly in place as his most trusted coven leader and Eldest Hunter, Remy would remember all the sarcasm and snide remarks. And he would take her whenever and wherever he chose, and there would be nothing she would be able to do about it."

His grin returned.

CHAPTER 4

*C*urious, Yako thought as he avoided swipe after swipe of his opponent's sword. Not more than ten minutes had passed since he'd released Jelani to check on his former human companions when the attack came. Four vampires—not Hunters, but four fighters obviously aspiring to the rank—had converged on his location, all equipped with swords made of pure silver. All with his death in their eyes.

Yako ducked a cut aimed at his neck and at the same time, stabbed his sword out to the left. There was a grunt, and the impaled vampire stumbled away and crumbled to the ground. When Yako straightened, he saw the mounting apprehension in the last assailant's eyes. They had attacked him as one, and now only this one remained.

Yako didn't bother to parry the forward stab at his midsection, he simply used a gloved hand to slap the blade aside, and countered with a downward swipe, cutting his adversary across the shoulder. The other man gasped and retreated, but Yako paced him step for step.

"Why are you here?" The Eldest Hunter demanded in an even

voice. In response, the other man spun and brought his sword around and down.

Yako sighed as he spun in the opposite direction, placing himself under and outside the descending sword. With his opponent's back to him, Yako struck him a shallow cut across his back. The would-be Hunter cried out and turned to face him again. Yako shook his head. The man's stance was better suited to pull a groin muscle.

"Whoever your instructor is, he should meet the sun for his lacking abilities as a teacher. I am unsure you would be able to defeat a human." He ducked another slash at his head, then leaned aside to avoid the returning stab at his heart. "You are slow and your technique is basic." He sidestepped a vertical slash. "You are unprepared and there are gaping holes in your defense."

As if to demonstrate, Yako snapped his foot up and kicked his opponent squarely in the face. He stumbled back and the Eldest Hunter again paced him. He dropped to a crouch and swept his leg around, tripping the other man and sending him crashing to the ground. As soon as the vampire's back hit the ground, Yako's black-coated blade was at his throat.

The Eldest Hunter saw in his eyes that the other vampire knew he would be dead if Yako had wished it. He glanced down at the sword, less than a hair's breadth from his neck. When he looked up, Yako read the question written on his face. "Yes," he said. "I am going to kill you. If you tell me who sent you and why, I will make your uncreation swift. If not, I will cut you apart and you will be conscious of it all. It will be infinitely painful."

Finally, the other vampire spoke. "I would pledge my allegiance to you, Eldest Hunter, if you would spare me."

"Your allegiance is not and never was an option. You broke it the moment your intentions were to oppose me. That decision was your death."

He touched the silver blade to the man's neck, and the skin

started to blister. The man growled in pain. "I had no choice! I was ordered to—"

"I will not ask again," Yako interrupted.

The other vampire considered him, then nodded. "Remy has taken control of the coven and was named Eldest Hunter."

Yako repressed his irritation. He knew this already. "What of the coven leaders? Where are Bakden and Clairese?"

"Dead," the other vampire said. "Remy arrived with an escort from Peles Coven and orders direct from the High Council to remove them."

"I'm finding it difficult to believe that Remy could depose Bakden and Clairese," Yako replied. "Not armed with little more than a forged note and a handful of disloyal Hunters."

The man shook his head, or tried to. He glanced down at the stinging blade and back to Yako. When he saw that the Eldest Hunter had no intention of moving the sword even an inch, he continued. "Remy arrived with a writ signed by the High Council, but not with a handful of Hunters. He was there with two Hunters and a Reaper."

Yako frowned, the equivalent of open shock by anyone else. He stared into the eyes of the man beneath him and saw no lie. How had Massius managed to send a Reaper with Remy? That would have required Vicken's consent, which was unlikely.

"I don't need to tell you that two good Hunters and a Reaper could probably take down a whole coven," he continued. "Or most of it, at least."

The statement jarred Yako from his private thoughts. Two Hunters and a Reaper? "You're certain?"

The other vampire misunderstood the question. He looked at Yako as if he were insane, but quickly erased the expression. "I don't think I could mistake anyone for Marcus and Berius."

Yet another shock, and this one the worst yet. "Marcus and Berius …" Yako repeated, more to himself than to his captive.

"Yes," the man responded. "I would rather be anywhere else

than in the presence of a Reaper, but those two? I'd rather be on the other side of the world than anywhere near them."

Yako found his cowardice distasteful, but he could understand the sentiment. He stood and held out a hand. The other vampire stared at the proffered hand in disbelief then took it. Yako pulled him to his feet.

"Eldest Hunter," he said, bowing in obeisance. "Please understand that I would have never—"

Yako spun away, his sword flashing in an arc at his side and then in its sheath on his back. He walked away from the now silent vampire behind him. "I understand," he replied to the heavy thud, as the man's head hit the ground.

🐾

YAKO WENDED his way through the downtown streets of Vancouver, moving in the direction of Richmond. It was a long walk, Richmond being a half-hour drive away in good traffic. There was no hurry, though. Because of the length of the flight to Romania, he wouldn't be able to leave till tomorrow anyway.

What he needed was time to think things through, and digest all that he'd learned. Remy taking control of the Northwest Coven, Hunters and civilian vampires following Remy's orders, no communication from either of the coven's leaders. Remy's continued presence in the city despite leading numerous vampires and Hunters to their deaths. And Marcus and Berius; and a Reaper.

"Hey man!" A random passerby stopped to admire the sword strapped to his back. "Is that a hand braided hilt—"

"Turn around and walk across the street," Yako commanded.

The human's eyes glazed over and he turned around and began walking across the street. Three cars slammed on their brakes, skidding to a stop barely five feet away. Horns blew and angry voices shouted expletives, but the man continued to make his dazed way across the street. Once he'd made it to the sidewalk, he stopped and blinked a couple times, looking in confusion at the angry stares and mouthed insults flying at him.

Yako never broke his stride. Buried in his thoughts, he was already over the hill and out of sight by the time the human had crossed the street.

Marcus and Berius. They were known as the savage twins, though the only thing that related them was their propensity for violence and a mutual distaste for harmony. They were true warriors, Yako had to admit, but in body only. In mind, they were imbalanced and volatile. The one time Yako had met them, he'd seen it in their eyes. The only thing that kept those two in check was the unity of the High Council.

Yako had even seen them sizing up Braggus Rayne on occasion, which left him to question their sanity. Only one living in the grip of madness would look upon Eldest Reaper Braggus Rayne and see a potential challenge.

The presence of a Reaper along with Marcus and Berius with that signed writ would have lent Remy the credibility he needed to take control of the Northwest Coven. As the elite and highest ranking enforcers of vampiric law, Reapers were answerable only to the Elders. If a Reaper arrived at Remy's back along with those two, it was because an Elder had sent them. High ranking purebloods they may have been, but Clairese and Bakden were outranked and stood no chance. Had it been a legitimate writ, sent by Vicken or one of the other Council members, there would at least have been a formal trial. That was, of course, the last thing Massius and Remy would have wanted.

A light mist started to fall from the sky and soon after, the rain came. Weaving his way between the numerous humans huddling underneath umbrellas or walking under the awnings of businesses, Yako was soon soaked through from head to toe; a slender black clad figure gliding through the throngs of oblivious mortals who — for reasons they couldn't understand—instinctively moved out of his way.

On occasion, a male filled with too much testosterone or a person under the influence of some substance or another would come too close, or look him in the eye in challenge. Yako never wasted his time on them. He would simply leave them rooted to the spot where they stood, or lying on the ground convulsing.

The street population began to thin as the hours grew later and morning approached. Finally out of the core of downtown, Yako stood at the highest point in the middle of the Cambie Street Bridge, and looked out at the water. Small boats and yachts lazed atop the gently rippling water.

Even though he was a pureblood, there were times when Yako grew weary of his own species. The posturing, intrigue, and elitism common in the covens was distasteful. Every time the High Council had approached him about ascending to the rank of Reaper, he had declined. The thought of living almost completely trapped within the compounds of a castle and its surrounding areas was the only thing Yako could relate to fear.

He leaned on the rail and looked up at the clouded sky, allowing the rain to rinse his face and cleanse his thoughts. Jelani would meet him at the airport in Richmond tomorrow. Though there was no physical bond of obligation tethering the fledgling to himself, Yako knew the man's heart. Jelani knew that Yako had not only spared his life, but had saved him from death on more than one occasion. There was honor and respect in him that Yako approved of, and he had no doubts that the fledgling vampire would hold to his word.

Thinking of the conflicted *shaquora* led Yako's thoughts to the current state of the Order of Hunters, and he considered the possibility that Jelani—his former target—might be the first result of his cleaning up of the order. How ironic.

The phone strapped to his arm vibrated. Darren Lacey. Yako hadn't expected to hear from his lycan ally until after speaking with Mariska, as was the arrangement. He clicked on his earpiece. "There is a problem."

"I never knew vampires were psychic in addition to everything else," Darren's voice said.

"I was born without that ability, Darren."

"Ah, then I must be right, and your sexy little viper has not contacted you either."

"What has happened?" Yako asked.

"That's exactly why I'm calling you now," Darren replied. *"Nothing. I haven't heard from your Second in four days and we were supposed to meet up three days ago. I think she may have sniffed her way into a problem."*

Yako considered the situation. "The last time you met, was she followed?"

"Nope," Darren said. *"We met in the woods more than ten miles from the castle, and I had sentries posted everywhere. They would have sniffed out a blood long before they could get close."* There was a pause. *"You mind keeping that little tidbit to yourself? I told Mariska that I'd only come with one other member of my pack. If she finds out she was surrounded by lycans, spread out far though they were, she might get upset with me."*

"There is no need for me to speak of it," Yako said. "Is it possible for you to learn of her whereabouts?"

"I can try but she may be dead already."

"She lives," Yako said. "She is my Second, and the only captive of worth. They would try to extract any information from her that would lead to me."

"Do you think she would talk?" Darren asked.

"Those capable of the level of mind compulsion needed to force her words lived a long time ago."

"Then they might just kill her."

Yako narrowed his eyes at a water taxi drifting toward Granville Island, as if were the cause of that undesirable notion. "Possibly."

"I could attempt a daring rescue—"

"And be slaughtered," Yako finished for him.

"Your lack of confidence in me is wounding."

"Your lack of understanding what it is to fight a Reaper is dangerous."

"Good point. I've heard the stories and I've never met a vampire that was given to exaggeration."

"I leave for Sinaia tomorrow," Yako continued. "Can you find out what happened and meet with me when I arrive?"

"Of course, my friend. How are things across the pond? Have you spoken with Imron?"

"Briefly," Yako said. "We fought together not long ago. He is formidable." He could practically see Darren nodding his head.

"Yeah, that he is. We met eighty years ago in Dubai of all places. Both of us were on vacation. Did you know they actually have indoor skiing there? When humans aren't making a concerted effort to become extinct, they do some amazing things."

"Will your Second pack leader remain here or will he join you in Sinaia?"

On the other end of the line, Darren sighed. *"We've really got to get you on a vacation or something. You're all business. No. If things are that out of hand over there that you and Imron and some of my pack had to fight together, I'm thinking I should leave him there to keep an eye on things. If any of "Braveheart's" minions decide to start trouble, he can handle it."*

Yako grinned at the sarcasm. Remy was known to have several notable attributes, but bravery had never been one of them. "How many of your pack are with you?"

"I sent for more, so I've got more than half of them with me. More than thirty. After tracking down the ones involved in your little skirmish the last time you were here, I managed to ... 'convince' two of the three packs into a merger of sorts."

Yako knew what that meant. The Silver Pack and Ghost Pack knew that Darren had obliterated the Woodland Pack who had led them against Yako's team. They could join with Darren or face a similar fate. For all his lighthearted personality, Darren was a vicious enemy with a reputation known throughout the lycan world. The fact that it was rumored he was descended from the wargkhull only added to his reputation. "That is good news. I appreciate your help."

"Don't go getting all mushy on me," Darren replied. *"I'm too used to the stone-like persona. You're going to scare me."*

Another tiny grin crossed Yako's features, then disappeared immediately. "Very well. I will see you soon."

"Until then," Darren said, and the call ended.

Yako glanced over his shoulder and shook his head. "Come out of hiding and speak to me. Now." After a few seconds of what was surely hesitation, a figure stepped from behind a nearby wall.

"How long have you known I was here?" the woman asked.

"Since you first arrived ten minutes ago," Yako answered.

"And you let me stand there the whole time?" she replied, irritated.

Yako continued to stare out at the water. "I could have killed you."

"Oh," came the nervous reply.

"You are Jelani's friend," Yako said.

"My name is Melinda," the woman replied. "I want to help."

In the blink of an eye, Yako drew his sword. The blade flashed. Melinda was too slow.

CHAPTER 5

From her vantage point high above, Saaya watched Daniel long after Jelani had departed. The conflicted man had taken Jelani's place, watching the two ladies across the street. She thought the men behaved more than a little creepy, staring at women through their window from across the street, but she knew them both well enough. They watched not as stalkers, but as those who had suffered loss.

Her vampiric nature could relate only to a small degree. Vampires did, after all, form relationships and couple, but it was different; not as emotional. Her human nature more easily understood. She wondered if it would have actually been easier if the two women had died in the conflict. Sure, Jelani and Daniel would have been devastated by Alisha and Wen's deaths, but there would have been a finality to it all.

That they still lived was a good thing, she supposed, but they were still lost to Daniel and Jelani all the same. Time passed and Daniel still remained rooted to his place. Even as the weather turned and the rain came heavier, he never moved.

Watching him, the *dampeal* wondered what it was like to feel such an intense love for someone that it could debilitate the person at the loss of their mate. She shook her head. Why would anyone allow themselves to fall into such a potentially damaging state? Why would they consider it worth the price? She had no answer to that, only the rationale that it was foolish to allow oneself to be open to what was an obvious weakness.

"When did humans begin to fascinate you so?" It was Kafeel who spoke. Her older brother towered over her. Unlike Saaya, he was not a *dampeal*, the spawn of the union of a Count and a human. He was the pureblood spawn of a Count and Countess's nobility. Among the vampire species, only an *Ancestor*, was more powerful than Saaya. For one such as Kafeel, however, it came down to age. Since technically he was an *Ancestor*—albeit a young one—only an older *Ancestor* would be more powerful.

"I don't know if it's humans that fascinate me, or the conditions to which they are subject," Saaya replied.

"Their emotions are one of their greatest weaknesses," came the expected reply.

Saaya continued to stare down at Daniel as she considered this. "Perhaps. Or perhaps enduring their emotions and continuing their lives in spite of them makes humans strong."

"You believe this?" Kafeel asked.

Saaya thought about what it would be like to lose Kafeel, her beloved brother. Although it was not the same as the loss of a mate, she still found the idea of it like a fist clamped around her heart. She looked up at him and smiled. "How much of that infrequently beating pureblooded heart of yours cares for me, brother?"

It wasn't often that the tall, statuesque Kafeel was at a loss for words—few that he spoke anyway—but he seemed not to have an answer to that question. Did he even known how to answer it?

"Let me rephrase," Saaya said. "How would you feel if I were to be killed?"

Kafeel's black eyes shifted lavender and flared so bright, Saaya actually took half a step away. "I would tear apart both heaven and earth if that is what it took to avenge your death."

Saaya nodded. "And then? After my unfortunate demise was avenged, what then?"

"I do not know," Kafeel answered. "Do not ask me this question again."

That was that, then.

A few minutes later Kafeel broke the silence. "The sun is rising. I will sleep through the day."

Saaya nodded, turning back to Daniel below. Though any vampire could move about in the day—so long as they avoided direct sunlight—it was unnatural, and thus difficult for them to function. The only exception was a *dampeal* and an *Ancestor,* the latter only needing to sleep through the day on occasion.

"I will see you at dusk, brother." There was no response, and she knew he had gone. So, that icy *Ancestor* heart of her brother's was indeed capable of something akin to love. A sad smile crept across her face. She couldn't blame Kafeel for not wanting to think of her death. She would go mad if she were to lose her beloved brother; her best friend.

Seeing Daniel standing there staring longingly at the woman he could no longer be with made the *dampeal* wonder just how strong his pain must be.

Her mind went unwillingly to that fateful day when first she'd met the then human Jelani, running for his life with the Eldest Hunter Yako on his trail. If she had simply killed the Hunter instead of toying with the situation, would things have happened differently? It was possible that the Northwest Coven would have sent another to hunt the human who had witnessed a feeding, but was she just telling herself that?

Looking down at the once human Daniel, she found that she pitied him. A tiny part of her, of her human nature, experienced an unfamiliar feeling. Guilt.

CHAPTER 6

Wen was just as beautiful as the first time he'd met her. He remembered last month when she'd said she wanted to cut her hair. He'd objected, preferring longer hair. Daniel smiled when he remembered her reaching up and patting him on the head and saying, "It'll be all right, honey. I promise you'll like it."

When she came home later that day with vibrant, outward curving shoulder length hair, he'd smiled and laughed. She'd misinterpreted his response, though. Her mouth had fallen open and he saw the hurt in her eyes. "Sensitive Wen", he sometimes called her.

Daniel had crossed the room and given her a big hug and kiss, assuring his then fiancée that he was laughing because she'd been right, and that he loved it.

The girls were sitting on the living room couch, probably watching one of those awful reality shows that girls loved to watch for some reason. Alisha had made tea and cookies, and they were having a girls night.

Daniel knew the routine. They had dinner, then they watched TV for a while. After their food had some time to digest, Alisha would make tea and they would have cookies and watch TV till they got sleepy. He wondered if they would recognize him if he went to see them. Would there be even a spark of recognition? That redheaded vampire had said they would have no memory of either him or Jelani.

As much as Daniel wanted to be angry with the female Hunter, she had shown a degree of compassion in allowing the girls to live and only wiping their memories. That compassion hadn't been extended to himself, however.

His mind flashed back to that moment when she had killed him … or thought she had. He would have died in a pool of his own blood if that big Pakistani guy with the thick goatee hadn't shown up. Daniel looked at his hands. They looked like normal hands, but they held more power in them than his human mind could have fathomed. Like Jelani, he was changed. But unlike his best friend, he was not a vampire, but a werewolf.

Best friend. Was Jelani still his friend? Daniel found that he couldn't answer that question, and that darkened his mood further. A close friend of his, Claire McMahon. Dead. In one night his fiancee lost to him. And all of this centered around Jelani. Jelani and that stupid nighttime jogging route he took almost every night.

Daniel wanted to punch something. He took a deep breath to steady his building temper. Was he being fair? Jelani was one of the least reckless people he knew, and beside that point, who could have guessed that vampires actually existed? When this first happened, Daniel hadn't even believed it.

He let out a sound that was half snort half chuckle. Vampires weren't the only things that came straight out of the stories. He was proof of that.

He sniffed the air, noting that Saaya was still somewhere nearby. Daniel wondered if the *dampeal* knew that he was aware of her presence. One advantage lycans held over vampires was their sense of smell. The second Saaya had arrived he'd known. She was watching him, most likely. Her brother had arrived a short time later, but he hadn't remained long.

34

Did she find all this interesting? Did she feel any kind of remorse or guilt, or did she even care? The gorgeous little *dampeal* had made it clear on more than one occasion that she didn't have the same stake in the situation that they had. She had simply found them … interesting.

Daniel thought about having a go at her, but quickly dismissed the thought. *What the hell is going on with me?* Saaya had helped them on many occasions and saved their lives more often than he cared to think about. She may have claimed indifference, but Daniel wouldn't have been standing there, longing to be with his fiancee, if not for her. His eyes narrowed. If Saaya had killed that Hunter when she'd had the chance, he might be enjoying a nice warm night with Wen instead of standing out here in the cold rain, wondering what his first full moon would be like.

He snapped out of his thoughts when the girls got up and turned the TV off. They moved away from the window and a few seconds later the light turned off.

Daniel sniffed the air again and rolled his eyes. "Look, Saaya. Even from your distance, I know you can hear me as well as I can smell you. Just come talk to me and quit watching from whatever shadow you're blending in."

Almost immediately her scent grew stronger, and in but a few seconds she spoke from close behind him. "Hello, Daniel."

Was that hesitance he heard? "Hello, Saaya."

She stepped up beside him and when he didn't look at her, she leaned forward to look up at him. Despite his mood, he laughed. "You're hard to be mad at, I'll give you that."

"It's a defense mechanism."

He snorted. "Like you need one."

She shrugged. "It's nice to have more than one tool at one's disposal."

"If you say so." Daniel felt a pang of regret in his chest. That was something Jelani would say.

A few moments of silence passed while Saaya stared at the

dark window and Daniel watched her do so. "I ... am sorry, Daniel."

He raised his eyebrows at that. *Did I just hear right?*

She kept looking straight ahead. "Perhaps if I had killed Yako that night, this may not have happened. Or perhaps it still might have."

Daniel didn't know what to say to that. He opened his mouth several times, then gave up.

"I don't know what you intend to do now," Saaya continued, "but if you plan to kill the Hunter Remy, I would see this through with you."

"Why?" The question sprang from his mind before he thought better of it. The *dampeal* seemed to take no offense.

"Because I had a hand in what your lives have become, and I would have a hand in seeing this matter through to its conclusion." She paused. "If you would allow me."

Daniel laughed though he found nothing funny about it. "Saaya, what could either of us possibly do to stop you from doing anything? Jelani and I are probably only a little bit less helpless against you now than we were before."

"I am not evil, Daniel," Saaya replied. "I am different. But that doesn't mean I have no feelings."

"Is regret what brought you here?" Daniel asked.

She nodded. "Regret." It looked like Saaya would say more, but she didn't.

Daniel blinked at her. He would never have believed the sometimes apathetic *dampeal* could be capable of such a feeling.

"Do you hate Jelani?" she asked.

The question gave him pause, for Daniel had asked that question of himself only minutes ago. "I don't know," he said.

"Every decision we make affects others in some way. I think if Jelani had known that vampires walk the night, he would have chosen differently."

"Of course," Daniel said, looking back at the dark apartment across the street. "But I'm standing here, looking at the building that houses a girl that might as well be dead to me. I'm glad she's alive, but it still hurts."

"You need time, Daniel," Saaya said, placing a delicate hand on his shoulder. "The pain is still near, and you have undergone a drastic change. The blood of a lycanthrope is hot, and rashness is not uncommon, especially for one newly changed. Give yourself time to think things through."

"Don't really have that luxury, do I?" Daniel closed his eyes. "I don't know what I want or what to think."

"I think you should speak with your Second Pack leader."

"My what?" Daniel said, horrified. "What the hell do you mean, my Second Pack leader?"

Saaya kept her features neutral. "Every person who receives the lycanthrope gene becomes a member of that pack."

"I don't want to be a member of anybody's pack!" Daniel's heart hammered in his chest. "I'm not some dog, Saaya. I'm a person, and I run my own life. I'm not somebody's slave."

"Calm yourself, Daniel. You do not understand, and you will not, until you speak with Imron."

"The one who turned me into this," Daniel said.

Saaya nodded. "Your feelings are conflicted, but you would have died if not for him."

"Maybe I was better off dead."

"That is for you to determine," Saaya replied.

Daniel was about to say more, but then he felt a tug in the back of his mind. He turned this way and that, looking for the source. It felt like someone was pulling him … south? Yes, the feeling was coming from the south side of the city.

"He calls you?" Saaya asked.

"Is that what the hell this is?" Daniel asked, nervous. "He can be in my head like this?"

"Not exactly. The Second Pack leader can call other pack

members to him, and has a level of authority, but it is the alpha who leads the pack."

Daniel's chest heaved with each nervous breath. "I can't handle this shit! What does it mean?"

"Go to Imron and learn for yourself," Saaya replied. As always, the *dampeal* exuded nothing but calm. "We will talk again soon."

Daniel took another deep breath. "I don't have a choice, do I?"

"No," came the response.

"Candid," Daniel said dryly, running a hand through his black hair.

Saaya gave him one of her half smiles. "Just go."

He went.

CHAPTER 7

Now he understood what the attraction was to the Shangri-La. Jelani knew that Saaya and Kafeel frequented the roof of the the tallest building in downtown Vancouver, but he had never really given it any thought. Standing there looking down on the sprawling city lights, he felt a sense of peace and a better perspective on things.

He blew out a puff of cold air. A few months ago it never would have entered his mind to be standing up here, right at the edge of the roof of a building that was over six hundred feet tall. He looked down at the private roof garden below. That suite must cost a fortune. He'd heard that the cheapest suites started at half a million dollars and were little more than large closets.

Jelani never understood that. If he was going to pay so much money, he wanted space and neighbors that were separated by more than an adjoining wall or ceiling. Why pay so much for a little box in a building? *Everyone is different,* he supposed.

He returned his attention to the carpet of lights beneath him. One of the things that had attracted Jelani to Vancouver was the dark patches where there were no buildings. All those dark patches were large wooded areas or parks filled with every manner of vegetation he could think of. A city in the middle of a rainforest, Vancouver was.

Daniel was down there somewhere. Thinking of his friend brought Jelani back to the moment he had looked down the stairwell and saw his best friend lying in a pool of blood, seemingly dead. As the scene replayed in his mind, it was more obvious what had happened. That big guy had been a werewolf, and had bitten Daniel to save his life.

Jelani wondered what the motive was in that. What did it matter to a random lycan if some human died? Did he want to add another member to his group, or pack, or whatever they called it? Or did he save Daniel at Saaya's request?

Whatever the reasoning, Jelani's life seemed just a little bit worse than it had been. His girlfriend had no memory of his existence, Daniel was in the same situation with his fiancee, and apparently hated him.

He was about to wonder where Saaya was when he felt her in his head. The feeling was getting stronger by the minute, so he guessed she must be getting closer. Now that he knew what had happened back at his apartment, he wasn't sure how he felt about her.

Saaya's presence in his mind kept getting stronger. He thought about the last thing he'd said to her, and wondered if he should avoid the *dampeal*. He'd told her that he would kill her for what she'd done to Daniel, but he knew that was ridiculous. Yako was practically helpless against her, and Jelani knew firsthand how capable the Eldest Hunter was, having fought him already.

He felt her in his mind and it was stronger still. She was probably on her way up. She seemed unusually serious. He was still getting used to the connection with her. Jelani couldn't exactly read her thoughts, but he could feel her moods. The more he focused, the better he got.

"Beautiful from up here, is it not?" Saaya said from behind.

"It is," Jelani replied.

"You are conflicted about me." It wasn't a question.

Jelani smirked at that. "And you're in my head."

"You are in mine as well," Saaya replied.

"Then you'll have to pardon my moroseness," Jelani said a bit more coldly than he intended.

After a brief pause, Saaya simply said, "I understand."

Jelani looked at her. In the time he had known her, this was the most serious she had ever been. It actually made him more uncomfortable. "I'm … sorry." He looked directly into her beautiful light brown eyes. "I'm sorry for what I said to you when we last saw each other."

He didn't know what response he was expecting, but her amused titter wasn't high on the list.

"You thought I had a hand in your friend's demise, Jelani. I wouldn't have expected anything less of you. I trust you have learned differently?"

"You know I have, Saaya. And I'm pretty sure you also know that he hates me."

"Why do you say that?"

Jelani snorted. "Why ask? You always seem to know my business."

Saaya offered a disarming smile. "Give him time. His life has been harshly altered. I suspect it is a more difficult transition as a lycanthrope. I cannot imagine what that first transformation will be like."

"Horrifying, I would imagine," Jelani said. "He's got a little while, at least. There's still some time till the next full moon." Jelani thought about that, and remembered his first encounter with a werewolf when he was stuck in the woods on the side of Grouse Mountain. "Then again, that's another myth. They don't even need a full moon."

"It is a partial truth," Saaya replied. "Their first full moon is when they undergo the transformation for the first time. It marks the completion of their transition."

41

"How do you know so much about werewolves?" Jelani asked. "Is it a 'know your enemy' thing?"

"Not at all," Saaya replied. "I don't pretend to know when lycans and vampires decided to become hostile with one another, but the *Ancestors* and the oldest lycans know better. If ever you meet a Count or Countess, you will probably meet their lycan friend first."

"I wish that little fact was more widespread. I was almost torn apart by one not too long ago."

For a while they stood side by side, silently watching the city below. "What will you do now," Saaya finally asked.

Jelani chuckled. "You won't believe this. I'm actually going to hop on a plane tomorrow with Yako and head to Romania."

Saaya arched an eyebrow and looked up at him. "Romania with your former stalker? You surprise me, *ja* ..." she hesitated, "Jelani."

Again he remembered the last time they'd seen each other. She often called him *jaan*, which in the hindi language of her mother roughly translated into "my love". He had told her never to call him that again.

Jelani might well be entitled to hate this woman, who had toyed with his desperate situation all those months ago. What would his life be like right now if she had just killed Yako? But then, what obligation did she have to him? She could have left him to his fate with the Eldest Hunter. Despite all that had happened, Jelani found that he was still fond of life, however bizarre his had become.

He draped an arm over her shoulders. She stiffened for just an instant, then leaned against him. "Does this gesture mean you do not hate me?"

"No. I'm just afraid if I don't make friends with you, you'll kill me."

Saaya laughed and wrapped her arms around his waist. Her head barely reached his shoulder when she pressed against him.

She may be tiny, but the woman had some distracting curves. She released him and stepped away. Now was his turn to be surprised. No flirtation, no innuendos, no attempted seduction. Was she actually restraining herself out of respect for his situation? He could hardly believe that was the case.

"You will need to be careful," she said. "You are traveling to the seat of vampiric power. As a *shaquora*, you occupy the second lowest tier in vampire society."

"I don't care about a bunch of snobs," Jelani said.

"But some of those snobs dislike vampires who were once human," Saaya pressed. "Some of them feel that *shaquora* are a lesser form of life and should be killed on sight."

"They're welcome to try it," Jelani replied evenly.

Saaya blinked slowly at that. "Your confidence is sexy but try not to let it lead to your uncreation ... *jaan.*"

"What?" Jelani said. "You're not planning to accompany me?"

She took another step away. "Perhaps," she said, then a towering figure suddenly landed behind her and draped his cloak around her. Jelani was thrown into darkness.

CHAPTER 8

"All three?" Alicia asked.

"My Lady, yes," the Reaper confirmed. "I was told that there was a struggle. They struck quickly and managed to kill one of the Hunters. Apparently they were rather … capable … fighters. Tara was forced to dispose of them."

"How very autonomous of her," Alicia said. "I would think that such an independently thinking Reaper would have *thought* to deliver this report in person."

"The prisoners had help from the outside, Elder," the Reaper said. "Tara went in pursuit of the traitors and sent me in her stead."

"I see," Alicia replied. "And where is she now, this loyal defender of the coven?"

"I do not know her exact whereabouts, Elder, but I believe the hunt took her out of the castle."

Alicia's eyes narrowed, and a thin smile slithered across her face. "Of course. How very convenient. With whom did she depart the castle to hunt down these … miscreants?"

"Layne and Michael, Elder."

Alicia nodded slowly. "Do see to it that they are found and exterminated immediately."

The Reaper blinked, but quickly answered. "As you wish, Elder." He gave a precise bow and turned to leave.

"One more thing," Alicia said, and the Reaper stopped and faced her. "Speak of this with no one."

"Of course, Elder."

She nodded again, a clear dismissal.

After the door to her private rooms closed, Alicia sat in her plush high-backed chair, tapping a finger to her cheek. The elder knew that Tara was no idiot, but what she didn't know was whether or not Tara thought *she* was an idiot. Mariska and her two remaining allies were not to be harmed until Alicia had an opportunity to question them. Four piles of ash covered by the prisoners' clothes had to have been the most pedestrian attempt at subterfuge she had seen in some time. She laughed silently at the child's little ploy.

At the far right of the room, Massius stepped from around one of her many thick, blood-red curtains. "If you would order the death of a Reaper, you must suspect a lie."

Alicia didn't even bother to look at the idiot. Of course it was a lie. Of all the captives, Yako's little pet was the most important, and Tara knew that. If she had been functioning as instructed, she would have killed the other two and brought Mariska before her. Instead, Tara had supposedly disposed of the prisoners and gone after the ones who had helped in the failed escape plan.

She looked over at Massius and favored him with a bored expression. This was the reason she had insisted on being informed of everything. If this report had been given to Massius, the imbecile would likely have believed it.

Alicia had spent the past several weeks trying to undo her biggest mistake, which was not taking a more active role in this business and keeping Massius on a tighter leash. She hadn't wanted to be seen having a direct hand in anything, but Massius had done a fine job of mucking things up.

The first and most crucial mistake had been in allowing the

fool to handle the matter with the Eldest Hunter. Alicia had mistakenly assumed that he would have had Yako killed quietly. Sending one or two Reapers would have been sufficient, and the High Council would have been left to speculation. Perhaps another coven, or a pack of lycans? Instead, the dolt had tried to be sophisticated, and had Yako brought before the High Council where he could speak on his behalf about a situation that the High Council—Alicia included—saw as nothing more than a formal waste of time.

"Do you not think the High Council will be suspicious at the death of a Reaper?" Massius asked. "And what of her sister?"

"Her sister will die as well, of course," Alicia said. "Familial bonds tend to outweigh rank. Let the twins enjoy uncreation in the same manner that they enjoyed creation. Together."

"And the High Council?"

Alicia masked her irritation. She wasn't given to providing a report of her thoughts and plans to anyone, but she needed Massius to be the face of change, repugnant though she found that face.

"The High Council will be angry that Tara and Meilana sided with the Eldest Hunter's Second, and so will understand the necessity of their uncreation during the fight that brought them down. The fact that they were seen consorting with lycans only strengthens the case against them."

Massius's mouth turned down at that last remark. Alicia mentally laughed at him. That down-turned mouth combined with the partially bald scalp and gray hair on the sides combed upward, and the bushy eyebrows gave him a worthy "grumpy old man" appearance.

It wasn't often that anything surprised Alicia, but her surprise had been complete when the High Council of Elders had unanimously voted in favor of granting Massius a seat. She didn't deny that he had been useful with his contacts that ultimately brought about the creation of the Order of Hunters, and later, the The Elite Order of Reapers, but to grant a mere *shaquora*—no matter how old—a seat at the High Council?

She glanced at the scowling old raisin. "Such a sour look does not become you, Massius. Perhaps if you were to see to it that your wolves were seen in her presence, the implications would make further explanation unnecessary." She could practically see the beginnings of a plan forming with molasses-like swiftness in that vacuous mind of his.

"Indeed," he replied. "I will have the woodland pack intercept them as indiscreetly as possible. If they appear friendly, your Hunters will believe them disloyal—"

"How you and your pets hatch your schemes is outside my province, Massius," Alicia lied. "Do as you will and I will see to our allies."

Massius looked as though he would challenge her, but thought against it and turned away. Already having mentally dismissed him, Alicia looked up in amusement when he stopped at the door and spoke again.

"Alicia. After things have been settled, I think it would be wise for you to travel to Vancouver and see to the Northwest Coven. Things are not yet solidified there. And with Remy returning here, our efforts may have unraveled a bit by then."

Alicia's smile was like a dagger coated with venom. "Of course, Massius. That sounds like a very wise idea." She and Massius locked gazes, the latter visibly deflating with every passing second. Finally, he offered a stiff nod he left the room.

Alicia stared at the tall oak doors after Massius closed them. The one useful attribute the man had was that he was particularly skilled at surrounding himself with those who had the skills he lacked. Unfortunately, he also lacked the skills necessary to lead, and the presence necessary to ensure obedience.

Ah well. He would learn the dangers of enlisting powerful allies that he could not control. That lesson would likely come too late. Immortal or not, fools never lived forever.

CHAPTER 9

Melinda stood perfectly still. She dare not look away from those brown eyes, though the black-coated silver sword burned her neck. The speed and precision of the man was unbelievable. Although she was no warrior, Melinda had taken self-defense classes for more than half of her human life. She knew how to defend herself.

This man was well beyond her. He had drawn that sword from the scabbard over his right shoulder and had the naked blade pressed against her neck before she could blink. If he'd wanted to, he could have had her dead and decaying on this bridge and been on his way. There was nothing and no one to stop him, and after the rain washed away her ashes, the world would be none the wiser.

She continued to stare at him, lips pressed tightly together. After what seemed forever, he lowered the sword a bit, but continued to stare at her. When the uncomfortable silence stretched, she figured he was disinclined to speak, so she did.

"I'm … I'm guessing you're making a point?"

He stared at her.

"Okay. So I'm not one of your elite Hunters, and am only a

newly turned vampire. Remy has made it clear on more than one occasion how you purebloods feel about *shaquora*. But I want him dead as much as you do, and I want the chance to try."

"You would die in short order."

She tried flattery. "I doubt there are many Hunters half as skilled as you are." Another cold stare. *This guy is a glacier,* she thought.

"Okay, look. If you don't like me, fine. I understand I'm a fledgling, unwashed *shaquora*, but I'm not helpless or useless. And Jelani is a close friend of mine. I'm more than sure he would want to kill the bastard as well. If you count me in, you can count him in—"

"Your suggestion is unnecessary," Yako interrupted. "Leave me, and remain discrete. Both will ensure your continued immortality." He removed the sword from her neck.

Melinda's mouth was still open. She closed it and just looked at him, trying to find some sliver of something, anything, that might be a hint that she could use to get this man to cooperate. Ice. She looked down at the black sword. The tip was pointed to the ground, but the threat remained.

M'kay. No point tempting fate. "Thank you for … not killing me, Eldest Hunter." She started away. After she'd gone several dozen paces she looked over her shoulder. He was still standing there, staring at her. She felt a shiver go down her spine, and turned and walked faster.

YAKO WATCHED the woman until she disappeared below the arch of the bridge. For a time he remained there, staring in the direction she had gone, considering her offer. He had no time to properly train anyone right now, which meant he had no use for any untrained would-be allies. He could tell by the way she carried herself that she was a student of some martial arts school, but that meant little. Schools did not train their students for the kind of combat that awaited him in Sinaia. Even without the presence of the werewolves, the threat would see the end of her.

He glanced to the east. The sky was starting to lighten, and the light bluish tinge of predawn had arrived. He continued across the bridge in the direction of Richmond until just before the sun crested the eastern horizon. Yako found a mid-rise condominium and made his way to the top floor. On one side of the building, bedroom bay windows protruded out from the brick facade, and at the top window, he found a space of about four feet between the roof and the top of the bay window.

Without a second thought, Yako slid into the dark space and shimmied sideways until he was six feet inside the space. Lying in the darkness of the gap, he considered the situation. Remy was on a plane to Sinaia where he would unite with Massius and make a move for Peles Coven and the High Council. If he had his way, Massius would eliminate Vicken and every other member of the High Council with the exception of Alicia.

Yako's eyes narrowed. There was something in Alicia's eyes that set him on edge. He didn't trust the Elder, of course, but when he looked at her he saw something dangerous. Perhaps he should have had Mariska extend her eyes and ears to keep track of the Elder as well.

He cast the thought aside. He would deal with the situation when next he heard from Mariska or Darren, or when he arrived in Sinaia. Thinking of the Romanian city led his thoughts to Remy's new fledgling, Jelani. Another mystery. As obvious as it was that the *shaquora* had been highly skilled as a human, Yako found himself impressed that the newly turned vampire had so quickly adapted his skills to his new immortal body.

If he was more inclined to expression, Yako would have smiled. With the exception of the *dampeal's* older brother, it had been a long time since anyone had lain so much as a hand on him in single combat. In their duel, Jelani had actually managed a two-footed kick to Yako's chest. The blow had had no affect on him, of course, but the fact that the fledgling had actually scored the hit convinced the Eldest Hunter that the *shaquora* would be worth the effort.

Indeed, he looked forward to training Jelani further. The former human may still hate Yako for targeting him for death all those months ago, or he may not. It didn't matter. As Eldest Hunter, Yako was charged with maintaining the integrity of the Order of Hunters. What he'd seen of the Order over the past two months left him disgusted.

After Remy and Massius—and possibly Alicia—had been dealt with, he would return to the Northwest Coven and scour it. Those that could be re-trained would remain. Others would not. He would leave the matter of leadership of the coven to Vicken.

Yako thought about another friend of Jelani's. The male named Daniel. Remy had been after Jelani and Daniel while Yako had forsaken that task in favor of eliminating Remy. Once the situation was done, Yako considered what to do about the human.

Imron reported that his lycans had happened upon the two female companions of Jelani and Daniel. Apparently their minds had been wiped of the incident. They were lucky.

The lycan second in command had said nothing about Daniel, so Yako suspected the human was still roaming free. He would need to do something about that. Daniel had shown a similar skill to Jelani and could be another asset. With little left of the man's former life, perhaps Yako would offer him the gift of immortality instead of killing him.

The Order of Hunters did not accept turned vampires, but Yako was considering bending that rule in this instance. Jelani and his friend had exhibited skills that shamed most of the Hunters he had seen of late. The two would be worthy assets.

He dismissed them from his mind and moved on. If Mariska was incarcerated, she had little time remaining, if she was even alive. Massius would want to find a way to leverage her against

Yako, but every time he thought about the troublesome Elder, his mind went from Massius to Alicia, whose eyes knew too much.

The way she had looked at Yako when he'd been brought before the High Council was something the Eldest Hunter would never forget. She hadn't been perturbed or irritated, but exhibited a calmness and calculating manner that Yako found to be a direct challenge.

The more he thought about Alicia, the more his suspicions nagged at him that she, and not Massius, was the true threat here whether Massius was aware of it or not. Whatever the case, Yako's business with Massius was of a personal nature that he would see to on behalf of his ancestors. But he would keep an eye on Alicia.

The sun had finally emerged from the east, and within the safety of his temporary lair, he saw the city brighten. He pushed his thoughts aside, closed his eyes, and slept.

CHAPTER 10

Damn girl, Jelani thought, rising from his bed. Whatever Saaya or Kafeel had done to him had left him in darkness for so long, he had barely woken and made it home before sunrise. Was she still having a game of all this? It was like she was playing with his life or something.

And then there were the dreams, or visions, or whatever they were. Ever since she had injected her essence into him to counteract Remy's, he'd not only had a mental connection with her, but he'd started having these dreams about her's and her mother's childhood.

He had to admit it was quite insightful to look into the *dampeal's* life as a child, but he wondered how in the world he was seeing into her mother's childhood. Was it some sort of vampire connection? He'd have to ask her later, if he wasn't still mad at her for leaving him on the roof of that building to fry in the sun.

He sat at the edge of the bed and ran his hands over his clean-shaven head. Ever since he'd been turned into a vampire, waking up had been a different experience. No more grogginess or forcing himself to get out of bed. Now, it was a simple coming of awareness. When he awoke, his mind was immediately alert.

He hadn't dreamed since being turned unless it was of Saaya's young life. Was it a symptom of being a vampire or that he just hadn't dreamt of anything lately?

He sighed—a distinctly human habit—and started making the bed. Saaya had giggled at him when she found that he still slept underneath the covers, but Jelani didn't care. He may not need the warmth, but he liked the weight of the blankets.

Once finished, he made his way to the bathroom, then stopped and shook his head. He was about to go brush his teeth, but there really was no need. Another phenomenon of vampirism.

He leaned close to the mirror, bared his teeth, then breathed into his cupped hand and inhaled. Perfectly clean teeth and fresh breath. *Another perk of being a vampire, I guess. No halitosis or butter-teeth.* The first few nights he'd awoken, he insisted on following his daily hygiene rituals until finally accepting that he was just wasting time. He did still shower, though. Not even vampirism could hold daily grime at bay.

He felt a brief but sharp ache in his stomach. The thirst. That was the first and most gentle nudge his body gave him to let him know it was time to feed. After that, the pains would become worse until it felt like he had fire flowing through his veins instead of blood.

Jelani turned on the stove and placed a saucepan on one of the ranges, then went to the refrigerator and took out a two-pint carton of blood. For a while he just stared at the carton, eagerness and revulsion warring inside him. *Two pints,* he thought. *Seems like a lot to drink, no matter what it is.*

He poured the contents of the carton into the pan and stirred. Saaya had been kind enough to give him some of her own personal stock, not having the need to feed as often as a full vampire, pure-blood or *shaquora.*

He tried to imagine that he was stirring spaghetti sauce, or barbecue sauce, but he couldn't fool himself. Barbecue sauce was not this red, and neither was spaghetti sauce. The texture wasn't right, either. Both sauces were much thicker, and gave off a rich, warm and comforting aroma.

The crimson contents he stirred in the saucepan were certainly comforting and smelled delicious, but in a more primal way. Every human knew that eating food was essential to maintain life. It was the same for vampires and drinking blood. But it was more than that. He'd never been driven to the point of bloodlust or madness after missing a meal or two. He supposed if he'd been stuck in a forest somewhere and starving, he might try to take out a deer or a bird or something.

This was quite different and infinitely worse. It took only one night to realize that the little nudge he just felt gave him a grace period of about an hour before his blood was on fire and he would be driven mad by the thirst.

Jelani blew out a breath through his teeth. Maybe he hadn't gone totally bloodlusting mad, but he had been out of his mind enough to attack a human. He laughed at the irony of her having been out jogging at night.

Once the blood was ready, he poured most of the warm contents into a tall glass. After taking a sip, he smiled with a sad satisfaction. Warm, but not hot. That's all that was needed. The blood only needed to be as warm or a little warmer than it would have been if it were being … extracted … from the body.

Jelani drank it down in one go, then drank the rest. Afterwards, he rinsed and washed the glass and the saucepan, replacing both in the cabinets. He looked around the spacious and lavishly decorated condo. Saaya's taste in decor was as appealing as the *dampeal* herself. He admired the elegance of the place, and its underlying sensuality that couldn't necessarily be seen, but was ever present.

He leaned his head back and felt the energy coursing through his body. Eating food provided a sense of satisfaction of hunger, or being filled. This was like being replenished. He could feel energy coursing through his body, like an infusion of life that spread through his entire being. In less than a minute, he felt invigorated.

Jelani went into the bathroom and looked in the mirror, studying his reflection. He chuckled when thinking about how he himself had thought that the mythical vampires would cast no reflection, or be burned by holy water or the cross. Pure fantasy. If a human tried to touch him with a cross, he'd probably be incapacitated by laughter rather than any power the cross would have over him.

Aside from the frequent bits of irony, there was little about his life that Jelani found funny these days, and thinking about it dampened his mood further. His good friend Wen no longer knew he existed. Alisha was alive but may as well be dead to him as well. And Daniel.

Jelani shook his head. He could call Daniel his best friend no longer. It came as no surprise that Daniel hated him, given what had happened to the man's life. But it hurt more than the bite of the purest silver. Daniel was like a brother to him; *was* his brother. Now?

He stepped out onto the balcony and looked around. The sweet refreshing smell in the air spoke of the coming rain. He closed his eyes and listened. He could hear no heartbeats or breathing in the general area, which meant no one stood on their balconies on the remaining five floors above him.

He stepped onto the rail, balancing perfectly, then jumped the ten foot distance to grab the next rail. Up he continued until he finally knelt at the edge of the roof, looking down on the quiet city. Soon, drops started to fall from the sky, and a few minutes later rain showered from the sky.

Clothes soaked through and tiny rivulets streaming down his head and trickling across his face, Jelani's mind went from place to place, cataloguing all that had happened to him these past months.

In his human life his mind might have wandered, occasionally coming to mental milestones that reminded him of past events. As an immortal, he found that he couldn't help but be focused.

He thought about all the vampires at the *dark rock*. All those vampires he had killed in his semi-controlled rage against a species he now belonged to. The moral implications of what he'd done had haunted him; still haunted him. Saaya had assured him that vampirism only sharpened what was already present in the individual. If a person was given to violence or theft, they would be even more violent. They would enjoy the thrill of stealing without being caught by much slower and weaker mortals.

If a person was given to kindness or benevolence, they may not necessarily become Santa Claus, but they would be the type of vampire that avoided feeding on humans, and generally either separated themselves from humanity, or sought to quietly integrate.

His thoughts moved on to Daniel being changed into a lycan, Alisha and Wen being lost to them.

He thought of Saaya and Kafeel, the powerful *dampeal* and her pureblooded brother, directly descended from the union of two *Ancestors*.

He thought of how Yako had gone from predator to something like an ally, and of Remy, who had forced this new existence upon him. Jelani's brow creased above his smoldering eyes. He could feel his blood heating at the thought of the latter Hunter. He knew he should equally hate Yako, but the Eldest Hunter had been after him in a purely business manner. Though motive mattered little when someone was trying to kill you, Yako was operating under vampire law.

Remy had made it more personal, using innocent people as bait, or just to torture him. He had taken pleasure in the hunt.

Jelani wondered if he would take equal pleasure in ripping the Hunter's heart from his chest, or if he would somehow feel empty and unsatisfied.

He leaped from his perch, gliding across the street to the next rooftop and making his way toward Alisha's apartment. He came to the same place he'd been the night before and waited until lights came on in her apartment.

Jelani felt guilty watching like this, but it was all he had left of his life with her. If she had been just a girlfriend, it might not have hurt so much. He'd realized in the last few days they had been together that he'd wanted to spend his life with her. After years of secretly hoping she would break up with her fiancé, it had finally happened. Jelani had been patient, and it had paid off. Shortly after her ended relationship, she and Jelani had come together, and it was like they had been together for years.

The blinds in her living room slid sideways and she opened the sliding glass door and stepped out onto her balcony. In the rainy night, Jelani saw her perfectly. That same beautiful dark skin. Those round, full lips that produced the most brilliant smile.

Her hair was pulled back into a ponytail, which he loved. She wore loose-fitting silk pajamas and a pair of house slippers with synthetic fur lining around the ankles.

When she turned her head to look in Jelani's general direction, he saw her captivating hazel eyes. Eyes he couldn't, and never wanted to lie to. He wondered what would happen if he met her now; happened upon her in a crowded coffee shop and asked to share her table. Would she be receptive? Could he try to rebuild his life with her all over again?

Jelani sighed again. No. This whole business was the reason her life had been in danger in the first place. Whoever the vampire was that had wiped her mind of any knowledge of the last half year and more, they had done her a kindness. For Jelani to reintroduce himself in her life would be selfish and endanger her all over again.

He clenched his teeth together, his eyes changing into their lavender hue whenever his new nature, his true nature, revealed itself. To him, Alisha was both alive and dead. She had her life back, to which he was grateful, but to him, she was no more.

Raindrops flowed down his face and down the inner corners of his eyes, replacing the tears he could no longer shed. His mind went to Remy, and the unbidden knowledge of the Northwest Coven came to him. This wasn't his own memory, but that of his re-creator.

I wonder if the asshole intended that, Jelani thought. Thinking of Remy and a whole coven of vampires who had gone to his former home and tried to kill himself and his friends lit Jelani's mind on fire. Many vampires had died in that fight, but not all. How many Hunters were left? Who led the coven in Remy's absence?

He continued to stared unblinkingly across the distance at Alisha. Gone to him. His newly gained memories bade him to look to the west. At the very top of the mountain where one of Vancouver's several wealthy communities resided, sat a mansion housing a coven of more than a hundred vampires. Forty Hunters had resided there, but not quite half remained.

Jelani narrowed his eyes into glowing lavender slits. If every Hunter was in that coven right now, there would be somewhere close to twenty. With the non-Hunter casualties accounted for and the death of the two coven leaders, Jelani estimated there were still close to a hundred non-Hunters left. No joy radiated from Jelani's smile, but smile he did. "Time to introduce myself."

CHAPTER 11

J elani crossed the many rooftops of downtown Vancouver until he came to Georgia Street. Boiling ramen noodles and freshly grilled shawarma drifted in the air to compete with the smell of brewing coffee from the corner cafe. Not long ago, it would have set his stomach grumbling. Now it was just another scent.

After ensuring that no one was around, he dropped fifty feet to the street. Traffic was thin, but cars and buses still flowed in both directions.

He thought to just sprint across, but noticed a girl standing at the bus stop where he needed to go. He waited until she turned her head to look down the street, then dashed across. In less than the time it took her to lean forward to look for the bus, then turn back, Jelani had crossed the distance and was gone by the time she jumped at the rush of wind where he'd passed her.

He ran over the small bridge that went over the bike lane leading to Coal Harbour, and moved a little into the trees. It wouldn't do for drivers to see him running at the same pace as traffic.

Soon, he heard the bus that travelled across the Lions Gate

Bridge, and he slowed until it came into view. At the last instant, he leaped out of the trees and landed softly on the roof.

Riding the bus across what looked so much like a miniature Golden Gate Bridge brought Jelani back to the night when so much had happened. He and Daniel had gone across this very bridge in hopes of somehow getting Melinda away from Remy. A long trek up the side of Grouse Mountain brought them face-to-face not only with Remy, but a small group of Hunters and a newly turned Melinda.

The night hadn't stopped there. In their retreat assisted by Saaya and Kafeel, they had come upon another figment of fiction come to life. On the dark wooded mountainside, they'd nearly been ripped to shreds by a werewolf, and in spite of all of this they made it to Daniel's car and got away from the mountain.

Remy hadn't intended them to get away. The bus passed an area of the bridge that looked newer than the rest, jogging another memory. Remy had punched through the metal roof of Daniel's car and reached in to grab hold of the steering wheel. The Hunter had sent them crashing into the opposite side of the bridge and then over sidewalk and rail. Their lives had almost been lost alongside Daniel's car, but through luck that was the stuff of divine intervention, they'd survived even that.

The bus entered the circular junction and continued west toward the mall, Park Royal. Jelani gazed up at the darkened mountain, lit by the houses and high-rises dotting the side.

He leaped off the bus and ran straight for the trees. Unlike the last time he'd hiked up the side of a mountain, Jelani didn't need a flashlight. He didn't need to be careful, or fear injury, and he needed no break to catch his breath. He ran up the mountainside as if on horizontal land, passing between the trees as silently as the settling haze.

With the benefit of untiring speed, he made it to the base of the hill that the coven rested upon in little more than five minutes. His eyes smoldered at the sight of the structure lavishing in self-indulgent arrogance while looking down its proverbial nose at the rest of the world.

Jelani's lips tightened. He was spared any moral dilemma this night. Through Remy's memories Jelani knew that many in that coven had gone to kill his friends. Thanks to his re-creator, he had a mental catalogue of each one of them.

His features smoothed, and an icy calm settled over him. He would find and kill every one of them. Let Remy find out that his little coven had been wiped out by the very fledgling he'd created. They brought trouble into his life. Tonight, he'd bring it back.

AFTER THE FIRST HOUR PASSED, Saaya lost track of time and interest in Jelani. He'd been staring at that human girl like a living —but equally still—gargoyle, standing sentry as her lone protector.

She knew she must be patient with him, but the *dampeal* wished he would move on. Such indulgences could undo him before he'd had a proper chance to fully grasp his immortality.

Saaya sipped at her mug of tea, enjoying the sweet and bitter taste. "S'cuse me, pretty little Miss," a man's voice said. "Mind if I share this table with you?" When she didn't respond, he spoke again. "I promise I don't bite—"

"Turn around and walk away, and I won't show you how I like to play." Saaya looked up at him and a glimmer passed across her eyes.

The guy's eyes glazed over. After his mouth opened and closed several times like a drowning fish, he smiled dumbly and left the table. Saaya watched his stiff-legged departure and returned to her tea.

Humans. Such simple ...

Her head snapped up and she looked to the west. After a moment, she shook her head. "Oh, foolish, *foolish* child."

CHAPTER 12

Tara and her two Hunters, Layne and Michael, weaved through the charming town of Sinaia, moving as though they had a destination in mind. She'd held out some conservative hope that the story she told Jeremy might at the very least slow pursuit. Alicia was no fool, and Tara held no doubts that the Elder would see right through her ploy.

It had taken less than an hour before pursuit had arrived. Tara knew what that meant. Vampires as a whole were not given to mercy, but Alicia was especially ruthless. She knew that Tara had betrayed her, so she wouldn't bother having them brought before her for questioning. She would simply have them killed on sight. But why hadn't they attacked?

Several men came around a corner in her direction. Tara knew immediately that they were not vampires, but werewolves. On either side of her, the two Hunters tensed. She was preparing for what would surely be a fight when one of them spoke.

"You Tara?"

"Why would I confirm or deny that question?" she asked him.

He and the other four dogs around him chuckled. "I wouldn't

expect any other answer from a blood." She made to move around him but he held out a hand. "Hold on, we need to talk."

"Make a move like that again and you lose a hand," the Reaper said. The remark earned several growls.

"Look," he said. "I don't like standing here talking to you either, but I don't have much choice. I have a message from your allies."

Tara arched an eyebrow. "And what allies would those be?"

"Darren Lacey—"

Tara's twin scythes were instantly in her hands and she took his head in one swipe. Before the others could react, Layne and Michael lunged forward, taking two more in the neck as Tara went for the remaining man on her left. She buried one of her scythes in his chest, and when he arched his back, she brought the other scythe around and down into his throat.

She held her weapons imbedded in him until the death spasms ceased. Lycans were also vulnerable to silver, but it was different than vampires. To a vampire, silver was more like acid. To a werewolf, silver was like a severe allergy. Brief exposure was painful but not lethal. The strike had to be precise or lingering in order to kill.

In a fight that had taken less than a minute, five werewolves were dead, and the three vampires dragged the bodies into a nearby street and discarded them into a dumpster. She would have liked to take them out of the city and bury or burn them, but there was no time.

Tara glanced up, wondering why their rooftop pursuers hadn't used the distraction to attack. She knew they were there even if she couldn't see them.

"A question," Layne said.

"Speak," she replied, still watching the rooftops.

Layne stepped in front of her. "Why did we just attack a group of Darren's lycans? I don't pretend to like the mangy animals, but they're supposed to be our allies in this, are they not?"

He looked understandably concerned. As dangerous as lycans were, even a Reaper would think twice before crossing Lacey. "They weren't from Darren's pack," she said absently.

"They weren't?" Michael asked.

Three figures dropped from the rooftop and came toward them.

"Every member of Darren's pack knows that we meet only with Darren."

"So who did we just kill?" Layne asked.

"Allies of Massius would be my guess," Tara replied with a smirk as she watched the three draw nearer."

"And lucky for you, the seven that Alicia had sent to follow you are not alive to report your fraternizing with lycans," Tara's mirror image added. They were so caught up in the dialogue between you two that we were able to strike quickly."

Michael snorted. "Why would they think we were friends with a bunch of dogs?"

"The lycans did not appear threatening toward you," Meilana explained.

"Which would lead our pursuers to report back to the Elders that I am consorting with a potential enemy," Tara said with a nod.

"An offense punishable by the sun's warm embrace," Meilana said.

"An offense Massius would surely exploit," Tara added.

"With Alicia's full agreement," Meilana added further.

Layne and Michael looked at each other, then back at the twins.

"You two could give a guy a headache," Layne said.

Meilana made a sound that could have been a huff, then indicated the man and woman on either side of her. "You have met Lydia and Barakus, if I remember?"

Tara nodded to each of them then indicated her two companions. "Layne and Michael," she said. The four Hunters nodded to each other.

"We need to move," Tara said. "Since you've killed our

pursuers, I doubt Alicia and Massius will need much excuse to send a full contingent to hunt us down."

"Where were you going, anyway?" Barakus asked.

"To meet with your Second Hunter," Tara answered. Meilana already knew this, of course, but she said nothing. The twins' connection was a secret they kept from all except their most trusted friend, Mariska, and Eldest Hunter Yako by extension.

"We're in a thick situation, here," Barakus said as they continued through the brightly lit nighttime streets of Sinaia.

Tourists made their way down the sidewalks, snapping pictures and pointing. A small part of Tara admired their sense of wonder about the world. They were able to enjoy a discovery for the first time and experience a sense of awe that no vampire could relate to. Even a *shaquora* had such memories, but a pureblood saw the world differently. Things were what they were, and though there was always something new to see and discover in the world, it was simply that, new and undiscovered.

"Because we just killed a group sent by an Elder to spy on us?" Michael asked.

Barakus nodded. "Which means they'll scour this city to find us. There is nowhere in Sinaia for us to go."

"And we dare not travel too far from the coven," Lydia said. "Whatever egg Massius has laid, we need to be near when he hatches it."

Tara glanced at the solidly built woman with the curly red hair. Her pale freckled face was both handsome and imposing. A capable Hunter, as was her closest friend, Barakus. Tara wondered how those two had met.

"The watchers I have in place tell me that the Second has fled the city. It's reasonable to suggest she seeks Darren Lacey."

Tara continued to scan their surroundings as her sister spoke to her through their mental connection. Tourists were typically out late, exploring, but tonight the streets were quiet. Humans had at least some pedestrian form of intuition that kept them indoors this night.

"Allies or not," Tara replied, *"I find it difficult to imagine the Second Hunter camped in a den of lycans."*

"The very den we may find ourselves camped in," Meilana's thoughts said. *"Where else would we or Mariska go? You know as well as I that Alicia and Massius will see every inch of this city combed for us."*

Tara knew Meilana was right, but she would explore every other option before resorting to that one. The Reaper caught sight of someone on the roof of a building ahead and to the left. Another spy? "Rooftop, eleven o'clock. Intercept."

The faster of the two Hunters accompanying her, Layne leapt away, scaling a nearby building and darting across the rooftops. Whoever watched them would find themselves face-to-face with one they could not outrun.

The group never broke step, and in a couple minutes Layne returned to her side. "Second Hunter wishes to meet us at The Casino," he said.

Tara frowned. The Sinaia Casino? Why would Mariska go there?

"A vehicle waits not far from here to carry all of us," Michael said.

"No," Tara replied. "Massius sent coven guards to watch us. When he finds out they're dead, he'll send Hunters to track us. I would not have the vehicle anywhere near our destination."

"Not to mention the tracking devices our brave Elder had placed in every vehicle the coven owns."

Tara almost smirked at the comment. None but the Elders and the Order of Reapers knew about the devices. When Tara had shared this little fact with her sister, Meilana had found it humorous just how paranoid Massius was. The only logic Tara could find in Massius's continued rank as a member of the High Council was that he was an Elder, and had aided in the blood moon battle that ended the war. Meilana had hinted that Mariska might have some insight on this, but the two hadn't had the chance to speak of it.

"We should move," Layne said. "When Massius doesn't receive any communication from them, he will act quickly."

Tara responded with a curt not. "Then let's move."

CHAPTER 13

"The whole pack?"

When the man nodded, Massius hissed through his teeth. He turned his back on the messenger and sat down in his armchair. An entire pack of lycans, killed to the last. The Woodland Pack was his oldest ally and the primary factor in Massius's formation of the treaty, as well as his acquisition of the services of the Silver and Ghost packs. He had been hoping to use the three of them to put pressure on another pack of wolves that he knew to be larger than most and particularly dangerous. They mostly roamed North America, but if he had been able to secure their loyalty, it would have made things much easier.

"Explain to me," Massius demanded, standing again, hands clasped behind his back. "How it is that three packs of lycans attack a lone party of nine Hunters, three of which were allies, and yet not only fail to kill them all, but were sent running after an ambush by only one pack of enemy wolves?" Massius turned back to the messenger. "How?"

The other man bristled at the insult. Calling a lycan a "wolf" was akin to a lycan calling a vampire a "blood". The tone determined whether there was insult given.

"Every one of them were a great deal bigger and stronger than any of us," the messenger explained. "Combine that with the fact that there were silver swords and silver bullets flying around everywhere, and it made for a tough situation."

"I'm not interested in your excuses."

"You just asked—"

"Be silent and be gone." Massius turned his back again and waved a dismissive hand. "You may pass along the message that I expected more from you. The Woodland Pack has been decimated? Find a new alpha to lead you and send him to me. I'll have no more second hand information via messengers. This is not the age of camelot."

The lycan growled deep in his throat. Massius saw an amused Alicia at the far side of the room. The Elder reclined in her leather cushioned chair, fingers interlaced as she watched the scene.

He looked a dozen feet to the side of the angry werewolf, where Braggus Rayne stood at ease. The lycan also spared him a glance, no doubt guessing that whether by speed or the reach of that long scythe across his back, the huge Reaper could easily close the distance between them before any attack could happen.

Massius grinned. There wasn't a coven anywhere in the world that didn't know of the mighty Braggus Rayne. He looked back at the flea-ridden messenger who likely understood that Braggus would have his head off his shoulders before the thought of an attack could finish forming in his simple brain.

Several tense seconds passed, then the messenger gave Massius one last glare and stalked out the door. They remained silent but for Massius's grunt of satisfaction. He turned to Alicia, who seemed to be looking into her own private thoughts.

He waved a hand in the direction the lycan had gone. "That is the very reason I wanted to bring the race of large wolves into an alliance. This problem would have been avoided entirely."

"Oh?" Alicia said. "Why do you think so, Massius?"

He frowned at her as if it were obvious. "Would having that group of big wolves as allies not prove a boon to us?"

"Would having them as supposed allies really ensure their allegiance?" she countered.

Massius began his sputtering response as Alicia smiled at him beneath those always narrowed red eyes.

"I ... how could they not?" he finally managed. "The treaty—"

"Is only as useful as those who allow it to be," the woman interrupted. "Promises and agreements do nothing to inspire loyalty. If you would align yourself with a former enemy, would it not be wise to treat them with respect?"

"They need to know that I tolerate nothing less than cooperation," Massius stated. "I have no interest in excuses for failure. If they wish to continue living their lives without the threat of being hunted to extinction, they will do as told."

Alicia stared at him for a long moment, then nodded. "Of course."

Massius ground his teeth and turned away. What was she getting after? The woman acted as though she had some extensive knowledge about the situation. Who knew better about dealing with werewolves than he?

"Do you think we should trust this ... 'messenger', Massius?" Alicia asked. "Do you really trust these lycanthropes so much?"

Massius raised his black and gray eyebrows. "You suggest I have him followed?"

"I'm sure you know what is best," the Elder said, rising. "Please excuse me. I have business to attend."

Massius watched her go. After she exited, he looked at Braggus. "Have one of your Reapers track and observe our messenger. See to it that the Woodland Pack is indeed no more, and that the other wolves have not decided to think too independently."

The Eldest Reaper gave a precise bow and turned to leave.

"Braggus," Massius said. The towering man turned back. "I have not heard back from the five that I sent after your little stray.

Send a Reaper with five of your best Hunters and five more of the coven guard. I want those vermin exterminated."

"Then, best I lead that party myself," the Braggus replied in his baritone voice.

"Of course that is the only way I could be sure the job is done right," Massius agreed. "Unfortunately, I cannot spare you away from the coven. There are too many things happening right now and I need you close."

"You suspect unrest?"

"Many things are possible," Massius said. "But only two of those possibilities need your attention. Send someone to track the lycan and send a group to deal with Tara and the other traitors. I want her and Yako's little puppet dead."

Braggus took it all in with a neutral expression. "You do not wish them to face trial for their transgressions?"

"Their betrayal is a clear fact. They must be dealt with swiftly before they can do any further damage."

The Eldest Reaper bowed again and left.

Now in the solitude of the windowless chamber, Massius sat back in his armchair and rested his chin on his fist. Could it really be possible that a pack as powerful as the Woodland have been wiped out while fighting alongside the Silver and Ghost Packs? Three packs of wolves couldn't defend themselves against a handful of Hunters and one pack of rogues?

There were already too many annoying little problems nipping at his heels. Yako was *still* alive, as was his Second. One of the Reapers had apparently defected, and now a rogue pack of were-wolves decided to make a play for dominance at the worst possible time.

This was a budding problem that needed to be crushed before it could germinate.

CHAPTER 14

"You are a girl who enjoys immortal life if ever I saw one."
Lounging on her velvet sofa, Nichelle glanced lazily at her friend over the top of her goblet. "Why shouldn't I?" she said. "Am I not an immortal? Why should we not enjoy the fruits of this world? We are nearly Gods."

Lisa scoffed. "To humans, maybe we are Gods."

"Or demons," Karie added.

Nichelle glanced at the third woman and waved a hand. "Gods, demons, it doesn't matter as long as they know their betters."

Lisa and Karie chuckled as Nichelle lit a cigarette.

"I think our Nichelle here has passed from enjoyment to decadence," Lisa said, looking her up and down. "You project the typical self indulgent immortal. All that's left is for you to have a red dress and a manservant."

Nichelle giggled, puffing a cloud out of her mouth. "Now, that would be something," she said, taking a long draw on the cigarette and letting the smoke linger before shooting it out of her nostrils. "A shirtless manservant to mindlessly cater to my whims."

Lisa licked her lips. "I know who could have been the perfect candidate. Sadly he had to be killed. You might have enjoyed making him watch as you drained his girlfriend before having him bound to you."

"That is horribly cruel, Lisa," Nichelle said to a round of tittering.

Lisa's laughter was cut short a moment later when a figure darted across the room and slit her throat. The shadow leaped backward and turned, imbedding a long silver knife into the side of Karie's neck, then lifted a knee into her stomach. When she doubled over, he stabbed her once in the back, then came at Nichelle.

The attacker was so fast that it all happened before Nichelle had time to move. The cigarette fell when she opened her mouth to scream, but only a grunt came out when she felt three hard blows to her body from her lower abdomen to the middle of her chest. One of those terrible silver knives sliced the air in front of her face and the already falling cigarette landed on the floor in two halves. A gloved hand clamped around her mouth and the assailant leaned in close and put a finger to his lips.

"I hate those disgusting things," the dark skinned assassin whispered. "Your friends have been bad. You haven't. Be a good girl, okay?"

He released her and was gone without a sound. Nichelle heaved a few shaky breaths. Her first thought was to alert the coven Hunters, but something in that man's eyes told her that if she did that, he would hunt her down and kill her.

She ran a shaky hand over her face and made for the door. Minutes later she was in her car and speeding away from the luxurious mansion.

※

I PROBABLY SHOULD HAVE KILLED *her*, Jelani thought for at least the third time as he passed through the shadows of the offensively opulent mansion. Just like any human, vampires were possessed of a range of personalities and many were on display. He passed a room of male and female vampires sprawled on the floor and on couches, kissing and sampling each other's blood, among other things. The scene fit perfectly in the mold that his human mind would have conceived.

In other rooms, however, groups sat in conversation, tinkerers built devices, scholars leaned studiously over desks studying who knows what.

He came to the door of a room where he heard two men talking. Despite the closed door and softly speaking residents on the other side, he could hear them easily.

"This situation is just going to get worse," one of the men said. Jelani leaned closer to the door, more an unconscious move than the necessity to hear more clearly.

"We don't have a choice," the other voice said.

"Like hell we don't. Since when has he ever had a brave bone in his body? That was not enforcement of law, but usurpation."

"Usurpation?" the second voice said, unconvinced. "Do you not think you're being a little dramatic?"

"He showed up with a Reaper and a couple Hunters at his back. All anyone had to go on was his word."

"His word backed by a Reaper, who would only have been there at the command of an Elder."

"I still don't buy it," the first voice said, a little less confident. "Something's wrong and he pulled us into the middle of it."

"What else could we have done?" That Reaper by himself could have wiped out most of those in attendance. Add those two psychos Marcus and Berius into the mix, and there would have been chaos."

"I think we should get out of here," the first voice said. Jelani arched an eyebrow. Interesting. Who were Marcus and Berius?

"Where would we go?" the second man asked. "We're guilty of nothing more than acting on orders given to us by our superiors.

It's not for us to judge or ask questions. We do as ordered. You know that. Besides, what do three humans matter?"

Jelani's eyes flared.

"You know it's more than just a few humans. He publicly denounced Eldest Hunter Yako and then declared himself Eldest Hunter. There was no trial and no opportunity for Eldest Hunter to defend himself."

"Be careful," the other man warned. "You know we cannot question law."

"I question what looks to be a perversion of the law. We have only Remy's word to go on, and that holds little credibility with me. You know him as well as I."

"I also know you are treading dangerous waters, here. What-ever we may feel about him, he has a Reaper and two of the worst Hunters at his back."

Jelani had a strong suspicion that the word "worst" wasn't used in the context of lacking in ability. He would need to be careful not to run into those two if he could help it.

A frown creased his brow as he mulled over what he heard. These two seemed to know what was going on, but it was unlikely they would just volunteer to tell him what he wanted. They were also involved in the attack on his former home. Maybe he could kill one and interrogate the other.

"I understand your point," the first voice said after a pause. "I admit that I have no desire to cross those two. Where did they come from, anyway?"

"I don't know, but there's always plenty of rumors. Some say the only reason why they are not Reapers is because they're too unpredictable. One thing everyone knows about becoming a Reaper is that you have to be stable; in total control. Those two are everything that is the opposite of control."

Jelani weighed his options. He wanted to work his way through this mansion quietly for as long as possible. If he kicked in the door, it would likely alert the whole coven.

He shrugged and knocked on the door. The talking stopped and a few seconds later the door opened. The pale-faced scowl of one of the men who had attacked his friends greeted Jelani. He looked into the vampire's eyes and saw pure malice. "You gonna stand there staring at me or speak?"

Jelani recognized the voice as the second speaker, the one that wished not to challenge the new status quo. "Well?" the man said again, frowning down at Jelani. "You gonna make some sound come out of that hole in your face? Otherwise, I'll just shut the door?"

Jelani's right hand flashed up and around, then back to his side. The vampire stumbled away as Jelani walked in and closed the door. There was a delayed reaction since the first man's view had been blocked by the other vampire, who now leaned against the wall and slumped to the floor.

By the time the other man realized that something was wrong, Jelani had a silver blade to his throat, the tip of his second blade pressed against his stomach. Jelani wanted to run his dagger straight through this guy's neck right then and there, but he held back.

"Remy sent you?" the other vampire growled, flinching at the sizzling pain of the silver pressed against his neck. "We've done everything he ordered. Why would he want us dead?"

"Is everyone that went to that human's apartment in this mansion right now?" Jelani asked.

The vampire studied his face. "I've never seen you before."

Jelani pushed the dagger into his neck a little more, and the man's body jerked at what was surely burning agony. He clamped his eyes shut, then opened them again, staring hatefully at Jelani.

"Do I need to ask the question again?" Jelani asked with an unfriendly grin.

"Yes," he growled. "Every one of us that was at that building is in the coven tonight. Why?"

Jelani nodded. "And the Reaper?"

"Auck! Yes! He's here too. You gonna take that thing off my neck, it burns like hell!"

"What does he look like?" Jelani pressed. "As you said, I've never been here before and I need to see him."

The vampire's eyes glowed. "Remy sent you to find Jamir by putting a knife to my throat?"

A thought came to Jelani that was helpful and horrifying at the same time. If he drank this vampire's blood, he would gain the other man's memories, at least for a time. This would be a more quiet and efficient way to get the information he needed. He shook the thought out of his head in disgust.

"You all right, mate?" the other vampire asked, seeing his internal conflict.

Jelani drove both blades home and was at the door before the man tumbled to the floor.

He paused next to the ash-covered clothes where the first vampire had died. "Jamir," he said under his breath. Why did he know that name? He'd never met anyone with that name before, yet it was familiar to him. Remy's memories.

Jelani turned away from the door and sat down at a nearby chair. He had to collect his thoughts. According to the connection he had from Remy, this Jamir guy hadn't been involved with the attack on his friends, nor were those two Hunters. That would have been a relief if he could be sure they weren't in the coven at the moment. As it was, Jelani had to assume they were.

"My luck isn't that good," he muttered, glancing around the room. Of those who had attacked, only eighteen had survived. Jelani glanced at what had been the man he'd interrogated a few minutes ago. He'd seen no lie in the man's eyes, which meant that all eighteen of the vampires were present. Of course, he didn't know if vampires displayed the same telltale signs of a lie that humans did, but it was all he had to go on.

"Eighteen," he thought aloud. "And possibly a Reaper and two crazy Hunters." He stood and took a deep breath. "Guess I'll have to play ninja and see how far it gets me." He stepped out the door and disappeared into the dark halls.

"YOU KNOW WHAT YOUR PROBLEM IS." Berius lifted his glass in toast, then took a long draw. "You don't know how to have any fun. You super disciplined lot never let your hair down and have some good ole fashioned, creatively brutal fun!"

Jamir made no attempt to hide his disgust as he watched the lounging Hunter wait for his glass to fill. His lifted his gaze to the slowly dying woman, strapped to the chandelier by her ankles and bleeding out of her wrists. Berius had four glasses in rotation as she bled out. As one filled, he would replace it with an empty one, passing the full glasses around.

Again, he offered the Reaper a glass. "Sure you won't have one?"

Jamir just stared at him.

Berius shrugged, swirled the blood around in his wine glass, and downed the contents in one long draw. The only thing sweeter than the coppery smell was the thick warm liquid going down. "You see?" he said to Marcus, wiping the corners of his mouth with his thumb and forefinger. "Stuffy, they are." He looked back at Jamir, who continued to stare. "Why are you lot so damn serious all the time? We're immortals for crying out loud. Enjoy yourself."

Marcus's black curly locks bounced when he jerked his chin at the still silent Jamir. "What's on your mind, Reaper?"

Jamir never stopped staring at the gluttonous Hunter in front of him as he answered, "the severity of the infraction I must have committed to be placed in charge of this cretin."

Berius coughed up blood through his nose and looked at Marcus, who roared in laughter. He looked back at Jamir. "Did you just call me a … cretin?"

Jamir didn't blink. "Is your hearing impaired?"

"You know I've killed more people than I can count for saying less than that?"

The Reaper gave him a look that could be nothing less than an invitation.

"Come," Marcus said, stepping between the two. "Let's have a walk and leave our handler to his thoughts. The smaller Hunter glanced at Jamir, who still hadn't taken his eyes off of his friend.

"You walkin' from a fight?" Berius accused Marcus after he closed the door.

Marcus snorted. "Correction. I'm walking before the fight."

"So you're afraid, then?"

The smaller Reaper rolled his eyes. "Berius, you know I would meet death willingly before running from a fight." Berius opened his mouth to speak but Marcus continued. "But I don't see any reason to throw my life away either."

"So, you are afraid," Berius accused.

"I'm realistic, you idiot."

"Watch it, now," Berius warned. "We're friends and all, but I'm not in too much of a mood for any more insults."

"Then stop acting the part, my friend." Marcus jabbed a thumb back the way they'd come. "That Reaper could skin us both and you know it. Even if we attacked him together, we'd be done. We might give him a little pain for his trouble, but that's about it. And then what?" He looked up at his white-haired friend. "Dust. We're dust blowing away on the floor. Even that long shimmering white hair of yours would be little more than straw sliding around to add to all the dust bunnies hiding in the corners. And all because you had to open your mouth."

"Hmph," Berius grumbled. "We could take him."

"Right," Marcus said. "Keep thinking that."

"And here I thought you wasn't afraid of no one."

"You know I ain't afraid of no man," Marcus replied.

"But here we are, walking the halls of this boring mansion."

"I ain't afraid of no man, but I know I'm not invincible either. Anyone can die."

Berius snarled at him. "Not me. I'll leave all that dying stuff to you."

Marcus chuckled helplessly. "I'll remember that when I'm sweeping you up with a dust pan …" he froze.

Berius continued on a few steps then turned to regard him. "What is it?"

Marcus remained perfectly still. "Someone's here."

Berius scanned the room, only his eyes moving. "Someone?"

"Yeah. I heard something. I think we've got a little intruder."

"Yako?"

Marcus shook his head. "No. If he was here I don't think I would have heard anything. This person's quiet but he's no Yako."

"Sounds like this night might not be so boring after all," Berius said, smiling. "Let's go find the fool and have some fun."

Marcus returned the smile. "You really think we can have that much fun with one person between us?"

"Better than nothing."

"True…" he trailed off again. "Damn. Whoever it is, I think they just killed someone. His footsteps are pretty quiet, but I can just make them out. Someone's definitely taking people out."

"Not much loss if you ask me," Berius replied. "The little vamps of this mansion are not much better than humans."

Marcus continued to stare down the hall. "No disagreement here. They're just turned humans pretending at being immortals if you ask me."

Berius shrugged. "Then why not let whoever it is clean this coven out and not bother?"

"Because there's no fun in that," Marcus answered. "Weren't you bored?"

Berius's grin widened. "Good point. Let's find the unlucky bastard."

"Yes," Marcus said, starting down the hall. " Let's."

They retraced their steps, passing the room that no doubt still housed the brooding Reaper. As they moved through the shadowy mansion, Marcus thought about Berius's most recent victim, the woman tied to the chandelier.

"Hey, Ber. Why is it you only feed on women? Every time I've ever seen you make a kill, it's always been a female." He frowned. "I don't taste any difference."

Berius wrinkled his nose. "Why would I desire to bite the scruffy neck of a man when a woman's neck is so much softer?"

"What?" Marcus would have laughed if they weren't tracking someone. "Last I checked, feeding wasn't a sexual thing. When I thirst, the last thing on my mind is savoring the feel of her spasming neck in my mouth as I'm draining her. Man, woman. Either way, they're food."

"If you insist," Berius said, glancing down a hallway to the left. The corridor was wide enough for ten men to walk shoulder to shoulder. He reached behind his back and drew his massive sword. "I think I heard him that way," he said, jabbing the tip of the silver sword past Marcus's chest.

"Easy now!" Marcus growled, staring down at the giant blade. "Watch where you stab that thing." He glared at the ancient weapon. "Why do you carry that antique around with you anyway? There are so many more inconspicuous swords crafted these days. And I *still* don't get your little feeding philosophy."

"I told you before," Berius said as they crept along the wall. "It was a gift from a Scottish Highlander. And who said it was a philosophy?" They heard what was certainly another vampire dying in a room at the end of the hall. "I don't enjoy putting my mouth on a man's neck." He shrugged. "I'm not saying there's anything wrong with it. You don't mind your lips pressed to a man's rough neck, I'm not judging you."

"You're so kind," Marcus said dryly, and Berius's thick shoulders bounced as he chuckled.

"There," the bigger man pointed farther down the hallway. Someone quietly exited a room and crept toward them.

The duo pressed their backs against the wall and waited. The figure paused for a moment then went into a larger set of doors, one of the mansion's several lounge rooms where many of the younger or more recently turned vampires liked to socialize.

The two Hunters looked at each other and then jogged down the hall till they reached the door. Marcus stared absently at the floor, listening. He looked up at Berius with glowing red eyes. "The bastard's quiet, I'll give him that. Sounds like there's at least a handful in there with him. Looking at the way he moves and what he's done so far, he could probably kill them all."

Berius's devious grin returned. "Wanna wait till he does and then go in?"

"What fun is that?" Marcus replied. "Let's go get him now. Any of these decadent idiots get in the way, we'll just cut 'em down, too."

Berius gave the arm holding his massive sword a little shake. "Let's have some fun."

CHAPTER 15

Jelani was feeling quite pleased with himself, having dispatched another vampire in a room only a few doors down from where he'd just left. He had to keep moving, keep himself busy. When he allowed his mind too much time to stop and think about what he was doing, the part of himself that still clung to his humanity would surface in horror.

As a human, he had never thought about killing someone. Sure, he'd had thoughts of strangling an idiot here or there. He'd even wanted to knock a guy out once for almost running him off the road when he was driving, then flipping him the middle finger when he looked at the guy in shock. But he'd never seriously contemplated killing a person.

Yet another thing about Jelani that had changed. In less than a week since he had arisen to his new existence, he'd killed more people than he could count. They'd all been vampires, granted, but did that make it any better? The vampires at the *dark rock* might have been predators, but he didn't know that for sure. He'd killed at least two dozen vampires that night. How many of them might have been just like him? Trying to deal with their existence as best they could?

Jelani took a deep breath and banished the thoughts. Self-chastisement would have to wait. Unlike at the *dark rock*, he knew exactly who had come to kill his friends and he would deal with them all without hesitation.

When he turned down yet another of the wide dark corridors in this ridiculous mansion, he grew more disgusted with every step. How much money did vampires have? Their financial resources seemed infinite. And the way they flaunted it! Were all covens this self-indulgent?

He heard conversation in the room and reached for the door, but stopped and glanced down the hall. He thought he saw something. He focused his hearing but only the conversation in the room was apparent, and there was no movement in the darkness further down. He turned back to the door. There couldn't be anyone down there or he would have spotted them, since he could see in the dark now.

Jelani opened the door and stepped in. His level of disgust deepened even further at the sight of almost two dozen people lounging on sofas and plush chairs, or standing around in conversation. Everyone had some sort of goblet style glass in their hand filled with crimson contents that definitely wasn't wine. Despite his revulsion, Jelani had to refrain from licking his lips at the sight and coppery smell of the blood in those glasses.

He stood there, frozen as several pairs of eyes turned toward him. One woman smirked, and the man standing next to her gave Jelani a dismissive look.

"Fledgling," he said in a lazy, nasal tone that Jelani instantly hated. "I can smell it all over him." He half turned toward Jelani as he spoke, head wobbling in that 'I've got a lot of money and power and you don't' kind of way. "Tell me, fledgling. What alley did you wake up in to discover your new existence?"

Jelani ignored him and continued scanning the room. There were two sets of curving stairs that led to a balcony overlooking the room itself. Three chandeliers, one on each end of the room, and two identical statues of some warrior or knight holding his sword extended out. Various paintings and tapestries adorned the walls, and there were even some wall sconces, though the lights were the modern electrical type rather than the torches he'd half expected to see.

"Looks like whoever bit him must have damaged his vocal cords," the male said, sauntering in Jelani's direction.

Jelani barely spared him a glance before dismissing him outright. The room had no windows except for the glass double doors on the balcony, and since the balcony reached halfway across the room inside, only a small ray of sunlight would touch the bottom floor. That meant the room had two exits; the balcony and the closed doors behind him.

"Nothing to say, have you?" the nasal vampire said, cutting through his thoughts. He stepped directly in front of Jelani, still holding his goblet of blood. "Newly turned fledglings are not typically invited to dine with us. Have you not been educated in the rules here?" He closed his eyes and took in a long breath as though smelling Jelani. "You're little more than a month or two old. How have you already found your way here?"

Jelani stared at him, and for a moment the two men's eyes locked. Then the other man broke contact and half turned toward the room to regard the many amused expressions.

"I think our unwashed friend here has wandered up the mountain, through the trees, and come in from the street by mistake." He turned back to Jelani and held up his hand, flicking his fingers away in a dismissive gesture. "Would you so kindly clean yourself before you further sully our—"

His words ended in a gasp as Jelani's right hand flashed up in an outward arc and came back to his side. His eyes never left the eyes of the other vampire, who gaped in shock at the stump where his hand had been only a few seconds earlier.

Jelani spun the dagger in his other hand and thrust it into the man's forehead just as he looked up from his missing hand. Jelani held him up just long enough to glance around and see everyone coming to their feet, then pulled the weapon free. The dainty man crumpled to the floor.

Fangs and claws extended, and over twenty hissing vampires approached. Jelani took the entire scene in, savoring it. A man to his right leaped at him. *Why do people do dumb stuff like that?* Jelani thought as he stopped the vampire mid air with a kick to his face. His head snapped back and he hit the floor. His back barely touched the floor when he immediately flipped back to his feet.

Jelani's silver daggers were a blur in his hands as dropped the vampire to the floor again with a flurry of stabs and slices, any number of them a killing blow. The man dropped into a decaying heap.

Some of the others hesitated, then everyone came at him at once. Jelani turned and ducked, spun and leapt away. For every injury he received, he dealt twice as many. Exhilaration at his newfound speed and strength filled him as he spun and slashed and stabbed. *I feel like I could do this all day.*

A female vampire died from a dagger in her throat. A male died from a double stab to the chest. Time seemed to stop as Jelani slaughtered the unskilled vampires. After being dealt a painful slash to the arm by one of Jelani's silver daggers, a female lost her nerve for the fight and tried to run. Jelani grabbed a male by the neck and flung him at her. The two fell in a heap.

While the entangled pair tumbled away, the doors opened and two men stepped in. Though the fighting didn't stop, it did slow enough for Jelani to get a good look at the new threat. He cursed under his breath and slashed another vampire across the throat, turning to face the two men. Judging by the grin on the smaller one's face, and the giant sword in the hand of the bigger man, Jelani figured he knew who these two were. "Marcus and Berius?"

The two looked at each other, the bigger one raising his white eyebrows.

"Sounds like our reputation precedes us," the smaller man said.

Now the fighting did stop, and the other vampires backed away. Jelani saw a few trying to inch their way to the door, while others worked their way up the stairs to the balcony doors.

He thought fast. These guys may or may not be better than him, but all he cared about at the moment was killing everyone in this room that came to his apartment.

"You think you can protect all of them from me?" Jelani asked, moving back. They paced him step for step. "Who said anything about us protecting anybody?" the bigger man said. "You just made too much noise and we got curious, that's all."

"Too much noise?" Jelani couldn't believe what he was hearing. He'd been careful not to make a sound.

"Ah, but we've all got our *talents*, don't we?" The smaller vampire tapped his ear. "Mine's hearing. I can practically hear the fear wafting from all these upper crusted cowards sidling for the doors."

"I think what my friend Marcus is trying to say," the big man said, "is that we don't particularly care if you kill everyone in this room. We're more interested in how many of them you can kill with us in here."

"You want them," Marcus said. His hand snapped out, grabbing a man by the throat. "Have at it." He hurled the helpless *shaquora* at Jelani, who ducked and spun away. His peripheral vision saved him. He stopped mid-spin and reversed his direction, feeling the rush of air where a giant sword almost cleaved him in two. *What the hell is that barbarian-looking thing?*

"Claymore," Berius said, reading the question in Jelani's face. "Pretty effective ..."

Jelani sent a dagger spinning end over end at the big vampire, who deflected it with his sword. When Berius brought his sword up to knock the blade aside, Jelani came in right behind it. The man's size belied his speed. What would have been a killing slash across the throat ended as a deep gash across Berius's cheek. Still, it caused him to stumble away just long enough for Jelani to recover his dagger, take the throat out of another vampire running by, then dive aside as the other Hunter, Marcus, came in from behind.

Jelani brought both blades around in a one-two swipe that he was sure would take the fingers off of his enemy. His surprise nearly cost him his life when the blades skipped off of the silver capped claws. Jelani ducked yet again. His feet pumped as he backpedaled, staying barely ahead of that massive sword and those wicked silver claws.

"I think you caught him by surprise with your little weapons, Marcus," Berius said, claymore working in angles Jelani wouldn't have thought possible for such a large weapon.

"Gotta give him credit," Marcus replied, raking his silver claws in a horizontal arc that cut through Jelani's shirt and left three scars across his chest.

Jelani grunted but kept moving. By now, most of the vampires in the room had simply taken to spectating, figuring there was no way for Jelani to best the two Hunters by himself. He was beginning to think they might be right.

Jelani sidestepped a downward chop of that horrendous claymore, but mid swing, Berius stopped the sword and brought it up diagonally. Jelani leaned backward and barely avoided having his face cleaved off. The sword passed so close in front of him he could smell the silver.

He straightened and brought his daggers around and down, keeping Marcus from following through behind Berius's attacks. These two had many years of fighting together. Jelani tried to discern some sort of pattern or rhythm to their movements, but the two moved too fast and were too savage for him to pick out any kind of telegraphed strategies.

When Marcus stepped safely away from his attack, Jelani leaped backwards. He turned and brought his right dagger around and into the neck of another spectator, nearly taking his head off. The vampire fell to the ground and began to decay. The woman standing next to him yelped and tried to run, but Jelani sent a dagger spinning after her. The instant it buried into the back of her neck he was there, pulling it free and leaping over her decaying corpse.

Marcus and Berius were close behind, stabbing and slashing. Jelani reversed his grip on both daggers and went on the defensive blocking and parrying, ducking and sidestepping. He sensed a presence behind him and stabbed one of his daggers backward at his left side. He heard a grunt, and immediately spun to his right, using his momentum to pull the dagger free as he came around behind the dying vampire.

He shoved the man toward the duo who knocked him aside without a second thought. Jelani was already on the move, trying to put some distance between himself and the two berserkers. Marcus jumped over and past Jelani and slashed the chain holding the chandelier in his path.

Jelani dove to the side just in time before it crashed. He looked up to see the large form of Berius midair, falling toward him. Jelani brought his daggers up in an **X**, and caught the sword between them. The other man was much stronger, and his sword forced Jelani's daggers down. He leaned aside and fire exploded in his shoulder where the thick blade bit into his flesh. Through the cloud of agony he heard Berius's voice. "And so he finally feels her kiss."

Jelani growled, trying in vain to lift the sword. It proved impossible with this beast of a man leaning over him.

"Will you stop trying to be poetic, you lumbering oaf." Marcus said. "You don't have the wit for it."

"And you do?" Berius replied, looking over his shoulder.

Jelani's knee snapped up and slammed into Berius's rear end. He stumbled forward just enough for Jelani to scramble from under him and get to his feet.

Marcus rolled his eyes at the bigger man. "You were asking me something about wit, my friend?" He indicated Jelani with an open hand, silver capped claws reflecting the light in the room.

Berius whirled and brought the giant sword around and down. Jelani stepped inside his reach and slammed the hilt of his dagger into the big man's nose. The blow had little effect, but it bought him just enough time to scramble around behind him.

Jelani was about to drive both his daggers home into the Hunter's back when he felt a hot raking pain down his own back. He turned, bringing both his blades around, but Marcus had already back-stepped out of reach.

Jelani didn't have time to hate that irritating smirk on the other man's face, for he knew that a claymore was very likely coming around for his head. He dove into a roll, came to his feet, and spun into a crouch. At the same time, he launched one of his daggers at the midsection of the larger Hunter.

His aim was perfect, but the big man—though not as fast as Marcus—was quick enough to move aside. The blade missed the center of his stomach, but still buried itself in his side.

Berius roared and snatched the dagger free. He threw it to the floor and charged Jelani. The sheer wildness and savagery of the onslaught forced Jelani to retreat. With only one of his weapons available, he didn't dare try to block or parry, so he avoided every strike, ducked every swipe at his head, sidestepped every down-ward chop.

Just as he was able to turn the fight in the direction of his other fallen weapon, Marcus entered the fray. They forced Jelani into a desperate retreat. All he could do was avoid Marcus's raking silver claws while trying not to be chopped into pieces by Berius's claymore. Another blast of white-hot pain tore down his leg, followed by that infuriating grin. Jelani narrowed his focus, and ignored the grin. His feet moved as his body twisted and turned.

From the periphery, he saw his fallen dagger only a few feet away. He dared not even glance at it for fear of being impaled, or worse, drawing his enemies' attention to it. He kept moving, working them in an arc toward his other weapon.

Marcus stepped in and slashed at his face, which Jelani easily leaned away from. Seeing his awkward position, Berius stabbed at his midsection, which was what Jelani had expected. He straightened and threw all of his weight into a downward parry, knocking the tip of the sword safely down.

He hopped back as Marcus came at him, slashing and raking. Jelani dove into a somersault and rolled over his dagger, finally recovering it. He came to one knee and turned, bringing first his left dagger, then his right, around to knock away one of Marcus's claws and force him back.

His kneeling position must have looked like an opportunity, for a female vampire came gliding down from the balcony toward his back. Jelani rolled backward, and when the woman landed and rounded on him, he was already on his back, feet tucked in, and kicked out with all his strength. The kick launched the woman away, and her grunt turned into a scream when her flight ended at the tip of Berius's sword.

The big vampire frowned at the thrashing woman and whipped his sword to the side, dislodging her. She hit the wall hard, leaving a dent in a metal panel that swung open. Judging from the lack of concern on the Hunter's face, Jelani figured these two truly were here either by their own curiosity, or Remy had sent them. Either way, he needed something to improve his situation. Fighting these two was difficult enough. With the occasional idiot lunging at him from the sidelines, it was too much.

Jelani stole a glance at where the now-dead woman had hit that metal panel. Circuit breaker. He remained crouched, circling around to put his back to the breaker. He studied the two Hunters who made no effort to be careful. Side by side, they approached.

"Looks like our little would-be assassin is having second thoughts," Berius rumbled.

"Probably because he's thinking about how he wishes he was

anywhere but here," Marcus said. "If he hadn't been so stupid, he might be able to enjoy the limitlessness of immortality instead of staring down his own death."

Jelani rolled his eyes. "I don't think I've heard anything more corny."

The grin on Marcus's face disappeared, and Berius laughed.

Jelani chose that moment to turn and run. Several vampires blocked his way. Daggers flashing, he slid, darted, and jumped over them, leaving decaying corpses in his wake.

He made it to the circuit breaker but his instincts screamed at him. Jelani ducked, narrowly avoiding the stabbing claws of Marcus heading for the back of his head. The Hunter overreached, and his claws dug into the electric circuit breaker.

Marcus spasmed in a shower of sparks before being thrown across the room. The lights flickered as the circuit breaker shorted. Jelani straightened and began dispatching any vampire near him. The flickering lights gave all in the room short darting glimpses at each other's movements.

Jelani leaped onto the rail of the curving stairs just as a woman turned in his direction. The flickering light first showed her from the side, then when the light caught her again, she was looking up in Jelani's direction. He sent a dagger spinning into her left eye. He hopped off the rail and landed on her shoulders. He drove his other dagger into her heart before her back hit the floor. He was on the move, leaving the decaying corpse behind.

Despite everyone being able to see in the dark, the flickering light still disoriented his prey. Jelani was in one place, then another, slashing a throat, stabbing a back, impaling yet another vampire in the chest. He glanced across the room and saw Marcus finally climbing to his feet, still twitching. Berius was looking for him but in the opposite direction.

Jelani looked up the stairs and saw a trio heading for the balcony. He ran up the stairs, then used his momentum to run partway up the wall. He kicked away and glided the rest of the way up to his targets. He slashed the back of the neck of the man closest to him as he landed. As that one fell, Jelani hamstrung the second man. Jelani drove his silver dagger into the man's neck on his way down. When the third vampire turned toward him, fangs bared, he whipped his hand out and sent a dagger straight into her mouth. He pulled the blade free and was gone before she hit the ground.

"There you are, little fly!" said Berius's rumbling voice somewhere in the flickering room. "Wait for me. I promise I'll not hurt you."

Jelani didn't have time to move from his position before the large form of Berius glided over the rail of the balcony to land next to him. Jelani ducked and air blew over his head where the claymore missed him. "Thought you weren't going to hurt me."

"I did not lie," Berius replied, stepping closer. "If my blow had struck true, you wouldn't have been hurt at all. You would've died instantly."

Jelani narrowed his eyes. "I'd make the same promise to you, but you're too damn big. I'll need to hack at you a bit. It'll be very painful."

"Oh?" Berius chuckled. "We shall see, little man."

Jelani noticed Berius's eyes were just a little too focused on him; as if he was trying not to betray his partner's position. He spun with a horizontal swipe of his left dagger, catching Marcus across the chest. "Now that's just playing dirty," he said as the Hunter stumbled back, hand over his smoking chest.

In the flickering darkness, only a handful of vampires remained. They had first thought to watch or join in against Jelani, but seeing that the two Hunters were not there to protect them, they were now heading for the door.

Jelani darted for the rail and vaulted over, gliding toward one of the two remaining chandeliers. As soon as his feet touched the giant ornament, he cut the chain holding it and leaped to the other one. He heard a loud crash, followed by several curses. Jelani allowed himself a smirk as he cut the chain to the final chandelier and rode it down.

After the impact of the first one, the remaining vampires were quick to leap out of the way. All but one. Jelani rode the chandelier to the floor and crashed on top of the head of a male that wasn't fast enough. He hissed and started lifting the broken structure as he pushed himself to his feet. Jelani drove both his daggers into the struggling man's back several times until he fell still and began to decay.

Up and moving, Jelani went from place to place, slashing and stabbing, kicking and diving, working his way through every one of the bloodsuckers that had attacked his home and his friends.

Then, Marcus and Berius were there. The duo quickly flanked him and began an expert offensive. Marcus slashed and Berius stabbed when the smaller Hunter retreated. They worked in perfect concert against Jelani. He had to admit to himself that it was effective. He was steadily giving ground.

"In case you're wondering," Marcus said, all humor gone from his voice, "that last cut from your little silver toothpick hurt, and now I'm sorta pissed off. We're going to kill you now. I'm sure you understand."

He slashed at Jelani's ankles, and when he hopped over, Berius's foot slammed into his back, sending him tumbling toward two vampires that had finally extricated themselves from the broken and tangled pieces of the chandelier.

As he tumbled past, Jelani took the foot out from under a skinny male, then he regained his feet and darted left, cutting the throat of another male, then snapping the neck of a female before driving one of his daggers through her heart. He just managed to finish off the one whose foot he'd severed when Marcus was on him again.

The relentless Hunter quickly overwhelmed him. Berius came in right behind his partner, claymore swinging down. Jelani barely avoided the chop that would have taken his arm, but it cost him.

Marcus's silver claws pierced his chest, but Jelani shoved the pain aside long enough to respond by cutting the Hunter's wrist.

Both men retreated, Marcus cradling his smoking wrist while Jelani similarly gripped his smoking chest. Both men glared at each other, then a large hand gripped the back of Jelani's neck and lifted him from the floor. Berius turned and hurled Jelani into two of the last five vampires who had finally made it to the doors.

The double doors burst open with Jelani's blades in the back of a male who thrashed wildly before going still as death claimed him. Jelani came to his feet and whipped his leg around, snapping his foot into the side of another man's face. He knocked the vampire into a spin and slashed him across the face before he hit the floor. Jelani straddled the man and drove his weapons home once, twice, a third time.

As his smoking victim decayed, Jelani hopped up and after the last three vampires fleeing down the dark halls. He looked over his shoulder and saw two sets of glowing red eyes approaching.

"Later," he said under his breath, and fled into the darkness.

CHAPTER 16

The tug grew so insistent, Daniel could have found its source with his eyes closed. He didn't know what it meant to be a member of a pack, but based on this feeling alone, he didn't like it. Would he retain his free will? Would his thoughts and feelings remain private, or would this alpha be in his head all the time?

The skytrain was practically empty. Only people on their way home from work, partygoers, or some of the more questionable members of society rode the trains this time of night. A Pakistani lady sitting in a seat across from him enjoyed a book so thick it could have been a dictionary. Daniel always found himself trying to figure out what people were reading, so it shouldn't have caught him off guard when an accented voice said, *The Ninth Star.*

He looked up to see the lady—quite attractive—smiling at him. She had thick black eyebrows, smooth olive skin, and a beautiful face surrounded by a colorful burka.

"Pardon?" Daniel asked.

"The book," she said, holding it up with a polite smile. "It's called *The Ninth Star.*"

"Oh," Daniel said, smiling back. "Good?"

"I would recommend it," she replied.

Daniel smiled. "Thanks. I'm kind of nosy when it comes to what people are reading."

"You're welcome," she said.

The train stopped at Yaletown Roundhouse, and the doors opened. Two girls and a guy stepped on the train just as the doors were closing. Daniel leaned back in the seat and closed his eyes. The pit of his stomach was roiling at the possibilities of what his new existence meant. Free will was something he took for granted. You just had it. He thought about other parts of the world where the government assumed more control of people's personal freedoms, and he couldn't help but snort. His freedom wasn't in question because of some government structure, but because he'd been turned into a monster.

He could feel the wolf lurking just around the corner, just a step behind his conscious human identity. It felt like something primal inside him sat waiting to be let out. The feeling was tiny, but when he thought about it, when his mind brought attention to it, it was like the beast inside looked up and took notice.

He shoved the thoughts away, but some tiny one still seeped through. Would he be able to control himself when he got hungry? Could he still just eat normal food, like a steak? And what about the change? Would he still retain his human mind and thus, control over himself? Or would he become some berserking monster?

He coughed. *Maybe I should just move out of the city, as far away as I can.* He coughed again, and his eyes started to water. *What the hell?* Was this part of his body's change? He coughed again, then he realized it wasn't anything to do with his new existence, but with the smoke of a cigarette.

Daniel looked down the other end of the car to see the guy that had gotten on the train with the two girls, smoking a cigarette. One of the girls looked at Daniel nervously and went over to snatch the cigarette out of the guy's mouth and put it out.

"You're not supposed to smoke on the train," she hissed at him, stealing another nervous glance at Daniel.

Daniel stared at the guy, who said nothing. He reached into his pocket, pulled out a pack of cigarettes and slid another stick out. He parted his smirking lips and lit a new one, taking a long draw and blowing it out into the car.

Across from Daniel, the lady he'd been talking to started to cough. After a few minutes she finally got up and moved to the far end of the car.

"Knock it off," the other girl said, frowning at him. "Quit being stupid."

He continued to slouch in his seat, eyes half lidded, and took another draw from his cigarette.

Daniel sighed. "Hey man. You mind putting that out?"

No response.

He tried to ignore the guy, but the smoke was starting to fill the car. Finally, he got up. As he approached, the two girls backed away to the other end of the car and pressed themselves against the far side next to the door.

"Hey, asshole. You wanna put that out?" He pointed at the no smoking sign. "You're being inconsiderate to everyone else. Put the cigarette out."

The guy took another draw and blew smoke out in a long stream with a smug grin. Daniel's temper was starting to take the lead. "Dude, seriously. Put the cigarette out and we can all relax."

"Just put it out, Travis," one of the girls said from behind.

The guy looked at the space next to Daniel and grinned. He put the cigarette to his lips and took another long draw, then lowered it. Just as he was about to blow the smoke out, Daniel's hand snapped out and gripped him by the throat.

"I don't like breathing smoke, *Travis*," Daniel growled.

Travis's face turned red as he struggled not to swallow the cloud of smoke trapped in his lungs.

"Tell you what," Daniel continued. "Since you like breathing smoke so much, why don't you just have it all. No need to share it with the rest of us."

The little man scratched and slapped at Daniels arm, kicking his feet out, but Daniel easily held his throat. He was surprised at effortlessly he held the other man. Daniel had a mental smirk at that. Man? This dude was, what? Maybe nineteen or twenty? He gave Travis's throat a little squeeze, and heard a strangled cough.

Daniel released him and watched the fit of coughing and sputtering while smoke puffed out of "Mr. Cigarette in the Train's" nose and mouth. A round of wheezing and Travis managed to take a long breath, then dropped the cigarette and hopped out of his seat.

"I wouldn't do that if I were you," Daniel warned, just as the fist came toward his face. He surprised himself by letting the punch connect. It felt like a baby had just punched him. The stupid little man rained several more punches, then stepped back, panting and rubbing his hands.

Daniel tilted his head. "Are you seriously telling me you're winded after whatever it is you just did?" He laughed. "Maybe if you weren't sucking on so many of those ..." he trailed off at the sight of the beet red face glaring back at him.

"Screw you!" Travis yelled, and threw another punch.

Daniel's temper spiked and he grabbed Travis's fist in his hand and crushed it. Travis screamed and dropped to his knees, holding Daniel's iron-like hand. The two girls screamed, and the woman at the other end gasped. Daniel looked over and saw the woman with her hand over her mouth, book pressed to her chest.

He looked back down at the pathetic figure kneeling in front of him. A soft ding indicating the next stop sounded, then the pleasant female voice of the train indicated the next stop. The train slowed to a stop and the doors opened. Daniel lifted the cursing and sobbing Travis with one hand and walked to the door. "Told you to just put the damned thing out," he whispered, then hurled Travis out the door. To his surprise, Travis flew across the walkway and slammed into the wall, where he dropped to the ground in an unconscious heap.

The two girls ran out of the train and knelt beside him. One of the girls looked back at Daniel, pure terror on her face.

He looked away and saw a similar look on the Pakistani woman's face. When he looked at her, she shrank back, pressed against the side of the car.

"My apologies, ma'am," he said, wrestling his temper under control. "I'm sorry to make a scene like that."

He knew she wanted to get away from him, so he stepped farther away and offered an apologetic smile. With a shaky nod of her head, the lady slowly moved toward the open door, then darted out.

Standing by himself in the empty car, Daniel opened several windows to air out the smoke, then sat back down and pondered his situation anew. Apparently this werewolf thing not only made him temperamental, but more aggressive as well. That was something he'd need to get a handle on. He couldn't go around beating on people because he didn't like them or what they were doing.

The train finally came to his stop at Broadway and Cambie. He made his way above ground and looked around. The streets were always quiet this late on a weeknight. He walked to the corner and looked around. The pull wasn't stronger, but it felt closer.

"Guess I'd better find this guy and tell him to find someone else to join his club," Daniel thought aloud. "I'm nobody's dog." As soon as the last words left his lips, he felt a powerful will press down on him so heavily it took all his strength just to remain standing. A deep voice spoke behind him.

"You believe that is so?"

CHAPTER 17

D aniel didn't bother to turn around. He just stared out at the quiet city. Vancouver being the hilly city that it was, from this corner he had a good view of downtown and the mountains beyond. It would have been a beautiful sight under better circumstances. After a moment, the heavy force lifted.

"Nothing to say?" the voice said. A large Pakistani man who looked halfway between six and seven feet tall stepped up beside him. They stood in silence for a few minutes until he took a deep breath and blew it out. "You know what's funny about this place?" He half turned toward Daniel and spread an arm out to encompass their surroundings. "Not just Vancouver, but the greater surrounding areas." Daniel gave him a sideways look then turned his attention back to the city below.

"It's the irony," he continued. "Vancouver is in the middle of a rainforest. It's a nature wonderland. Not many places in the world can you be at the beach, then the mountains in less than fifteen minutes." He smirked. "Well, barring any traffic, which there is plenty of. But really, Vancouver has it all. Lots of trees and beaches and mountains for the humans." His thick black goatee stretched to one side when he smirked. And, plenty of rainy cloudy dreary days for the vampires if they want to come out during the day every once in a while." He took another long breath and sighed. "Plenty of forest and mountains and wilderness for the lycans."

"Wonderful," Daniel said.

The other man chuckled. "So dry, my friend. You seem like a guy that can look at the bright side of things, yet you're so dismal."

Daniel's responding laughter held no mirth. He turned to face the man. "I hope you can excuse me. I'm standing next to the dude who infected me with a disease that will have me changing into a giant wolf at the next full moon. Maybe some people find that prospect attractive but I'm not one of them."

"Of course you aren't." He offered a hand. "I'm Imron, by the way. We didn't exactly get to exchange pleasantries when we first met."

Daniel looked at the hand, then at Imron, amazed that he would think Daniel would touch him in any way but to kill him.

Imron smiled. Surprisingly, there was no aggression in the man's eyes. He looked ... amused. "I'm sure you think of me poorly for changing you into what you are, but let me assure you that had I not, you would be dead." He held up a hand as Daniel opened his mouth. "Please, spare me the 'I would be better off dead' routine. I've heard it enough times to throw up if I hear it again."

Despite his anger, Daniel genuinely laughed at the comment. He had to admit the guy seemed rather likable. "I won't say it, then. Can't say I don't feel it, though."

"That is because you've had no one to help you consider the prospects, my friend."

We're not friends. "I'm listening."

"Consider that you are still alive. I heard from the little *dampeal* shadow that your girlfriend's memory has been wiped." He saw Daniel wince at the mention of Wen and shook his head.

"You may not believe this, but I do understand. Believe me, I do. But that Hunter who wiped her memory did her a huge favor.

The big thing about our world is that humans must remain oblivious to it. If the bloods don't see her as a threat, they won't bother her."

"You were telling me things I should consider about my new existence?" Daniel replied, wanting very much to change the subject.

"Yup. As I said, consider that you're alive. Consider that barring any exposure to extreme violence involving silver or the removal of your heart or head, you'll live forever. Also consider that unlike a blood, you can walk the day and the night."

Daniel looked up at the sky. "And I'll only have to howl at the moon once a month."

Imron barked a laugh. "It's always funny when a one who has been newly changed brings their human lore with them into their new existence. No, my friend. You don't have to howl at the moon once a month, though some do." He looked up at the sky where the moon drifted lazily between the clouds; there one moment, gone the next.

"You telling me it has nothing to do with werewolves?" Daniel asked, following Imron's gaze at the nearly full moon.

"Oh, it does, but not in the way humans think. You see, in their stories, werewolves are human except during a full moon. When the big bad werewolf gazes at the moon, all human intellect and emotion and morality goes out the window. He transforms into a wolf and prowls the night, killing randomly and feeding on humans and animals alike. The stories also mostly tell of us being smaller than we actually are."

"And that's not what happens." Despite the situation, Daniel felt himself hoping for some sliver of possibility that his fate might not be what he thought.

Imron smiled again. "In some form, yes." At Daniel's crestfallen look, the big man chuckled and placed a hand on his shoulder. "The first time you look upon the full moon, you will indeed undergo the change. The transformation will be painful and terrifying. You will feel your sense of self slipping back and a primal part of you stepping forward. When the transformation is complete, you will feel a sense of freedom and power like nothing you can imagine. The change will leave you hungry, and you will hunt and kill."

"I should just kill myself now," Daniel said, thinking of Wen. Every time his mind strayed to his former fiancée it was like a stab of ice through his chest.

"Take heart, Daniel," Imron said. "You will not undergo the change alone. You will be surrounded by companions, and you will be guided through your first night."

"Companions," Daniel repeated. The word was dry and bitter in his mouth. "You mean pack."

"We use both terms," Imron replied. Both carry the same meaning. A group that looks after its members."

"You make it sound like a club," Daniel said.

Imron shrugged. "Think of it however you like. There are many who consider their pack family."

Daniel snorted. "I don't know how anyone could consider the person that bit them and turned them into a monster as family." He turned to fully face the much larger man. "And what if I don't want to be a member of your pack?"

Imron never blinked. "That could be a problem."

Daniel prepared himself for what would surely be an attack, but it never came.

Imron shook his head and looked away. "You can release your fears about retaining your free will, pup. Yes, you are tied to me because I am the one who has brought you to the pack. Yes, you are bound and answerable to Darren, who is the alpha of the pack. But no, you are no one's slave or servant. No one will attempt to dominate your will except for two instances."

Daniel had been waiting for that. There was always fine print. "And those two instances are?"

"If you ever go berserk and attempt to go into the human population in your lupine form, or if you attack a member of the pack without cause. Both will earn you death."

"So that's it, then?" That sounded totally fair, and Daniel was afraid to believe it. "No picking fights and no slaughtering innocent civilians. Sounds too good to be true."

"But again, your desire to not join the pack will present you with a serious problem."

Daniel's fading apprehension flared again. "Why is that?"

Imron's smile melted away. "As I told you, your first transformation will be difficult. You will struggle and fail to hold on to your human intellect. If there is no one to guide you, you will attack and kill every living thing close enough until your hunger and bloodlust is satisfied. When the night is done, you wake and either remember nothing or everything. Some can't handle the memories and try to kill themselves or simply go crazy. Some are driven crazy by the holes in their memory and the presence of the wolf in the back of their consciousness."

"So I won't be able to control myself at all?" Daniel felt his apprehension turning to into panic.

"During your first transformation, probably not. Most lose their humanity the first time they see the moon, though it's not unheard of for some to retain their intellect."

"So, I need you there to hold my paw," Daniel said.

Imron chuckled. "If that is the way you wish to see it, yes. I know you think what I've passed on to you is an infection, or a curse. In time you will come to see the truth of it. The gift of the wolf is a great thing." He waved a hand over Daniel.

"You've already discovered that your strength and speed are greatly increased. Am I wrong?"

"Yeah, that's true," Daniel admitted. "But you neglect to mention the part of me that is this primal animal clawing to get free, or that I'm starting to get hungry and don't know if it's for a rare steak or a human leg." Daniel's stomach lurched at that last part. "Can you stand there and tell me I shouldn't be disgusted?"

The big lycan's smile said that he understood Daniel's feelings. "Your human mind sees it as cannibalism. The wolf sees it as devouring prey. It is difficult for you to understand, but you are in no way human when you are the wolf."

Daniel's mouth fell open. It took everything he had not to empty his stomach right there on the ground. "You're really making me long for that silver bullet more and more, buddy. I don't want to turn into something that's going to go around eating people."

"Heheh," Imron's massive shoulders bounced as he chuckled at Daniel's mounting discomfort. "There are those who hunt humans, but most don't. I've never consumed a human, and I was born a lycan."

"You can be born a werewolf?" Before his mouth fell open wider and he swallowed a bug, Daniel closed it. Would there be any end to the shocking revelations tonight?

Imron looked at him as though he were slow-witted. "How do you think the species exists?"

"I thought it was something about—"

"A man being bitten by a wolf," Imron interrupted dryly. "And I suppose you think the bloods came into being because some poor fool was bitten by a bat. Instead of rabies, he was changed into a creature of the night that drinks blood and changes into a bat to traverse long distances." Imron closed his eyes and shook his head. "I don't know where humans think this stuff up."

He gave Daniel's shoulder a squeeze. "Come. It's time for you to meet the pack."

"I thought you'd gotten the message by now that I don't want to be part of a pack of animals." He noticed the frown crease the brow that was well half a head above his own and added, "no offense, man. I just don't see myself running with a bunch of giant wolves through the woods."

Imron's hand slid away. "It'll help you understand. There will be a full moon tomorrow, and with it comes your first transformation. We will be there. After that night, if you wish to shun us, that's your choice."

"And if I go it alone from here?" Daniel asked.

"It's likely you will hunt humans without discretion."

Daniel's palms started to sweat. "Gotcha."

"Good," Imron replied with a nod. His normally relaxed expression darkened. "Because if you do anything to endanger us, you will be hunted."

CHAPTER 18

I nteresting. Yako thought over what he'd just heard as he sat perched on the roof of the skytrain station, several minutes after Daniel had departed.

Imron stood to the side of the skytrain station, gazing down at the city below. "How long will you stare at the back of my head, Eldest Hunter?"

The words were spoken in a soft voice but Yako heard him as if he were standing beside the man. He smiled the tiniest of smiles. A lycan's sense of smell was nothing short of amazing.

The Eldest Hunter dropped from the roof of the station and approached the Second Packleader. "That was a good deal of explaining you did," Yako said, stopping beside Imron. "I don't remember you ever offering details of the like to anyone before."

"That one is different," Imron replied.

Yako waited, but Imron said nothing more so he let the matter drop. It was not his concern. "I leave for Sinaia."

"I thought you would have already gone," the giant of a man said.

"I was expecting a foolish fledgling to have joined me by now," Yako replied.

"That one may be intent on his own destruction," Imron said. "Whether he's conscious of it or not is another matter."

Yako stood beside Imron and looked out at the city. "On some level, he wishes to die. I want to make him one of us before his own fire burns him out."

"You are the coldest blood I know," Imron said.

"The world is cold. I do what must be done."

"Of course." A pause of silence stretched between them for several minutes before the Second Packleader spoke again. "I doubt you've found me to report your departure, Eldest Hunter Yako. What has brought you here?"

Yako thought about the recent events, and how Remy had insinuated himself into a position of power in the Northwest Coven. Some even referred to the traitor as Eldest Hunter. Despite how laughable the claim may be, Yako never underestimated an enemy. Remy had accumulated a good number of Hunters and civilian vampires to his cause. Yako would do the same.

The Eldest Hunter's brown eyes began to smolder as he glared out at the forest of highrises and office buildings shrouded in the night and lit by the endless sea of lights. "Alliance."

CHAPTER 19

Like clockwork, the sun had barely dipped below the western horizon when Melinda opened her eyes. She glanced at the two sets of thick black curtains she'd nailed to the wall to cover the window. She remembered enjoying waking up to the warm sun shining on her face. Now the thought made her shiver.

She put her pillow against the headboard and sat up. As a kid, how often had she wished she could live forever? Funny how things change. As an adult, she couldn't fathom wanting to live forever. Every year seemed to bring new problems or some new difficulty. Or nearly just as bad, the same thing as last year. Who would want to live in such a state forever?

And here she was, sitting in her bed trying to figure out what she was going to do with the rest of an endless life. Of course, it might not be endless if she got caught up in all this business with Remy and Jelani and that lethal Eldest Hunter. Thinking of Yako gave her chills. Never had she met someone so cold and matter of fact. There was not a single doubt in her mind that he could have and would have killed her before she could lift a finger to stop him.

And yet he was the best option she had to be rid of Remy and get her life back. She sighed and swung her legs over the side of the bed. What would she do with the rest of her existence, assuming she did get her freedom back? She still needed to earn money to live somewhere, and purchasing blood from the coven-owned blood markets—something humans knew nothing about—was less expensive than traditional groceries but still required money. The thought of an immortal working an average nine to five job seemed so silly she could have laughed.

"Hmph. Maybe I'll fight in the female Ultimate Fighter." Who could beat her? *An older and stronger vampire, that's who.*

She walked into the kitchen and reached past the aging turkey bacon and carton of—no doubt yogurt-like—almond milk to grab a pack of blood out of the refrigerator. She looked at the other items and sighed again. How long had it been since she'd been turned? Three months? Four? Such a short time and already she couldn't remember. Melinda stared at the two items—now inedible—that represented what she had once been. What she would never be again.

Melinda closed the refrigerator door and turned on the stove. "How bad can it be, really?" she said to the dark apartment. "I'll live forever, which is plenty of time to do something great with my life ... hopefully. All I have to worry about for sustenance is blood. I'm pretty damn strong and fast, and I'll never age." She looked around. "Hell, I can even see in the dark." *And all I had to give up was ever seeing and feeling the sun again.*

If she'd put it on paper, it seemed a good tradeoff. She did live in Vancouver, anyway. How many days of dreary rain and clouds did she have to endure before the sun came out anyway?

That thought drew her mind to Jelani and she had to smile. She knew exactly what he would say to that thought. "If the weather makes you unhappy, you're not doing enough. You've got the mountains, snow, beach, biking, hiking, huge trees, tulips, and cherry blossoms. I could go on and on, girl. You need to get out and live in all this!"

"Wanted to slap him every time he said that," she muttered. He was right, though.

She poured the pack of blood into the saucepan, thinking about Remy. Maybe she could just stay here and hope for the best. She'd seen Jelani in action. With him and Yako on Remy's trail, there was a good chance they would kill him. But they were going into the heart of the storm. The Sinaia Coven. Through her disgusting link with him, Melinda knew that Remy had some kind of status with one of the Elders there. Massius, his name was.

She thought about Yako again. That one hadn't lived so long and gotten those skills by being careless. He would have some kind of backup when he went after Remy. But should she sit in a corner and wait, or do something about it?

With all these thoughts troubling her mind, Melinda poured the lightly warmed blood into a glass and drained it. As the warm blood went down and energized her body, Melinda's worries melted away. Her thoughts grew clearer, and the instant vigor made her smile.

"To hell with waiting," she thought aloud. She went into the living room and turned on the computer, checked her bank account, then started surfing the web for flights to Romania.

CHAPTER 20

*I*s this a mansion or a damn castle? Jelani thought as he jumped from beam to beam along the high ceiling of the darkened mansion. The last three surviving vampires must have made a sprint for it after they'd escaped the room. Jelani had been trying to pick up their trail for twenty minutes now. He knew that he had eluded the two crazy Hunters for the moment, but the still burning wounds on his body reminded him not to rest on his laurels.

He leaped to the last wooden beam in the hallway and stopped to listen. There was movement all around the mansion now, as word must have spread about the fight in that big banquette hall. At least some of the ones he'd killed were probably being missed by now, or would be soon.

Two men came out of a doorway to the left and turned in his direction. Should he let them go or take them out? It would be two less vampires for him to have to deal with later. He tried not to grind his teeth as he considered it. He'd gotten a good look at them, and from the memories he'd inherited from Remy, he knew these two had nothing to do with the attack.

Still. From their body language and the way they were creeping down the hallway, he knew they were looking for him. He decided to let them go. If he had gotten word of someone killing up a bunch of people in his house, he'd be doing the same.

After the pair disappeared around the corner, Jelani started to drop to the floor, but then he heard talking.

"… told you he went this way. Just shut up and listen to me for once."

"Watch it little man. Don't let your frustration cloud your judgement."

"You're damn right I'm frustrated, Berius. That unskilled idiot not only got away, but we've lost his trail. If you'd listened to me—"

"Will you stop complaining, already? It's not going to help us find the little fly, and with you bantering like this he's probably already heard us and fled."

Jelani stifled a laugh. Berius had no idea how close to the truth he was. He carefully lowered himself to lay flat on top of the thick beam. Vampires could see in the dark but not through solid objects.

"Whatever, husky man," Marcus snapped. "I think I heard someone going down that hallway." He pointed in the direction the two other vampires had gone earlier. "I can't be sure though, since word spread so fast and now all these fools are out looking. I can't pick out one person from the next. I just hear a bunch of footsteps and talking."

"Let's make toward the front door. He's probably trying to get out of here."

"And I'm sure he'll want to walk right out that way," Marcus replied, his tone laced with sarcasm. "Since he can't just jump out any number of the windows in this oversized house."

"Then, maybe if we hurry," Berius said. "We can look around and catch him when he gets out, if he isn't already."

"Fine," Marcus replied. "Not much of anything else we can do anyway. It's like trying to pick out one rat amongst a den in here anyway."

Jelani almost dropped on top of the Hunter for that, but he

reigned in his temper. At the moment, he didn't want to deal with those two again. He forced himself to admit that they might be a little more than he could handle. For now.

He waited till the dangerous Hunters were well out of sight and —hopefully—earshot, then dropped down. As soon as his feet touched the marble floor he darted to the side and waited in the darker shadows against the wall. After a few moments pressed against the wall next to a pillar, he silently chastised himself for forgetting that shadows didn't matter to vampires. Once sure no one else was nearby, he made his way down the hall.

Berius had been right. As much he wanted to get ahold of those last three who had gotten away, he had to get out of here while he could.

After weaving his way through the many hallways, Jelani realized he was lost. He looked around, and saw a window just under the roof. With any luck he'd be able to open it without making any noise. Better still, there was another row of beams overhead, one passing near enough to the window.

The sound of footsteps around a corner drew his attention. Jelani didn't bother to look. He leaped the thirty feet and swung himself over the beam. Crouched above, he waited. A man appeared down the hallway. He didn't seem to be looking for Jelani, or concerned about anything, given his casual stride.

Jelani didn't move a muscle, just watched as the man passed underneath his position. He relaxed and straightened a bit when the man continued on, but then he was suddenly gliding backwards. No, not backwards. Up and backwards. Before Jelani could move out of the way, the man turned as he glided toward him with a roundhouse punch that knocked Jelani from his perch.

He flew away and crashed through the nearby window, plummeting into the dark forest. The sting to his face faded under the chaos of his body ricocheting off tree trunks and limbs. His head bounced off the trunk of a redwood tree, then his legs hit a fir, spinning him sideways to slam into another giant redwood.

Jelani gritted his teeth and ignored the pain of slamming into a branch as big around as his body, and wrapped his arms around it. His legs swung underneath him and he used the momentum to swing them back and hop onto the branch. The tiny bit of pain from what should have been a body full of crushed bones was rapidly dissipating. He forced the grin from that recognition away from his face and scanned the surroundings, not daring to move from his crouched position.

The woods were quiet, and he didn't see any sign of pursuit. *So, what the hell was that?* he thought. How had that guy known he was there when he'd not made a sound? And even more peculiar; why hadn't he pursued? Jelani had been practically helpless by the surprise attack and by the time he'd recovered, that guy—whoever he was—could have had him dead the moment Jelani had stopped his fall.

He looked up as though he could see through the canopy of trees that blocked his view of the mansion up the hill. He still half expected to see his attacker descending through the trees to give him another shot to the jaw.

Jelani rubbed the side of his face. *Never been hit hard enough to send me flying through a window.* He thought again about the last three that got away. He'd find them. He didn't know how, just yet, but Jelani would find them.

He started to drop to the ground and make his way back to Vancouver, but then he remembered that there were giant wolves that liked to stalk less trafficked woods on the mountains. He decided to take the slower route of leaping from branch to branch.

It took him nearly half an hour before he finally made it back down, and he stopped on a branch at the edge of the tree line. The dark woods were replaced by open grass awash in the pale light of the waxing gibbous moon. Looking at that moon made Jelani think of his best friend, and what it might mean to him when it was full.

"Probably be full tomorrow," he said under his breath. And then what? After what he'd seen, Jelani had no doubts that

Daniel would change into a giant wolf, but would he have the same level of control as the guy had on the mountain? It seemed like a lifetime ago when they were trying to rescue Melinda from Remy. They'd all been human back then. Now, none of them were. He shook his head at the thought. *Life sure can take a turn.*

After one last scan of the area, he dropped from the branch and started across the grass. A circle of trees surrounded the little grassy patch, and on the other side would be another cluster of trees, then the street.

He kept his steps even and calm, better for an enemy to reveal themselves while he was in the open.

The thought hadn't fully formed in his mind when a woman stepped out from the far side of the tree line, directly in front of him. He reflexively reached for his daggers, then relaxed. She stood with a hand on her hip. Short, lithe, and with curves that would make a sculptor hang up his hammer and chisel. "Hello Saaya," Jelani greeted.

"Hello, fool boy," the *dampeal* said, walking toward him. The pale light seemed to glow around her. Was this another one of her mind tricks? Was she doing something to make the light shimmer over her like that? Or were his vampire eyes seeing something his human eyes could not?

"You look at me with starved eyes, *jaan.* Are you hungry for something?"

"No. I was just—"

Saaya was suddenly right in front of him. Even now, a vampire, Jelani still couldn't follow how fast she could move when she wanted to."

She smiled up at him and he struggled against a wave of, what was it? Desire? More like lust. He forced the feelings down, thinking of Alisha.

Saaya looked up at him with beautiful brown eyes with whites so bright they practically glowed. How had he never noticed such a majestic presence? Or had he simply not allowed himself to see it before now?

"How long, *Jaan?* How long will you punish yourself? How long will you torture yourself?" She slipped her arms around his waist and pressed her body against his. "How long will you deny yourself?"

Jelani clenched his jaw, afraid his mouth would betray him, like his body. She pressed tighter against him. So tight. It was all he could do to keep from ripping her clothes off right there.

She looked up at him with a devious smile and Jelani groaned. Of course she could feel everything he was feeling toward her. She knew what he was going through and enjoyed every second.

"You know this isn't playing fair?" he said, voice as stiff as the rest of him.

"Oh?" she said, trailing a finger down the middle of his chest. "What am I doing that is unfair?"

"You're doing that dazzling thing you do."

She fluttered her long eyelashes. "I'm doing nothing of the sort, love."

"I'm having a hard time believing you," Jelani said through clenched teeth.

That precise, angled smile returned. "I agree, you are having a …" she glanced down, "hard time."

Jelani swallowed. "Why is it I'm not even human anymore and you still affect me like this?"

"Because being a vampire does not make you immune to desire," came the melodious answer. Her nails trailed down his chest. "Why do you resist? Am I so repulsive?"

"Gimme a break, Saaya."

"Well? I would like to know." She trailed her nails up his chest, then down again. "I must admit that in all my years I have never met a man so intent on loneliness."

Jelani let his head fall back. *Gotta look away. Full moon.*

Gonna be a full moon, soon. "I think you know better than that, Saaya."

"What do you hope for?" She grabbed his hands and guided them to her hips. What do you want?"

Jelani looked down into the depths of her brown eyes. "Do you not know?" He felt her go still. It was subtle, but he felt it.

"This true love you so obsess over is not outside your reach, Jelani," she said crisply. "You need simply to wake her to the night, and all will be perfect. You can enjoy eternity together."

Yep. Wrong thing to say. "I'm sorry, Saaya." He shrugged helplessly. "I really am. I'm not trying to be like this—"

"But you cannot help how you feel and who you love." She stepped back and his hands slid away from her hips. It was like a bucket of iced water fell over him. "Trust me, I understand it better than you. Go. Find your love and remake her. It is within your power to do so. If you like, I can help you get it right so that you do not kill her."

At that moment, Jelani would rather end his own existence before inflicting this one on Alisha. "I would never ask you to do something like that."

Saaya's expression grew bored. "I assure you the process would be less painful for her than the endless headache I would endure of your moral agony, should you not."

Jelani took a deep breath. "I'm not going to turn her, Saaya. I would—"

"Never do something like that," she finished for him. "Of course not. That would be bad." She ran her fingers through her silky raven hair. "I must say that you have a hidden *talent* I hadn't seen before. I have never met someone who has made me so weary."

Jelani held his hands out and let them drop. "Look, I'm sorry I'm pissing you off, Saaya. But I don't know what else to say or do. My life is well beyond upside down and I'm trying to make sense of everything while dealing with this situation with Remy.

My best friend is a werewolf on top of it all. I'm not intentionally trying to make you upset with me, but I need you to cut me some slack. I feel like I haven't been standing on solid ground for months."

She took another step back, and for some reason this one seemed a little more absolute. "Very well. I may have been selfish and pushed you too hard. Search your feelings and do what you must. I wish nothing but the best for you, Jelani."

He stared at her. "You're … you're not ending our friendship, are you?"

Saaya made a sound that was part laugh and part sigh. She smiled at him, but there was regret in her eyes. "Friendship. No, Jelani. I am not severing our …friendship. You have a good heart and a beautiful spirit, and ever will I be your friend."

"Okay," Jelani said carefully. "Well … that's good to hear—"

"Goodbye, Jelani. Good luck hunting Remy. Good luck with your life."

"Saaya …" Jelani took a step forward, but then she started to fade from view directly in front of him. There was the slightest of afterimage, like her silhouette was still there, but then it moved away. After only a few feet, even that was gone as if she'd never been.

Jelani stood there for a long time, staring at the spot where the *dampeal* had been standing. *Well, that went great.* A drop of rain spattered on his head, then another. He looked up at the dark sky, and as if by invitation, the clouds let loose. Instantly soaked, he lifted his hands and let them drop again, this time with a wet splat.

"Seems like this has happened before." He continued across the grass and headed into the trees. "Very good, Jelani. You've got to be the only man alive who not only opted not to 'get it on' with a beautiful woman who likes you, but for the sake of a girl you can't even have anymore. Can't say I blame her for being pissed off. I'm me, and I'm pissed off at myself."

᠅

Saaya watched Jelani until he disappeared into the trees, rambling and berating himself. Not for the first time had she asked herself how she'd come to have feelings for such a difficult man. What was it? He was physically attractive, but that was meaningless in a world of hundreds of millions of men.

What was it, then? Intelligence? Surely he was smart, but again, that was not necessarily a rare trait, though she could probably argue that point with herself. She thought about those first days when he had been so torn between his feelings for two women, and how he had been obsessed with not doing either of them wrong, even if it meant his being alone.

"Fool," she said, but she knew it wasn't that simple. And then she understood. It wasn't his appearance, or his mind, or his personality, or even his spirit, though all of those things were attractive. The *dampeal* sighed and made her way into the trees. What was it that so drew her to him?

His heart.

CHAPTER 21

"Lemanda?"

Mariska nodded. "I think she will stand with us."

"You think." Tara leaned against the wall and crossed her arms. "So you think Lemanda, an Elder, and member of the High Council *might* stand with us? You do understand that speculation can be deadly, given our circumstances?"

"I understand well," Mariska replied.

"Do you?" The diminutive Reaper moved to stand in front of Mariska. The top of her head came barely above the Second Hunter's shoulder, yet she seemed to tower over her. "Massius has at least one pack of lycans left at his disposal. He has a good number of allies in the coven, and his coward lackey has taken the Northwest Coven. From all reports, he's done this with the assistance of a Reaper and two Hunters. And, there is no longer doubt that Alicia has sided with him, though she hides it well."

"I believe that sums it up, Reaper," Mariska replied.

Tara stared at her. Through her. "Our position is fragile."

"Reaper, may I speak?"

Mariska didn't dare break eye contact with the woman, but she knew the voice of one of her few allies. Akin.

"Speak, Hunter," Tara replied.

"As Second Hunter has reported, we have the allegiance of Darren Lacey's pack, as well as the two whom he has absorbed into his own. A good number of the Peles Coven side with us as well, and Eldest Hunter will be here soon."

Tara arched an eyebrow at Mariska, though her response was directed at Akin. "Are you repeating all this in case my comprehension is slow?"

"Of course not, Reaper," Akin quickly replied.

Tara nodded. Get quickly to the point, Hunter." Tara said.

"We have powerful allies, and once the rest of the High Council becomes aware of Massius and Remy's actions, they will most certainly stand with us. Are we not in a more favorable position?"

Tara held Mariska with her icy gaze a few seconds longer, then turned away. It felt like being released from a vice she hadn't known was compressing her tighter and tighter until it was gone. She resisted the urge to sigh.

"Your point makes sense," Tara said, "but you have neglected one detail." She turned her iron gaze on Akin. "When hunting prey that are larger and stronger, you attack the most vulnerable parts." She looked over her shoulder at one of her own Hunters. Layne. "Which is?"

"The eyes and neck," Layne answered, then shrugged, "Or genitals. But for our purposes, the head."

Tara turned back to Mariska. "There is no more basic a concept, but it has escaped you, Hunter. The High Council of Elders is composed of five. Any *one* of them could kill everyone in this room by themselves. But they are not gods, and they are not omniscient or omnipotent. We would be well served to assume Massius and Alicia have planned for their … removal, before they make a move."

"And knowing Massius," Mariska added, "it will happen in such a way as to point to some other party, should the effort fail."

That brought a round of chuckling and even a smile to Tara's youthful face. "Indeed. And there is nothing more dangerous than the plotting of the cravenly. What we don't know is when he plans to move."

"And, there is danger in organizing in any way before he does." This time it was Meilana who spoke. "The Elders aren't fools. They suspect Massius may be up to something."

"But they cannot simply have him removed ..." Tara added.

"Because he has Alicia at his side ..." Meilana continued.

"And the coven knows of his influence with the Order of the Hunters and the Order of the Reapers," Tara finished. "Even if they don't know that he created it,"

Mariska kept her features neutral. Sometimes, following the twins when they got going could be dizzying.

"Unfortunately we don't know how long Massius has been nurturing division in the coven," the twins continued, leapfrogging each other.

"Or, how many lycans he has at his back ..."

"But disposing of two Elders would rightfully raise serious questions ..."

"And eliminating two Elders that happen to be members of the High Council ..."

"Would raise dangerous questions."

"So, perhaps one of us should speak to Vicken in private about our concerns," Mariska offered, breaking the twins' momentum. "We can set our Hunters and Reapers to guard the High Council."

"That has already been done," Tara replied. "There is one whose name I will not mention who remains close. I'm led to believe that the Elders are prepared to deal with the situation, and hopefully it can be resolved before any conflict has a chance to escalate. Our hope is that Massius and Remy can be revealed for what they are before their insurrection has a chance to gain momentum."

"There may be another option," Mariska said. She and Tara locked gazes again.

"Leave us," the Reaper said.

After the Hunters had filed out of the room, Mariska caught a snippet of conversation. "Do you two read each other's minds or something?" It was Akin who'd asked.

"It's not uncommon for twins to think in tandem," Meilana replied. "Even human twins are known for this."

"Strange," the Hunter remarked.

"To you," came the responding quip.

Mariska gave a mental nod in appreciation of the skillful deflection. No doubt the sisters had many years to have perfected the technique diverting attention away from their connection.

"Need I guess that your option involves a certain Eldest Hunter?" Tara asked.

"Yes, Reaper."

Tara waved a hand. "Cease with the formality, Mariska. It's only us, here."

Mariska nodded. "I can think of no one better suited to discretely silence Massius and Alicia."

"Careful," Tara said. "You're dipping your toe into acidic waters, Mariska. I want nothing more than to be done with those two the same as you. But we must be cautious." She walked past Mariska toward a nearby window.

"I do not fear Massius. For an Elder, he is palpably weaker than the rest of the High Council. His strengths lie in manipulation and collusion."

"Then, perhaps we should eliminate him first and figure out how to deal with the other head of the hydra," Mariska suggested, moving beside the Reaper.

"Alicia makes me nervous," Tara said, and Mariska couldn't hide her surprise at the admission. "She shares Massius's strengths as well as age and power." She glanced at Mariska. "Yes, I admit I fear her. But I fear more for the coven's well being, should those two succeed."

"You think it would be a risk to eliminate Massius and not both of them at the same time," Mariska said. "In removing him, we risk angering her?"

Tara responded with quiet laughter. "You can believe me when I tell you that we could kill Massius a thousand times and it would not anger Alicia. There is something about her that seems ... elevated. I believe she has no particular attachment to anything, the coven included. She sees us not as enemies, but obstacles. She sees Massius not as an ally, but a tool."

"Your words suggest we have been concerned with the wrong threat," Mariska said with growing apprehension.

Tara nodded. "Massius is a threat, yes. But I'm of a mind that Alicia is the concern. I cannot be certain, but when I am around her I feel off balance."

Mariska frowned in concern for the Reaper. "You don't think—"

Tara shook her head. "No. If she knew about Meilana and me, we would be long dead, possibly before any of this began."

The two stared out the window for a few minutes. Mariska wondered what thoughts the woman was having. She knew better than to ask about any business concerning the Order of the Reapers, but she wondered how many had sided with them. Tara was obviously with them, and Mariska could be reasonably sure Braggus Rayne would fight beside them as well, though the giant man made her nervous.

"Have you ever wondered who should fear death more?" Tara suddenly asked.

"I'm not sure I follow," Mariska replied.

"Us, or humans," Tara clarified. "Have you ever thought who should fear death more? A human, whose fragile existence is but the blink of an eye in eternity, or us, whose life potentially spans that eternity? Who has more to lose? The mortal, or the immortal?"

Mariska didn't know where this was coming from, but it was a perplexing, if disturbing question. "I would suppose the immortal would have a greater stake at life than one who's life might reach no more than sixty or seventy years."

"You think so? Because they live so few years, would those few years not be even more valuable?"

"I suppose," Mariska said, eyeing her. "May I ask what this diversion is about?"

Tara's answering smile was anything but humorous. "Just a thought. I sometimes wonder if the cattle we ignore might have the right of it."

"Humans live their lives in perpetual obliviousness," Mariska said. "Most of them know little to nothing about the world around them."

"Do you think the decadent fools infesting our covens are any different, lounging in a constant state of hedonism?"

Mariska opened her mouth, then shut it. She really had no answer for that. Where was all this coming from?

The Reaper waved a dismissive hand. "I can see the confusion practically seeping from your ears, Second. Do not concern yourself. I was simply voicing my musings, nothing more. You said yourself that most humans are in a constant state of obliviousness. Most, not all. But to what good do most immortals put their lives is all I am asking. We so elevate ourselves from the human cattle, but are we truly?"

She cast Mariska a sidelong look. "You and I, my sister, Braggus and Yako. Yes, we put our lives to use in the protection of our species through discipline and devotion. But is there not more to existence than this? What good is an infinite life if it is simply for the pleasure of experiencing no pleasure?"

"You … raise an interesting point, Tara," Mariska replied.

More quiet laughter. "Let's leave it there, Mariska, lest I be responsible for your immortal life crisis. I would hate to place myself on Yako's bad side."

Mariska nearly scoffed at that notion, but she couldn't avoid wondering who would win that fight. "You bring an interesting perspective I'll have to think on further once this is all over," she said.

"I would recommend it," Tara said. I've known a human warrior or two in my time, and there were some who, at the end of their lives, had regrets. The regrets were always the same; not to have lived life a little more. Not to have allowed themselves to smile more, or experience joy and love. To see not only the darkness in life, but also the light."

She turned to Mariska. "I find little warmth in my heart for anything. Perhaps that is just an inherent trait of our species. I do not even pretend to comprehend the meaning of joy. But I do know that even we can find something about life to enjoy. And I know for certain that we are not above, or beneath, love."

She started away. "I would not recommend your Eldest Hunter moving on Massius alone. I would not recommend he go anywhere near Alicia. I do recommend we all convene when he arrives, and that includes your pack of wild dogs as well."

"There is one more," Mariska said, and Tara paused. "Yako's former target."

"The human Remy turned?" Tara asked, skepticism clear in her voice. "What good could he possibly serve? Even if he had been turned by someone more powerful than that idiot, what good could a *shaquora* do other than aid the enemy by being in our way?"

"Yako tells me his skills are adequate," Mariska said.

Tara, who had started away again, stopped and turned back. "Does he? Now, that is interesting. I should look forward to meeting him, then."

The Reaper left the room, and Mariska alone to her thoughts. *So do I.*

CHAPTER 22

L aura. Remy could have thought of a handful of individuals assigned to escort him back to the coven, but the black-haired woman standing at the bottom of the steps hadn't been one. She looked up at him with eyes so blue, they practically glowed against the contrast of her pale skin and black hair.

"So, it is true," she said. "I have the pleasure of being the first to meet with our newest Eldest Hunter."

"Pleasure?" Remy descended the last steps from the plane and stopped in front of her. He was so close he could see every detail of those ocean-colored eyes. "That is one word to describe it. I would think that privilege is the more appropriate term, right?"

She smiled and bowed her head. "Of course." She looked him up and down. "But I wouldn't write off the pleasure part just yet."

Remy restrained a smile that certainly spoke of a brief stop on the way to the coven. "Perhaps we will see." When Laura's expression turned sour, Remy guessed that Scarlene had come up behind him.

"The coven must think highly of us, Eldest Hunter, judging by our escort." Her tone was filled with a similar cheerfulness to that of the laughing sound of a hyena.

Laura smiled, showing teeth. "Hunter," she said, bowing her head again.

"Tart," Scarlene replied, staring down at her.

Remy's mouth twitched. Laura didn't dare speak a word of defiance. Not only did Scarlene outrank her, but the crimson-haired woman could rip her to shreds before she finished the insult.

Laura raised her head and pointedly looked past Scarlene to Marcos De La Vega, who had come around to Remy's right side. "Hunter," she said, showing a little more deference in her bow.

Remy's eyebrows raised. *You play with fire, you get burned,* he thought. Beside him, Scarlene's eyes blinked lazily above a smile so venomous, he thought the younger woman would burst into flames right there.

If the foolish girl noted her dangerous position, she didn't show it. "It is good to see you again," she said.

De La Vega's lips parted for a moment, and then he let out a breath that sounded like a laugh. "And you, Laura. I hope to see you in the future."

Laura made an uncertain expression, then glanced at the still smiling Scarlene, and looked back at Remy. "Please follow me, Eldest Hunter."

Remy fell in step behind her, enjoying the sway of her hips. Yes, he would send his subordinates on an errand and enjoy this one in a hotel for a couple hours before his arrival at Peles Castle. Whatever was brewing at the castle wouldn't spark in the couple hours he spent unwrapping his little tart, as Scarlene had called her.

Laura led them to a stretched Chrysler Navigator. A pair of humans jumped out of the vehicle and opened the doors on both sides.

Marcos looked around inside the vehicle, nodding in appreciation. "This is the luxury afforded the Eldest Hunter, hmm?"

Remy smirked at Marcos, who sat on the couch along the side. "You're fortunate to be my closest two. Now, which of you I make my Second will depend on your performance during all of the fun awaiting us at Peles."

"Between our Eldest Hunter and Elder Massius, I'm sure we'll see any difficulties easily handled," came the reply.

Remy's smirk disappeared. The statement was neutral, but he wasn't sure if the man's tone was mocking.

"I have every confidence in our Eldest Hunter's abilities," Laura said.

"Of course it will be handled," Scarlene cut in, rolling her eyes at the simpering young woman. "A member of the High Council of Elders and his chosen Eldest Hunter will ensure that whatever our enemies are plotting will be quelled."

Remy eyed Scarlene. He really didn't like her tone, but she was always obedient. She had done away with the humans linked to Jelani, ensuring the task that Yako had failed was completed. She did what was ordered of her, but he would need to help her adjust that saucy demeanor.

The privacy slot separating them from the human driver slid open. "Please pardon, Eldest Hunter," the passenger said in his thick Romanian accent. "There is a call from Peles Castle from Elder Massius."

Odd. Why didn't Massius simply call him directly? Remy nodded to Laura, who crept to the front of the vehicle to get the phone. Again, he admired her attributes as she turned away and leaned forward in the low-ceilinged vehicle. Beside him, Scarlene snorted, but when he looked at her, she was looking out the window.

Laura returned with the phone and handed it to him.

"Yes, Elder," Remy said.

"You have arrived," the cantankerous voice said through the phone. *"This is good."*

"You doubted I would come, Elder?"

"I doubt everything until I know for certain, which is why I called you through the driver. I will fully believe your arrival once

you are standing before me. Learn this, and you will live a long time."

A long time in paranoia, Remy thought. "Of course, Elder. I hope to one day achieve your wisdom." His eyes wandered toward Laura's crossed legs, her hips, her breasts. By the time his eyes found hers, those blue orbs were staring back at him enticingly.

"Yes yes, of course you do," Massius replied, rather impatiently. *"And you can begin achieving this wisdom by focusing while in the presence of distraction."*

Remy's eyes wrenched from the girl. "Distraction, Elder?"

"Am I beginning to stutter in my ancient years?" Massius asked. *"Yes, distraction. There is a great deal happening in the coven that will require your immediate attention. I've sent that empty-headed little girl to retrieve you and bring you directly to the coven. Directly, Remy."*

Remy closed his eyes. He could swear the old bastard was reading his mind. "Of course, Elder. I had no other intention but to come directly to—"

"The castle after you finished mauling and grappling with that stupid girl," Massius interrupted. *"Why do you think I'm on the phone with you now? I'll tell you. It is because of your dependable ability to focus your undivided attention in absolutely the wrong place at the wrong time."*

Remy felt his anger budding. "I can assure you I would not—"

"Save your lies for the fools that follow you. I can hear it forming in your throat before it escapes your mouth. You will come directly to the coven and present yourself before me. Then, you will come before the High Council of Elders and present yourself before them as if you came to them immediately upon your arrival. Once we have finished with those idiots, you and I have a lot to discuss and not a lot of time to do it. Too much has happened that you know nothing about."

"Of course, Elder," Remy said, trying not to growl. He glanced at Scarlene and Marcos, but the two were looking out the windows, far too interested in the scenery. Laura sat erect, legs still crossed, playing with her phone. How long ago had she been turned, anyway?

"Yes," Massius said. "Of course."

Remy was about to hang up the phone when the crabby voice spoke again. *"And one last thing, Eldest Hunter."* There was no doubt to the mockery in his tone. *"If you manage to find the wit and focus to match the challenges ahead, you will see rewards that go much farther than being Eldest Hunter in full, and not just title. And before you argue that point, consider how you would feel if you were a member of the Northwest Coven and saw your leaders killed by an upstart. How would you measure your loyalty under such circumstances?"*

The line died. Remy tossed the phone to Laura, who crept back to the front and knocked on the little screen and gave it back to the human up front. This time Remy didn't give the girl a thought.

As the Navigator made its way through the streets of Sinaia, Remy couldn't stop the feeling of insecurity creeping up on him. He knew that his two closest subordinates may or may not like him, but they were obedient, and that was all that mattered. But he couldn't ignore the truth of Massius's last words. How many in the Northwest Coven hated him because of what happened? Would Yako arrive at Peles with an army of angry vampires at his back? He glanced around and felt foolish sitting in the ridiculously long vehicle with two Hunters and a rather dull-witted girl who may be the only person that liked him at the moment.

He slammed his finger on the intercom. "Driver."

"Yes, Eldest Hunter?"

"Pull the vehicle over."

After a pause, the driver responded, "Of course, Eldest Hunter."

Scarlene looked at him. "Pining for a coffee? You'll only find twenty-four-hour coffee shops near the tourist part of town—"

"Marcos," Remy interrupted. "You will take Laura and deposit

her in a safe location where she will remain until I say otherwise."
He said this while looking at the young vampire, hoping she would
have enough brains to understand he didn't want to repeat or
explain himself. She seemed to get the message and bowed her
head nervously.

"Once you have done this," he continued, "you will rejoin me
at the coven."

"Of course, Eldest Hunter," Marcos said. He climbed out of the
vehicle with Laura close behind.

Once he closed the door, Remy turned to Scarlene, clamped a
hand under her chin and squeezed. "Not one word, do you understand?" He squeezed a little tighter. "There is a pack of wolves
waiting for our call. You will remain at the edge of town and be
quick to meet with them unless I tell you otherwise.

"I don't want to waste time with someone leaving the castle to
come this distance when you can be here now. You will find a
place to stay and you will speak to no one. I don't care if that
means you sitting in an inn or a motel day to night waiting for my
call. When I need you to act, you will do it swiftly. You understand, yes?"

With his hand clamped under her chin, she couldn't easily
speak, so she stared at him with baleful green eyes. He smiled at
her. "You'll have to excuse my lack of manners, Scarlet." Her eyes
practically blazed when he spoke her nickname. Odd woman. "I
have a lot to do in not much time, and I have no patience for
sarcasm at the moment. Now, be a good girl and do as I tell you.
When all this is done, you'll see that your reward will by far
outshine this little offense."

He released her chin and opened the door. Her eyes never left
his as she backed out of the Navigator and closed the door.

"Drive," Remy said into the intercom. He turned to look out the
back window. Scarlene remained where she stood. The windows
were tinted, and it was night, but he could have sworn she was still
staring into his eyes even as the vehicle pulled away.

CHAPTER 23

Scarlene watched the stretch Navigator carry that cretin off into the night. A small part of her found it amusing that Remy actually believed he was as forceful as he thought he was. Amazing that he could really believe his own bluster! If not for the need for discretion, she would have snatched Remy's hand off of his wrist and fed it to his little half-witted pet that Marcos was very likely disposing of now.

She watched the Navigator round the corner and almost laughed. She could envision Remy reclining on his plush seat, trying to convince himself he wasn't afraid he might actually have to fight for his little power grab.

She turned away, lost in her thoughts as she made her way aimlessly through the streets of the sleepy little tourist city. Occasionally she came across a pair of tourists who wanted to see the city while it was asleep.

Four blocks away, a man and woman holding hands turned onto the street, walking toward her. She could hear them quietly disagreeing. It had been his idea to explore a little bit of Sinaia without the crowds of tourists. The woman had agreed at first, but had gotten a bad feeling.

Once they were half a block away, the man discretely pointed at Scarlene while the woman whispered her objections. "Don't bother her. We don't know her."

"She obviously knows where she's going," the man said. "Why not just ask?"

Scarlene's lips thinned into a smile.

"S'cuse me, Miss," the man said, smiling. "We couldn't sleep and were looking for a late-night coffee shop. Do you know if there's one around here?"

Scarlene looked at him and then the woman who had taken a firm grip on his arm. She smiled nervously and said, "Hi. Sorry to bother you."

Scarlene could smell the anxiety on her. Never mind encountering a vampire. If they continued on with this woman wafting fear off of her like this, they ran a good chance of being sniffed out by a lycan.

They were healthy eaters, she could tell. The blood was different depending on what a person ate. She suspected they wanted a coffee shop for tea and not actually coffee. Their blood would be rich with oxygen, slightly sweet, and just the right balance of thin and thickness. Yes these two were healthy, and their blood would be delectable. She imagined how smooth and silky it must be, coursing through their clean arteries and veins.

She licked her lips and took a step forward. "There is a coffee shop that way," she said, half turning and pointing behind her and to the right, "but nothing is open at this hour. "You should come back when the sun is up."

She smiled and nodded as they thanked her. The woman smiled back and muscled the man back in the direction they'd come from while he protested, wanting to explore a little more.

Scarlene drew in a deep breath and blew it out with a snicker. Just as a fully gorged lion would walk right past a deer, so too had she let a free dinner walk away.

The woman glanced over her shoulder and Scarlene tilted her

head and waved, waggling her fingers. The woman smiled nervously and pulled at her husband to walk faster. The red headed vampire turned down another street, still tittering to herself. Yesterday, she had fed. Those two had eluded death by less than twenty-four hours.

After turning another corner, she looked into the distant night, and the castle wrapped within it. Peles. It stood as the unmovable presence it had always been, though the future was uncertain. She wished she could head straight there and kill Remy and Massius and be done with all this. Those two had already caused so many problems. She wondered why the other Elders of the High Council had not dealt with the situation, but as a Hunter, she had not the privilege of rank to know what went on behind those doors.

"I don't think you want to go in there yet," a voice said from behind and above. Michael's voice.

"Oh?" she replied.

"There's a lot going on that you don't want to be involved up in."

Scarlene stared at the distant castle without seeing it. "You think I don't know that?"

"I'm sure you do," Michael said.

"Then, we're just talking to hear our own voices," Scarlene said. "Or have you found me for another reason?"

"Am I to continue this conversation staring at your back?" Michael asked.

"Yes," she said, "if you plan to remain on the roof of that building. I'm not going to crane my neck back to talk up to you."

He chuckled at that. "Fair enough."

She turned around as he dropped from the roof and approached. "Why have you found me, Michael?"

"Found you? I was thinking to ask you the same question, Scarlet."

Despite her mood, the flame-haired vampire smiled at his use of her nickname. "Maybe I'd had enough of languishing in Remy's presence and needed to escape."

He laughed that deep breathy laugh that she liked. "I can't think of a better reason to be out here. It's good that you didn't continue on to the castle. It's getting dangerous there."

Scarlene waved a hand. "Massius and Remy together aren't the most desirable duo to tolerate, but I don't think I would be much worried about my safety from those two."

Michael frowned at that. "You must not know."

Now he had her attention. "Know?"

"I think you should come with me," Michael said.

Scarlene stared at him, wondering why his tone had gone so serious. "Know?" she repeated.

Michael didn't offer anything else. "Follow me."

CHAPTER 24

After waiting for an hour, Jelani figured Yako had gone. The Eldest Hunter had said to meet him as soon as the sun descended below the horizon, but Jelani had had other things to do. Unfortunately, he hadn't even completed that job, and now he was here, across the street from Alisha and Wen's building, half hoping that Yako would show up, and half hoping he would not.

He sat down on the roof, not feeling the coldness or hardness of the stone in the near freezing rainy night. Alisha didn't appear to be home, but Wen sat on the couch with the TV on, playing a game on her phone. Jelani smiled sadly. It was probably one of those puzzle games Daniel had accused her of being addicted to.

Thinking of his friend dampened Jelani's mood more than his rain soaked clothes. A year ago if anyone had told him that he would be sitting on a rooftop in the freezing rain, a newly turned vampire watching over his best friend's former fiancée while his best friend—who now hates him—is dealing with whatever issues he's having after being turned into a werewolf, Jelani would have told them to write the screenplay.

Vampires. Werewolves. He hated them for what they'd done to his and his friends' lives. Did that mean he hated himself?

In the back of his mind he felt Saaya. The *dampeal* felt, what was that? Conflicted? *That's new.* Was he the cause of her mental discord or was something else going on? He thought about their last meeting and decided he was probably the cause.

Jelani chewed his bottom lip. All he'd ever wanted to do was live a good life. He'd gotten quite good at avoiding trouble and keeping life simple. He'd been blessed with a nice home in his beloved Vancouver BC, had his own home-based web design business and had been gaining traction with Alisha. Things had been great and getting better.

Now his life was the epitome of chaos. The more he tried to do what was right the more it seemed like what was right slipped away from him. Should he keep looking out for Alisha? Maybe one day her memory would come around and they could be together again.

Across the street, Wen stood up from the couch and turned out the light.

JELANI STOOD, and with an effort, turned his back on the dark apartment. Time to go. Whether Yako was still waiting for him or not, Jelani would fulfill his promise and make his way to Romania. He just had to figure out how to do it so that he wouldn't get burned alive on the plane.

He did a mental note of his bank account and figured he would have to pay for first class on one of those jumbo jets where they had private cubicles with a bed, chair, desk, and more importantly, private use of a window shade he could keep down during the day.

That flight would cost more than many people made in a year, but weighed against the prospect of someone opening the window shade and frying him, he could think of far less valuable things he'd spent that kind of money on.

He froze. Someone was here, he could feel it. He kept still and scanned the dark surroundings. Someone was definitely here. "You gonna come out and talk or do I have to find you?" He'd said it under his breath, but he knew the watcher could hear. Sure enough, someone stepped out from behind a pillar on the other side of the roof.

"You are surprisingly aware, for a *shaquora*." The voice had a tinge of a Middle Eastern accent to it. "And a fledgling, at that."

The hairs on the back of Jelani's neck stood. "You're the guy that launched me out the window back at the mansion."

The man stepped closer, and Jelani's hands moved toward the silver dagger strapped to his waist.

"There will be no need for that," the man said.

"My left jaw disagrees," Jelani retorted.

"My fist could have easily held a weapon of silver," came the reply

Jelani thought about that, then shrugged. No arguing that logic. "Would I be a narcissist for assuming you came here for me? If not to fight, then to talk?"

"It might be that I came here for both."

"I'm not much of a mind to make small talk with someone who wants to fight me," Jelani said.

The man offered no reaction to that. "Sometimes we don't have a choice in what we want."

Jelani's hand remained near his dagger. "You're not making these pleasantries easy."

The man continued toward him and Jelani held up a hand, which did nothing to slow his progress. "Say, bruh. You need to back it off or we *will* be fighting."

"That would be unfortunate." And then the man was standing right in front of him, no more than a foot away.

Jelani reared back. *What the hell? I thought only Saaya and her creepy brother could do that to me now.*

"Very unfortunate," the man continued, "if you considered I could have had you dead three times over by now."

Jelani blinked. "Uh … thanks for that. What do you want with me? I'm pretty sure you know who I am."

"I do not know exactly who you are, but I know that you've caused a big stir amongst the inhabitants infecting the coven."

Jelani raised his eyebrows at that. "I take it you don't care for them?"

"Anyone who commands respect for themselves was not present when you made your attack," the man replied. "To your point, I am here out of curiosity. How a newly turned vampire could move about the coven dispatching targets one after the other, then kill almost everyone in that lounge while fighting off Marcus and Berius alone is something I have never seen."

Jelani shrugged again. "Luck?"

"Don't irritate me," came the darkened response.

All pride out the window, Jelani felt he'd better comply. This guy could be a problem if he really wanted to be.

"Simply put," the man continued, "I haven't killed you because it would be a shame to uncreate such potential. What is your name?"

Jelani's mind raced. What would this man do if he knew who he was? "I can't remember," he lied. "When I awoke for the first time, my memory was fragmented. I don't remember much of who I was."

The man considered this then looked directly into Jelani's eyes. "You are still new, so I will pass on a piece of advice. Until you have walked the night for a time, do not assume all of the myths are true. I will ask once more. What is your name?"

Jelani readied himself. "The name's Jelani. How about you?"

The man nodded. "That is interesting. Jelani. The former target of former Eldest Hunter Yako. You fascinate more than a few of us, my friend."

So we're up to the "my friend"thing now? "Why so?" Jelani asked. "And, you still haven't told me your name. It feels like you've got me at a disadvantage."

The man blinked at him. "I am Jamir of the Order of the Reapers of Peles Coven."

Ho ... ly ... shit. "So," Jelani swallowed the lump in his throat. "You're a Reaper. I hear you guys are pretty tough."

Jamir chuckled and it actually seemed genuine. "It is a trait we are noted for."

"So you're here because you're curious about how a fledgling like me has done what I have and am still alive?"

"The fact that you're alive despite being hunted by a legendary Hunter is enough to afford you a great deal of respect," Jamir said.

You definitely don't know the whole story, buddy. "Yeah well, we've kinda made a truce about the whole thing."

Jamir perked up at that. "Oh?"

"Yeah. And since Remy turned me ..." he trailed off at the Reaper's reaction to that little bit. "I take it you didn't know that?"

"An interesting little fact that Remy failed to mention." Jamir seemed to be speaking to himself. "Hmm." He looked back at Jelani. "I didn't know. The fact that he used Yako's failure at killing you as a springboard for what was done at the coven is especially interesting, considering he should have been able to compel you to come directly to him, given he is the one who re-created you." He frowned. "You're sure?"

Jelani looked at him as though he'd lost his mind. "You think I'd forget something like that?"

"I suppose not," Jamir said. Remy's little situation grows even more tenuous."

And then, Jelani saw it in his mind. Jamir on his right, Marcus and Berius behind and to the left and right. The mansion. Bakden and Clairese meeting them with surprise, then outrage. Jamir swiftly subduing both leaders of the coven while the two Hunters ensured no interference. A swift trial followed by immediate execution. The denouncement of the absent Yako as Eldest Hunter and the order for him to be executed as a traitor to the High Council.

Jelani blinked the vision away and focused back on Jamir, who silently watched him.

"I doubted whether you had truly been turned by Remy or not," the Reaper said, "but I see you've just experienced a shared vision; likely one involving my participation in the restructuring of the coven."

Jelani didn't miss the change in tone. "You didn't approve?"

"It is not for anyone to question an Elder of the High Council." Every word he spoke sounded forced.

"That's an easy way to be manipulated, my friend," Jelani ventured. That seemed to anger the Reaper, but Jelani didn't feel it was directed at him. "Am I hitting a little close to home?"

Jamir frowned. "What?"

"About the manipulation thing," Jelani said. "Is that what happened? One of those Elders sent you riding a lie to help Remy secure the coven?"

The Reaper's gaze turned icy. "That isn't your business."

Jelani held up his hands. "Hey man, you're the one who came here up in my business. I'm just trying to follow the thread. Let me just tell you this. Remy turned me away from the sun but has no power over me. I'm not going to lie to you and say I'm thankful to him for what he did to me. I'm planning to skin him alive, metaphorically speaking, of course." That earned a smirk. "He ran away to the coven, what's it called? Peles Coven? Yeah. I'm planning on catching a plane to go say hello.

"As for Yako. He hasn't betrayed anyone, and the only thing that diverted his attention from me was Remy, as far as I know. If you want my take, I think you've been had."

"Quite a story," Jamir said, seeming to make an effort to control his anger. "Are you sure you're not just trying to gain an ally?"

Jelani snorted. "Dude I'm still not even sure I like any of you after everything I've been put through these last months. The only thing that concerns me at the moment is screwing Remy's head off his neck for himself. I'm not particularly interested in help, mostly because I don't want anyone else beating me to the guy."

"You may have a challenge, there," Jamir said. "I've never met anyone better at making enemies."

"Then I'd better get moving," Jelani said.

Jamir nodded. "You probably should."

He regarded the Reaper more carefully. "You're not exactly all in with Remy's camp, are you?"

"What?"

"On his side," Jelani clarified. "You're not really on his side so much as you were following orders. You didn't know about him turning me, which makes me think it was something to hide. Is it that unusual not to be able to control someone you turned?"

A corner of Jamir's mouth twitched. "I would say it does not look very good not to be able to control one's own fledgling. I would say it is extremely embarrassing to have one's fledgling hunting you down. If word got out that Remy's own *shaquora* was trying to kill him and there was nothing he could do to compel you to stop, I cannot fathom the humiliation."

Jelani grinned. He actually felt excited. "Well, I'll have to work on that."

More quiet laughter, from the Reaper. "You are the most unusual *shaquora* I have ever met."

"How so?" Jelani asked.

"Vampires who have been turned from the light are typically more grim. They strive to portray the persona of what they think it is to be an immortal. Instead, they become caricatures. This is why you're unlikely to see purebloods mingling with *shaquora* who have seen less than a century or two, and also why we often kill them on sight."

That was unexpected.

"So," Jelani said, frowning, "you kill them on sight because you don't like them?"

"Some of us do. But mostly it is because *shaquora* are more often than not, a danger. They tend to become intoxicated with their newfound power and use no discretion. They are like a virus that must be held in check."

"That's a harsh way to put it," Jelani said. "You call us a virus, but what does that make you?"

"More than you can understand," Jamir answered. "What I say may have given you offense, but your feelings mean nothing against the real possibility of this world being overrun with low-blooded vampires."

Jelani just looked at him. "I didn't take you for the dramatic type, Jamir."

"It has happened before," the Reaper said. "And though we have managed to shroud our existence into myth, there are some humans who remember."

Jelani frowned. "Remember what?"

"You want to know more about it?" Jamir said, turning away. "Try to at least pretend to yourself that you don't want to die. You may survive long enough to discover the history of the species of which you're now a part of."

"Who said anything about wanting to die?" Jelani asked as Jamir departed. "I never said anything about being suicidal."

"Breaking into a coven housing two skilled Hunters and a Reaper for the sole purpose of revenge is not what I call somebody that wants to live a long life." He dropped from the roof.

Jelani stared in the spot where the other man had been. He'd been so caught up in the conversation that he hadn't realized the rain stopped. "Life just gets more interesting by the minute."

"You must be the luckiest person I've ever seen, blood."

Jelani whirled, daggers in his hands. A man much larger than Jelani felt comfortable being near stood at ease, despite the brandished silver. *How did he creep up on me like that?* "Look," he said. "I know I'm new to this 'creatures of the night' thing, but the mysterious sneaking up on folks from behind is not working for me."

The man took another step forward into the light shining from the roof lights. Thick goatee, curly black hair, olive brownish skin, bear-like size. Jelani instantly knew him for the big Pakistani guy that had turned Daniel.

Jelani didn't know whether to attack him or wait and see what happened. The big man's shoulders bounced as he laughed. "Grudges are unhealthy, my friend."

Jelani narrowed his eyes. "I'm not your friend."

He shrugged. "Fair enough. But allow me to speak before you attempt to kill me."

"Fair enough," Jelani echoed.

The man laughed again. "Such an icy tone. You are definitely a worthy blood. Look. Your friend had been broken up pretty bad when I found him. He'd already had a foot in the grave."

"And you make a habit of infecting anyone you find who's knocking on death's door?" Jelani asked.

"Infecting." He shook his head. "You know, it's the same with us. Our newly turned lycans take some time to stop thinking as humans do. Viruses and infecting, curses, monsters, walking dead, that sort of thing." He slid his hands in the pockets of his coat. "It's not that simple."

"Enlighten me," Jelani replied.

The big man responded with a frowning smile. "What am I, a school teacher? You've got, I dunno, an unlimited lifetime to learn all this. Supposing you survive long enough, do your own research and find out how we all came to be, if such a body of work actually exists. If you're really the Road Scholar you act like you are with all these questions, you might seek out one of your vampire *Ancestors* to sit you down in a big leather chair and impart your history orally in between puffs of a tobacco pipe."

Jelani continued to stare at the man, unamused. "My ancestry is mostly African."

The big man rolled his eyes. "A griot, then?"

Jelani snorted, then laughed. It was a hearty and much needed laugh. "Okay, homie, you got me." He sheathed his daggers. "This definitely isn't going to be a fight, so why are you here? Does this have something to do with Daniel?"

"Ah, so the blood has figured it out. I'm sure there are a million reasons a lycan would seek out a vampire for reasons other than to kill each other, but none come to mind. Yes, it's about your stubborn friend."

"What's going on with him?" Jelani asked. "I was going to try to find him but I've had some things going on." He looked out at the colorful city, glowing in the night. "And what's your name, dude? Everyone comes at me wanting to talk about whatever, and no one volunteers a name."

"Imron. Happy?"

"Thrilled," Jelani answered. "Cool name."

Imron smirked. "I know."

Jelani snorted again. "What's the deal with Daniel?"

"He and I need your help," Imron replied.

Jelani's smile disappeared. "Is he in trouble?"

All humor left the giant lycan's face. "Not yet."

CHAPTER 25

A good day.

Daniel leaned his head back into the sun. It was so warm that he'd donned shorts and a T-shirt. He glanced at a Caribbean couple walking by, both dressed as though winter still held sway. They reminded him of Jelani, and he smiled when he remembered how his best friend would often say, "dude, black folks don't do the cold. If it's under eighty degrees, we're cold."

Of course, Daniel would point out places like central Canada and the east coast, but Jelani's response always went down the road of "people fly in planes, too. Doesn't mean we're naturally supposed to be up there."

Daniel smiled wider when he thought about how in the last three years he'd been living in Vancouver, Jelani had begun to wear shorts and a T-shirt when the temperature had barely risen over seventy. His smile faded.

Best friend.

Was Jelani his best friend anymore? Daniel had asked himself that question many times lately, and he still wasn't sure of the answer.

He shoved his hands in his pockets and continued down the

boardwalk in Coal Harbour. Nothing that had happened to them was Jelani's fault. Rationally, he knew this. How often had Daniel himself gone for a walk down the very boardwalk he was on right now, at night, alone? Could he just as easily have stumbled across a vampire? The events of the past half year made it seem almost a certainty.

He tried not to think of Wen, but there she was, in his head. Her dimpled smile and slightly wavy hair from where the curls she insisted on having had fallen out. He saw perfectly in his mind, her brown eyes and straight white teeth.

Daniel closed his eyes and clenched his jaw to force the anger down. Apparently having a wolf inside you had a particularly nasty side effect in that it gave you a temper. Daniel had never been the excitable type, but this thing inside him was like a crouched predator, waiting for him to let his guard down so it could pounce and take over.

Jelani came to mind again and the anger buckled his knees. He leaned against the rail overlooking the ocean and took deep breaths. The anger focused at Jelani, not solely because of what had happened, but because he was a vampire. Were all bloods and lycans predisposed to dislike each other?

Daniel wrestled the anger under control and looked out at the water. "What the hell am I going to do?" he muttered. "Do I continue on as usual? Go back to work?" He had done most of his work from home, claiming injury from snowboarding. His boss had been great, saying for him to do everything from home as long as he needed to. It was getting harder to focus, though, with this thing inside him.

He thought of Wen again and wanted to throw his head back and howl at the sky, which was horrifying. How the hell did Imron and other werewolves deal with this? It seemed like he was fighting to keep his identity against this thing inside him that wanted to take over. Daniel took another deep breath and let his head hang.

This thing inside him. A confrontation between himself and this "thing" inside would happen soon, he could feel it.

Daniel looked up at the sky. It was like something up there tugged at him. Full moon? It seemed ridiculous, like all those untrue myths about vampires.

Some of them were true, though. Jelani hadn't seen daylight since that fateful night at the shipping docks. Daniel thought about his friend's plight with the sun and took at least a little comfort in the fact that he could still walk around any time, day or night, without having to worry about being fried. If anything, his blood seemed to be running warmer than before. While everyone suffered the post winter sicknesses and allergy problems around him, Daniel had felt nothing of it.

He looked down at his arms, which were more muscular than they had ever been. He glanced at his legs, where his quadricep muscles were beginning to strain against his shorts. Every muscle in his body had become bigger, harder and stronger. He placed a hand to his chest, feeling the indent in the center, and smirked.

In all the years he had trained and worked out, he'd only ever been able to get definition in his chest, but never any size to it. The familiar smell of sweet flowers and rain, and personal scent interrupted his thoughts.

"There are others who would enjoy rubbing your body, love. You need not do it yourself."

Daniel dropped his hand away and tried not to blush. "Hello Saaya. What can I do for you?"

She came up beside him. Closely beside him. "Hmm."

Daniel sighed. "I said what can I do *for* you, Saaya, not *to* you."

The *dampeal* pushed her bottom lip out. "Pity."

"You enjoy being a tease, don't you?" Daniel said, looking down at her.

She returned his gaze with a flutter of her eyelashes. "Who said I was teasing?"

"I thought you had the hots for Jelani," he said.

In response Saaya brushed her shoulder up against him. "Who says I can't have the hots for the both of you?"

As much as he tried to deny it to himself, Daniel enjoyed the contact, even if it was only a shoulder. He cleared his throat. "So, you're trying to start your own male harem, then?"

"Two men hardly make up a harem, silly boy."

"Doesn't matter anyway," he said. "Guys don't take well to that sort of thing, you know."

"What sort of thing?" she asked innocently.

Daniel gave her a bored look. "You know exactly what sort of thing, but I'll spell it out for you anyway. You're not going to find many straight guys willing to share one girl. First, because we don't want to see another naked guy. Second, there's too much chance of getting touched by the other guy's junk, and that's just … hell no."

"Do you not have community showers in some places?" Saaya asked.

"Yeah we do, and we also pretend the other guy doesn't exist. If for some reason we have to talk, we don't look at each other. Now, if you're serious, I know a couple of really cool bi guys …" He stopped and sighed when he heard her giggling. "I've been baited, haven't I?"

"Oh, my silly boy," Saaya said. "It's too bad your heart lies so completely with another."

"Not like it matters now." When no response came, Daniel glanced down at her. The *dampeal* seemed to be in thought. "Something I said?"

"Perhaps," Saaya replied absently, tapping a finger to her lips.

Daniel waited, but she said nothing further. "What did I say?"

She shook off whatever she'd been thinking about. "Nothing. Just a thought."

"About?" Daniel pressed.

Saaya smiled and blinked those light brown eyes at him. "You seem well on the outside. You hide your turmoil well."

Daniel decided to let the deflection hold. He really wasn't in the mood anyway. "Yeah, right. Thanks for that. Don't know how long I can last, but I'm doing my best."

Saaya grabbed his hand. "All will be well."

He flinched at the contact, but then relaxed. There was no lust or provocativeness in her eyes. Was this friendship? From Saaya? "You the resident authority on lycans?" he asked, looking back out at the water.

"Hardly that," she replied, "but I have learned some things in my few years of life."

"If it'll help me deal with this thing inside me," Daniel said, "I'm all ears."

She gave his hand a squeeze, then released it. To his surprise, he found he didn't want her to let go. "Once you've completed your first transformation you will find balance again."

"You make it sound like it's an easy thing," Daniel said, trying not to let anger creep into his voice. "I didn't want it, and now I have to deal with this ... thing, inside me. I can't even describe what it's like, Saaya. It feels like there's a raving animal inside, waiting for me to slip so it can come out."

"It will get easier—"

"Once I complete my transformation," Daniel interrupted, nodding his head dramatically. "Yes, yes I get it. But what if I don't want this "transformation"? Who in their right mind would want to transform into a monster?"

He put his head in his hands. "What if I don't remember anything while I'm a ... you know?" He couldn't bring himself to say it. Now he knew how Jelani felt when he had first been turned.

A rare note of sympathy coated Saaya's tone. "You have no choice about it, love."

Daniel felt the heat of his anger rising again. "I remember. That choice was taken from me."

"You would have died, Daniel."

"Maybe that would have been better." He didn't mean to snap, but his anger bubbled to the surface. "Maybe I would have been better off dead than prowling the night as a monster."

Saaya's face darkened, and Daniel thought maybe he'd pushed too far. He frowned and looked back out at the water, realizing he really didn't care if he'd upset the *dampeal* or not.

"There are ways to alleviate your plight, if you wish it," Saaya offered. "You still carry your silver daggers?"

Daniel opened his mouth, then closed it. "I'm sorry. I didn't mean to cry all over you." Maybe he did care, a little. "It's just that I feel like my life isn't my own and that there isn't anything I can do to get it back. I can feel that it's only a matter of time before this thing comes out."

"Do lycans not help each other through this?" Saaya asked. This time, her inquiry was genuine. "Why haven't you spoken to Imron?"

Daniel felt mixed emotions at the mention of that name. Right now he wanted to rip the iron rail off and throw it into the ocean. "He did talk to me, but what am I supposed to do with that? I don't know him or anyone else in this supposed pack I belong to. The only thing I can think of that's worse than transforming into a monster is doing it surrounded by other monsters."

They were silent for a while, looking out at the water. It felt unusual having a conversation with Saaya without it diverting onto a sexual route.

"I recommend you reconsider your stance on this," she finally said. "It could mean the difference between you retaining your sense of self and becoming something else."

Daniel considered it and shook his head. "He is the reason I am what I am. Yes, he saved my life, but at a cost that's pretty damned high. I don't know what I'm going to do. I just need time to figure this all out."

"Unfortunately, you don't have much time," Saaya replied.

"Then I'll just have to deal with this as best I can," Daniel said. "If something happens, it happens. This is a personal thing, Saaya. I'm gonna have to deal with it alone."

"You have a friend," came the response.

"I'm not really sure about that eith …" he trailed off when he realized she was gone. "How the hell does she do that?" he thought aloud. "And in daylight?"

He looked back out at the ocean, taking in the sights. The cherry blossoms were in their final stage before falling and the trees turning green. Soon tulips would be planted throughout the city for the remainder of spring before summer arrived.

Seeing couples holding hands walking up and down the board-walk felt like a knife twisting in his chest, and he suddenly felt like being alone.

Before he knew it, Daniel had left Coal Harbour and headed over the Lions Gate Bridge. He realized that he was moving directly toward Grouse Mountain. He'd had moments when he wanted to be away from people, but that usually meant a trip to the interior of Stanley Park, or just going home. But he was walking toward the mountain, and it was getting late.

"What does it matter," he said to himself. "I got nowhere to be anyway."

He kept walking and staring at the mountain ahead. What once was a place that held year-round outdoor fun now sent chills through him.

CHAPTER 26

By the time Daniel reached the base of the mountain, dusk had nearly arrived. He watched the busses filled with snow-boarders and skiers pass him by, wishing he was heading up the mountain for the last few days of boarding before the season ended.

He turned off the main street and started weaving his way through the residential neighborhoods. He and Wen had often gone for drives through these streets, looking at the homes and picking out what type of house they would buy one day.

Walking through the quiet neighborhood actually made him feel better. He drew in a deep breath and blew it out. Maybe Saaya was right, and this would all get easier over time. Daniel didn't know how long he could take living with an animal inside him clawing to get out.

At the end of a cul-de-sac he came to some stone steps that looked to lead up into a hiking trail. He followed them up until he came to the trail, then followed it until it started to turn away from the mountain. He continued forward, hiking straight through the woods.

Despite the steepening terrain, Daniel increased his pace until he found himself jogging up the mountainside. Something pulled at him and he needed to move faster. *What the hell am I doing?*

He jumped over a fallen tree and stopped to look back at it. Then he turned and looked up the hill and the steep slope. It was an impossible jump, but he'd just done it. He looked around the darkened woods. Unlike the last time he was in this place, he felt no fear. Somewhere inside Daniel knew that there was no animal on this mountain or anywhere in the world that could harm him. He shook his head and continued on until the terrain leveled off and he came to a clearing from the woods.

Please tell me I didn't just come to the same spot where we found Melinda. Daniel looked around, unable to believe he'd come back to this place. He started out of the trees, then stopped. The full moon bathed the glade in its pale light. It should have been beautiful instead of terrifying.

"What now?" Daniel slumped down against an evergreen and pulled his knees against his chest. It had rained up here recently, he could smell the dampness. He heard species of birds roosted somewhere in the distance, and he could smell a squirrel under the fallen tree limbs.

Somewhere across the grassy glade, he smelled a rabbit, or rather, the rabbit's fear. He laughed under his breath at that. He might look human, but you couldn't fool an animal.

Daniel had to force himself to block out the endless smells and sounds assaulting him from everywhere. He could hear and smell things that were miles away, and in the olfactory equivalent of high definition.

He glanced up in the general direction of the moon. If he went out there, the thing inside him would gain the upper hand and he'd be lost. He could feel it stirring now, so close. The moon was only a few steps away, and if he cast his eyes on it, he and the wolf would switch places.

"Why did I come here?" Daniel rubbed his sweaty palms on his legs and forced his breathing to slow down. What if the wolf completely took over and he couldn't get back to himself? Would he be the one inside while the wolf kept him at bay? How long would it last?

A distant howl rose above the rising insect chatter, followed by another. Wolves. The normal kind. It went on for a few minutes and then the night went quiet again but for the insects.

Then he heard it.

It was the most terrifying sound he'd ever heard, yet a part of him felt comforted by it. A wolf's howl, but ten times deeper, ten times heavier, if sound could have weight. If Daniel had heard that with human ears he wouldn't have known what to make of it except to get the hell out of the woods immediately.

Another howl, answered by another. Daniel felt his answering howl creeping up his throat and he fought it down. The howls were getting closer, but after a few minutes they stopped. He sniffed the air, disgusted that the action came so natural to him and that he could smell everything around him.

Daniel felt the pull again, and before his human mind could react, he was on his feet and out of the woods. Several steps brought him fully into the moonlight. It felt invigorating. Slowly, his gaze lifted. His human mind screamed at him to fight it, to not look up, but he may as well be fighting against the urge to breathe.

His gaze lifted up and up until he saw it. Never had he seen the moon like this; huge and perfectly round. Its power washed over him, burning away his weaknesses and filling him with strength and vigor.

So fixed on the power of the moon, Daniel didn't realize he'd begun to shake. Ragged breaths came out in huffs and his knees buckled. He dropped to the grassy earth, eyes still held in the moon's powerful grasp. His breaths slowed, came deeper, more guttural.

He looked at the back of his hand where tiny hairs grew thicker and longer. The horrified human part of Daniel rapidly diminished until it was nothing more than a tiny voice deep inside.

His back heaved with each breath, and he felt the muscles moving, reforming. Pain exploded through his body as cartilage twisted and stretched to accommodate the growing muscle. He heard a popping sound as one by one, every joint dislocated and shifted.

Mind-splitting pain replaced his very existence. Even his mouth pulsated with agony. His jaw dislocated and began to reform, pushing his human teeth back as row upon row of much larger canine teeth slid into place. His body heaved, and with each heave, it became bigger.

His clothes stretched to their limits and tore around him. His shirt ripped apart around his reforming back. He slammed his hands to the earth, and saw that they were no longer hands, but claws. His pants ripped at the seams and his phone tumbled out. He looked down at the unfamiliar thing and saw a pair of golden eyes above a muzzle covered in pitch-black fur staring back at him.

He gasped, struggling not to drown in the pain of bone and sinew stretching and twisting, breaking and re-knitting. Finally, mercifully, the pain stopped, and then a wave of shivers rippled through him. Still on all fours, he gave his body a shake, and felt the rustle of long black fur. He placed his rear feet—not feet, claws —beneath him, then steadied himself and stood.

As he straightened, his senses came into focus. As acute as his sense of smell had been only minutes before, now he smelled everything for miles and smelled it with such clarity and distinction, he could have picked a single ant out of a colony for its distinctive scent. His golden eyes could see every detail in the darkened woods as if it were day. He looked down at claws with fingers that were twice their human length.

The air misted around his muzzle as he took ragged breaths, then threw his head back and roared at the moon. He howled out a long, deep proclamation of his arrival, his power.

Nearby he smelled a male black bear. It smelled him, too, he knew, and it ran away. Neither black nor brown bear could challenge him. He could hunt either down and easily catch it, easily kill it and feast. He smelled the sweet and pungent fear of rodents, insects, birds, and every small animal in the area aware of his presence.

The wolf's ears twitched. They swiveled of their own accord, picking up sounds in every direction. He sniffed the air and smelled them. They were coming fast.

He turned left, then right, snapping his jaws at the night air. He smelled a power greater than his own drawing near, and he crouched, growling deep in his belly.

Two giant wolves emerged from the brush and stood on their hind legs. He whipped his head around to see three more emerge to his right, then two to his left and two behind. They closed in, then stopped, keeping their distance.

He looked at each of them, males and females, and not a one that could challenge him. This was a pack, but none of them had power over him. He could smell the challenge in the two in front, and the fear in one of the two behind him. One of the wolves to his right smelled of attraction, while another smelled of uncertainty.

Daniel turned, looking each of them in the eye, growling, snapping his jaws. Several snapped in response, but most just watched him. He crept toward the largest gap in the circle, and one of the wolves moved to tighten it. Daniel snapped his jaws and barked a challenge. The slightly bigger wolf backed away. More barking ensued as the pack grew agitated. Daniel kept his eyes on the challenge. This one would move out of his way or he would fight.

A roar shattered the relative silence. It made the insides of the wolf that was Daniel vibrate, and he struggled not to lower himself to the ground. Around him, the other wolves were doing just that.

A giant black wolf just over a head taller than Daniel emerged from the woods and towered over him.

It barked a challenge and Daniel was instantly repelled. He crouched, snapping his jaws, but there was no challenge in it. He barked at Daniel again, and again, Daniel felt his insides shake. He backed away, struggling against an unseen force compelling him to lower his belly to the ground.

Hungry and confused, and not willing to submit, Daniel shook his head and struggled to rise. The wolf growled and barked at him yet again, but Daniel resisted and rose to his full height. He looked into the yellow eyes of the larger, more powerful wolf for an instant, then bounded to the side.

The wolf that had challenged him earlier moved to intercept and Daniel plowed into him, knocking him backwards. Once free of the circle, Daniel took off in a full run. Hungry. So hungry. Prey everywhere. He could smell the fear in the small animals all around, but he wanted something more substantial.

Behind him, he heard the barking and howling of the wolves in pursuit. His ears flattened atop his head and he tore down the side of the mountain, darting between trees, leaping over logs and springing to the side as soon as his claws touched the earth. Behind him, the pursuit dropped farther and farther back.

Daniel smelled the air. Prey nearby. Two-legged prey. They smelled cautious but little more. Easy prey to sate his hunger. He altered his course in that direction, salivating at the promise of warm, bloody flesh to fill his grumbling stomach.

A two-legged prey dropped out of the trees and darted left, then right, then left again, coming toward him. Daniel growled and lowered his head, prepared to lunge. This was not prey, but it would sate his hunger all the same. It smelled different, though, almost familiar.

The trees thinned and on a path directly in front of him, the two-legged ran. Daniel opened his maw and lunged. He would take the two-legged's throat or snap him in half.

The figure jumped forward, Daniel snapped his jaws shut, then saw the ground rushing to meet him.

CHAPTER 27

Jelani's eyes snapped open. He didn't know if he'd awoken because the day had passed or because someone waited for him outside the building, but what he knew for sure was that someone was there, for him. He could feel it, or sense it, or whatever it was he did now. He sat up and threw his legs over the side of the bed.

Seemed like he'd been doing that a lot lately; sensing things. On his way home the previous night he could sense the fear in just about every animal nearby. How they knew what a thirsty vampire was, he didn't know. Maybe they could sense things like he could.

Jelani thought about that for a moment as he threw on a pair of jeans and a T-shirt. How was it that animals had such superior senses than humans? And why did a human have to become a vampire to get these amazing senses and strengths and all that? So much about this supernatural business was a mystery and he doubted the oldest vampire would know everything about it.

"Why would they know?" he asked himself. He stepped out of the hotel room and locked the door. "Who knows how they first came to be, anyway?"

The hotel was comfortable and expensive, but worth it. Jelani had managed to get a room that faced exactly north, where less sun shined in. That, combined with a thick set of drapes, and he could safely sleep through the day.

Saaya hadn't kicked him out of her place, but he still thought it best to leave for the same reason he left his old place he'd shared with Daniel. It was just an awkward situation. After one last check through his backpack, he zipped it up and made his way to the lobby.

Another cool thing about the room he got was that it was ground floor and there was a nice big tree and a walled courtyard in front of the window. The front desk attendant must've thought him crazy when he'd asked for the room with a wall in front of the window.

He stepped outside the building and immediately spotted a woman sitting on a bench to the right of the front door.

"How'd you know I was here?" he asked.

Melinda let her head hang back and smiled at him. "Luck."

Jelani came around to sit next to her. He'd forgotten how much he liked her smile. "Luck?"

"Yup." She tapped a finger to her cheek. "Well, not all luck. I needed to find you and I know you're the sentimental type, so I waited around your old girlfriend's apartment in case you decided to show up and play crying sentry."

Jelani's mouth fell open. "Crying sentry? What the hell is that supposed to mean?"

Melinda gave him a look. "Oh, come on, Jelani. You know as well as I do that you've been agonizing over everything that's happened over the past half year. You've probably been blaming yourself for everything bad that's happened to everyone around you as if you alone could protect us all. And I'm sure you could have. Only you, as a human, could have stopped Remy from turning me. Only you, as a human, could have stopped everything that has happened with those Hunters. You. Jelani. One man."

Jelani just listened, staring off down the street. When she

finished, he leaned forward and rested his elbows on his knees. "I am who I am, Melinda. Who wouldn't try to protect the people they care about?"

"But you obsess over it like it's your life mission," she said. "When all this started, you were human and practically helpless. Now you walk the night, but you're still only one person, and surrounded by purebloods that have a lot more years ahead of you."

"It's only going to get worse," Jelani said.

After a lengthy pause Melinda said, "because you're going there, too." She looked at him. "Sinaia, right?"

Jelani stared at her. "How did you know I was going there?"

"Part of it I got through that nasty little mind link with Remy. It's gotten really faint since he left, but before he took off, a few things slipped through his mind that I picked up. He and an Elder are planning some kind of thing and he went to Peles Coven to meet up with him."

"The idiot is planning to cause a whole lot of trouble over there," Jelani agreed.

"And you plan to stop him!" Melinda said, feigning determination in her voice.

Jelani laughed. "Hardly. They can all kill each other up and go extinct as far as I'm concerned. I just want to remove Remy from the planet."

"Too bad you couldn't have done it while he was here," Melinda said. "Would have been easier."

"Actually it might be easier there," Jelani replied. "Here, he has a whole city to hide in. He can run and hide and strike when and wherever. Over there, when everything comes to a head, he'll have to play a part, even if it's a small one. I'm sure I can get him to face me."

Melinda's face brightened when Jelani's intent dawned on her. "Because if you make it known that you were re-created by him, and he can't control you ..."

"It will be embarrassing for him," Jelani finished.

"And, to take it a step further," Melinda continued. "If you call him out for a fight and he avoids you, he looks like a coward who is afraid of his own creation."

Jelani nodded. "Exactly."

"You do realize he's going to have backup," Melinda said. "I wouldn't doubt he knows you'll come after him. Knowing him, he'll probably have someone waiting for you the minute you step off the plane."

"I'd be surprised if he didn't," Jelani agreed. "I'm not concerned about it, though. I know he's going to try to kill me before I can get anywhere near the coven. I will admit that it would have been easier if I'd gone with Yako."

He noticed Melinda's grimace at the mention of the Eldest Hunter's name. "Something I said?"

"No." She ran a hand through her sandy brown hair. "No. He just makes me very uncomfortable."

Then you've definitely had a conversation with him, Jelani thought. "Ran into him?"

"Went looking for him," she replied.

"Ah," Jelani tried not to laugh. "I imagine that didn't go over too well."

"He let me know really fast how useful I'd be to him," Melinda said, a tinge of bitterness in her tone.

"I'm sure he did," Jelani said. "Probably said it with as few words as possible."

"Yup. I tried to tell him that I could probably get you to come if he included me ..." she trailed off when he started laughing. "Glad you're finding humor in this."

"Sorry," Jelani said, recovering. "I'm sorry. It's just that I'm indebted to him. He's saved my life more than once already and I kind of owe him. When you went with that little bargaining chip, it was almost like finding a shark and trying to bribe it to carry you."

"Not sure that's the right analogy," Melinda replied dryly, "but I get your point, and I got his too … literally."

Jelani whistled through his teeth at that. "Glad you're still here to talk about it."

"You don't seem too concerned," Melinda said. "You didn't even ask if he hurt me."

"You're sitting next to me," Jelani said, his tone sober. "Yako may give the rare uncharacteristic warning, but he doesn't inflict non mortal injury." He laid a friendly hand on her leg and gave it a pat. "But yes, I'm glad you're all right. Just … probably just stay away from him. I don't think he's an evil guy, but he has a very cold, matter-of-fact way about him that doesn't leave a lot of space for mistakes."

They sat in silence for a while, and Jelani wondered what Melinda was thinking. He had practically felt the electricity shoot through her when he'd touched her leg. After all this time and all that had happened, she was still drawn to him. And when he was honest with himself, he felt drawn to her as well.

"When are you leaving?" she asked.

Jelani started to answer, then studied her. "You're planning to come, aren't you?" He patted the air between them as soon as he saw the defiant look coming. "No, no no. I'm not trying to tell you what to do and I'm not saying you can't handle yourself. But do you realize what's waiting there?"

"I have an idea," Melinda said.

"Then you realize there are individuals there that outrank Yako, and are possibly more dangerous?" She gave him a look that said she thought that was unlikely. "Girl, you need to listen to me on this," he said. "I hate to reach into the bag of cliché, but it's the truth. This is the lion's den, and it's going to be crawling with Hunters, Reapers, and Elders. Not to mention plenty of other vampires who are much older and stronger than us."

"You're still going?" she said.

Jelani opened and closed his mouth a couple times. He didn't want it to come to this, but he didn't want her to go over there and get killed. "Look. I know you can handle yourself—"

She lowered her eyelids at him. "You already told me that."

"But," Jelani continued, "You need to be honest about whether or not you'll be in a little too deep."

"So you think you can deal with it and I can't. That's pretty much what you're saying."

"All right, Melinda," Jelani said. "I'm not arguing with you on this. You want to go, cool. Go for it. Your wit will help you a good deal, but if it comes to a fight, you might be in trouble. I've had my ass kicked a couple times already and I'm not too proud to tell you that. And that's *here*. If you think you can beat me in a fight, then you've got a better chance than I do."

"Is that a challenge?" she said, arching a slender eyebrow.

"Only if you want to test your odds." He had no ego in the statement. No desire to show how good he was. He waited patiently as Melinda considered him for a long time. She knew him well enough to know when he was serious, but would she take him seriously on this? The girl could be remarkably stubborn.

In a flash of whirling brown hair she was on him, fangs bared, claws going for his throat. She was quick. Surprisingly quick. Jelani slipped his right arm between them and wrapped it around her neck. In less than two seconds he had her in a helpless position, back arched over his lap, arm wrapped around her neck, and the tip of a silver dagger hovering over her heart.

When she went still, he slowly released her and sheathed his weapon. She sat up in his lap and glared at him, and he tried not to laugh. "I'm sorry, but you need to know—"

She wrapped her arms around his neck and kissed him, her tongue finding his. Just as quickly as it started, she pulled away.

"Try to give me just one reason why we're not in your bed right now. Just one, Jelani." When he opened his mouth to speak, she held up a hand. "Actually, don't. You'll just piss me off. Let's leave it where it is. You're a good kisser, you still want to bang the hell out of me and I know it by the way you look at me. For whatever reason you choose to continue with this solemn vow of chastity—"

"I'm not following a vow of—"

The hand came back up. "Knock yourself out. All this," she waved her hand over her body, "obviously is not much of a temptation anyway." She stood, and Jelani groaned. "By the way," she leaned over and gave his groin a friendly pat. "Your friend disagrees." Jelani groaned again.

"I'd appreciate it if you let me in on this little adventure of yours," Melinda continued, turning away in a manner that was *certainly* not meant to be enticing. "So, please include me when you go. Oh, and I'd be interested to know how you figure out the whole thing with being on that plane during the day. Last I checked, daylight is not a friend."

"I'll figure it out," Jelani called after her.

He leaned back on the bench and sighed, then caught sight of the full moon. Jelani stared at it for a moment, then remembered his conversation with Imron the previous night. "Shit!"

CHAPTER 28

R ooftops.

Jelani was starting to wonder if this would be the routine of his life, sprinting and jumping from rooftop to rooftop like some wannabe superhero. *Seems like I've done this before,* he thought sarcastically, reminded of his recent little adventure to the coven on the side of the mountain. He leaped a forty foot gap between two buildings, gliding over the street, and hit the next roof in a run.

He neared the end of downtown and would need to get to North Vancouver quick. Daniel would go someplace where there weren't any people.

Once sure there were no humans nearby, Jelani dropped from the roof and dashed across Georgia Street. Since he'd first awoken to the night, he'd gotten better. Faster. His body had gone through changes he wasn't even aware of, but he could feel it more every night as his mind grew better attuned.

He ran further up Georgia Street where it passed through the woods of Stanley Park and leaped to the lowest branch of a redwood tree. There, he waited till a bus passed by and hopped on. Jelani allowed himself a self-satisfied smirk. A cat couldn't have landed softer. His smirk faded, however, when he thought about how he could actually *afford* bus fare, but instead rode on top of it for free. *Practice*, he thought. *I'm not actually a jackass. I just need practice with this vampire thing. That's all.*

He rode the bus all the way to the Lonsdale Quay exchange and hopped off, looking for the next bus going up to Grouse. "Ten minutes," he said, reading the schedule. "I don't have time for this." He looked at the passing cars heading down the street and sighed.

A few minutes later he was gently laying an unconscious man behind a bush and driving toward Grouse.

"Where would you go, man?" he thought aloud, eyeing the mountain just ahead and trying to guess the path Daniel had taken. He turned onto Capilano Road.

Jelani knew that Daniel wouldn't have gone to Stanley Park because people could still be around. That left one of the mountains, and the nearest one was Grouse. He could make it up there in decent time where no humans were likely to venture, and on a guess, Jelani figured he would probably gravitate to the place they had once been. The only place they knew that was off the trails and rugged enough terrain that no one would think to go.

He pulled the car over and jumped out, sprinting into the woods. Occasionally the moon would shine through a gap in the canopy of treetops, bathing him in its pale light. He looked up at it and felt a sense of dread that deepened when he heard a wolf howl. It was a normal wolf, but it felt like an omen.

Another howl rent the air that made the hair on the back of Jelani's neck rise. That was definitely not a regular wolf. Another howl answered, followed by another. Several minutes passed and a monstrous roar brought him to a stop. Daniel. Jelani didn't know how he knew, but he did.

He started up again, then his senses picked something up. *You have got to be kidding me.* He instinctively looked in the direction he'd sensed them. "What the hell are humans doing on the side of this mountain and at this time of night?" The longer Jelani experienced his new existence, the more it seemed like humans were bent on their own undoing.

Another roar, this one practically made the air shake. Jelani didn't have to think. He changed his direction, heading toward the human hikers. He remembered the terrible thirst when he'd first awoken, and how he would have attacked anyone nearby to satisfy it. He had no doubt that in his newly transformed state, Daniel was having a similar experience. The result would be the same, only in this instance, messier.

He heard barking and chuckled despite the situation. It sounded like a bunch of giant dogs arguing. He focused his hearing, and moments later heard the thuds of giant paws. They were on the move, and judging from the sound, directly toward the hikers.

Of all the places for a night hike. Jelani sprinted forward until he found the four hikers, two shining flashlights out into the darkness like beacons while the other two gathered their gear. *At least the fools have sense enough to get out of here after hearing that.*

He came into their camp so quickly, they never saw him until he was in their midst. "You guys better hurry up," he said. The four men yelped and dropped gear and equipment, grabbing for bear spray and guns.

Jelani closed his eyes and tried to ignore the enticing sound of blood racing through their nervous veins. Delectable, oxygen-filled blood. He shook it off. "Trust me," he said, still drinking in the sweet smell of all that rushing blood, "none of that is going to do any good. Just get off this mountain."

"Thanks, mate," one of the nervous hikers said. "But who the hell are you?"

Another roar split the air and all five heads turned up the hill. "You wanna sit and talk about it?" Jelani replied, and the men went back to gathering their gear. Before the man could ask any more questions, Jelani was gone. He didn't worry about them wondering how he disappeared so fast. If they were lucky enough to survive this, no one would believe them anyway.

The giant wolves were close, he could smell them now. He leaped onto the branch of a tree to get a better look. He got one.

A huge black wolf weaved through the trees. Behind it was an even bigger one, and nine or ten more behind and to the sides. They were coming straight toward his position.

"This isn't one of my smarter ideas," Jelani muttered under his breath. He dropped from the tree and sprinted forward, darting to the left and right around the foliage, trying to draw its attention away from the hikers directly behind him.

The wolf never altered its course, so Jelani came back in its path and ran straight for it. Once they were within thirty feet of each other the wolf leaped and Jelani leapt to meet it. Huge jaws filled with teeth like serrated knives opened to swallow him.

Fangs bared, Jelani tucked his legs up so close his knees were against his chest. He slammed his feet down on the top of its head just as it snapped its jaws at him. The wolf's head went down into the earth and Jelani went up and over it.

He didn't have time to see how effective the stomp had been, for as soon as his feet hit the ground, he had to dive to the side to avoid being bitten in half by another wolf. This one was smaller, but fast. It came after Jelani, easily weaving through the trees. Jelani felt the air behind him whip as jaws snapped at his back.

An angry lavender glow smoldered in Jelani's eyes, and he dug his right foot in the earth, skidded to a stop, and brought his fists around in a double axe-handle swing that connected with the side of the giant wolf's head. The blow sounded like a gunshot that split the silence of the mountainside and the werewolf tumbled away.

Another wolf came in behind it and jumped at Jelani. He dropped flat onto his back and kicked up as it passed over. His feet connected with the wolf's midsection and launched it into a tree. Jelani was already on the move when he heard the resounding crack of the splitting trunk.

Apparently he had dazed the wolf he thought was Daniel. It was just regaining its feet, shaking off the dirt from its muzzle from where it looked like its head had shoveled into the ground. Jelani came up beside it but pulled up short.

"A little dirt in the mouth never hurt anyone. You gonna come outta that fur coat, homeboy?"

The giant wolf's lips curled back to reveal teeth longer than some of Jelani's fingers. It issued a low growl that gradually grew louder. Though Jelani no longer possessed the same degree of emotions as a human, he had to fight down the urge to get as far away from that monstrous growl as possible. "It's me, buddy," he tried again. "I know you've got to be massively hungry, but look at me. It's me, man."

The wolf slowly, deliberately, turned to face him, teeth still bared. The hackles on its back raised and vibrated as it growled deep in its belly.

Jelani circled with it, eyes darting left and right. The other werewolves had arrived and were creeping forward. A bark came from farther back in the trees, and the wolves stopped, then retreated a few steps. It was the big one. Jelani didn't know why it stopped the others from coming in and ripping him apart, but he wasn't about to complain.

"Dude, it's me. You know me. It's Jelani. Focus, man!"

The wolf lunged, swiping a clawed paw across his chest. It was a lot faster than Jelani had expected. Four claws sliced through his skin as if they were knifes through soft butter. Jelani clenched his teeth against the pain as he spun through the air and crashed to the ground.

He was up in an instant and slammed his fist into its muzzle. Jelani ignored the burning pain as his wounds slowly closed up. The wolf made a sound that could have been a dog's version of "ow!"

Jelani kept his eyes on it, shaking his hand. "You've got a hard head, my man. But you know that by now. How many times have I told you that?"

For a second, just one second, He saw a spark of recognition in the wolf's glowing golden eyes. The moment passed and it lunged at him again. The sudden shift from familiarity to aggression caught Jelani off guard.

The wolf plowed into him, and Jelani held on to the thick neck with both hands. His fangs extended again as he clenched his teeth under the strain of keeping those snapping jaws from crushing his skull. He didn't know if he could endure a bite like that and heal. He also had no desire to find out. He pushed with all his strength, but those snapping teeth were right in front of his face.

Jelani's eyes smoldered, and a hiss escaped his own throat. His nails extended from his fingers and dug into the wolf's neck. The snapping didn't slow.

Jelani hissed again and pulled a hand free. With as much speed as his arm could pump, he thrust his claws into the werewolf's neck and flank. One two three four five. In less than a few seconds he had stabbed his friend more than a dozen times.

The wolf hopped off of him and leaped aside, favoring its left flank.

Jelani was instantly on his feet, hissing. He held his bloody claws out at his sides, fangs bared, lavender eyes glowing. He watched the wounds heal on his friend's side even as he stalked in a circle, looking for an opening to attack again. The two circled each other, neither making the first move.

"Fight, dammit!" Jelani said, his voice gone guttural. "There's all kinds of animals up here you can eat."

The wolf leaped and Jelani ducked the swiping claw as it flew past. He raked his own claws along the wolf's side, and heard the closest to a yelp that a monster like this could make.

The wolf hit the ground in a tumble and Jelani hopped on top of it. He retracted his claws and balled his fists. His fists were a blur as he punched his friend repeatedly in the side of the head.

"I'm not … going … to … let … you regret tonight for the rest of your life!"

The wolf tried to stand, but Jelani dazed it with his repeated barrage. He put enough power into every punch to fell an elephant, but the wolf finally rose with him on its back. For a moment it seemed the wolf that was Daniel would rear up on its hind legs, but then it stumbled and fell. Jelani pounded it on the top of the head. "I said fight it!" He clasped his fists together and brought them down in a double axe-handle punch to the top of its head.

The wolf let out a heavy grunt and slumped. Jelani hopped off and took a few steps back. It shook its head and made a coughing sound, then turned toward him. Whatever pain he'd put on the thing was already wearing off.

Jelani lowered his stance, ready for another go. The werewolf regarded him with more recognition. He felt a spark of hope. "It's me, bro." He spread his hands. "It's me."

The wolf barked at him in response, but there didn't seem to be any aggression in it. Jelani relaxed just a bit. "Try to think, man. Try to think about what you're doing."

The wolf growled and curled in on itself, then looked back up at Jelani. There was pain in its golden eyes. Pain and hunger.

"I know, man," Jelani said. "Oh, trust me, I know! But you don't want what's down there." He pointed further down the hill in the direction of the fleeing hikers. He could sense they were farther away, but not moving nearly fast enough. *You fools better get some pep in your step. I can't guarantee the whole pack won't dine on your slow asses.*

"This mountain has all kinds of animals on it. Go find bigger prey; more satisfying prey."

The wolf that was Daniel barked again, then half turned away. It turned its big golden stare on him one last time.

"Do what you gotta do," Jelani said. "I got you. You know I've always got your back, my friend."

The wolf bounded off in the opposite direction. Almost immediately Jelani sensed the terror of the nearby animals that weren't far enough away. He almost felt sorry for them. As a mortal, he would have. As the predator that he'd become, he couldn't, not completely.

Half a dozen black blurs flew past him. They were joining in the hunt. One remained behind; the biggest. It stalked up to Jelani and stopped less than a few paces away. Even on all fours it was nearly Jelani's height. It stood on its hind legs and looked down—way down—at him.

"You're a big one aren't you?" He looked more closely at the werewolf and considered its size and rank in the pack. "Imron. It's you, isn't it?" The giant wolf turned and stalked away, disappearing into the trees.

Jelani stared after it. There was something particularly disturbing about watching a nine foot wolf walk on two legs, away from him or not.

CHAPTER 29

Saaya remained perched in her tree long after Jelani, Imron, and his wolves had departed. She'd lived long enough to understand that nothing happens at random. That she had been drawn to Jelani enough to keep him alive had been a conundrum she'd struggled with for months. Though she had found her answer, she was still finding layers to it, and Castle Peles was yet another.

Coincidence was illusion. It wasn't coincidence that she happened upon a fleeing human and remained in his life to the point where she would save him time and again.

Even at the point of his re-creation, she'd saved him from a terrible fate of subservience to the Hunter named Remy. Why was it so important that Jelani retain his free will? She thought about what it meant for Jelani to have been turned then have his re-creation altered by the essence of one such as herself. He still didn't quite understand what it meant. He still didn't understand the gift she had given him.

There were other questions that needed to be answered. She thought about the Eldest Hunter, and why she'd spared him. She could have easily killed him and been on her way, and there wouldn't have been a soul the wiser of it. Yet on three different occasions she had not killed Yako. She feared nothing of reprisal from the local coven, or even the High Council of Elders. There was something to that one as well that had stayed her hand.

Now it seemed fate had given Jelani a powerful ally. She looked in the direction Daniel and his new pack had gone. Whether he and Jelani knew it or not, their lives were inextricably bound.

She had no doubt that Jelani would go to Romania and Daniel would join him. There would be a lot of excitement at Peles Coven, and the *dampeal* had no intention of missing it. Even her stubborn brother, for all the pureblooded *Ancestor* that he was, could not deny the potential of what was going to happen.

"Foolish of me to hope you were done with your little pet," Kafeel said from behind.

A smile spread across Saaya's face. "Think of the devil and he appears."

"Is that what I am, sister?"

She didn't bother to turn around. "Aren't we all, to them?" She waved a dismissive hand in the direction of the city. "The spawn of the devil? The lapdogs of Satan? Demons? Some form of thinking zombie; revenants walking the earth in our insatiable search for sustenance?"

Kafeel's voice remained as uninterested as usual. "Likely, though it matters not at all."

She sighed. What was it about purebloods, particularly the warrior types, that made them so ill-natured? She imagined a night of conversation between her brother and Yako sitting around a fireplace in leather chairs sipping warmed blood. The image made her giggle. "Oh, Kafeel. One day. I have an eternity to draw some kind of emotion from you. A laugh, or even a smile that wouldn't freeze the sun."

She let the conversation drop, having sorted through her feelings and deciding that no matter how stupid Jelani might be in regard to his own feelings, she would keep an eye on him. That meant a trip to Peles Coven and the High Council of Elders, the last place she wanted to be.

Few immortals knew that the *Ancestors* were more than figures out of myth. Kafeel was the youngest living *Ancestor*, and like his predecessors he was more the solitary type. How would Kafeel react if they went into the seat of vampiric power?

Questions for later. Saaya looked back to the northwest, then south to downtown Vancouver. In his rashness, Jelani had actually stumbled upon something useful. Upon her arrival at the coven, Saaya had learned quite a bit from the shadows. Apparently Remy had taken over the Northwest Coven and left a few minions to keep things in check. That was interesting. But even more so was the fact that he had virtually no loyalty from its denizens, only obedience ensured by the word of an Elder of the High Council.

Then there was Jelani's conversation with the Reaper. The fact that a high-ranking warrior in the Order also thought little of Remy was interesting. The Northwest Coven teetered on a knife's edge, chaos on one side, restructuring on the other. The right hand would guide it in either direction. One inexperienced but intelligent person came to mind. Inexperienced, yes, but intelligent and cunning.

The more Saaya thought about it, the better the idea felt. *Time to make a friend out of an enemy.*

CHAPTER 30

"Tell me. What must be done to impress upon you the weight of this situation? You seem not to have a full grasp on it." The old gray haired vampire lifted a hand at Remy in a gesture that was intended as exasperation, but instead gave the impression of a shaking old man scolding a grandson before giving him candy money. Kneeling several feet away, Remy swallowed his smirk.

"In fact," the Elder continued, "you seem rather nonchalant about it."

"I don't know what you imply, Elder," Remy said.

"Bah! Spare me your foolishness, Remy. Your intended dalliance with that girl was another glaring indication of your casual attitude about this. Have you no idea what is at stake here? Do you not know who our enemies are?"

"I believe you have imparted that wisdom to me several times over the course of these last months I was away, Elder." Massius went quiet, and Remy thought he might have pushed his luck a bit too far.

The silence stretched for a few moments longer before Massius spoke again. "Do you know what it means to be an Elder?"

Remy frowned. "To have attained knowledge and experience

through a millennia and more of life, and to have refined the wisdom gained therein."

After another few moments of silence, Remy dared look up from the floor. The old man was smiling at him. It was the most wicked smile he'd ever seen, like a decrepit scarecrow on the verge of maniacal cackling. "Have I spoken ill, Elder Massius?"

"No," Massius said, holding the Hunter fast with his gaze. "You have spoken true, but not in full. You've neglected one important attribute." He approached, and Remy found himself frozen by the Elder's eyes. He couldn't even blink.

"Why do you think I have been a member of the High Council all these years, child?" It had to have been a rhetorical question because at that moment, Remy supposed he wouldn't be able to breathe if Massius willed it so.

"Perhaps it was given to me," Massius said. "Perhaps one or more of the female High Council members bore an undying attraction to me. Perhaps the High Council felt sorry for an old wayward vampire come to their halls seeking shelter." The vice-like clamp around Remy's entire being vanished and he had to fight not to fall over.

"Of course not," the Elder said, chortling as if he'd told a joke that only he could understand. "I had a little more to offer than that. A lot more, actually."

He turned back to Remy, and as soon as their eyes met, the Hunter felt something clamp down on his mind. A tiny trickle of blood streamed down his nose.

"Some things can be done by force," the Elder said, and he released Remy's mind. "But some things must be done with tact."

This time, Remy felt a presence creeping on his mind, like tendrils of mist sliding around his cortex, enveloping his brain and then sitting there like a low lying cloud at the top of a mountain. It floated there, unmoving in the back of his awareness.

Remy would swallow liquid silver if the Elder had wished it. If Massius had told him to drive a silver blade through his chest, slowly, inch by inch, he would do it without hesitation. He also knew that his mind could be crushed into a gelatinous pool and left to seep out of his ears if the Elder willed it.

The fog retreated from his brain, and Remy released a breath he didn't know he'd been holding. This time he did fall to his hands and knees. *That was educational.*

"Good," Massius said, clapping his hands together. "Now that we understand each other, I would like you to meet with the new alpha of the Silver Pack. I have taken the liberty of assigning four Hunters to accompany you."

Remy hid his disgust but the Elder laughed. "My elitist little Hunter. You think us above the lycans, don't you?" He clasped his hands behind his back and turned to face Remy. "Rise."

Remy stood. How long had he been kneeling there? The Elder stood squarely in front of him, resplendent in his white and gray robes. What was it about Massius and robes? Remy couldn't think of a single instance when he'd seen the Elder dressed in anything else.

"Well?" Massius said, and Remy had almost forgotten he'd been asked a question.

"Ah," he knew that Massius had close relationships with several packs of the savages. "No, Elder. I do not believe we are above the lycans."

"Then you are a fool." He laughed at Remy's surprise. "But no, you are not a fool, are you? You don't believe that lie sliding off your tongue any more than I do."

Massius grinned that scarecrow grin again. "Of course we are above them. They're animals. But what you mustn't forget is that they are thinking animals, and as such, are prone to things like pride and social status. To constantly remind your subordinates that they are inferior to you does not foster loyalty or a healthy relationship.

Then what the hell did you just do to me? Massius arched an eyebrow at him, and for a moment a spike of alarm shot through

Remy's stomach. Could the Elder actually read his mind? When the old vampire turned away, he relaxed.

"Just because another is inferior to you does not mean you must remind them of it at every opportunity. Whether or not they agree with their status, let them believe what they will. So long as their actions move in line with your will, that is what's important."

"I see, Elder."

"No," Massius snapped. "You do not see. You think to tell an old fool what he wants to hear. Why do you think I went to all this trouble with tarnishing Yako's reputation instead of killing him outright?" He didn't wait for Remy's answer, which was good because he didn't have one. "Appearances, Remy. Think! There are plenty I could have enlisted to discretely hunt down and kill him, but not a one of them were skilled enough to do it. Any who might be equal to the task would never undertake it without the complete approval from the High Council."

He made an irritated gesture. "I had to wait a long time for a slip, and it happened when he failed to eliminate a simple human target. It seemed almost too good to be true."

"There is one thing that confuses me, Elder Massius."

"Of course there is," Massius said. He waved an impatient hand." Speak it."

"Why bother Yako at all? I admit that I had aspirations to be Eldest Hunter," Remy refrained from grinding his teeth at the amused expression the Elder took on, "but I could have bade my time; waited for the right moment to arrange an … accident."

"Because," Massius answered, "there was too much call for Yako to become a Reaper."

"He's refused every time," Remy replied. "Why would he change his mind now?"

"It was only a matter of time," Massius answered. "None with skills such as his could be allowed to remain a Hunter forever, even Eldest Hunter. Sooner or later, he would have undergone the ritual to become a Reaper, and that would have been to disastrous effect."

To whom, Remy wondered. *And why?* "Of course," Elder.

"Of course," Massius echoed, eyeing him closely. "Go." He waved Remy away. "I have already sent word that you will meet with the Silver Pack. Go and see what can be salvaged of our animals."

"Yes, Elder Massius."

"So respectful," the Elder said just as Remy opened the door. He didn't miss the sarcasm.

As MUCH AS he hated to admit it, even to himself, Remy realized he'd better be careful. Because Massius had never used such an overt show of force before, Remy figured him for an Elder in age only. With Vicken and the other Elders, it had been different. Their presence commanded respect. Massius was always less noticeable outside of seeming like a smart but cantankerous old man. Remy hoped that whatever the old vampire had done to his mind was temporary. The thought of Massius in his thoughts all the time was enough to make him want to walk into the sun.

He scowled at the stone columns and tapestries on the walls of the castle. Normally he would have basked in the wealth of Peles Coven and all its adornments. Now they seemed to mock him. Remy had hoped his return would include at least some luxury. When Laura had come to meet him at the hangar, he'd thought her a welcome gift. A reward for work well done. Instead it had been a tease that neither of them had anticipated.

It didn't matter. He would finish this filthy business with the lycans quickly and then have Laura brought to him. After his needs were met, he would set about securing his place in the coven. A large part of that involved making sure Yako was dealt with the moment he set foot off that plane. The former Eldest Hunter was a danger that had to be removed quickly.

Remy stepped out into the cold wind and wrapped his dark blue cloak tight around his body. The cold meant nothing to him, but it wouldn't do to have the cloak whipping about.

The gray stone bridge arched away, leading over the water that separated the castle from the grassy grounds beyond. Four men waited in the middle of the bridge. The escort Massius had set up for him, no doubt.

"What leader goes anywhere without a group of goons to accompany him?" Remy muttered in a tone as dry as the cold night air.

"Remy," one of the men said, bowing his head. The others did the same.

"Eldest Hunter," Remy corrected. "There is a large body of water separating you from the events in the Northwest Coven, so I will tolerate your error this once."

The four men glanced at each other. "Of course ... Eldest Hunter," came the stammering reply.

Remy wanted to strangle the fool. He would need to be more forceful, more lethal in how he dealt with transgressions. These four would never have reacted to Yako in such a way. "Of course," he said, eyeing the other man. He was dressed in simple black clothes from head to toe, and a waist length leather jacket that looked like he was about to jump on a motorcycle. Remy looked him up and down, wondering why his species was so unimaginative at times. Always black.

Remy resisted the urge to shake his head. All this idiot needed was a pair of shades. When he glanced at the other men, he did shake his head. One of them was wearing shades.

"You do realize that sunglasses are for the sun," he said. The boy couldn't be older than twenty. Young enough to be stupid even in the ephemeral life of a human.

The young Hunter glanced at his comrades as if they might

feed him an answer. Before he could say anything, Remy pushed past them. "Come. We have dogs to leash and I would prefer to have it done sooner rather than later." To his relief, they fell in step behind him without a word. If he was lucky, he could be done with this business without having to speak much. He really wasn't in the mood.

"If I may ask, Eldest Hunter?"

Remy's lips tightened. *No such luck.*

"Why would the Elders wish to enlist the wolves to fight with us? Is it wise to trust them?"

"History tells of a time when vampires and the lycanthropes lived in harmony," another Hunter said. "Maybe that time comes again. I see no reason why we need to fight them."

"We fight them," yet another of the group said, "because they do not know their place and think themselves our equals."

There was silence. Remy guessed they were waiting for his response, which of course he was not going to give. He quickened his pace until they came to the end of the bridge where his stretch Navigator waited. He wished he could make these twits ride in something else so he could be left alone. He needed to think things through.

Fortunately, the human drivers were already briefed of their destination, and Remy didn't have to speak a word to them. The driver from the night before opened the door and he climbed inside. After the other four Hunters climbed in after him, the driver shut the door, and a minute later, they were pulling away from Castle Peles.

"I suppose we could use the coming conflict to exterminate the animals," the younger Hunter said, breaking the blissful silence.

Remy sighed. *Why can't these idiots shut up?* He wasn't near old by immortal standards, but Remy found that the older the vampire, the less they spoke unnecessarily.

"Smart idea," another Hunter said. "You propose to break a

perfectly useful tool simply because you don't like it? You have wisdom beyond your years, kid."

"It was a thought," the young Hunter said.

Remy almost laughed at that. The young fool would likely die if he didn't wise up.

Lost in his thoughts, Remy didn't know how much time had passed before the Navigator crunched onto a gravel path off the road. A few minutes later it came to a stop and the driver opened the door.

"We have reached the destination, Eldest Hunter," the human said.

"Obviously," Remy replied, not bothering to look at him as he climbed out. "I'm sure I don't have to tell you to wait here for our return," he said, turning his back to look over the dark woods.

"Not at all, Eldest Hunter," the human replied. "We will be right here."

"Yes, you will be." Remy waved his hand to the other four Hunters. "Come."

❧

THE TREK HADN'T GONE AS QUICKLY as Remy had hoped. Unfamiliar with these woods, they had to move more slowly to ensure they continued in the right direction. Finally, they came to the meeting place, a fairly large patch of open ground, as agreed to by both parties.

A lone figure sat facing their direction, the flames of a tiny campfire dancing in his blue eyes. "My warmest greetings, Hunters of Peles Coven. I am Jason."

Remy stared at him. *He's a jovial one.*

"Things are proceeding well in the coven, I hope?"

"Our proceedings are not your concern," Remy replied. "We are here to talk about how you will be of use to us."

Jason stood, and Remy resisted the urge to back away a step.

Jason wasn't much taller than six feet, but he was covered in layers of thick muscle straining against every stitch of clothing he wore. "Of course, Hunter," he said. "But if we are to be of use to you, shouldn't we know how things proceed so that we don't come in blind?"

"Blind or not," Remy replied nonchalantly. "Does a dog not have a better nose than eyes?"

The werewolf shrugged, seeming unaffected by the insult. "If you wish to fight beside a handicapped ally, so be it. We will bleed for you, Hunter, but we will not die needlessly. We are your allies, not your fodder." He spread his hands toward Remy.

Remy studied him. This one was odd. Absent was the usual gruffness that lycans usually displayed. He seemed very much in control of his temper, and was subtle enough to let Remy know they could spar words all night if he wished.

"Things at my coven proceed as we intend them. You have no need for concern about that. What we need from you is an assurance that you will be ready when needed."

The other man nodded. "And as I promised before, we will be. And if I may ask, when would you like us to be on standby?"

"I'm presuming you can use a phone. I will be in contact."

"Quite the diplomat, you are," Jason replied.

Remy grinned at the remark. He could almost like this man, if he was more than just a well-trained animal. "From this point forward," he said, "you will deal with me. And you will address me as Eldest Hunter." The corner of the man's mouth twitched, but he nodded.

"And speaking of such, the former Eldest Hunter will likely be here in the next night or two. He is of Japanese origin and his name is Yako. His skills are formidable, so I recommend that when you engage him, you bring help."

"Help?"

Remy didn't blink. "Quite a bit of it."

"How many do you believe he will be traveling with?"

Remy thought about it. Yako's little assistant was detained at the coven, as were two of her allies. Several more had been hunted down and killed. Yako had no friends that Remy knew of back in Vancouver that he could bring.

"Likely he will be traveling alone. He might have dug up a friend or two, but I doubt it."

Jason's mouth fell open in a silent laugh. "I mean no offense, Eldest Hunter, but how many fully formed lycans do you think this one Hunter could fight?"

Remy frowned. "Were you not present during the attack on Yako in these very woods not that long ago? You should have witnessed his skills then."

"I must admit that I was not present. Our packleader at that time had sent me off on other business and I returned to find out that an unexpected situation had occurred that placed me at the head of the pack."

"Then you are at a distinct disadvantage as to what that man is capable of. I would bring as many of your lycans as you can spare."

Jason nodded. "Fair enough. We will keep watch for him, and I will await your call to move into position." The man gave Remy a look as if to ask if there was anything else.

"I must admit that I am surprised you've come to meet with me alone," Remy said, looking around. "I don't sense or smell any of your ... friends, around."

Another smile. "A show of faith," he said. "We stood with Elder Massius for more years than I can remember, and we trust him."

Remy scrutinized the man's face. "I'm sure you knew I would not arrive alone."

"Of course not," came the reply. "But it would not do to insult our friendship by arriving in force to a simple meeting."

"Of course," Remy said. There was something about this one that made him uneasy. He displayed nothing but confidence despite being in the presence of not only five vampires, but five Hunters, the very Order specialized in fighting lycans. "When you have dealt with Yako, immediately get your wolves into position near the coven and contact me. With the threat of Yako neutralized, we will start our internal restructuring."

"Fun times," Jason said.

"Of course," Remy repeated. He was about to leave when he caught sight of the big man's expression. His nostrils twitched. The movement was so subtle he'd almost missed it.

"I guess this concludes our business," he said, and Remy suspected he was trying to hurry things along. "I will inform you the moment this Yako has been dealt with."

"On second thought," Remy said, stalling for time. "I think it might be a good idea for a few of my Hunters to accompany you on this particular hunt. Yako is quite dangerous."

"I'm sure I can handle it, Eldest Hunter," came the reply. Remy could clearly see he was trying not to appear hurried. What was happening?

"I'm sure you're most capable," Remy continued, having fun seeing the formerly composed man squirm, "but one can never be too careful, hmm?"

"Perhaps you're right," Jason replied, his face darkening.

Remy opened his mouth, then stopped. He caught it. The scent was faint, but he caught it. Someone was coming, and fast. Apparently, his friend here didn't want the new arrival to make an appearance. "Something wrong?" he asked.

"There is a rogue pack of lycans roaming these woods, Eldest Hunter," Jason said. "I'm afraid you might be in danger. I think you should leave."

"My Hunters are well equipped to deal with such a situation I assure you," Remy said. "Let them come."

"I should insist—"

The transformation must have happened at the last possible moment, for they only heard the big wolf crashing through the trees seconds before it burst into the little camp. Remy and the four Hunters behind him went into a defensive crouch, silenced guns ready. To their surprise, the wolf didn't attack them, but Jason.

It leaped the last dozen feet at the big man. Jason lowered himself and whipped his left hand under and up, knocking its head —and gaping jaws—upward. He reached his right hand up, grabbing hold of its throat and squeezed. There was a crunching sound, and Jason snatched out its throat. The wolf fell to the ground where it began to revert to its human form, as all lycans did in death.

Despite the oddity of this new development, Remy was impressed and more than a little unnerved. The man hadn't even bothered to transform to deal with a fully formed werewolf.

They heard what sounded like two more sets of paws pounding the earth just before they burst through the woods and threw themselves at Jason. To Remy's amazement, the man still didn't transform. The five Hunters watched in shock as the man ducked a swiping claw and delivered an uppercut punch that doubled the standing wolf over. He whipped his arm around and knocked it aside just in time to duck the snapping jaws of the second wolf.

"Shouldn't we help him?" a Hunter behind Remy whispered.

"And do what?" another Hunter replied. "Get in the way?"

Remy agreed. He wanted to see what their 'ally' was capable of.

The fight lasted less than a minute. One more lycan lay dead and transforming on the ground, and the third was already limping. To its credit, it lunged faster than Jason could react and dealt him four deep gashes across his torso.

Jason's eyes glowed, and he bared his teeth. The sight so unnerved Remy that his trigger finger twitched.

Jason stalked toward the wolf, who actually backed away.

Remy couldn't believe his eyes. A werewolf in lupine form *should* be exponentially stronger than in human form. After all, that was their major physical advantage. Not here.

Under that angry blue-eyed gaze, the big wolf actually shrank away. As Jason moved in, it recovered some of its courage and lashed out.

Jason caught the foreleg under his arm and snapped it with a subtle twist of his body. Before the wolf could let out as much as a yelp, Jason yanked it toward him and punched it in the side of the head.

When it stumbled sideways, he stepped around it, grabbed it by the back, and lifted it over his head.

Remy's mouth fell open as he watched the lycan in human form hold the giant wolf over his head, and bring it down on his shoulders. The sound of snapping vertebrae echoed through the woods. The big lycan dumped the wolf to the ground and walked around to kneel beside its head. Without hesitation, Jason raised his hand—now sporting elongated claws—and snatched out a good portion of the giant wolf's throat.

"I apologize for that, Eldest Hunter," he said, tossing the grisly bits aside.

"For what, lycan?" Remy interrupted. "Having to kill three of your own kind who attacked you instead of us?"

"I told you that there is a rogue pack out there that do not want the alliance. They would kill me and my pack to prevent it. If they had managed to kill me, they would have come after you."

Remy watched him. This whole situation was wrong and now he knew why. A single lycan that felt confident enough to meet with five Hunters. Not only that, but he had apparently just become packleader yet was easily the strongest lycan Remy had ever seen.

He thought about the conversation he'd had with Massius over the phone months ago when Yako had been attacked. The Elder hadn't gone into detail, but he had mentioned that a pack of lycans had attacked and tipped the scales in Yako's favor.

"Don't you wolves decide who leads the pack based on strength?" Remy asked. "Is it not the rule that the strongest and most dominant of your kind must lead?"

Jason raised his bushy eyebrows at that. "You want an education of our society?"

Remy almost laughed. Was that what they called them now, societies? "I don't doubt your honesty about this pack of rogues," he finally said, pointing his gun at Jason.

"It is traditionally considered rude to point your weapon at a friend," Jason said.

Remy fired. The silver bullet knocked the big man back a step. He looked down at the wound, then up with murderous eyes. Remy fired again and the other Hunters did as well, peppering the man with silver bullets.

"Never been much for tradition," Remy said, turning his back. "This night turned out better than I had hoped," he said to the others. "I think we just killed the alpha of Massius's rogue pack."

"Not likely," said a strained but angry voice from behind.

Remy's already infrequently beating heart skipped. He whirled, and fired, but the man was already on the move. His gun emptied just as Jason came right in front of him. The fist that took him in the chest was already transforming as it hit him, and Remy was launched up and away. He had just enough time to see the man transform into the biggest black wolf he'd ever seen before he crashed into the treetops.

He bounced off of several limbs before righting himself and making his way back to the ground. He didn't bother to turn and help the others, for he could hear them being ripped apart. He sprinted in the opposite direction, hoping he had enough of a head start to reach the car before that thing ran him down. He pulled out his phone and called to the driver.

"Yes, Eldest Hunter?" the voice said through the phone.

"Have the car ready," Remy ordered, trying not to sound panicked. "As soon as you see me, take off. I will catch you."

There was a pause. *"Yes sir."*

Remy felt the ground thud every time one of its massive paws hit the ground. He didn't fool himself for a second into believing he could fight that thing. He and the others had filled the man with at least twenty rounds of silver while he was in human form. Lycans had gotten tough enough to survive perhaps a single round in human form, maybe four or five in lupine form. This was unheard of.

On pure instinct he changed direction and ducked and darted left. He felt the rush of air as a claw swiped the space where his head had been. He ran up the trunk of a tree and jumped off of it just as the wolf came on him again.

Remy used his momentum to push off one tree trunk to the next, zigzagging his path. He hit the ground without slowing and chanced a glance over his shoulder. The wolf was a little farther back, but closing in again. It was black as the night, and huge. The wolf was so big that it plowed through anything smaller than a full sized redwood or maple.

Remy cursed. He was good at evasion, but the one thing he wasn't good at was the attribute that would have made his escape easier. All that size and strength wouldn't do much good against him if he was able to travel through the trees. Another skill Yako had that he did not, and he hated the man for it.

He continued to zigzag his retreat, in some cases even doubling back. When the wolf was nowhere in sight, he sped quietly through the woods until he finally came to the open road. Fortunately the driver had been intelligent enough to turn the vehicle around. As ordered, as soon as Remy came into the open, the Navigator kicked up gravel as it sped away.

Remy sprinted, barely catching the vehicle, and leaped onto the roof. His nails extended and he dug them into the metal to steady himself. He looked over his shoulder and saw the massive black wolf tearing down the road behind him. Remy freed one hand and drew his second gun. He took aim and fired.

His aim was perfect, and the silver bullet struck the werewolf in the center of its skull. It stumbled and shook its head, but continued on. The Navigator lurched forward. The human must have caught sight of the massive beast gaining ground on them.

Remy fired again and the wolf dodged. It couldn't avoid every bullet, however, and it finally slowed and veered back into thick cover of the woods. Remy fired into the woods for safe measure, then holstered his gun and reached down to open the door and climbed in. The car phone rang just as he shut the door.

"Get us back to Peles Castle," he said, and hung up before the driver had a chance to speak.

Remy took one last glance out the back window and relaxed when he saw no sign of pursuit. *That went badly,* he thought. He pulled out his phone and dialed Massius.

"I trust things went well," the cantankerous voice said.

"That depends on your definition of 'well'," Remy replied.

DARREN LACEY STEPPED BACK into the fire-lit camp. Things hadn't gone exactly as planned. He stood for a moment and concentrated. That blood had filled him with at least another seven silver bullets. It wasn't enough to kill him, but it hurt like hell!

He concentrated, and willed his body to push the bullets out, one by one. He threw his head back as an agonized roar tore from his throat. After the last bullet fell out of his naked body he dropped to his knees, his thick muscled shoulders heaving with every gasp. It would take him a day or two to recover from this.

He glared at the three dead lycans. Woodland Pack. Darren thought he had killed them all but apparently he'd missed a few, and to potentially disastrous consequences. He'd almost had them. That Hunter hadn't given up as much information as he'd hoped, but at least it could have been a nice little surprise when the call came and Darren turned the tables on them. It would have been doubly as sweet when he appeared beside the supposedly dead Yako.

He growled and kicked one of the dead males. A shallow promise of status among a coven of vampires and they come with lowered heads and tails tucked between their legs like domesticated dogs. How they could not see that the promise was as empty as their heads was a mystery to Darren. He could practically smell the sense of superiority wafting off of that Remy character.

He heard his phone ring, and searched the camp till he found it lying next to another of the three corpses. He picked it up and got straight to the point.

"The plan failed. Be ready as soon as you get off that plane."

CHAPTER 31

It felt familiar but at the same time not. Jelani looked around the place that he used to call home. A place barely lived in. The dishes looked like they hadn't been washed in days, the floors were unswept, and dust—one of Daniel's biggest pet peeves—had collected on the entertainment center.

Jelani slouched on the couch and stared out the large window of the living room. Even Daniel's bed hadn't been made. It was amazing how the place could go from "abnormally neat for a bachelor pad", as the girls had put it, to a warm and fun home after they'd moved in, to a barely lived in shell, now.

"One minute life's good, the next it's upside down." He didn't bother to get up when he heard Daniel get out of the elevator down the hall. He smelled his friend when he was about a dozen feet from the door, but Daniel no doubt smelled him long before that.

The door opened and closed.

Silence.

"Can't say I'm surprised to see you here," His best friend said from the kitchen.

"Good to see you again buddy," Jelani said.

"Is it?"

Jelani continued to stare out the window at the dark waters and the lights of North Vancouver beyond. He smelled the raw steak before Daniel had begun to pull the plastic off of it. He heard the sound of teeth biting into the raw meat, chewing, swallowing. "Yeah, it is. I miss you, man."

Another bite, chew, swallow. "Our last meeting wasn't a good one, was it?" Another bite, this one crunching through bone.

"I suppose not," Jelani said. He could smell the blood from the steak, but it was old and dead, not appetizing at all. He didn't know what it was like to be a werewolf, but he suspected eating a package of dead steak was the equivalent of himself drinking a carton of blood off the shelf of a grocery store. Flat and low in nutrients. "How's that steak?"

"It makes me not hungry," Daniel said. "But if you're referring to how enjoyable it is, it's awful compared to the poor deer I slaughtered last night."

Jelani felt saddened, both for the deer and for his friend. One of the many things that drew them together to become best friends was their mutual respect and love for nature. He couldn't imagine what it must feel like to come back to his senses surrounded by the carnage he'd inflicted. "Everything has to die to feed something else."

"Yeah, I know," came the bitter response. Jelani heard water running in the sink, then Daniel drying his hands. "I know," he repeated, sitting on the couch on the left side of the room. Such a familiar scene yet so different. "I've been telling myself that for the last day now. When'd you get here?"

"About a half hour ago," Jelani answered. "Thought I'd come see how you were doing."

They sat in silence for a while, Jelani wrapped in his thoughts while Daniel sifted through his own. He tried not to wish this was just another night; that the girls would be home any minute now and catch them playing video games. He tried, but the memories were too strong.

"Thinking about how things were?" Daniel asked.

Jelani made a sound that could have been a huff or a snicker. "You read my mind."

"Hardly," Daniel replied, his tone as dry as their current living conditions. "I was thinking the same thing. How could I not?"

"Yeah."

Daniel forced a grin. "You think every new vampire and werewolf sit around like this? Moping and wishing they had their old lives back?"

Jelani shrugged. "I suppose some do, but I think there's plenty out there whose lives turned a lot more interesting after the change. I imagine this existence is more desirable to people of lesser character. Just a hunch."

"You're probably right," Daniel said. "So, I'm imagining you're off to chase Remy across the pond?"

"Yeah."

Daniel leaned forward and propped his elbows on his knees. "Need a hand?"

Jelani finally looked at him. He saw no anger in his best friend's eyes. No hatred or blame. He was afraid to believe it.

"Don't look so surprised," Daniel said. "I needed some time to come down off the shock. You only had to go through the internal change and adjust to nightlife. Imagine your whole physiology changing on you twice. It felt different when I first awoke, but when I saw the moon ..." he shook his head. Dude, I can't even describe it to you. And the *pain*. Oh my god, the pain!"

Jelani tried to imagine what it must be like to change into a huge wolf. "That bad huh?"

Daniel grabbed the sides of his head. "I didn't know how a person could endure going through that pain every single time they transformed, but Imron told me it's only that bad the first time. Thank goodness for that."

He stood and moved beside Jelani and held out a hand. "Thanks, bro. For guiding me through."

Jelani looked at the proffered hand and up into his friend's—his brother's—eyes. If he'd still been human, he might have had to fight back tears. He grabbed the hand and Daniel pulled him up from the couch into a crushing hug.

"Damn, dude!" Jelani said in a strangled voice. "Did I lose a hundred fifty pounds or are you ridiculously strong now?"

Daniel laughed. "If there's a benefit to all this, it's that I'm probably ten times stronger than I could ever have dreamed of being. Seriously, I think I could lift a car." Jelani stared dryly at the devious grin that always preceded some foolish suggestion. "I bet I'm stronger than you are," Daniel finally said.

Jelani rolled his eyes. "Yeah sure. We'll have to arm wrestle one of these days. To answer your question, yes I can use a hand if you're up to it."

A glint passed over Daniel's eyes. Whether it was a trick of the city lights outside or not, it gave his devious look a dangerous edge. "Let's get moving, then. I'm assuming we need to find a night flight."

"It's a little tricky," Jelani said. "It'll take a little over twelve hours to get there, so if I'm going to get out of the airport without getting fried, we're going to have to be on a plane that lands at night."

"Which means we have to catch a day flight." Daniel rubbed his chin. "That's a problem. Hmm." He snapped his fingers. "Got it! Why don't we just fly to … oh I dunno … Toronto, and then fly in to Romania. We'll leave and land at night."

Jelani groaned. "How the hell didn't I figure that out?"

"You've had a lot on your mind," Daniel said, giving him a slap on the back. "And I'm the smarter one, so don't worry about it."

"Yeah right," Jelani said, shoving him away. It felt good to have his friend back. At least some part of his life was starting to resemble what it was. "Let's jump on the computer and do this now."

Daniel went into his room and came back with his laptop. "When do you wanna leave?"

"It's already too late to leave tonight," Jelani said. "So first thing tomorrow night."

"We can leave tonight," Daniel said, typing. He scanned the screen. It's only a four-and-a-half-hour flight from here to Toronto and there's a flight that leaves in an hour and twenty minutes."

Jelani looked at his phone. "We can't make it in time."

"It's not an international flight," Daniel said, looking at the screen. "It won't take long to check in since we won't be going through customs. We can make it. Taking the time zone difference into consideration, we'll get to Toronto with at least an hour left before dawn. And there's a hotel inside the airport, man! It's accessible from terminal 3, so we don't even need to leave. And tomorrow we can just leave the hotel and jump right on the plane to Europe."

"Good job," Jelani said. "Book my ticket and I'll reimburse you later."

"Already done, my friend." Daniel powered his computer down and went back into his room. He came back a few minutes later with two duffel bags and tossed one to Jelani. "I'm a little taller than you but not much bigger, so you can wear a few of my clothes till we get you to a store. And stop looking all sentimental, all right? Or I'm taking my bag back!"

"Gotcha," Jelani said, still grinning. He couldn't help it. He felt like a kid who was best friends again after a fight.

Daniel snarled at him. "What're you *grinnin'* at?"

Jelani tried to stifle his grin and only succeeded in wrinkling it. "Heh. Nothin', man. Thanks for the stuff. Let's go."

"Melinda's gonna be ticked off," Jelani said, but he wasn't much concerned. The woman wasn't a pushover by any means, but she would be in over her head in Peles Coven in the middle of a bunch of Hunters and Reapers. And if what Imron had told Daniel was true, there would be werewolves involved as well. Jelani wasn't even sure he would survive this. It felt odd that he didn't really care. He wanted to live, but he wasn't concerned about the possibility that he might die.

"She'll get over it." Daniel leaned his head back against the headrest and stared out the car window. "Probably for the best anyway. From what you tell me, Remy could mess up her head."

Jelani nodded. "Yup."

"So what should we expect going into this?" Daniel asked.

"My best guess," Jelani said, "is that we probably won't have a problem getting from the airport to the castle. In fact, if we play our cards right, we might be able to take Remy out before he even knows we're there."

"What makes you say that?" came the skeptical response.

Jelani took the exit to the airport and followed the signs. "Because I'm certain he's keeping an eye out for Yako. He doesn't know for sure that I'm coming after him, and even if he did, he would see Yako as the bigger threat. And he would be right."

"So he'll be too busy dealing with Yako to be concerned with us," Daniel reasoned.

"That's my thinking," Jelani replied. "Yako's probably there now, or almost, anyway. Let him slaughter as many of Remy's goons as possible while we slip into the castle and handle the sneaky bastard. Once I take him out, my debt with Yako will be fulfilled and I'll have no more business with him."

"And then?" Daniel asked.

"I'll worry about that later. Right now I'm just focused on Remy's uncreation."

Daniel looked over at him. "You're starting to sound like a blood again."

Jelani gave him a sidelong glance. "Blood, huh? Well, you're starting to sound like a lycan."

Jelani turned into the extended parking lot and nosed the car into a spot. He tried not to think about how much the parking would cost when they returned. They grabbed their duffel bags and hurried through the airport. As luck would have it, flying midweek was the best time. Not only was the airport not crowded, but the flight was barely half full.

"I have to admit," Jelani whispered as they fastened their seat belts. "In my new existence I hadn't imagined riding in coach."

"Last minute flight," Daniel said. "Keep your fingers crossed for the flight out to Bucharest. The planes going that far are bigger, but I still don't want to sit for that long in coach."

The flight attendant went through the routine of informing the passengers of the various safety measures and facilities of the cabin while no one listened. Jelani had usually made a point of paying attention out of courtesy, but tonight would have to be an exception. "How long is the trip from Bucharest to Sinaia?"

"I looked it up after booking this flight and it said it was a little over an hour and a half. Like an hour and forty minutes or so, but by rail."

The captain's voice sounded over the intercom. "Flight attendants prepare for departure."

"I think I'll catch a nap," Daniel said. "See you when we land."

"I got you," Jelani said, looking out the window as the plane sped down the tarmac. He lost himself in thoughts and concerns. He looked out at the sprawling city lights of Vancouver as the plane lifted into the air and angled its way east. Day or night, it was a beautiful city. Jelani wondered if he was looking at it for the last time.

CHAPTER 32

Mariska waited patiently for Yako to emerge from the airport. She assumed Remy had sent men to kill him even if Michael's fire-headed friend had not told them of his plans. She looked at the building across the street to her right and saw the woman crouched at the edge next to the other man she had just met, watching.

She looked over her shoulder and, once again, caught Reed eyeing the woman. She cleared her throat. He looked back to her and she stared at him.

"I'm sorry, Second."

"How much weight do you suppose your apology would hold with Eldest Hunter?" Mariska asked.

Reed deflated a little. "None, Second."

"How much weight to do you think your apology holds with me?"

"None, Second."

"Be careful your lust does not end your life, Hunter." The threat had the desired effect, and the young Hunter kept his attention fixed ahead.

Mariska turned back. She didn't know if Yako would truly kill

Reed for such a small indiscretion, but it was possible. Eldest required focus at all times when in the field.

She looked to the left and confirmed the twins' position. Tara and her two Hunters waited at the edge of the closest building. Somewhere hidden from the streetlights, Meilana, Lydia, and Barakus also lay in wait.

Mariska studied the entrance while considering the possibilities. If it came to a fight—as she was sure it would—the redhead, Scarlene, would wait with Marcos and only join in if needed. Remy still believed them to be his, and that was an advantage neither Mariska nor Tara wanted to lose.

"That's him," Akin said, pointing.

Mariska tensed. A man dressed in charcoal gray jeans and a black sweater came out the front doors. He had a long duffel bag strapped across his back. Yako.

A woman walked up to the Eldest Hunter and the two spoke. Mariska strained to hear but it was too far.

"I wish I could hear what they're talking about," Reed whispered.

"Why don't you ask him when we're done here," Akin retorted.

Mariska refrained from throwing a glare at them, keeping her attention solely on Yako. If something happened she would need to act immediately.

The two talked for what seemed to be several minutes, then the woman turned as if to leave, but stopped and looked back. Yako hadn't moved. She said something again, but the Eldest Hunter remained where he was.

"Looks like she's trying to get him somewhere discrete," Akin said.

"Which means there are others," Mariska replied.

"Should we find them?" Reed asked.

"If you were concealed and waiting to attack,"Mariska replied, "what would you watch for?"

A brief pause, then came the answer, "my target, and anyone who came to neutralize my attack."

"So we wait," Mariska said.

Humans came out the doors around them, carrying bags and pulling luggage on wheels. More than a few glanced at Yako and gave him a wide berth. He had that effect, even on unperceptive humans.

"Looks like whatever she's saying must be convincing," Akin said. "He's following her."

"She's dead," Mariska said.

"What makes you say—"

Before Akin could finish the question, Yako had followed the woman a short distance around the corner from the entrance where there was little lighting. As soon as they were obscured from the light the woman rounded and pointed a gun at Yako. She stood there, and Mariska saw the shock on her face the instant before her head and left arm fell from her body.

Akin whistled through his teeth. "I almost feel sorry for her. I didn't even see that happen and I was watching the whole time."

Mariska allowed herself a self-satisfied grin. She was closer to Yako than anyone. If the Eldest was the least bit hesitant about you, it meant your death. If you were more dangerous, you would die before you could speak. That girl was fool enough to even turn her back on him, but still he'd waited for the instant she made her attempt. It was an amazing thing to watch.

"Looks like the snakes are slithering out," Akin said, nodding his head toward the top of the terminal where six figures dropped into the darkness. Mariska touched her earpiece. A moment later, Tara answered.

"Time for action?" the Reaper's voice asked through the device.

"We should hold our position," Mariska said.

"He is being engaged by six Hunters, Second."

"Even if their skills are better than I suspect, we will still have time to move in." Mariska ended the call and glanced at Scarlene and Marcos De La Vega. She could see the thinly veiled amazement on their faces. When she returned her attention to the fight below, admiration filled her.

No more than two dozen feet away from the lights of the terminal, the Eldest Hunter silently engaged six Hunters who were fast realizing they were losing the fight. One went down, grabbing at the wound in his chest before falling over to decay. A second lost his right arm to that deadly black-coated silver blade.

"I cannot deny my amazement," Akin said. "I think most of us have heard of the Eldest Hunter's prowess, but it has been understated."

When the fight finally ended, six Hunters lay on the ground, death greedily claiming them. Yako replaced his sword in the hole in the top of his duffel bag and continued down the street as though nothing had happened.

"Let's move." Mariska was up and headed toward Scarlene and Marcos's position. They leaped the distance between the two buildings and continued past the pair. Without a word, the two Hunters fell in behind them. Mariska knew that Tara and the others would make their way around from the other direction, ensuring that the two groups would secure the area in a large circle.

Something wasn't right, though. Sending what was obviously an inexperienced woman for what was the worst attempt at an assassination Mariska had ever seen was insulting. Or was that the point?

She heard a whistle so faint she almost missed it. Mariska dove to the side and an arrow passed through her hair. She rolled to a stop against a nearby wall and scanned the higher rooftops. Nothing.

"Second!"

Mariska looked behind her to see Scarlene, kneeling over Akin, two silver tipped arrows protruding from his back and another in his side. On his other side, Reed clasped his hand tightly. Akin's body trembled as little tendrils of smoke crept from the wounds.

"Use your head," he groaned at Reed, "and you'll keep it." He looked at Mariska and nodded. She nodded back and drew her gun. One silenced silver bullet put his agony to rest and death rushed to claim him. Reed stood and glared at the seemingly empty rooftops above.

"Those arrows were meant for me," Reed said.

"How many will have a claim on your survival?" Mariska asked.

"None other, Second," came the reply.

Mariska nodded. He had just declared that he expected no aid in the fighting to come. If death found him, no one would save him from the killing stroke. Mariska found a flicker of respect for the young Hunter.

She turned to Scarlene, the woman had wrapped her telltale fiery hair into a black scarf. "It galls me to admit that I'm probably only alive because I saw you dive to the side," the woman said.

"As long as their position remains hidden from us," Mariska said, "they will use arrows because they're harder to hear. Once we've found them, they will use guns."

"Even silenced, the bullets are louder, but faster," Reed said. "Silence won't matter once the fighting starts."

"Is your *talent* stating the obvious?" Scarlene asked, glowering at Reed before turning to Mariska. "The arrows came from behind."

"They will have moved," Mariska added. She touched her earpiece and waited. The line rang, but there was no answer. She saw a tiny flash of light in the distance, and turned off the device. Another flash. The others followed her gaze and Reed swore.

"Looks like Tara found someone to play with," Marcos said.

Mariska looked down the street and found a curse of her own stuck in her throat. Yako was engaged in a fight with four enemies, and now she saw shadows moving everywhere, converging on his position.

It was a bold move, but also a smart one that had depended on Yako's devotion to the species and the coven. It was very possible that Massius and Remy were so desperate to be rid of him that they would have sent the attack whether the Eldest Hunter was surrounded by humans or not. The risk of discovery by mortals was great, and it was a risk Yako would not take, even if it meant his own uncreation.

Mariska's anger rose. The Eldest Hunter lived by what was right for the vampire species while those two cowards lived only for what was best for themselves. They would die, and she would deliver that stroke side by side with the true leader of her Order.

"How many have turned against us?" Scarlene asked.

"Those are not all vampires," Mariska said, noting how some of the attackers moved differently, more direct. Vampires could run fast, jump high, but lycans in human form could run just as fast and jump higher. What they saw in the distance was a mix of traitorous vampires fighting alongside their dog allies.

Her eyes lit in red flame. "Come."

"You know as soon as we step out from this spot they'll be on us," Marcos said.

Mariska drew her sword. "I will cover your descent. Aid the Eldest Hunter."

"I stand with you, Second," Reed said.

"Then do as you are told," she replied.

Marcos put a hand on his shoulder and turned Reed away. "Plenty of fighting down there, young Hunter. Let us go and do our leader proud."

Scarlene stared into Mariska's eyes and nodded, her eyes smoldering crimson as well. Mariska nodded back, then stepped out into the open.

For decades she'd trained personally with Yako. Early on he

had seen the potential in her and had taken her on as his personal student.

She went within, drawing upon the years of training, discipline, repetition, focus. She brought her mind to awareness of every muscle in her body, and they responded by coming to attention. Every tendon, ever muscle fiber, every joint. She felt every inch of the black two-piece spandex that hugged her body for warmth that she didn't need, but allowed for the uninhibited movement that she did.

Mariska faced the street below where her mentor battled three of the four who had attacked him. Scarlene, Marcos, and Reed blew past her and an instant later the quiet sound of seven arrows slicing through the air followed.

Yako felled another enemy just as three lycans entered the fight. Mariska cut apart the arrows while her three remaining Hunters dropped over the edge of the building. Yako ran a lycan through the chest and drew his blade away and in a horizontal arc, decapitating a vampire behind him.

Four more arrows raced through the darkness. The Second Hunter became one with the sword in her hand. The arrows came for her. She met them.

CHAPTER 33

Tara didn't know if the stroke of luck was good or bad when a handful of humans happened upon the fighting. She'd had a second to glimpse the dumbfounded mortals watching Yako's swordplay, phones out taking pictures and video. They must have thought it was some street show.

Ironically, the presence of these human bystanders kept the fight from getting much uglier, for they lycan attackers wouldn't change into their lupine forms with mortals in sight. The amazed murmurs and clapping ended when Yako delivered a killing blow.

Meilana had spotted the rooftop threat first and had warned Tara through their connection. Her twin had taken a more round-about route and came up behind a group of lycans accompanying two Hunters. Once they'd engaged, everything happened at once. The fight was on in full, with at least seven human witnesses, a panicked stampede, and a rapidly locking down airport terminal.

Tara slapped a silver bullet aside and ducked a sword that would have taken her head. It was a trick she'd been taught by a vampire who had known a gunsmith back when the gun had first been invented. Bullets traveled fast, and with destructive force, but a little known fact was that if your timing was right, you could slap it out of the air.

She laughed, ducking and spinning away as more silenced guns fired in her direction. How ironic that humans could discover such facts that were practically useless to them, but invaluable to one such as herself.

The Reaper grinned as she took half the leg of her nearest attacker and hauled him around to shield her from another barrage of silver bullets. "Not fast enough are you?" she hissed, and dropped the decaying vampire.

A burly man with two machetes rushed in, hacking and swinging. He was fast. She leaned away from a vertical swipe that missed her neck by inches, then ducked and rolled between his legs, slicing him across the front of the knee with one of her hand-scythes.

He staggered, then his back arched as a blade punched through his back and out of his chest. He wailed as Tara used her deadly silver scythes to climb up his back. The lycan's agonized cries ended abruptly with a swing of her weapon that sent his head dropping to the ground. Unlike the death of a vampire, the lycan's lifeless body simply dropped and bled out onto the ground.

She hopped off the corpse, not wanting to get blood on her boots. Michael and Layne were each fighting a lycan, and two vampires had just emerged from over the side of the building.

The diminutive Reaper was there in an instant, disemboweling one of them, and bringing her left weapon around to take the head of the other. This one—a slender male—was the faster of the two and easily leaned away from the attack. He stepped in and stabbed with a dirk, and when Tara knocked it aside, he pointed a 9mm handgun at her midsection.

Tara bared her fangs and brought her right hand around and let fly the bloody scythe. At the same time she released the weapon, she jumped straight into the air.

The blade struck true, and on reflex he fired. The shots were erratic and one of the bullets hit a lycan Michael had been fighting. The missile passed straight through and hit the Hunter in the chest. Midair, all Tara could do was note the death of her Hunter as she descended on the dying traitor below her.

She brought her remaining scythe down and sliced him in the front of the chest, grabbing the other embedded weapon. Her enemy fell back, kicking and hissing as his body decayed around the grievous wound.

She heard sirens in the distance and assessed the situation. Michael was nearly ash, and the right side of Layne's face was gradually healing from a deep gash. Wounds inflicted by werewolves were always slower to heal for some reason. "We've got to move," he rasped.

She sent her thoughts to Meilana, who still fought. Her twin was a little worse for wear, but she still lived, and had registered the contact. They would begin their withdraw.

"Come," Tara said to Layne.

The Hunter fell in step with her. "If our enemies follow us?"

Tara's face darkened. "One can hope.

SEVEN HUNTERS and one Reaper occupied the plush chairs and large sofa that crowded the red and purple meeting room. Cross-legged on the floor, Yako cleaned his blade as he listened to the others discuss the attack.

"I don't understand the logic," Meilana was saying. "Why send a single girl who obviously knew nothing about combat to die, then send groups of vampires and lycans to attack us at the airport with plenty of human witnesses?"

"Arrogance," Layne said. "I've had a strong enough dose of Massius to know that he's not above trying to prove a point."

"That point comes at a high cost." Meilana argued.

Reed shrugged. "Any humans that witnessed the attack would

reveal themselves when they talk to the police and be eliminated. Seems easy enough to me."

Scarlene's lips twitched and she looked away.

"And every witness will most certainly come forth," Layne said, his tone suggesting he were talking to an infant. "Every single one of them will go to the police, and I'm sure *none* of them will have taken pictures or videos of the incident."

Reed glared at him but held his tongue. Good. There seemed to be at least a sliver of wisdom in him.

Yako took note of the silence of Mariska, Scarlene, and Tara, as well as Barakus and Lydia. "What are your thoughts, Reaper?" he asked, addressing the highest-ranking warrior in the room.

Tara inclined her head, returning the respect. "Should I murder my ego to speak the truth, it would force me to admit that Massius sees you as the primary threat. Where his protégé errs on the side of idiocy, he would rather strike a decisive blow and deal with the consequences thereafter."

He felt Scarlene's eyes on him. "Eldest Hunter, a question, if I may?"

Yako nodded to her.

"With respect, I have witnessed your skill for the first time today, and it has been greatly understated by all accounts. However, I cannot figure why an Elder of the High Council so fears you. Despite his age and the power that is borne of it, he holds a seat of influence and is protected by the Order of Reapers. In fact, he is personally protected by the Eldest Reaper himself."

A tension filled the air to which only Mariska and Tara seemed immune. Apparently he must have a reputation for unbridled ruthlessness. It was a humorous thought.

Yako considered Scarlene a moment before responding. "Either Remy had an uncharacteristic spark of wisdom in placing you by his side, or it was Massius's doing." The woman replied with a precise smile. "I suspect," he said, addressing everyone, "that Massius fears the threat of my lineage more than myself."

"Your lineage, Eldest Hunter?" Marcos asked.

Yako kept his features neutral as he stared at the space in front of his crossed legs. "Massius is not an Elder." He looked into the eyes of the Hunter named Marcos De La Vega; reading his reaction. He was also aware of Layne and Scarlene, who had stiffened. The words he had spoken were akin to blasphemy.

He resumed cleaning his sword, one hand concentrated on the blade, the other gripping the hilt. Ever ready, ever vigilant.

Consternation twisted Marcos De La Vega's features, and the redhead had a similar reaction. Layne's mouth simply dropped open.

The room settled into a deathly silence and Yako let it remain so. Best to know his true allies from enemies now.

"Ha! I suspected as much!" It was Barakus that spoke, his booming voice caused Lydia to smack him in the head.

"Quiet yourself," the stocky woman said. "You only suspected it after it was already said."

"Those are … strong words, Eldest," Marcos replied.

"They are words spoken true, Hunter," Yako said. "And they are also words that demand the swift execution of the speaker by all who are loyal to the Elders and the coven."

Barakus glanced at Marcos and Layne, the fingers of his sword hand twitching. Lydia eyed Scarlene.

The flame-haired woman rolled her eyes. "Okay, enough with the standoff. We're all here because we are loyal to the coven, and that very loyalty puts us against Massius. I will admit that the laws are ingrained in me as strongly as anyone else, but however shocking it is that the old man is just that, an old vampire, it doesn't change the fact that each of us plan to coat the floor with his ashes."

Her words snapped Marcos from his stupor and he nodded. "Of course. My apologies for the hesitation, Eldest Hunter. This news is, as Scarlene has said, shocking."

Of course it was. It could lead to the question of who in fact was an Elder and who was just an immortal who happened to be turned much earlier than anyone else. The thought of a non pure-blood as one of the leaders of the coven was unsettling.

"Eldest Hunter," Scarlene said. "Might I ask how you came to find this out?"

"When this is over," Yako answered, "look to the histories that are older than those at the surface. I suspect he tried to destroy all the evidence but there is always something hidden or overlooked." He looked at Tara, but the Reaper held up a hand.

"I will offer suggestions or advice when necessary, but in this, I cede command to you, Eldest Hunter."

Yako nodded in deference then addressed the others. "The night is almost, ended and Massius will expect us to attempt to enter the castle tomorrow as soon as the sun is down. It would be ideal if we were able to find a way in tonight."

"If we left at this moment I'm not sure we would make it before the sun caught us out," Reed said.

"He's right," Scarlene said.

"Why not give him what he expects," Meilana suggested.

Yako looked at her, an indication to continue. Next, came the rapid-fire thoughts listed and expounded upon by the twins.

"WHEN THE DAY WANES," Meilana began.

"Brace yourselves," Layne said.

"And the night holds sway," Tara continued.

"A few of our number will converge upon the castle."

"And when they are seen ..."

"The front guard will not engage ..."

"For their duty is to protect ..."

"And only protect ..."

"The coven grounds."

"Massius will be notified ..."

"And he will likely send some of his Hunters and lycan allies in pursuit."

"We need not fight, but only withdraw …"

"While you, Eldest Hunter …"

"And those who accompany you …"

"Will take the tunnels underneath the city."

Marcos held up a hand. "I'm sorry to interrupt. Tunnels?"

Tara nodded. "A network of tunnels span a good portion of Sinaia. During the early ages of the city's history, the coven was much smaller and existed underground; a safe haven from the sun and discovery by humans."

Reed frowned. "Sounds like our forefathers were squatting in a sewer in fear of being seen by a bunch of cattle."

Yako cast the boy a withering stare. "Would you like to test the High Council's sense of humor with your observation of their previous existence?"

Reed seemed to turn to stone, then he came out of his seat and knelt, head down. "Of course not, Eldest. My words come without the benefit of wisdom to guide them."

"Look at me," Yako said, and the young Hunter obeyed. Minutes passed while Yako held the boy fixed with his icy glare. He sensed Mariska's resolve. She felt the boy had transgressed too far and that Yako would surely kill him. He was tempted.

"I doubt you understand your proximity to uncreation," Yako said, "so I will say this plainly. Your next foolish words will precede your death."

"Yes, Eldest Hunter." He looked like he was about to rise and sit back down, but wisely remained where he was.

"Why do you kneel?" Yako asked him.

"Respect and humility, Eldest Hunter."

"Remain and contemplate this."

"Yes, Eldest Hunter."

He turned to Scarlene. "Are there others outside Peles Castle that are loyal to the coven?"

"Only those in this room, Eldest."

"And I might add that there are more than a few that are fostering misguided loyalty at the moment," Tara said.

Yako nodded at that. "How so?"

The Reaper stood and walked past him to look up at a large painting of a mountainous landscape dotted with yellow and white flowers growing in an ocean of green grass. She turned back. "Massius and Alicia. I have a growing suspicion that Massius has a way of playing with the mind. Several times I have had a conversation with him and felt something creeping in my mind. A fog filled with whispers and suggestions."

Meilana looked horrified.

"Calm, Meilana," Tara said. "I would not succumb to his subtlety."

"Mind compulsion in its various forms is not uncommon among us," Mariska said.

"But the degree of subtlety to which Massius seems capable of is a dangerous thing," Tara countered. "It can creep on you, slowly. Patiently. If you are vigilant you may resist it, but at the risk of tipping your hand that you are aware of what he's doing."

"You believe he may have used some form of mind compulsion on members of the coven?" Yako wondered what would happen upon Massius's uncreation. Would those he had influenced come back to their own minds? Would they be aware of what had been done to them?

"Some, yes," Tara answered. "But many who side with him think he will grab control of the coven. They want to be on the winning side."

Yako was getting an idea of how he would approach this. "Do you know where the Reapers stand?"

Tara thought about that for a moment. "Doghden and Serena will stand with us, as well as Gulghin and Lugar. But Syphera, Mesha, and their cronies must die."

That was undesirable. Yako had hoped not to have to cross blades with any of the Reapers, not out of fear, but out of respect. Anyone who had gone through the *Trials of the Ancients* deserved the utmost respect. But then, if they followed Massius out of their own desires, they perverted the very power they had attained. A deeper question also remained of how a Reaper could turn against the Elders.

That brought his thoughts to Braggus. Yako looked at Tara expectantly, and she responded with a subtle grin. "Yes, Eldest Hunter," she said, reading his expression. "I do believe the Eldest Reaper's magnificent scythe will be drawn beside your sword and not against it."

Yako nodded and stood. "That is well." He looked at Mariska. "Second. Assemble the Hunters and formulate a plan for next night. We will come at them from every angle, and the following night, we enter."

"We enter in two nights, Eldest?" Tara arched an eyebrow.

"In two nights," Yako replied.

Mariska called for the Hunters to leave the room. Yako stopped her as she moved to leave. "Eldest?" she asked.

"A word."

After everyone had left, the two women turned questioning looks on him.

"What would you have of me, Eldest?" Mariska asked.

Tara's eyebrow rose a little higher. "You have my full curiosity as well, Eldest Hunter."

"Are you certain he does not know of these tunnels?" Yako asked the Reaper.

Tara nodded. "Only two members of the current High Council know about them, and one of them is dead. When Lord Ordine was killed, Elder Vicken did not want the knowledge of the tunnels to fall into obscurity, should he fall."

The mention of the fallen Elder Denry Ordine set Yako's blood hot. He looked at Mariska, who shared his fire.

Tara looked from him to the other woman and back. "Is there something I should know?"

"Lord Ordine was not simply killed by a lycan," Yako said.

"With respect, Yako, I was there to see him die of his wounds after being severely mauled by one of those rabid dogs."

"He was killed by a lycanthrope," Yako clarified, "but his fall had been plotted carefully."

Tara's eyes narrowed. "Are you about to tell me that Massius had something to do with that?"

"Consider the timing of all of it," Yako said. "Massius's relations with the lycans, Lord Ordine's fatal wounds. The plots of Massius reach back hundreds of years."

A pale red glow crept into the tiny Reapers eyes. "I will give him a hundred deaths combined into one."

"Exact your revenge however you may," Yako said, "but he is still powerful. He is not an Elder, but he is still far older than any of us, and that gives him a notable advantage."

Tara responded with a curt nod. "Your warning is duly noted."

A thought occurred to Yako. "You said Elder Vicken passed on his knowledge of the tunnels, lest their existence be forgotten. Who knows about them now?"

"Everyone that was in the room when I spoke of it."

Yako stared at her. "With respect, Reaper—"

She waved an irritated hand at him. "Yes, Yako. I am well aware of your propensity for formality, but there is no one else in this room but the three of us. For the sake of my sanity, relax the titles?"

Yako saw the corners of Mariska's mouth curl up. "Very well … Tara. Is it not strange that Elder Vicken would choose someone other than the Eldest Reaper to pass this knowledge to?"

"A good question," Tara replied, "I asked him about it when he first told me of the tunnels. He asked me how much I trusted Braggus. I told him my trust was tentative." She indicated Yako. "And how about you? How far does your trust extend to the giant?"

"Until several months ago," Yako said, "I had only considered trusting him a possibility."

She laughed. "Then he must have been at the very least, reliable. You are the most mistrusting person I've ever met, Yako. It is a good trait, if not a lonely one."

"What will we do when the night returns?" Mariska asked.

"As soon as night has fallen," Yako said, "you will split into two groups and approach the castle and search for any unguarded entry points. You will likely be spotted, which is the plan, but if you actually do find something, enter if you feel you can."

"And you?" Tara asked.

"I would have you accompany me to a meeting with a friend," Yako answered.

"A friend?" Tara looked at Mariska in disbelief. "You may only reveal crumbs of information about yourself, but every morsel is shocking. Who is this friend?"

"Darren Lacey," Yako said.

Tara frowned. "That name means nothing to me."

"He is the alpha of the most powerful pack to roam here or North America," the Eldest Hunter explained.

"Lycans?" Tara said. "Of all the unlikeliness of you actually having a friend, you make friends with a wolf? I don't know whether to laugh or be horrified."

"I would recommend you be relieved," Yako said. "He is better our ally than our enemy." He looked at Mariska. "Go and form the groups. After our meeting, we will convene there."

Mariska nodded and left.

"Of course," Tara said. "Massius and Remy would expect nothing less than for you to be there with your Hunters, but not necessarily at first." She walked over to the window. A beautiful and deadly glow lined the eastern horizon.

"Time to go." She faced Yako again. "Disloyalty in the North American Coven as well as here in Peles. Civilian, Hunter, and Reaper alike. When this is done, what do you plan to do with those who remain? The Hunters who stood against us, I mean? There are many who might swear loyalty, and there are ways to bind that loyalty."

Yako turned away and started toward the doors leading to the rooms underground. Loyalty lived and died with the individual. He had no use for someone who would switch alliance simply because they were on the losing side of a conflict. Better to die with honor.

"They have sided with the enemy and made me theirs. In this, they have bound themselves to Massius. They understand what my coming means.They will stand against me, and I will deliver them. All."

CHAPTER 34

"How long has it been since we last walked these streets?" Saaya asked. "Intriguing, is it not? How humans can so change their civilizations in but one or two hundred years."

"In appearance only," Kafeel replied.

Saaya poked out her bottom lip. "Sour as always, brother."

Kafeel's stony expression never changed. "Sour, or presenting a sour truth?"

"Does finding the sour in the sweet not make one sour?" Saaya asked.

"Does seeing only the dot of light in a vacuum of darkness not make one naive?"

"Oh," Saaya replied, "but that tiny dot of light is a beacon in the darkness for one to follow."

"To what end?" her brother asked.

That brought a look of surprise to the *dampeal's* face. Kafeel was rarely so talkative, and she couldn't remember him ever posing her a question, much less engaging in a philosophical discussion.

"They struggle for what?" Kafeel continued. "For whom? You see them as well as I. Do you not find them humorous?"

"Humorous in what way?" Now Saaya was genuinely curious what direction this was going.

"I admit that here, humans seem more tolerant of each other," Kafeel said. "But how many places have we been where their disdain for each other is evident? The larger the population of humans, the less happy they are. They struggle and fight one another to own things that don't make them happy, to live an existence of toil and conflict in the hopes of living out some portion of their ephemeral lives in a measure of comfort dictated by colored pieces of paper upon which they attach value."

Saaya arched an eyebrow. "That was a mouthful for you, brother."

"More than I care to discuss, but I wish for you to see this for what it is, and I wish to understand what joy you find in it." He spread a hand out in front of them.

Saaya looked around the sunlit streets of Bucharest. Stores sold goods ranging from smartphones to clothing, and everything in between. People walked down the street tapping their fingers on the screens of their phones, almost heedless of the environment surrounding them. A man discussed personal matters on his phone loud enough for all to hear, while a woman spoke sternly to a child who barely listened.

Then there was a couple sitting at a patio of a coffee shop. The woman leaned her head against her companion's shoulder and he kissed her on the top of the head. A mother rocked her baby in her arms until its crying stopped while a passerby smiled at both of them.

"It is their experience to have, brother," Saaya said. "There is love and hate, joy and sadness in their lives. They kill and maim each other while others heal and protect one another. They are to themselves two sides of the same coin."

"They are darkness and light," he agreed, "but more darkness than light."

"Are you sure?" Saaya countered. "Every ill deed is countered by a good one."

"Every?" Kafeel looked away. "I think not. The light you see in them is there, but the underlying darkness is not far away."

Saaya clicked her tongue. "Cynicism."

"Truth."

"Light cannot exist without darkness, Kafeel."

"Only because they do not allow it to be so. Answer this, Saaya. What would humans do with themselves if there was no conflict in their lives; no opposing force to struggle against? What would they do without something in their lives to fight? Even their lore is filled with struggle and pain."

"It is what they know. It is their history, brother. Their past and present … and their future."

"An existence they create," Kafeel said. "A darkness they fashion upon themselves."

"Are we not part of that darkness, *Ancestor*?" She stopped walking, and her towering pureblood brother turned back to face her. She looked up into his dark eyes. "What are we, if not a darkness to them? Do we not stalk them in the night? Do we not feed on their lives to continue our own? We are predators to them, no?"

Kafeel stared down at her. Anyone else, including another vampire, would find his hard eyes threatening, but she knew his heart, even if ever was it wrapped in iron. "We are a balancing force," he said.

Saaya laughed but he continued. "Vampires have used their influence to prevent human destruction on a scale that could have destroyed the world twice over."

"Out of benevolence, I'm sure," Saaya replied dryly.

"It doesn't matter," Kafeel argued. "What matters is that they are balanced by those who are above them."

"And now we come to it," Saaya said. "Vampires have always thought themselves above humans."

"Are we not?"

She winked at him. "Of course we are. But arrogance is deadly."

"It is," her brother agreed. "And with that, we come to the reason the *Ancestors* have nothing to do with the vampire world at large."

A breeze carrying the scent of roses, roasting food, and general city smells flitted past, knocking a few strands of hair over Saaya's eye. She brushed them aside with a finger. "I'm glad we've come to this point. Our father never would explain to me why he so disdained contact with his own people."

They turned a corner where tourists snapped pictures of just about everything, no matter how mundane.

"Has this discussion not given you an idea why?" Kafeel asked.

Saaya shrugged and looked up at the Athenaeum. Saaya remembered her parents bringing her here as a child. She had marveled at the beautifully detailed hand-painted depictions on the ceilings and floors, and the pale pink colored stone pillars inside. The concert hall was the landmark of the city, sitting in the very center of Bucharest.

"Perhaps arrogance?" she finally said. When Kafeel didn't bother to reply, she looked up at him. He walked in silence beside her, and she sighed. "Oh, brother. Have you no humor in you?"

He actually seemed to think about that. "I don't know if that's a trait I was born with, little shadow."

Saaya smiled up at him. He'd managed to find a little affection for her despite their debate.

"It is not arrogance that keeps the *Ancestors* away, but knowledge. They see things from a perspective others do not."

Though the sidewalks teemed with milling tourists and locals, everyone gave them a wide berth. A man who couldn't help himself took in Saaya's 'adequately' covered figure. His eyes soaked in every inch of her, lingering on the visible muscles of her exposed stomach, then continued up. The effect seemed similar to a paintbrush sliding up a wall. The *dampeal* might have been offended if she didn't find it amusing.

Only after he made eye contact with her and she winked at him, did he notice the towering presence walking next to her.

"Go away," Kafeel said in his baritone voice. The blood drained from the man's face and he did indeed turn and walk in the opposite direction.

Saaya placed her hand over her heart. "My dear brother. Are you getting protective?"

"Why must you dress like that? Do you truly need the visual molestation you receive when you expose so much skin?"

"I will admit that I like the attention, but it is my sense of humor that enjoys it more than my ego." She indicated the man who was now farther up the street, making an effort not to run. "Did you not find it funny how his mind nearly melted at the sight of me?"

"No ego, you say?"

Saaya shrugged. "I try to find humor where I can, Kafeel."

"Is that what they are to you?" Kafeel asked. "Humorous playthings?"

"That is exactly what they are to me, brother. But that does not mean I wish them any ill will. They are what they are and I am what I am."

Kafeel's lips tightened at that. "The fact that you care even a little about their world is something I will never understand."

"How could you?" Saaya replied. "I am a *dampeal,* and you are an *Ancestor.* Part of me is a part of the human world, but I cannot imagine anyone less able to understand my interest in it than you, beloved."

As they drew nearer to the train station, a tiny presence in the back of her mind became more substantial. It felt aware of her on a more subconscious level. She repressed a smile, but her connection with her brother couldn't hide it.

"While part of me would like to reduce that *shaquora* to ashes, another part of me wishes you would have whatever it is you want from him and be done with it."

"Oh, Kafeel. If you would see past your prejudice of turned vampires just this once—"

"It is a prejudice well earned," Kafeel pressed on. "They are a reckless side effect of our kind."

"He is different," Saaya insisted.

"He is conflicted and irritating."

"You have spent a small amount of time with him and he still lives," Saaya said. "Your words belie your true feelings."

There was a long pause before Kafeel responded to that. "You believe he would be yours if he can find a way to detach his heart from the past, don't you? And you wish this?"

Now it was Saaya's turn to pause. Would Jelani turn to her when he finally let go of his mortal life? Would this man that she was so drawn to finally be hers? Did she want him; truly want him? Or was it the conquest that attracted her? There had never been a man that would not have fallen over himself for her, human or immortal. Why was this one different? Were her feelings born of heart, or ego?

"I don't know," she finally said.

CHAPTER 35

"She's here."

Jelani stared out the window at the brightly lit city of Bucharest. His eyes could make out every detail as if it were daylight. He couldn't help wondering, though, what it would be like to see such an amazing city in the day.

"How do you know that?" Daniel asked, still wrapped in the covers of his twin bed. Apparently lycanthropy hadn't altered his sleeping habits.

Jelani tapped the side of his head. "She's in here, man. I can feel her. When I slept, it was like a part of my mind that's dormant when I'm awake could sense her. Almost like a dream, but not really. Then, when I woke up she was still there. She's somewhere in Bucharest."

"You planning on doing anything about it?" Daniel yawned.

Jelani continued to stare out at the city as if it held the answers to Daniel's question, and every other question that hung on his shoulders. "I don't know."

"Maybe you don't have to do anything," Daniel said. "You know, it's not easy being friends with a vampire. It's just not normal sleeping the day away and getting up at night. You're screwing up my biorhythm."

"I have to do something," Jelani said absently as he finished dressing and slipped into his shoes. "I have to go meet with her. Make things right."

"Well, why don't you do that and I'll hang out here." Daniel yawned again.

"We need to get to Sinaia," Jelani reminded his friend. "Or have you forgotten, already?"

Daniel rolled over. "Go talk to her, or do more than talk. Either way, it'll be good for both of you."

Jelani glared at his friend's back. "You just want to go back to sleep."

"That too," Daniel mumbled.

"I shouldn't be too long since I can practically track …" he trailed off when he heard his friend's rhythmic breathing. Jelani chuckled and left.

❧

As soon as he stepped out the door to the hotel, Saaya called to him. It was faint, and gentle, and altogether terrifying. *"You wish to see me,* jaan*? Do you want to find me?"*

"I need to talk," he said, wondering if she could hear his response in her mind. He also wondered if he was crazy.

"Come to me."

Jelani looked at the sprawling city. "Now, how in the hell …" A crow landed on a streetlight in front of him. It looked directly into his eyes and let out a loud "Caw!"

Jelani looked up at the night sky and chuckled. "Can't get a stronger hint than that." He looked at the black bird, still staring down at him. "I don't know if I'm talking to you or Saaya, but either of you can lead the way."

"Caw!" The crow hopped from its perch and glided over his head, causing him to duck.

"Funny," Jelani muttered.

The crow glided down the street then angled to the right. Jelani jogged behind it, still keeping a wary eye on the surroundings. All the conflict may be in Sinaia, but that didn't mean Remy might not have goons wandering around here as well.

He passed high-rises and a tall glass office building that must look amazing in daylight. Jelani began to suspect the crow was leading him on the scenic route when it finally landed in a tree in front of a tall inwardly curved building.

"Hotel Intercontinental," he read. Then he noticed a particularly odd-looking statue of a man in a suit reclining on a narrow wooden bench of some sort. The crow cawed at him again, and Jelani patted the air in front of him. "All right, man, get it." He walked up to the tree where the crow perched and stared down at him.

"So, you gonna go fly up to the window or balcony where she is, or do I have to guess?" In response, the crow hopped to a different branch, then flew up to the top of the tree and ruffled its feathers, clearly huddling down for the night.

"Thanks," Jelani said dryly. He turned to the building and immediately spotted a woman looking at him from the top floor of the hotel. "There you are."

A moment later he stood at the base of the hotel, about to walk through the front door. "Why bother?" he said to himself, and jumped the twenty foot distance to land on the edge of the first balcony. *Yup. I like this part about being a vampire.*

He jumped from balcony to balcony, ascending the hotel until he finally came to where the *dampeal* stood.

Statuesque and practically glowing in the moonlight, she stared at him. Her pink, purple, and gold sari was woven around her body like a second skin, with thin wisps of transparent silk cloth blowing gently in the night breeze.

A wave of calmness washed over Jelani, and he felt his nerves go still. She smiled at him, a tiny, almost hesitant smile that made her full brown lips all the more enticing. She blinked at him. Even her eyelashes seemed intent on seducing him.

"This is the part where I say something stupid," he said, though he had no such intention.

The smile deepened, and she walked up to him, but stopped about halfway. For a moment they both stood staring at one another. Then Jelani took a step forward, then another, until he had closed the distance and they were directly in front of each other. She looked up at him, and her gaze pulled him into another world.

He reached out a hand to touch her hair and she stepped aside. He went to touch her with the other hand, and again, she avoided him. Smiling, she stalked a circle around him, her eyes taking him in. He turned, following her until they were walking a circle around each other. Her lips parted and her brown eyes slowly shifted into the soft smoldering lavender that revealed her nature. As a human he had found it alluring yet frightening. Now he found it the most beautiful and irresistible thing he'd ever seen.

An invisible blanket of energy settled over him, like tiny sparks of energy all combined into one large invisible cloak. When she went to touch him, he grinned deviously as he moved away. She smiled back and gave a slow nod of her head, then she was instantly in front of him.

Jelani's hands snapped up and he grabbed her arms. "Gotcha."

Her eyes flared, and she grabbed him by his jacket with both hands and spun him in a circle. There was a tearing sound and he flew away from her, through the doorway, and landed sideways on the king size bed. He lay on his back in disbelief, then curled up to see the woman still standing in the sliding glass doorway, the two halves of what was once his jacket in each hand.

She let the pieces fall, and before they touched the balcony floor, she was on top of him. "Gotcha," she whispered.

This time, instead of a blanket of energy washing over him, he felt it directly from her. Tiny sparks of energy jumped from her body and exploded against him. She pulled his shirt off and tossed it aside. The sparks of energy stung his skin with pleasure. He slid aside one layer of her sari, unwrapping it from around her body. With each layer came a better view of her flawless form.

She slid her hands up and down his muscled chest, letting her fingers bounce over the gaps between each muscle as they slid down his stomach. He slid his hands up her back and she arched, throwing her head back and pushing her breasts forward.

His slid his hands over them, and she grabbed his wrists and guided his hands down; down the tiny muscles of her stomach, over her tiny waist, and down the sides of her curved hips. He slid more of the exotic wrapping from her body till finally, she sat naked atop him.

He took her in, every curve, every inch of smooth soft brown skin. She slipped her hands into his pants, her eyes on his while she stroked him. Finally, finally, she slid his pants off and guided him to her.

A faint cry of pleasure escaped her lips and glided on the air. It swirled around them, over them, caressed their skin. He felt the ecstasy of the sound sliding over his skin like fine silk. She shuddered, then another cry of pleasure came, this one even more powerful.

Her hips rocked back and forth, sending wave after wave of soft and electric pleasure through them both. Energy pulsated from her body and flowed into his, and it was like nothing he had ever felt. She lowered her head and looked into his eyes. And he surrendered.

Bodies joined, they moved in unison, each sending waves of pleasure through the other. He felt the force of her will upon him, but not like before. There was no sense of power or seductive compulsion. This was a part of herself laid bare before him. She let him feel her body, both physical and ethereal. He felt her life energy swirling around his, caressing, joining, intertwining.

Through the joining of their bodies came the joining of mind and spirit. He could feel her stronger in his mind than before, intuit her feelings, emotions. He felt her very essence coalesce with his own.

Her mouth fell open and a tiny moan seeped from her throat that became louder and louder.

"Don't shatter the windows this time," Jelani managed to say through the haze of pleasure.

"Then I release it into you," *jaan*. Her voice caressed him as if it was the air itself, sliding over his naked skin.

She exhaled and a flood of ecstasy assaulted him. It took everything he had not to be swept away in it. And then he released, and two swirling torrents of sensual vigor entwined with one another, sweeping them away in passion that could no longer be denied.

When the tide subsided and they lay spent, Jelani allowed himself to feel her mind and heart. For the first time in a long time, he felt no guilt, no sense of having betrayed another. Life had dealt him a hand and he'd done the best he could.

The night ended and morning arrived. He lay in bed with a beautiful woman curled in the crook of his arm. So feminine and delicate she looked, half of which couldn't be farther from the truth.

He looked to the sliding glass door, where a thick curtain and one of the blankets from the bed hung in front of the closed blinds. They had coupled the entire night and now the light of the sun burned away the shadows. He carefully slid from under her and pulled on his underwear and pants. She still lay there, pretending to sleep, for he could feel her mind and knew she was awake.

"Guess I didn't do my job well enough," he said.

Her eyes were still closed, but through their link, he felt contentment. A smile crept across her face. "Why do you say that?"

Jelani couldn't help but smile at her voice. A voice like silk. "You had the presence of mind to get dressed and cover the sliding door so I don't get fried."

"I wouldn't want you to be uncomfortable," came the reply.

Jelani snorted. "That's one word for it. Though I think being incinerated is a little more appropriate." He looked her over. "I think you might have been a little hasty getting dressed so soon. I think I've got a little more ..." he trailed off at the worried look that crossed her features. "What?"

"We have a problem," she said calmly.

"What do you mean?" he asked, a sense of dread creeping over him. He looked around but saw nothing.

"I can't move," Saaya said.

The *dampeal* had barely spoken the words when they heard a card slip into the card key slot in the door. It opened and a man in slacks and a white button shirt stepped aside to admit a woman who looked to be in her mid forties. She stepped past him and patted him on the head.

"My thanks to you, Lex," she said.

The man, an employee of the hotel judging by his attire, turned a vacant stare on her. "It is my honor, my lady," he said.

The woman placed a hand on his cheek. "I do so love old world politeness. Now be on your way, and I'm sure you will never remember this encounter." The attendant turned and left the room, closing the door behind him.

For several heartbeats she stood with her back to them, then finally she looked over her shoulder. Her thin red lips were stretched in a wicked half smile.

"Who the hell are you?" Jelani said, making an effort to control his fear. He glanced at Saaya, who lay stiff and immobile on the bed. He didn't think there was a vampire alive that could do such a thing to her.

The woman tsked. "That is such an unmannerly way to speak to your elders, young man."

"You'll have to excuse me for the shock of having someone barge into our room," Jelani replied.

She tapped a red-nailed finger to her cheek. "That was rude," she said. "Unfortunately, I'm forced to cast manners aside, this day."

Jelani lunged forward, or tried to. He'd only moved a step before every muscle in his body locked. He stared at the woman. The external effect was the same as what Yako had done to him when he'd still been human, but the sheer power was beyond anything he could have imagined. What Yako had done to him had been like nothing compared to what he felt from this woman.

She tsked again. "What has happened to chivalry in this age? Are you so willing to strike a woman?"

"Find me one and I'll be more polite." He regretted the insult immediately when his body suddenly felt like it was being burned from the inside out.

"Careful now," the woman said. She flipped a handful of long auburn curls over her shoulder. "You wouldn't want to die before your time, would you?"

"And you know when that is?" Jelani asked, still trying to buy time to figure a way out of this. If Saaya could somehow break free and distract her, Jelani could get to his daggers.

"Oh, I would say several minutes from now."

"Why the hostilities?" Jelani asked. "I'm pretty sure we've never met. You positive you've got the right guy?"

"Indeed I do," the woman said. "And it seems your ill manners have influenced me, for I have not properly introduced myself. My name is Alicia Magnus Lerae."

"Yeah, cool. Nice to meet you," Jelani said. "You mind relaxing the mind deal on me now that we're familiar?"

The woman named Alicia looked down at Saaya. "I admit there is a charm about him. I can see why you would want to lay with this child, *shaquora* or not." She turned her attention back to Jelani.

"As much as I would enjoy watching Remy squirm under the widespread knowledge that his personally turned *shaquora* is not only beyond his control, but is hunting him, I must unfortunately put a stop to it. Your vendetta with him is your own, but sadly, it falls into conflict with me."

"I've never even met you," Jelani argued. He glanced at Saaya, willing her to break free. "If you just let me take care of my business with him, I'll be on my way. You don't seem to like him either, so I'd be doing you a favor."

"A compelling argument," Alicia said. "Unfortunately I must endure his existence a bit longer. When the time comes I will deal with him myself." She pointedly looked at the sliding glass door, covered with a blanket, curtain, and closed blinds.

"And speaking of time, yours has come."

An invisible force slammed into Jelani and sent him flying across the room. He tried to reach for something, anything, that would stop him, but there was nothing. The blankets tangled around his body and muffled the sound of shattering glass as he crashed through the sliding door. His back slammed against the rail and he flipped over it, plummeting from the top of the hotel.

Jelani grabbed and pulled at the blanket, trying to cover himself, but as he twisted and rolled in the air, the blanket caught on something and ripped away. For the first time in months, Jelani saw the world bright and radiant, and the once welcome gaze of the sun was now a infernal glare turned upon him.

CHAPTER 36

"Now what, my dear, am I to do with you?"

Saaya didn't bother to answer the question. Instead she strained to find even a tiny crack in the other woman's will that restrained her. She had met Elders in her time, but none had the kind of power that could even approach what she felt from this woman.

"Nothing to say, little girl?" Alicia sat at the foot of the bed and smiled at her. Saaya smiled back and pressed harder. She may as well be pressing against a wall. She narrowed her eyes at Alicia's mocking titter.

"Come, child, be still. You are strong, but you're not that strong. Mind your elders and behave."

"I would have no trouble behaving were I not restrained for no reason," Saaya replied.

"Finally she speaks." Beneath her long white and pale blue dress Alicia crossed her legs and leaned back on one hand. "I'm certain you know that this visit isn't unwarranted."

"I don't know you," Saaya said. "If I have wronged you in some way it was not intentional."

"Of course you do not know me, nor I you. But I know of you." Alicia slid a finger through one of her auburn curls and moved it from in front of her face. Despite her obviously ancient age, there was a radiance to her that complimented her youthful presence. Despite her dangerous situation, Saaya found that interesting. Most Elders didn't particularly care about projecting youthfulness. What did that matter to an immortal?

"And, your existence is the core of our little problem, the woman went on. "The fact that I have not heard of the existence of a *dampeal* in almost a thousand years is exciting. The fact that she decides to enter into a situation in which she does not belong is unfortunate."

Again she stared at Saaya, then shook her head. "After a millennia, a true *dampeal*. You've presented me with quite a dilemma."

"I do not know why that is," Saaya replied. "One of my parents is a vampire, the other a human. What does this matter?"

Alicia frowned at her. "Don't take me for a fool, girl. I know what you are, which is not a lowly *skiek*. The *Ancestor* blood in you is strongly present. That those two fools would neglect to see the seriousness of your involvement is amazing yet not surprising. Which leads me back to my quandary. What am I to do with you?"

Saaya wondered what 'idiots' Alicia spoke of. She figured one of them would have to be that second Hunter that had come after Jelani. She didn't figure Yako for a fool, but Remy certainly fit the description. Who was the second player?

Alicia chuckled. "I can practically see the wheels turning in that pretty little head of yours. If our woman-to-woman session was of a more friendly nature, I would like nothing more than to share with you the stupidity of those with whom I've had to surround myself with. As things stand," she shrugged. "There are other matters to consider."

She studied Saaya, pursing her lips till a dimple appeared on her cheek. "It would be a shame to dispose of such a rare gem as yourself, not to mention it could create a problem with the immortal who sired you. On the other hand, I cannot allow you to interfere."

"Release me and I will trouble you no further."

Alicia laughed at her. "Were our situations reversed, you'd be a fool to believe me, little hybrid. You have involved yourself in this business from the start, and just watched me dispatch your lover. I doubt you will simply walk away."

Saaya would have shrugged if she could move. "He was enjoyable while I had him. I am not happy that you've broken my toy, but I can find another."

Alicia never stopped smiling as Saaya spoke. "I'm almost tempted to take you at your word," she said. "That I sense no lie in what you've said actually surprises me. I don't feel any anger or remorse from you at the mention of such an undoubtedly lovely companion."

"He is gone. There will be more."

Alicia seemed to think about this, and after a moment, Saaya felt her invisible binding released. She drew in a deep breath and sat up. "Thank you, Elder."

The other woman nodded. "I am sure you understand that any attempt to strike at me will result in your utter destruction. Now, with that unpleasantness out of the way, let us talk."

Saaya put on an earnest expression. "About what, Elder?"

"My original problem," the woman said. "What I am to do with you? I cannot simply arrive at Peles with you at my side. Not after your actions that prevented the Eldest Hunter from completing his task in disposing of that," she threw her hand up casually to indicate the balcony. "You could be useful to me, however."

Saaya felt Kafeel drawing near and willed him to stay away. "How would I be of use to you, Elder?" she asked.

Alicia tilted her head. "So willing to serve. For one with the blood of an ancient flowing through your veins, you are remarkably humble."

"I do not recall indicating I would be eager to serve," Saaya clarified, "only curious as to how you feel I could be of use to you."

"Is that so?" Alicia said, her tone amused.

"Since you know what I am," Saaya continued, "you would know that I am intrigued that an Elder could be so powerful." She tried flattery. "I have never met an immortal, pureblood or otherwise, as powerful as yourself."

Alicia smiled at her. It was the type of smile that could precede further conversation or obliteration. "I suppose so," was all she said in response.

"A question," Saaya ventured. "If I may." The Elder nodded. "How did you know where to find me?"

Alicia stood and walked toward the balcony, stepping fully into the brightness of the sunlight that shined in from the patio. *Interesting*, Saaya thought.

"One doesn't live as long as I and not learn a few things, *dampeal*. Your unlucky *shaquora* plaything would of course wish revenge upon the one who turned him; the one who is so remarkably weak that he cannot control the one whom he himself re-created." Alicia shook her head, auburn curls sliding across her back and shoulders.

"I cannot deny my fascination at how Remy could have attained the rank of Hunter while hosting so many inadequacies."

Saaya resisted a smile.

"I do not doubt the fun you must have had at his expense. Considering your dealings with the Eldest Hunter, Remy must have been comical to play with."

"Until he eluded me," Saaya replied. "I've never encountered a Hunter so adept at avoiding capture."

"A tactful way of saying he is a coward," Alicia said. "I will say this to his credit. He is not a complete craven. He will chance conflict, but only when he is sure it will end in his favor, or he has no other choice." She turned back to Saaya. Sunlight glowed around her body like an aura.

"I should not be surprised at your tolerance to the sun, Elder," Saaya said. "But I am."

"It is not unheard of among Elders," Alicia said.

"But not common either," Saaya replied.

"That as it may be, here I stand."

Saaya came to her feet, slowly. "And, where do I stand?"

"A good question," came the reply. "Part of me asks myself if you are worth the risk. I want to uncreate you here and now, yet at the same time, keep you at my side. I am so curious to learn what little half-breed tricks you've inherited from your sire. The last *dampeal* I met so long ago could adapt the color of his skin to his environment, much like a chameleon. It was an odd but valuable trait."

The thought of another *dampeal* in the world fascinated Saaya. She had never known another of her kind to walk the earth. "What happened to him?"

"I don't know," Alicia replied. "Those were more dangerous times when humans were more apt to believe in superstitions. I suspect he might have fallen victim to a witch hunt, or one of the vampire crusades."

Saaya nodded. "I see."

"Little hybrid." Alicia closed the distance between them and placed her hands on Saaya's shoulders. "One thing all half-breeds have in common, *dampeal* or *skiek*, is that you are conflicted from birth. To be born of two species who could not be more opposite must be difficult. Part of you experiences life in moment to moment, worrying little about the future that you know will come and go, while another part of you is connected to the feelings of fragility and ephemerality. You must feel very alone."

She felt Kafeel's concern, but he remained on top of the building. "Such little time together we've spent, and already you read me so well."

A venomous smile crept across Alicia's face. "Indeed."

Saaya felt the invisible force return. It clamped around her neck and lifted her into the air.

Alicia turned her now crimson gaze up at Saaya. "With that simpleminded mortal blood flowing through your veins, you actually believe you can hide from me, don't you?"

The pressure tightened. Saaya pressed the whole of her will against the other woman. It was barely enough to keep her throat from being crushed.

"Impressive," Alicia said. "You actually are quite strong. I regret I'll have to destroy you. Your ruthlessness is your greatest asset, but you have lied to me at least once. The fact that I cannot discern what you've lied to me about is what I find discomforting.

"So I wonder how one goes about killing one such as yourself. You would only tan that beautiful brown skin of yours should I throw you over the balcony as I did your little toy. The touch of silver is meaningless to you, and you would heal from any wound I would inflict on you."

Again came the tsking. "It looks like the only method left to me is a gruesome one. I fear I'm forced to remove that pretty head from your shoulders, or the heart from your chest."

Saaya felt her windpipe pop. She winced at the pain, but stared into the flaring red eyes of the Elder. She smiled when she felt her brother brother rapidly drawing near. She watched Alicia look past her when her brother dropped soundlessly onto the balcony.

She heard heavy footsteps as Kafeel stepped into the room.

"One of your lies finally reveals itself," Alicia said. "Not so alone as you would have had me believe, are you, little flower?" She showed no concern at all at the sound of Kafeel's long silver sword sliding from its sheath.

Alicia continued to stare into Saaya's eyes, but the pressure stopped. Still Saaya couldn't breathe, and asphyxiation began to take her. As her vision narrowed, she saw Kafeel lunge toward the

Elder. Alicia threw her force against him, but Kafeel merely stumbled back, then came on again.

A look of surprise crossed Alicia's face, and Saaya suddenly fell to the floor in a heap, coughing and choking as her throat repaired itself.

When Kafeel struck downward with his sword, Alicia leaned toward him and faded away. She became substantial again as she passed beside him.

Saaya didn't know if the woman had actually become incorporeal, or moved so fast that she seemed to disappear. Either way, Alicia managed to come behind Kafeel and threw her will at him. He flew over the kneeling Saaya and crashed face-first into the wall.

Her brother planted his feet and sprang backward, turning midair and bringing his sword around and down. Again Alicia seemed to pass through his sword and came around beside him. Kafeel quickly reversed his motion, thrusting the hilt of his sword backward. The blow seemed to strike some kind of invisible shield, as his weapon stopped several inches short of the mark. Kafeel grunted as he lifted into the air.

"Consider me impressed," Alicia said. "It has been more centuries than I can remember when last I met someone worthy of—"

Kafeel growled and suddenly dropped back to his feet.

Though her face remained neutral Saaya saw that the Elder hadn't expected that.

"Impressive," Alicia hissed.

Kafeel came at her again, but this time he was stopped and thrown left to crash into the wall, then right. Now the Elder didn't smile. Her eyes glowed brighter as she concentrated her will upon Kafeel, throwing him around the room.

His head snapped back as the invisible force slammed into his face, and he dropped onto his back. By the time Kafeel regained his feet, Saaya had healed and was beside him.

Alicia stood on the balcony. Death radiated in her eyes. "You have proven to be more formidable than I anticipated. I expect you know where to find me. Come to your death if you wish." She didn't jump over the rail so much as her feet left the floor and she glided over it. Alicia faded from view, but her laughter rang through the air.

CHAPTER 37

J elani's breaths came in short haggard gasps as he stared wide-eyed at the bright sunny day just a few feet away from the shadowy alcove in which he hid.

He inspected his hands and body, afraid to believe he was alive and not a disembodied spirit who would look down in horror at his own ashes any moment now. He ran a hand up and down his arm, touched his face. *How?* He looked back out at the sunlight. *How's this possible? I'm no pureblood. Even Yako can't walk in the sun!*

He looked at a piece of the shredded blanket lying at his feet. Maybe it sheltered him? Jelani shook his head at the thought. That blanket had caught on a rail and unravelled off of him. The only reason it lay on the ground now was because he'd grabbed it and torn a piece of it off. No. He'd been fully exposed to the sun.

Even when Yako and Remy had been hunting him, Jelani had never felt so close to death. He inched his way toward the edge of the shade and looked down at the line on the ground where sunlight and shade met. It was like standing at the edge of a bed of lava, trying to decide whether or not he could touch it and come away with nothing burned off. It seemed ridiculous, and yet …

He lifted his hand and slowly, slowly reached out to the light.

The instant his finger felt the warmth of the sun he snatched it back and inspected his unburnt hand. "I don't believe it," he whispered, turning his hand over.

His amazement was cut short when he felt a presence descending from above. Jelani retreated further back into the shadows just as the woman who'd thrown him over the rail landed less than a dozen feet from where he stood. Jelani's mouth fell open, for it seemed more like the woman came to a stop just above the ground and placed a foot down than actually "landing". *What the hell is she,* he thought, *a friggin ghost?*

Jelani instinctively held his breath as she turned in his direction, then silently berated himself. It's not like he needed to breathe more often than every few minutes. She looked in his direction and he pressed himself tighter into the alcove, willing himself to sink into the stone wall. After what seemed like forever, she turned away.

Jelani waited several minutes before daring to move again. He slid along the wall back to the edge of the sunlight and peeked around the corner. When he saw no one there, he slipped his hand into the sunlight again and experienced nothing more than the welcome warmth of a sun he hadn't seen or felt in what seemed like years.

He stepped fully into the light, and this time it was like stepping into a warm embrace instead of a fiery death. The sun welcomed him, caressed him in its warm perfect light. Jelani closed his eyes and leaned his head back, basking in it. How long had it been? How many months? "I wish I'd known about this sooner," he said to himself. "I spent all that time hiding from the sun and now I'm standing in it."

He thought about what he'd just said and snorted. Months of sun wasted. That was how a human thought. What was months, or years, or even decades or centuries to an immortal? "I'll get the hang of this, eventually."

Saaya's voice drew a smile to his face. "My lovely fledgling makes a new discovery."

Jelani didn't bother to turn around. "You knew."

"Of course," she said. He didn't have to hear the amusement in her voice, he could feel it.

"You might have let a brotha know," he said.

"There are some discoveries best learned on your own," the *dampeal* said.

Now Jelani did turn around, his face scrunched up in a frown. "What difference would it have made if you'd saved me the trouble of running from the sun all these months versus me finding out right now?"

"I do not expect you to understand this now," Saaya replied, "but you will value discoveries such as this when you have lived more. You have spent months living a life wary of the deadly sun. You learned to think and act differently; as all vampires would. You have an understanding you would not have gained had I told you from the beginning. Your experiences these past months were valuable."

"If you say so," Jelani replied. He glanced in the direction that lethal woman had gone. "Who the hell was that?" he jerked his chin in the direction she'd gone. "And, what happened between you two? I'm guessing you must've got the drop on her, since she took off and you're still alive."

"She is formidable," came the reply.

That threw Jelani back on his heels. Coming from Saaya that was practically an admission that she'd had more than a bit of trouble with the other woman. "She that tough?"

"I ... was assisted."

As if that was his cue, Kafeel landed behind her. Jelani found it odd to see him without his long, flowing coat that seemed so much like raven wings.

"So, you sent her running, then?" he said to tall man, to which he received no answer. Not surprising. Jelani looked to Saaya for an answer.

"She is formidable," the *dampeal* repeated. Apparently that was all the answer he was going to get.

"I'm going to venture a guess that this is another person we have to worry about when we get to Sinaia," Jelani said.

Saaya shrugged a shoulder at that. Such a cute gesture. *Focus, fool,* Jelani chastised himself.

"True," the *dampeal* said, "but you have an advantage."

"Oh?" Jelani replied.

Saaya winked at him. "Yes." She stepped closer and lifted up to her toes and wrapped her arms around his neck. She leaned in close and whispered in his ear, "because you are dead."

CHAPTER 38

Yako listened as the alpha of the Shadow Pack told of his meeting with Remy. As disappointing as the failure of the meeting might be, it wasn't necessarily a surprise.

"Of all the packs that live around here, the Woodlands have got to be the stupidest," Darren was saying.

That drew a snort from Tara. Doubtlessly she, like most vampires, thought all lycans were stupid to begin with.

"The idiots really believed that they would attain a level of status in that coven." Darren shook his head in disgust. "Why any of us would desire to be granted status and live in the same place as a crowd of bloods is beyond me." He glanced at Tara and favored her with a half smile. "No offense intended, Reaper."

"As you say, lycan," she replied. Despite her cool tone, Yako could tell his friend had grown on her. Darren had that kind of effect. His strong but amicable personality could win over human, lycan, or vampire alike. Even Mariska, despite her show of feeling otherwise, rather enjoyed his company.

"I have to point out," Darren continued, "that there is something to be said about possessing the right blend of cowardice and paranoia that makes one particularly intuitive to danger. That guy was sent by Massius to coordinate with me, and despite the Elder's orders, he told me just about nothing of what they're planning."

Darren leaned against a towering pine tree and crossed his arms. Everything about the man was muscle. He reminded the Eldest Hunter of a lycan equivalent of Braggus Rayne.

"You are correct in your assessment of Remy," Yako said. "His hesitancy for trust lies in a cowardly paranoia that makes him difficult to catch off guard. I am to assume he, and by extension Massius, knows that I am here and that your pack stands with me."

"Unfortunately that is the case, old friend," Darren said. "But fortunately he does not know anything about my particular species, or how many of Massius's allies I've absorbed into my pack."

"I question the wisdom of trusting a former enemy and traitor to your species as an ally," Yako remarked.

Darren nodded. "I expect you would not understand, Yako. Things with us are different. You have direct control only over those you have personally turned. I have complete control over those who are of my pack in much the same way, but not necessarily because I personally changed them."

"That is interesting," Tara said. "I would like to know more if you are willing to share."

Darren looked at her, the smile returning. "Such a request would normally invoke nothing more in me than uncontrollable laughter, Reaper." He glanced at Yako, then back at her. "But the discretion of our Eldest Hunter goes a long way with me. If he trusts you enough to bring you here, then I trust you as well."

"Then, perhaps one day we may speak of your most interesting … species."

"Why, my most honorable Reaper," Darren said dramatically. "That could have been interpreted as a compliment."

"The ears of a wolf are not as sharp as I have been led to believe, then." Despite the quip, Tara smiled.

"You've been holding out on me, old friend," Darren said to Yako. "I had no idea there were more than two likable bloods in your species." His smile broadened as he continued to stare at Tara. "You will have to tell your Second that she has competition for my affections."

Tara threw Yako an incredulous look that brought on a round of laughter from Darren and the tiniest of smiles from Yako. Tara looked back at the big man and she too was smiling.

"I believe," Yako said, sobering the meeting, "that you may find trouble positioning yourselves near or inside the castle now. Since Remy escaped you and will have gone running back to Massius, he is less likely to deal with any of your kind until his little insurrection has succeeded. After that he would set about hunting you down and filtering you out."

"I think you're right," Darren said. "But we can still position ourselves near enough not to be detected. Our sense of smell is many times stronger than yours. We'll be able to get close."

That statement was both useful and an eye-opener as to how dangerous a pack of enemy wolves could be. They could hear and smell a vampire long before the vampire knew they were there; much like a canine could detect a human. He didn't have to look at Tara to know she was thinking the same thing.

Darren looked from him to the Reaper at his side and shook his head. "Yes, my vampiric friends. I have just given you something to think about for the future. I hope you recognize it as a gesture of faith, and my value of friendship and loyalty. I do not take it lightly. When I named you friend, Eldest Hunter, that was as close as naming you an honorary pack member without cursing you to fits of nausea at the mere thought it."

Yako smiled a bit more at that. "I believe we will enjoy count-less years of alliance and friendship when this is done … my friend. And if you can get as near to the coven as you claim, That would be a boon to our cause. I will contact you when the time is right."

"If I may?" Tara interjected. The gesture showed Yako a great deal of respect, as the Reaper needn't have even asked. He nodded in deference. "Having known our taciturn and mistrustful Eldest Hunter as long as I have, I will take his confidence in you as a step in the direction of alliance as well. There is a passage that leads to the castle from Sinaia. On your word that you would speak of it with no one, not even the others of your pack, I would have you accompany us directly into the castle. Just you."

Darren rubbed his chin. "I am honored by your gesture, Reaper, but that may not be possible. Trust between our respective species is still tenuous. My pack would not agree to my venturing alone through a secret tunnel surrounded by vampires." He looked at Yako, then back at Tara. "How many of your number would even for a second, consider the prospect of your Eldest Hunter traveling in the middle of a pack of lycans?"

"If we are to truly trust one another, it must be done completely," Yako said. "I am unconcerned with the relations of our respective species as a whole; at least not now. At the moment, however, we can take a larger step forward, but the step must be sure." He looked at both of them in turn as he spoke. "If we are to fight together, we must be fully committed."

"What do you suggest?" Tara asked, but Yako knew the question to be rhetorical. Darren was already smiling. He knew Yako well enough to not to be surprised by what he was about to suggest.

"We fight together," Yako said, "not separated. Vampires will converge upon the castle beside our lycan allies, not on opposing sides."

"You mean to place some of our number with them," Tara replied.

Yako nodded. "And some of their number among us."

"True allies for a common cause," Darren said. "I like this."

"There are some details that would make this venture slanted in one direction, Eldest," Tara warned.

"Only until we have entered the castle, where our numbers will increase." Yako could see that the Reaper was still unconvinced.

"A tentative alliance is a weak one. We cannot afford weakness." He looked at Darren and saw agreement. "If both sides enter conflict separately, there would be little to keep them from killing each other by mistake, or not. I will not have discord in this venture."

"Is that so, Eldest Hunter?" Tara said.

Despite the challenge in her tone, Yako held firm. "It is, Reaper. I will not have our strength fracture because of the feelings between our species. Feelings and emotions are a weakness I will not allow our enemies exploit. Both sides will deal with their emotions, or deal with me." He bowed. "If you find my stance unsuitable, Reaper, I will step down to make room for another whom you deem suitable to the task."

Tara glared at him, but he saw playfulness in her eyes. "Ever the serious Eldest Hunter. You are perhaps the greatest warrior of our age, Yako."

"Hardly," he replied. "There are others of greater skill—"

"Enough, Eldest. You know as well as I that skill is only one aspect that defines a warrior." She looked at Darren. "What say you, lycan?"

"What say I?" the big man echoed. "Ah, the old speech. I love it! You must've seen several ages come and pass to speak like that. Yes, I believe the course Yako suggests is the best one. I won't deny that it'll take some convincing."

"Are you not fully in control of your pack, Darren Lacey?" Tara asked.

Yako silently approved of the Reaper's effort by calling him by name and not simply by his species.

Darren smiled, showing normal human teeth. "They will do as told." His tone held an unmistakeable edge of danger to it.

After discussing the details together, Yako and Tara left Darren to meet with his pack and prepare.

"Do you think he will be able to control his wolves in this venture?" Tara asked.

Yako thought about his long time friend. "There was a time, a little over a hundred years ago when he was faced with the choice of giving a rogue from his pack a second chance by killing one of my Hunters, or intervening. He killed the rogue, and my Hunter returned to me unharmed. Not one member of his pack voiced objection."

They came to the edge of the woods. A car would have been preferable, but Massius most certainly had scouts watching for any late-night activity. A car traveling to and from the outskirts of Sinaia would draw suspicion.

Yako looked up at the waning gibbous moon, shining it's majestic orange-tinted light upon the earth. The final turn of the Hunter's Moon cycle. "Darren will tolerate insubordination only as long as it takes him to rip out the throat of the offender."

Tara stared at the moon for several moments, then grinned at him. "If I thought you could appreciate it, I would say it is a romantic sight, this Hunter's Moon."

Yako didn't respond other than to say, "a cycle that comes rarely, but brings power to both our species when it does. Vampires and werewolves. We are more alike in some ways than we wish to acknowledge."

Tara's grin turned disappointed. "Pity," she said, laying a hand on his shoulder, then letting it fall away as she turned to walk down the road. "A great Hunter, a great warrior, and a great man. I wonder if it is all wasted on a shell with no soul."

Yako frowned and allowed his eyes to fall from the moon to the departing Reaper's back. Soul? In all the years Yako had lived, never had he any use for contemplating such a thing. Was concern for the soul not the province of one such as a short-lived human, who would find their lives at an end in less than a century?"

He started down the road after her. His mind and heart were focused, his resolve, iron, and his commitment unshakable. But the diminutive Reaper's comment lingered in his thoughts.

CHAPTER 39

"I am quite aware of what is happening, Lemanda," Vicken stated.

"I cast no doubt on your competency, High Elder," Lemanda replied. "But I feel compelled to underline the severity of the situation regarding his activities of late. His actions do not grow more bold so much as they gain momentum."

The leader of the High Council of Elders stared out the window at the night beyond. Lemanda wondered what thoughts ran through his mind.

"His actions are worthy of the sun's embrace," he finally said. "But my hands are tied, for now at least."

"Always is there politics in our society," Lemanda said. She took a seat on one of her plush couches. "It is an inhibition to our ability to act."

"In this case, yes," Vicken agreed. "But it goes deeper than that. For better or worse, Massius is a member of the High Council. I cannot eliminate him without proper cause, and I don't have a shred of proof. He is as slippery as his cravenly subordinate."

Lemanda made a disgusted sound. "I don't wish to speak of

that one. Whatever Massius sees in him escapes me. He is not worth sullying my own efforts to destroy him."

"And that may well be what makes Remy all the more dangerous."

Lemanda thought about that. "Perhaps. But we must do something about them both, even if it means starting with his little pet serpent."

"What message would be conveyed if we executed a member of our own High Council, Lemanda?" Vicken turned to her, and she saw the frustration in his face. "We are the foundation of the coven. Every coven. If we resort to this action, we show discord among us, which is weakness."

"The alternative is to gamble on winning a fight that is certain to come, if we fail to act now." Lemanda folded her hands in her lap. "Massius has poisoned the minds of the coven. I don't know how many stand with him, but I don't feel good about the prospective number. And he has lycan allies as well. We *must* act."

When the muscles in Vicken's neck tightened, Lemanda thought the man might lose his cool, right then.

"Massius's presence is a poison," he said. "Whenever he is near me, I feel as if my mind grows cloudy. I don't know if it's my general dislike of the crusty old creature, or my mistrust of him."

Lemanda went still and kept her features neutral. "Indeed," she replied carefully. "I too, find that when he is near, I tend to become more irritated. Surely a side effect of my dislike of him."

"If all you experience is irritation, count yourself lucky," Vicken said. "I think I dislike him so much that my thoughts become unclear. Half the time I want to agree to whatever he wants just to see him gone from my presence."

Ah, my dear Vicken, Lemanda thought. *How could it be possible?*

"What is it?" Vicken asked. "You seem distracted all of a sudden."

"You've said something that reminds me of a matter I must attend to," she said, which couldn't have been more true.

"Then you'd best attend to it now rather than later," Vicken said. "I know you don't like it, Lemanda, but there is no choice. Massius has been clever enough to create allies under our noses for who knows how long. And he has done it discretely enough that we cannot move on him without it looking unprovoked."

"We will handle him in one way or another," Lemanda said. "I have eyes and ears to keep me informed of the mood of the coven. There are apparently three loyalties here."

"Three?"

"Those who are loyal to Massius," Lemanda clarified, "who believe they will attain a position of power when he usurps you. Those who are loyal to the coven but may have been influenced by him into thinking that his rule would be the most beneficial. And lastly, those who are loyal to the coven and its current leaders. Namely, us."

Vicken's crimson eyes narrowed into slits. "Loyalists to Massius who would see themselves in the very seats we have occupied for centuries."

"It's not uncommon for a populace to long for a new rule."

"We are not fickle, disorganized humans that need a fresh start every so many years," Vicken said. "The rule of the current High Council has brought nothing but strength and solidity to our species."

"You know well that all of these accomplishments are meaningless in the eyes of those who desire to fashion their own vision of our society," Lemanda said. "A powerful empire still has glaring weaknesses in the eyes of those who have not built its foundation. From the first day Massius arrived at our gates, his eyes were on your seat at the High Council. We just failed to see it before now."

"Because he has been patient," Vicken replied. "I wonder if that is a *talent* of his. I've never seen anyone possessed of such a patience that he could wait hundreds of years before making a grab at the power he so covets."

"Massius is not the type to play his hand until he is absolutely certain he can win," Lemanda said.

"Let him believe what he will," Vicken said, his voice calm and quiet. "Neither vampire nor lycan nor the sun itself will stop me from bringing about his uncreation."

Lemanda knew that tone and thought it best to make her exit. "And with his uncreation, so too will this problem die, High Elder," she said, inclining her head. "And now if you will excuse me, I must attend to a few things."

Vicken made his way to the door. "Be done with this quickly that we might speak again, Lemanda," he said. "The High Council has stood strong since its inception. I will not have one such as Massius undo it in one stroke." He opened one of the tall double doors and closed it behind him.

Lemanda stared at the spot where he'd stood. *More than one stroke, Vicken.*

CHAPTER 40

Fun times had been rare lately, so Jelani enjoyed the dumbfounded look on Daniel's face when he walked through the door in the middle of the day. The two stared at each other until Jelani figured his friend was too stunned to speak. "Yes, it's me, and no, I'm not a ghost."

Daniel looked at the nearby sliding glass door, and the sunlight flooding in. When he looked back at Jelani, his mouth was still hanging open.

"Dude," Jelani warned, "if you keep that expression too long, a bug is going to think you're trying to provide lodging."

"How the hell?" was all his best friend could manage.

"Now we're talking," Jelani said. He walked over and slapped a hand across Daniel's back. "Have a seat before you fall down. We've got some stuff to talk about, and you can trust me when I say you'll want to hear it all."

Daniel listened quietly as Jelani rehashed the events of the day. After he finished, Daniel continued to sit there, looking at him expectantly.

"What?" Jelani asked.

"I was just waiting for you to tell me why you passed over the part about you and Saaya getting it on before that woman showed up and ruined the party."

"What?" Jelani repeated, a little weaker, this time.

Daniel rolled his eyes. "You leave to go find the woman and are gone for the rest of the night and into the day. When you didn't show up by dawn, it wasn't hard to figure out what was going on. C'mon man. Give me a little credit here."

The tiny seed of guilt that was beginning to sprout must have shown on Jelani's face because Daniel held up a hand. "*Please* don't go into guilt mode. I wouldn't expect anyone to hold on to something that can't happen. The girls are safe and oblivious, and their lack of knowledge will keep them that way."

Though he tried to hide it, Jelani could see the pain in Daniel's face when he spoke of Wen and Alisha. He couldn't imagine what it must be like to lose a fiancée to a situation like this. In a way, he thought it might actually be easier if it was a breakup. At least there would have been some form of dialogue instead of the person being taken away.

"Saaya thinks we have an advantage because that Elder thinks I'm dead," Jelani said, in an effort to change the subject. "I don't know how much difference she thinks I can make in a coven full of vampires much older than me. I'll admit I know my way around a fight, but from the knowledge Jackass passed on to me, the place is teeming with all kinds of warriors that would probably eat my lunch."

"Then we'll just have to be better, and smarter," Daniel said. "I've got your back. You know that. From what you've told me, she'll be expecting to see Saaya and Kafeel, and we know she's waiting for Yako and his cronies. She's got Massius and Remy and some portion of the coven on her side, which is something else to look out for."

Daniel pounded his fist into his palm. "But she doesn't know about us, and no one in the coven except Remy knows who we are or what we look like. If we pick our shots, we can make a big difference before anyone knows what side we're on."

"Yeah, and whose side is that?" Jelani asked. "I'm still not too sure I like any of them. As far as I'm concerned, if I walk out of this the only vampire alive, I'm fine with it." He thought about it, then amended, "actually, one of two remaining vampires. I'd hate for something to happen to Melinda."

"Well, she's safe back home, so no need to worry about her." Daniel leaned back on the sofa and smirked his young Russell Wong smirk. "You're pretty lucky, you know. If you're going to be a vampire, now is probably the best time in history."

Jelani gave him a dry look. "Yeah. I timed this perfectly."

"You know what I mean," Daniel said. "I know it's not the same, but you've got the whole blood bank businesses and underground stuff going on where you can get your fix."

"You make it sound like a drug addiction," Jelani said.

"It isn't?" Daniel replied. "How long after the thirst could you hold out till you go crazy and start slashing?"

"Not long," Jelani admitted. "And what about you? How long into the hunger before you start stalking like a lion in the savanna?"

A shadow passed over Daniel's face, and tension filled the room.

"Sorry, man," Jelani said. "Didn't mean to say the wrong thing."

Daniel sighed. "Don't worry about it. It's still a little hard to swallow. I know you've got the whole bloodlust with fangs and claws and all that, but this …" He shook his head. "This, you can't imagine what it's like feeling every part of your body shift and dislocate and pop and readjust." He winced at the thought and looked up at Jelani.

"You've seen a fully formed werewolf before. You know how their limbs get longer and the legs have that extra bone that bends backward just above the ankle?" Daniel bit his bottom lip and squinted his eyes shut. When he opened them again, Jelani wasn't sure what he saw in the other man's face.

"I'll tell you," Daniel continued. "The transformation, among other things, involves bone breaking and knitting back together again in new shapes. More bone is also produced in the process to create the larger and stronger limbs, skull, all that stuff. It all seems crazy, but I felt every bit of it. It happens so fast.

"The best way I can describe it is that you know how when you break a bone, the body takes time to knit the two pieces back together? Well imagine that happening in seconds rather than weeks. It's insane."

Despite the morbidity of the subject, Jelani found himself fascinated. "So what happens when you revert to human form again? Where does all that bone and muscle go?"

"That's the interesting part," Daniel said. "I asked Imron that same question." He let out a half-hearted laugh. "Apparently nature is perfect, even with its perversions. The bone actually goes through some sort of dissolving process similar to when a human experiences bone loss. Can you believe it?"

"Would it be inappropriate to say that I find this really interesting, maybe even a little cool?"

"Interesting, yes it is. Cool? Only because you haven't had to go through the process. It feels like someone is snapping you into pieces and putting you back together again."

"Sounds awful," Jelani said. "Also sounds like you'd be vulnerable during the transformation."

Daniel was shaking his head before Jelani could finish. "Nope. That's the one sliver of good news about the process. The first time is the worst and the slowest because your body is undergoing a complete physiological change. The shock and pain and everything else makes it more lengthy and agonizing. After that, your body and mind become accustomed to it, and the transformation comes quicker."

"What about the pain?" Jelani asked.

"It's there," Daniel said. "But according to Imron, you can't just change on the spot. Not really. You actually have to get your mind right."

Jelani frowned.

"Rage," Daniel clarified. "You learn to grab hold of the rage and channel it, focus it, into one direction. And if you're not feeling it, you find it."

"So you just get angry and focus it?" Jelani asked.

Again Daniel shook his head. "The rage is more primal. I felt some of it back on the mountain. It's like there's an animalistic side to a lycanthrope that's much more developed than in a human. Though for me, it just kinda moved me aside and took over, Imron says we tap it and pull it out. And, from what I felt," Daniel laughed mirthlessly, "trust me, once you've grabbed hold and woken it up, it's like riding a river rapid. You just have to concentrate on not falling in and drowning in the current."

"Speaking of drowning in a current," Jelani said, "we need to put our heads together and make sure we don't drown in the one that's brought us halfway around the world."

Daniel nodded. "You're right. If this woman is powerful enough to subdue Saaya and give Kafeel a run for his money, we'd better be really careful."

"Careful?" Jelani said. "How's this? I don't want to go anywhere near the woman. I just want to get in, handle my business with Remy, and get out."

"What about your little promise to Yako?" Daniel asked. "You planning on keeping it, or are you planning on bowing those shoulders with more guilt for reneging on a promise?"

"Oh yeah, right," Jelani said, sobering. "There is that. I suppose I need to find him and square things up. I kinda do owe him a few times over."

"Then we'd better get to Sinaia asap," Daniel said. "And since you waited till now to figure out that you can go in the sun, maybe we can get going sooner rather than later. It's not even noon yet."

"Yeah, we might as well hit the train," Jelani said.

"What about our little *dampeal* shadow?"

Jelani smiled, knowing that Daniel had no idea he had just spoken the actual meaning of Saaya's name. "She knows where we're headed. If she's not already on a train out, she'll be there not long after we are."

"All right, then." Daniel made for the door. "Let's get out of here now, and get to Sinaia and grab a hotel. We can be there maybe before twelve."

As they gathering their belongings, Jelani made a mental note to thank Saaya. Despite what he had become, she'd made his life so much easier after his re-creation. Not only was he not bound to Remy, but he was stronger than any fledgling *shaquora* had any right to be, experienced the thirst to a much lesser degree, and could walk the day. He may not be as powerful as her, but she had given him invaluable gifts that granted his life no small degree of normalcy.

Squatting in front of his duffel bag, he smiled and sent the strongest feelings of gratitude that he could. He was rewarded with amusement and ultimately, something that actually approached a human feeling. Warmth.

CHAPTER 41

"Are you sure that is the whole of your story, Hunter?" Massius enjoyed Remy's frustrated growl. It helped with his anger at how the Hunter had managed to bungle so simple a task.

"I don't know how I might forget an event that cost me two Hunters and nearly my own life," Remy replied.

Massius's gray eyebrows rose. "Speaking of such, you lost two Hunters and managed to come away unsullied. One would assume three Hunters could kill a single lycanthrope. That is a large part of what you are trained to do, is it not?"

To Massius's immediate left, Alicia sat with legs crossed and fingers entwined. He knew the woman had her menacing gaze leveled on Remy. Likely the fool was feeling as if he were being dissected more by her than Massius, though he was doing all the talking. He couldn't blame Remy for that, having felt the same discomfort under the woman's stare. The left corner of her lips stretched into a smile. It wasn't a friendly sight.

"Elder," Remy said. Judging by his measured tone, he did indeed feel the weight of her gaze. "I may not have properly relayed the situation, so I will try again. That lycan was formidable even in his human form. I've never felt strength like that from one of them."

Massius waved a hand. "Humanoid or lupine, all lycans are strong."

"Not like this," Remy pressed. "He killed three of what I have to guess were our real allies, all in their wolf bodies, and he had little trouble doing it. We filled him with enough silver bullets to take down at least four wolves, and he just shrugged them off and transformed into the biggest wolf I've ever seen."

"So you've said," Massius replied. "You suggest a lycan that is considerably larger than a normal one, which themselves are quite big. Your story is rather grand. Are you sure your mind has not embellished the event because of your desperate situation?"

Remy took a deep breath and opened his mouth to speak again, but quieted when Alicia stood. "I see no point in continuing with this interview." She gestured to the door behind Remy with an open hand. "We have other matters to attend, and so do you. See to the final preparations. Our enemies converge."

Remy bowed and left.

As soon as the door closed, Massius turned on the woman. "Might I ask why you excused my Eldest Hunter from my own chambers?"

Alicia barely suppressed her smile at the mention of Remy's title. "My dear Massius. Let us be clear on something. While we are dealing with this situation, I care not whom you name as Eldest Hunter. Grant one of your lycan pets the title if you see fit. However, when this is done you will find a suitable replacement for Yako." She seemed to think about that last part, then added, "as suitable as is possible, anyway."

"You think Remy a poor choice, then," Massius said, more than asked. The woman gave him a look that suggested she'd play this game if he chose to. "You seem to admire the disgraced former Eldest Hunter," he pressed on.

That venomous smile returned. "I see things as they are, Massius, not as I wish them to be."

Massius narrowed his eyes at her. Slowly, carefully, he extended his will toward her mind. Like a snake made of smoke, his will seeped into her mind as it had every other member of the High Council. It was a careful and painstaking process that was not without risk. Elders were not simple *shaquora* or infant purebloods having lived no more than a few hundred years. Push just a little too far, get just a tiny bit too greedy, and you were discovered. He couldn't control the mind of an Elder, but he could influence one with enough subtlety.

Slowly, cautiously, he made contact with her mind and began wrapping around the small part that was open to suggestion. He needed her to be more cooperative than she had been. He'd hoped not to do this to an ally, especially one that he might make his queen, but he needed her moving with him completely, not questioning him.

Once the contact was made, he began laying subtle suggestions upon her mind, like one might lay upon the skin a sheet of silk so thin it was transparent and barely felt.

"True words," he said. "But I can't help but see the benefit of having one that is malleable to our needs." He smirked at the double meaning of his words as his will sank deeper into her subconscious.

Alicia smiled. "Indeed."

The connection shattered and Massius made an effort not to fall over. It was like every glass window of a building bursting to shards at the same time. It took every ounce of his concentration to recover without revealing his shock.

She made her way to the door and stopped, half turning her head as she spoke again. "It would be good if you ensure your little pawn accomplishes his tasks properly, but you may want to give him something simpler to handle. You are placing him in waters a little too deep. He may drown."

After she left, Massius slumped down in his armchair. That went badly. The violent way in which his connection with her had been destroyed left no doubt that she knew what he was doing. He wondered if she knew that he had been doing the same thing with other members of the High Council.

He'd delved every mind in the High Council except Alicia, since she had already shown interest in change. Stavros was like an iron door. Impenetrable.

Lemanda he could never be sure about. He knew the woman didn't like him, but when he'd attempted a connection with her mind, he hadn't met resistance. In fact, he had planted his suggestions quite easily. All signs showed that she was cooperating in some fashion, and suspected nothing of his mental incursion. Still, there was something about that one that made him wary.

Oddly enough, the one that was the most susceptible to influence had been Vicken. The oldest and strongest of the Elders, one would think the High Elder would be an impossible task. Ironically, the demands and wearying nature of leadership on such a large scale can leave one vulnerable at times. Massius had waited for well over two centuries, testing and watching. When fully alert, Vicken was like nothing Massius had encountered. If Stavros's mind was an iron door, Vicken's steel was a mountain. Still, there was one moment, one short window of time just before he took sleep, when the powerful Elder was vulnerable.

And then, there was Alicia. He'd known she was powerful, but what Elder wasn't? Still, there was something off about her, and Massius was beginning to doubt his wisdom in including the dangerous woman in this venture.

His wrinkled mouth turned down as his sour mood deepened. If Remy was even partially to be believed, a big problem waited out there beyond the city. Taking down a fully formed werewolf was not easily done, and if the tale of this new formidable packleader carried any truth, his presence created a complication Massius didn't need.

Perhaps he should send someone more capable to find out what was going on in those woods. The two that came to mind for this task were both well suited and undesirable at the same time, yet Massius desperately needed to know what was going on with the Woodland Pack. One simple messenger sent to them wasn't enough. He needed trustworthy eyes from the coven to find out where things stood. Despite his foreign resources, if he didn't have the lycans to back him, this could be far more difficult.

He frowned at the door, where just outside, his champion Braggus Rayne stood sentry. Maybe he should send the Eldest Reaper on this important errand. He knew Braggus would not fail, and would be a match for any lycan, no matter how powerful. But dare Massius send his most trusted guard from his side?

He dismissed the idea. Better to send another, or even two if need be. Again, he thought of another option that had been on his mind. He didn't like the idea of awakening the two ancient Reapers. It was the last thing he wished to do, but he needed to regain control of this situation before it deteriorated further.

"Braggus," he said.

On the other side of the room, the door opened and the giant Reaper stepped through and knelt in the middle of the room. "You summoned, Elder."

"Rise, my champion."

Braggus stood. Closer to eight feet tall than seven, the man was imposing, and even more formidable than his appearance suggested. Resplendent in his dark blue and black cloak, cinched at the waist with four dark green strips flowing from the top of each shoulder over the front and back of his body to stop just above the ankle, the man cut a regal figure despite having the frame of a barbarian.

"Whom do you serve, Braggus?" Massius asked.

The man looked at Massius with icy blue eyes that could freeze a bed of lava. "I serve the High Council of Elders, I serve the coven, and I serve as personal guard to you, Elder Massius."

A precise and accurate answer. Massius had delved his mind as well, and never once had he sensed a lie in the man's words. Even now, as the Eldest Reaper spoke, Massius had delved his mind and found no lie.

"Awaken Tannis and Denari. Some of my resources have proven to be ill suited to the task of establishing the state of the Woodland Pack. I need to know if they will come to our aid and whether they still lead any of their remaining allies."

Braggus bowed. "A question, if I may?"

Massius nodded.

"Would it not be best if I go? I trust no one to do this more than myself."

Oh, how Massius agreed with that. "I have considered the same option, Eldest Reaper. But you are needed here." The man bowed and turned to leave. Massius stopped him at the door. "Braggus."

He turned back and bowed precisely. "Elder?"

"What is the situation just beyond our walls?"

"Patrols report that the renegades have appeared in several locations around the castle. The back, the sides, on the other side of the bridge and under it. There have been a few attempts to enter in secret, but all have been repelled."

"They are testing the integrity of our defenses," Massius surmised.

"And they will enter the castle if they happen upon an opportunity," Braggus added. "In every instance the Eldest Hunter has not been with them."

"That is because the Eldest Hunter is already inside the coven serving me," Massius reminded.

Braggus bowed. "Of course, Elder. It has been many years and old habits die hard."

"Ah," Massius responded. "See that this particular habit dies a quick death, my Eldest Reaper. When our disgraced former Eldest Hunter arrives with his band of traitors, you may need to take his head. Are you up to such a task?"

"I serve the coven and the High Council," Braggus answered. "If we cross blades, *Dor Vacus* will find his heart."

Massius glanced at the giant scythe strapped across the Reaper's back. It was the most intimidating weapon ever created, and perfectly suited to the towering man who wielded it. Massius looked into Braggus's icy blue eyes again. No lies, only loyalty. He motioned to the doors.

"Go."

CHAPTER 42

The phone rang until the voicemail picked up. Again. "What the hell is that damned girl about?" Remy thought aloud. He'd been trying to reach Laura for an hour, and the stupid girl hadn't answered her phone. He needed a pair of eyes and ears outside the coven, and this was one task he felt she'd be good at.

Grinding his teeth, he shoved his phone in his pocket and glared down the road leading Peles Castle to the mainland and Sinaia below. The cold, crisp night air carried a moaning breeze across the road, bringing with it, the smell of the surrounding forestry and burning wood in distant fireplaces.

Remy snatched his phone back out of his pocket and dialed Marcos De La Vega. Fortunately the man picked up on the second ring. At least someone knew to hop when their Eldest called.

"Yes ... Eldest Hunter?" Marcos's voice said through the receiver.

Remy could tell that the man had used his title as an afterthought. Too many Hunters seemed to forget that Remy was the new Eldest Hunter. He would have to see to that once this dirty business was done. "You housed Laura in Sinaia, did you not?"

"I did, Eldest. She is housed in an Inn not far from the location you dropped us off."

"Is there a reason she neglects to answer her phone?"

"I do not know. I was told nothing about any correspondence between the two of you. The last her name was mentioned to me was to drop her off at an inn, which I did. All else has been outside my province unless Eldest Hunter deems it otherwise."

"I'm deeming it otherwise," Remy snapped. "Get to wherever you left her and make sure her silence isn't the result of an untimely death."

"It shall be done, Eldest."

"And Marcos," Remy added before the man could hang up. "I see no need to take Scarlet with you. Send her to me."

After a pause, Marcos responded, *"Of course, Eldest."*

Remy ended the call and smirked. Scarlene was likely still incensed at Remy after their last encounter. He saw challenge in that one, and he meant to rip it out. She would learn her proper place or he would kill her.

Remy started away to begin the final preparations, then stopped. On a whim, he pulled out his phone again and dialed another contact. After several rings, a low voice answered.

"Eldest Hunter."

"Jamir. I want you, Marcus, and Berius on a plane out here immediately."

Pause. *"We will be on the soonest flight available, Eldest."*

"You will board the coven's other private Jet," Remy said. "I will text you the location. I expect you on that plane post haste and standing in front of me tomorrow night."

"We meet tomorrow ... Eldest."

Remy ended the call, struggling to control his temper. Why did everyone pause before responding to his orders? It was fast becoming yet another irritant he needed to deal with.

He noted the approach of two cloaked and hooded figures and turned away from the distant city lights. Despite his outward show of confidence, Remy felt a stab of cold fear rush down his spine. The pair stopped a few feet in front of him. If ever there were two individuals that were suited to the rank of Reaper, it was Tannis and Denari.

Both looked like personifications of Death, standing almost as tall as Braggus Rayne. Though not even close to the massive Eldest Reaper's size, they were nonetheless imposing. Nothing could be seen of them but the hooded cloaks they wore.

They stood in front of him, uttering not a word. They might have been cloaked statues, for they made not a move or sound, showing no indications of life. Though Remy couldn't see their eyes, he could feel them looking at him.

"Good hunting," he greeted, trying to keep the trepidation from his voice. The two said nothing; just stood there. "Ahem. Do you wish something of me, Reapers?" Still silence. "Do … has Eldest Reaper requested my presence in your task?"

"Eldest Reaper is not in the habit of requesting the inclusion of weakness in any task," the almost whispering voice of Tannis replied.

Remy stiffened. "I assure you, Reaper Tannis, it wasn't—"

"Nor are we in the habit of hearing lies and excuses," Tannis spoke over him. The hood lowered a bit more toward Remy, and he felt the eyes in the shadow of that hood boring into him.

"I strive to do better for the coven," Remy stated, having nothing better to say.

"Yet you exist," Tannis whispered.

Remy opened and closed his mouth several times before settling on silence. What could he say that wouldn't result in his immediate uncreation? There was no way to deny, even to himself, that either one of these two could cut him down before he could begin to move against them.

The silence lingered. *What the hell do these things want out of me? Why are we standing here?* "I only wish to serve the coven and the High Council," Remy ventured.

"The day may yet come when you earn the rank of Hunter," Tannis said.

"Perhaps you are unaware, Reaper," Remy said in as respectful a tone as he could manage, "but I have attained the rank of Eldest Hunter—"

"A rank you will never earn," Tannis replied.

Remy clenched his jaws, willing his pride not to kill him.

"Eeeldeeest."

A debilitating fear settled over Remy's body. It was all he could do not to stand there trembling. He had thought the descriptions of Denari's wicked voice pure embellishment. The way the hissing Reaper's voice penetrated Remy to his core made him believe that perhaps the descriptions were understated.

Denari made a sound that could have been Death Himself laughing.

Remy turned aside as the two Reapers seemingly glided by. He watched them go, noting the double-edged scythes strapped across their backs. He'd never seen either of them use the weapons, but there were no shortage of stories about the two. There were some who speculated that they were some sort of sub-vampire, akin to the type of immortal that human lore spoke of.

Remy scoffed at the idea. The notion of anything being undead was ridiculous. You were dead or you weren't. That a vampire was some sort of thinking zombie was frankly insulting. He may not care for the two creepy Reapers, but they were thinking living beings, not some revenant carcasses that climbed back out of the ground.

After the Reapers were far enough away, Remy turned back toward Castle Peles, nodding to the two posted sentries as he entered through the front gates. After his conversation with Tannis and Denari, Remy wondered how many others shared the opinion that he was not the true Eldest Hunter. Were such feelings indicative of loyalty to Yako? It must be, for why else would there be any doubt that Remy was the rightful Eldest Hunter since Yako had been disgraced and removed.

He turned a corner and came face-to-face with Lemanda. Remy took a deep breath and knelt before the Elder. How many unwelcome encounters remained, today?

"Elder Lemanda," he greeted.

"Rise, Remy," Lemanda said, omitting not only his title of Eldest Hunter, but even his basic rank of Hunter as well.

He stood, controlling his anger. This one would fall with the rest, but that didn't mean she couldn't turn him to dust right here, alone. "How may this unworthy one serve you, Elder?"

To his surprise, she laughed. "Don't be silly, Remy. You needn't play so hard at humility. It rings as false as your claim to the title of Eldest." Remy's nostrils flared and she laughed again.

"You think I insult you, yes? I know you do. You are trying to control your rage even now, for fear I would rip you apart. I only speak the truth. How much deference has been willingly shown you since your promotion? How many have come to you of their own accord to pay respect to you upon attaining your new title?" Her smile suggested an adult speaking to a child.

"Would you react so differently were someone else to simply arrive proclaiming they were the new Eldest Hunter, leader of your Order, with nothing more than the backing of an Elder to support it?"

"The Elders' words are law, Elder Lemanda," Remy said in a strangled voice.

"Of course," she agreed, "but our words alone do not inspire respect toward you, Remy, especially considering the position was recently occupied by one who is considered to be one of the greatest Hunters in our history. Be assured it is not a trivial claim. You will find respect difficult to come by while the former Eldest still lives."

Remy forced himself to incline his head. "I thank you for your wisdom, Elder."

"Still attempting humility?" She continued past. "If you believe that it matters not whether Yako simply dies, versus dying by your hand, then you are indeed a fool."

Remy's left eye twitched. If he could have snatched Lemanda's heart out of her chest right then, he would have. The notion was laughable, even to him. What grated on him even more was the truth of her last statement. How could he hope to command the respect of the Order of Hunters by simply showing up and claiming he was now Eldest Hunter with only Massius's word to back him?

The realization presented him with a big problem. Did he really believe he could best Yako in a fight? Yako's skills were legendary, and while Remy was possessed of *talents* of his own, would they be enough to see him victorious in a fight with the former Eldest Hunter?

"There's always a way," he muttered to himself. "Everyone has a weakness begging to be exploited."

CHAPTER 43

Yako stared into the darkness. Several hundred feet away at the driveway balcony overlooking the road stood Remy, alone. "You're sure?"

"Beyond doubt, Eldest," Mariska said.

Yako narrowed his eyes. This was uncharacteristic of the cravenly Hunter.

"What do you think he is about?" Tara asked.

"I do not know," Yako answered.

"She has almost reached his position," Mariska said.

Yako looked a little further down the road, where Scarlene made her way toward Remy. As soon as Marcos De La Vega had received the phone call and relayed Remy's order for Scarlene to meet with him, Yako had sent him away. Best not to take a chance of him being seen with the rest of them in case they were discovered. The longer Remy believed that Scarlene and Marcos still served him, the better.

"This could be a trap, and we may have sent her to her death," Tara said.

Yako wasn't so sure. "I doubt Remy believes anyone is enough of a threat to force himself to deal with those two."

"As if dealing with The Wraiths was even his choice," Tara said, referring to the nicknames of the already departed Tannis and Denari.

"Few willingly find themselves in their presence," Tara continued, "and when I think of Remy, my mind doesn't readily think anything other than laughter."

"That is what makes him a threat," Yako said. "He is a coward and an opportunist. Those two qualities alone are contemptible. Combined, they are dangerous."

The flame-haired woman finally reached Remy's position and the two started talking. Unfortunately they were too far away for Yako and the others to hear, and they couldn't take the chance of moving closer; not while Tannis and Denari were now lurking about the city.

Yako had no doubt that Massius had called for their departure into Sinaia. Likely, he'd sent the Wraiths to search for Yako and his band of renegades. Or perhaps to hunt for Darren's pack. Remy would have relayed his recent experience with Darren, and Massius would have sent someone more capable to assess the situation with his lycan allies, or lack thereof.

Perhaps he should warn Darren—

Blood spattered on his back and on the tree in front of him. Yako spun and brought his sword around to knock aside the silver curved blade of a scythe, inches from is face. He brought the sword back around to parry a second curved blade. The attacks came so fast, it was all he could do to keep them at bay. On one knee and fighting off the double-ended scythe, Yako dared not take his eyes off the cloaked figure for even an instant.

Behind his enemy, Barakus swore. "Dammit! What the hell ..." he bit off the rest, and Yako guessed that the other Reaper must have found him.

Tara came gliding between the trees and brought her twin hand-scythes down. The towering Reaper whirled the shaft of his weapon around his back to parry her attack, and kept it so close to his body that one of the blades came around quickly enough to knock Yako's thrust aside.

Fast, he thought. *Very fast.* Still, the tiny instant was enough for the Eldest Hunter to gain his feet. The Reaper's black cloak whipped as his right foot snapped out and connected with Tara's face. She tumbled away and Yako heard her ricochet off the nearby trees.

Yako pressed forward, attempting to gain an advantage. He found none. The Reaper matched him step for step, attack for attack. That double-ended scythe met every thrust, every counter, with little effort. It forced Yako to work twice as hard, for with every block or parry of one of the blades, the other came around. It was like fighting two enemies at once.

"Auck!"

That was Michael's voice. Yako heard the sound of a blade slicing through the air, and then the thud of something hitting the ground. The Hunter had just been beheaded, no doubt.

"How many of these things are there?" he heard Lydia ask, just before he heard her pained grunt.

Two, Yako thought. *Only two, and enough for us all.*

Tara had just regained her feet when Layne whipped out two suppressed 9mm handguns and let fly. The result was something Yako had never seen in all his years. The Reaper blocked another of Yako's thrusts, brought the scythe around and sliced two of the bullets in half, midair, then leaned backward to allow the final two bullets to pass in front of his face. At the same time, he had brought the scythe spinning horizontally over his leaning body to slice Yako across the leg and then kicked out, connecting his foot with the Eldest Hunter's midsection.

Yako went flying away to crash into the trunk of an oak. Tara leaped back in the fight, and fortunate for Layne, for her presence alone kept him alive. The Reaper had sliced the muzzles off of one of his guns and forced him to dance away. Layne cursed as he barely kept out of range of the whirling scythe.

Tara brought her own scythes to bear, blocking and parrying, ducking and moving in closer. Her greatest advantage was her speed, size, and being in close.

She worked to close the distance between herself and the frightening Reaper, but Tannis or Denari, whichever it was, knew her game and kept her out of reach. He kicked out at Layne and snapped his head back, then thrust his scythe straight out. The head of the weapon connected with Tara's chest so hard her feet swept out in front of her as she flew back.

Yako growled as he leapt into the fray. It was difficult to use his enemy's body language to predict his attacks when he was concealed in that robe, but not impossible.

The Reaper leaned away and Yako sidestepped as the scythe sliced vertically through the air where he'd been standing. He jumped forward and kicked the Reaper three times in the face, then landed and sliced his sword diagonally upwards. The Reaper avoided the followup and never broke his rhythm.

Yako gave a mental nod of appreciation. This one was good, and judging from the sound of Barakus's agonized growl, the other Reaper proved just as formidable.

"Eldest," Tara yelled. "Opposite shoulder!"

Yako knew that to mean help came from over his adversary's right shoulder. He moved left, and the Reaper stepped with him just as Meilana glided past. Her sword drew a horizontal cut across the Reaper's back.

Despite what had to be a painful cut from the silver blade, the cloaked figure made not a sound. He whirled his scythe around and slammed the head into the woman's chest, halting her flight and dumping her to the ground. A short distance away, Tara let out a sharp cry that she bit off quickly.

Yako snarled and redoubled his efforts. He thrust and swiped, kicked and punched between swordplay. For a moment, he had the Reaper on his heels. His adversary swiped low, and Yako turned, stepping over the passing blade with his left foot, then right. He spun and whipped his sword around and down.

The cloaked vampire leaned away, narrowly avoiding being cut in half. He brought his weapon up in a circle, spinning the shaft across his body. Yako sliced his sword in the same direction as the spinning shaft. He cut the Reaper across the left shoulder, the chest, then the right arm.

The only sign that he had done any damage was the hiss of his adversary. Denari, then. Yako's eyes glowed crimson. He pushed the offensive, beating his opponent back. Tara appeared but Yako stopped her. "Take the other."

"Eeeeeeldeeeeeeest," Denari hissed, and widened his stance.

Yako came in again, parrying and spinning away, thrusting and swiping down, then up. Denari met him stroke for stroke, spinning his weapon around his back, over his left shoulder, under the pit of his arm in an upward swipe. It was a dance of death, its music the clash of blades.

Yako ducked a swipe that would have taken his head. He continued the motion, crouching low and sweeping his leg out. The Reaper glided backward to avoid being tripped, and Yako came up and forward, his sword leading. He scored a shallow stab to the shoulder but it cost him. Denari hissed in rage and brought his scythe up and in a circle, knocking Yako's sword to the left.

Seeing his vulnerability, Yako threw himself into the stumble and turned his back to the Reaper, who brought one of the blades in a downward arc, running it through Yako's left leg. The Eldest Hunter gritted his teeth at the searing pain and spun his sword into a reverse grip. He thrust it upward into the back of the pit of Denari's arm.

The Reaper half gasped half hissed, and pulled his scythe free, stumbling away. Yako, too, stumbled away and turned to face his adversary, but the Reaper had already leaped backward and disappeared into the trees.

A few dozen feet away, the other cloaked Reaper, Tannis,

suddenly spun a circle, whipping his two-bladed scythe out with one hand. Every nearby Hunter hurriedly retreated, lest they be cut in half by the lethal weapon. Tannis leaped away into the darkness, and as quickly as the fight had begun, it ended.

Yako scanned the area. Mariska knelt, holding a bloodied right arm. Layne seemed barely alive, but looked as if he might recover. Meilana and Tara had survived and were recovering as well. Michael hadn't been so fortunate, judging from the the dusty remains covering his clothes, and a large tear in the center of his shirt.

He found Lydia, still in a squared stance, twin axes still clenched in her fists and her shoulders rising and falling with each heaving breath. Her red eyes glowed hatefully as she stared down at what remained of the rapidly decomposing Barakus.

"I will kill him." She looked to Yako watched her in silence. "You will grant me that, Eldest? The one who killed my best friend. He will die by my hand alone!"

Yako nodded and she replaced her axes at her sides, stooping to retrieve Barakus's greatsword. A movement through the brush had everyone leveling their weapons until Reed limped into sight. Yako had forgotten about the young Hunter. Interesting that he had survived.

"Before everyone gets suspicious," Reed said, holding up his hands, "I was in the fight until one of them stabbed me through the shoulder and slung me into the woods. Maybe they thought they had gotten me through the chest, maybe they just wanted me out of the way. Either way, that's why I'm alive, and this hurts like hell."

Given the relative size of the young man, Yako didn't discount his words. That didn't mean he trusted him, though. "Very well." He turned back to see that Remy and Scarlene were gone.

"What do you think happened with those two?" Tara asked, coming up beside him.

"I don't know," Yako said. "But we need to move fast. I don't like the tone in which this battle has begun."

"The Wraiths will not give up easily," Tara said.

"They will not give up at all," Yako replied.

"Then we must—"

Yako spun and drew his sword in one motion, just in time to see the two-and-a-half-foot blade of a scythe descending upon him.

CHAPTER 44

Scarlene's mind raced as she followed Remy through the halls of Peles Coven. Something was wrong about this whole business, but at the moment she could do nothing about it. Why would Remy send for her now? After their last parting, she hadn't expected to hear from him for a while.

"I expect I will have to kill Yako soon," Remy said.

"Was that not a priority before we came here?" she asked.

Remy responded with a casual shrug that Scarlene didn't believe for an instant. "Not enough so, apparently. He's proving to be more of a thorn in my side than I'd expected."

You're an idiot if that's true, or an idiot if you think I believe it. "I see," Scarlene replied.

They turned down another hallway lined with smooth granite pillars that reached from the floor to the thirty-foot ceiling. Many a night had she spent enjoying the extravagance of the castle. Now she could only wonder how much blood would stain the beauty of Peles.

She could have spat at the thought of vampire blood and lycan fur sullying the vast intricate stonework and tapestries. Bullets would crack and ruin the pillars, hand painted canvas art would be shredded. Stained glass windows would be shattered. "Now that you are at the heart of our power, can you not convince Massius to send a Reaper or two to deal with him?"

"I have a feeling that may have already been arranged," Remy replied. "If not, then I will deal with him myself."

Scarlene almost laughed, but she kept herself in check just as Remy glanced at her, no doubt judging her reaction. "How do you expect to draw him out for this duel of yours?" she asked.

He smiled at her. "You don't think I can do it, do you? You don't think a fight between your Eldest Hunter and that incompetent renegade will end in anything other than my uncreation."

"You speak your own words, not mine, Remy—"

He grabbed her by the neck and whirled her around, slamming her into the wall. The stone cracked from the impact. She stared into his eyes, trying to decide if she should just kill him and be done with it.

"If you utter my name again without some variation of the title Eldest Hunter before it," Remy growled, "I will rip you apart." He tilted his head as he studied her face. "Anger. You don't fear me at all, do you?"

"How effective a Hunter would I be if I were to feel fear?" Scarlene asked, avoiding addressing his name altogether. She didn't think she could bring herself to call him Eldest Hunter. Just the thought made bile rise to her throat.

Remy chuckled and released her. "You have a point. Perhaps I will make you my queen when this is done."

Now Scarlene did laugh. "Your queen? When have you shown me anything befitting a woman holding the respect of man who would have me as his queen?"

Remy shrugged a shoulder. "I've tolerated your flippant attitude till now, and still you live. Isn't that enough?"

Scarlene started to shake her head at him, but hid the motion by running a hand through her hair. This fool knew nothing about leadership. "You still haven't spoken of how you plan to arrange this duel with Yako," she said, deflecting the conversation. She almost referred to Yako as Eldest, but caught herself.

She almost felt sorry for Remy. No matter what he did, no matter how ruthless he tried to be, he would never be Yako's equal. Mercilessness was not what defined a leader. Yako inspired loyalty through his actions and his own personal code of conduct. He led his Hunters with competency and fearlessness, while Remy led with what he perceived as strength.

"I expect I'll have him brought to me," Remy answered. "I doubt he would simply offer himself up freely, so I will have to ensure that we meet."

Scarlene kept her eyes forward. Remy must be joking. Yako had spent weeks hunting this fool back in Vancouver, and Remy had used every evasive trick in his repertoire to elude him. Now he claimed that Yako wouldn't want a fight? Scarlene couldn't bring herself to believe Remy was this delusional. Power may be an intoxicating substance to him, but even Remy wasn't this stupid. Scarlene decided all this banter was for her sake, for some reason. "I see."

Remy laughed. "Do you? Or do you only see one dimension to my plans? I know what you're thinking."

I certainly hope not, Scarlene thought.

"I avoided that fool back in Vancouver to goad him into becoming angry. Once I finally get him here, he'll be spoiling for a fight, and more than eager to come to me where I can deal with him in a place and at a time of my choice, not his."

Yet, you just told me you'd have to have him brought, because he's avoiding you. Scarlene was beginning to wonder if every conversation with this man would result in her struggling not to fall into laughter. "You seem to have it all figured out where I did not."

"Your patronizing attitude is a dangerous attribute, Scarlet."

A spike of anger shot through Scarlene, but she repressed it. Only a friend addressed her by her nickname. This craven was anything but.

Remy's smug expression said that he knew he'd struck a nerve. "You do not like me, but you will come to change your mind in time. We have forever to become better acquainted, do we not?"

"True," she replied, though she would rather walk straight into the sun right then and there than spend the entirety with this cretin. "But, aren't we getting ahead of ourselves? You speak about making me your queen, yet not even Vicken makes such a claim of power as to consider himself royalty."

"His shortsightedness is his own issue," Remy said. "Which is why he will be removed. He has no knowledge of what is about to happen to him." The smug look deepened. "Not once has he questioned Massius or myself. I think he may be totally oblivious."

Like yourself. "Interesting," she said. Oh how she wanted to kill this twit.

"No need to worry your pretty red head about it, Scarlet," Remy continued. "Everything will be taken care of soon. Massius will become High Elder with Alicia at his side. Lemanda and Stavros will see the light of loyalty, or the sun. It really doesn't matter. And I will attain my place at Massius's side and you at mine."

Scarlene gave him a warning look. "Ahem. I thought Massius's side was already occupied."

"The old man has two sides," Remy replied, totally nonchalant. "The big man has nothing to fear from me except having to deal with someone with more wit."

At that moment, Scarlene realized there was nothing to fear from Remy other than that he might bungle into an opportunity to do real damage. Such a scenario would be purely accidental, for sure, for anyone who could so easily misjudge the intelligence or formidability of Braggus Rayne was someone racing to oblivion.

"It looks like you've got it all figured out," she said again. "What do you need of me, if not to keep an eye on our little renegade band?"

"Meet with our supporters and tell them we move tomorrow night," Remy ordered. "This business needs to be ended, soon."

Scarlene nodded. "And yourself?"

"I have business of my own to deal with, not the least of which is figuring out how to handle this situation with Yako."

Scarlene grinned at him. "As you've said, I'm sure if you just ask him, he will walk right in here to fight you."

Remy responded with a sly look. "Would you like that?"

"Who wouldn't?" Scarlene replied sincerely. "A duel between anyone with the confidence to cross blades with Yako would be far more worthy than anything humans watch on their 'pay-per-view' arena fights."

To her surprise, Remy actually laughed at that. "Fair enough. We'll see what we'll see concerning myself and our disgraced former Eldest Hunter." They stopped at an intersection of four hallways.

"Go and speak with Sorsha. I have given him responsibility to organize our allies in my stead. Ensure that he's done his job competently."

Scarlene nodded. "Tomorrow night, then."

"Tomorrow night." Remy started away, then stopped and looked over his shoulder. "And … Scarlet. Try not to betray my wishes to Yako. It would be a disastrous mistake."

She placed a hand on her hip. "The leader of a small band of renegades against our seat of power. I'm smart enough to know where the odds are in favor."

Remy grinned at that. "Spoken like a true opportunist."

"Pragmatist," Scarlene corrected. "Life's greatest insurance policy."

CHAPTER 45

The small but charming city of Sinaia sat under the watchful eye of its ominous sentry, Peles Castle. To a human's eyes, the castle would be a beautiful accent to the town, but Jelani and Daniel knew better. In that castle slept enough vampires to slaughter the entire population if they were inclined to do so.

Jelani still hadn't put together why they hadn't done so. Of course there was a need for discretion, but why the denizens of that castle hadn't been gradually feeding on this town escaped him. They passed a jewelry shop with no shortage of crosses or cross-shaped merchandise that placed even more questions in his mind. What did the populous know?

"I'm starting to get the impression the locals are the silent but vigilant type," Daniel said, as if reading his mind.

A well-dressed woman approached and smiled at them, noticing their interest in a necklace with a simple yet well crafted cross. "Would you like to try?" she asked in her Romanian accented English.

Jelani held up a hand and smiled. "No, thank you, but it is very nice."

"It will bring God's luck to you," she said. "It shines brightly, even at night."

Jelani and Daniel shared a look. "Thank you," he said. "I will remember. It is very nice." The woman smiled back and he absolutely *didn't* enjoy watching her walk away.

"Uh, why don't you ask her to tell you all about that cross over dinner?" Daniel asked.

"Hey, she probably works hard for all that," Jelani discretely waved a hand in her direction. "Why shouldn't I appreciate ..." he looked at Daniel to see his friend also admiring the woman's ... aerodynamics. "You're a hypocritical bastard, you know that?"

Daniel seemed to snap out of a trance. "Huh? No I was just asking why don't you ask her out."

"Right."

"Well she was nice enough to give us that little warning," Daniel said.

"Yeah. She should probably be careful, though, considering ..." he indicated himself.

"Yeah," Daniel agreed. "But there aren't many like you that can walk around in sunlight, knucklehead."

"I got your knuckled head," Jelani said in a playfully warning tone. "C'mon. I googled a weapon shop where people buy swords and other souvenirs. I'm hoping to score a few more daggers."

"So, where do you think Yako and his crew are sleeping right now?" Daniel asked as they continued down the street.

Jelani rubbed the back of his neck and leaned his head back, enjoying the warmth of the sun on his face. "I don't know. I doubt they're in that castle, and Yako doesn't strike me as the type that would just dig a hole. They're probably posted up somewhere in one of these larger buildings. Maybe that one over there." He indicated a building off to their left and Daniel pulled out his map of the city.

"Casino Sinaia," he said. "It's apparently not even a casino anymore, but houses the International Conference Center, whatever that is."

"Interesting," Jelani lied. "Let's swing by there and have a look. We've got nothing else to do, anyway."

"You don't think it would be a good idea to maybe get inside the castle while it's daylight?"

Jelani shook his head. "I know not many vampires walk the day, but the ones that do are extremely powerful, buddy. You don't want to run into one of them in there, trust me. We'll figure something out."

"I hear you," Daniel said, "but you know what I think? I think we should still consider doing this in the day. According to Imron, the pack has not only absorbed a couple other packs of lycans, but they are ready to go whenever Yako gives the word. What if we were to convince Yako to let us move on them in the day, and when night comes, if there's still any fighting left, Yako and whoever is still loyal to him can join us."

Jelani thought on that. "It's a good idea,"

"And one that will not work," a feminine voice replied.

Jelani let his head fall backward and Daniel just laughed.

"Hello, Saaya," Daniel said.

"Hello to you, handsome," she replied.

"How long have you been riding our conversation?" Jelani asked.

The only answer she gave him was a wink. "Anything is possible, but I have strong reservations that you will be able to convince Yako to go along with such a plan, no matter its merits."

"Why wouldn't he?" Daniel asked. "It would give us a huge advantage."

"Try to imagine this," Saaya replied to Daniel. "A newly turned vampire comes to you with a plan to aid against an enemy. It calls for you to allow vampires into the den of your pack, en force, while almost all of you are helpless. You must trust this new fledgling even though you sought his life not long ago."

She blinked slowly at him. "How easily would you find this trust to come by?"

"Not easily at all," Daniel admitted. He looked at Jelani. "But didn't you say that you had a debt to him and that he didn't doubt you'd repay it?"

"That makes no difference, man," Jelani said. "Saaya's right. There's not enough trust in the world that could get *me* to agree to that, and Yako is about as untrusting as you can get. It's a good plan, but it ain't gonna happen."

"So I guess we're doing this the hard way," Daniel said.

"Looks that way," Jelani replied, still staring at Casino Sinaia.

"We have no small part to play," Saaya said. "Alicia thinks you are dead and knows nothing of Daniel."

"How's that going to help us?" Jelani asked. "Unless you were about to do something really special back there in Bucharest, my memory tells me that lady had the drop on both of us. I couldn't even think of trying to break her hold."

"She will not have the luxury of sneaking in on us off our guard," Saaya replied, ignoring several men who admired her dimensions in detail as they passed.

"That doesn't bother you at all," Jelani asked, indicating the men, "does it?"

"Should it?"

Jelani shrugged. "I guess not."

Saaya looked down at herself then looked back up … before they could look away. Jelani quickly glanced at Daniel, but his friend just gave him a look that said "don't bother, we're both caught." She smiled at them. "Is it any different than the way you two look at me?"

Daniel's face changed colors and Jelani thought it best to deflect. "So, find Yako and the others and crash the coven. When is this going down? Tonight?"

Saaya's beautiful brown lips twitched, and she nodded at him. The look said she saw his diversion for what it was. "It is likely they will make their move tonight, and that the coven will be ready for their arrival."

"It's not like he's gonna just go up and knock on the front door," Daniel said. "Yako's smarter than that."

"Exactly," Jelani agreed. "That's why we need to find him before they make their move, otherwise we risk getting there late in the game."

Daniel took a deep breath and let it out in a sigh of resignation. "All right. I'll go and … find Darren Lacey."

"Who?" Jelani asked.

"The leader of your pack." Saaya asked.

Daniel winced. "Yeah, the leader of the pack. Imron told me he's going to be leading them in the attack, so it would be best if I find out how they're going to do it. Maybe we can get in with them if we can't find Yako."

"You, maybe," Jelani said. "But I doubt they'd welcome me to just mingle in."

"Darren and Yako are friends, and you are tied to Yako, at least for now. He won't do anything."

Jelani gave him a skeptical look. "If you say so."

"I do," Daniel insisted.

"This is a good idea," Saaya said. "There is still half the day left. You should meet with him as soon as possible."

Jelani looked at Daniel and shrugged. "Looks like we've got a task. Let's get moving." He turned to Saaya. "You coming?"

The *dampeal* looked away. "No. I have a task of my own, but I will see you tonight." She moved closer and kissed Daniel on the cheek, then Jelani. "Be careful, my two favorite boys."

"Make sure you follow that advice yourself," Daniel said, likely sounding a little more gruff than he intended. "I'm going to grab a quick steak across the street." He looked at the two of them. "Come get me when you're done, here."

"I got you," Jelani replied, and his best friend left.

"It is a more difficult transition," Saaya remarked, staring after him.

"Yeah. And bundle that in with the situation with Wen," Jelani replied.

Saaya nodded, a few strands of her silky black hair falling over her left eye. She slid them back behind her ear with a delicate-looking finger. "There will be time enough for love, *jaan*," she said, turning her light brown eyes on him.

Jelani looked down into those eyes and saw endless depth. Part of him wanted to fall into those depths. Part of him was disgusted at that part of him because of Alisha, and yet another part of him didn't know what to feel.

"So conflicted," she said, placing a hand on his cheek. "Your honorable soul is what makes you both frustrating and alluring."

"Alluring?" Jelani chuckled. "Can't say that's a word I hear every day."

"You would like a definition?"

"Saaya, I know what the word means—"

True desire fell over him. He stared down into her eyes, and a glimmer of light passed over them. He felt heat and energy radiating from her small body, and it settled over him like a blanket. So invigorating and enticing was it, so potent and irresistible, that it took every bit of discipline for him not to fall over her right there. His body screamed at him to take her to the nearest room and make love to her right then.

The threat of the coven in the looming Peles Castle, the impending conflict, the powerful Elder that had nearly killed them both, all of these things were pushed into the background of his mind. There was only Saaya. Only this magnificent woman, daughter of a human and a Count.

When the connection broke, Jelani fell back a step, panting. He looked around and found an older woman smiling at them.

"Awe," the tourist said. "Young love. I remember being there. You two enjoy it and hold on to it." She placed a hand on Saaya and Jelani's arms. "Hold on to that love. It will help you through the tough times." She smiled at both of them again and gave their arms a friendly squeeze, then continued down the street.

"How odd," Saaya remarked, watching the woman depart.

"Nice lady," Jelani said.

"She did not know us at all."

Jelani moved closer and wrapped his arms around her. She looked up at him, and even if he didn't see it in her eyes, he felt it through their connection. Affection. Deep affection, but controlled.

"No, she didn't, but she was a nice lady who took the time to show us a little kindness."

"Such a thing is unheard of in the vampire world," she said.

"I imagine there isn't much love floating around in the vampire world either," he said.

"It is a very rare thing," Saaya agreed. "My father's love for my mother was unusual. But I'm sure you already knew that, so privy have you been to my childhood."

She was referring to the dreams he'd had a while back. Jelani hadn't known what was going on at the time, having not known of or understood the nature of the connection they shared. "Yeah, that was a little weird. Especially the parts about your mother's childhood."

A tiny frown creased her forehead and she tilted her head at him. "My mother?"

Jelani nodded. "Yup. Making her way at night to present her offering to a healing God whose name I'm not going to try to pronounce, getting caught by a man who was more compassionate than the others. I'm really sorry about your grandmother not making it, though. That was really hard, I could feel it. Your mom had to grow up fast." He stopped talking when he realized Saaya was staring at him.

"That is interesting," the *dampeal* said.

Jelani frowned. "What is?"

"Through our connection, you have gained memories that I have through my own connection with my mother. An indirect connection, so to speak. I've never heard of such a thing."

"How many other humans have you sampled?" Jelani asked. He'd meant it as a joke, but Saaya didn't react. "Sorry."

"No need to apologize, *jaan,* but I find this unusual. I must look further into this later."

Jelani had a thought. "If I'm privy to your mother's memories through you, then why not your father's?"

Saaya's thoughtful look turned amused. "Not even his daughter has access to any of the memories he does not wish to be shared. The older the vampire, the more control they have over this. An *Ancestor* has absolute control. There are times when there is a sharing of blood. When knowledge gained through an age must be shared with a long sleeping *Ancestor.* The level of control they have allows them to pass on knowledge and information in detail to the recipient."

"I kind of know what you're talking about," Jelani said, having had the disturbing experience a while back when he'd attacked that woman jogging in Stanley Park. The thought of what he'd almost done, and the fact that he would have done it if not for Saaya, made his body go colder than it already was.

"Magnify that experience with a hundred times more clarity and focus, and you will have an idea," she said.

"I can't even approach that," Jelani said. "And since I can't, let's come back to why you were putting the dazzle on me a few minutes ago …"

He looked around, suddenly aware that everyone nearby was looking in every direction but them. Jelani glanced around nervously. He didn't see anything that would draw so many people's attention. Was Saaya doing this?

"I wanted to give you a better definition of 'alure'," the *dampeal* teased, stepping away.

Before Jelani could utter a response, she faded from view.

WRAPPED in the light that she had bent around her body, Saaya watched Jelani walk across the street, muttering to himself about how the hell she was still able to do that to him in spite of his new existence. He talked to himself a lot, whether vocally or in his own mind. Saaya couldn't imagine what it must be like to have constant dialogue running through her mind all the time, but it explained his personality.

She sighed, and her heart finally slowed. Everything he did, every decision he made, was driven by careful thought to the consequences of the action. While that may be a good thing, it was an excess that he didn't realize he was prone to. Fate was an amazing thing when one recognized it while in action.

That fate could bring together two men, then a third who had the qualities of both was as unbelievable as the fact that not one of them saw it for what it was. Jelani was as careful in every way as Remy, but in a more selfless manner, where Remy was purely selfish.

Jelani was also as honorable as Yako, but in a more compassionate way, whereas the Eldest Hunter was cold, ruthless and pragmatic, yet not cruel.

Saaya watched him disappear into a sandwich shop where his lycan friend would be tearing into a very rare steak. Yet another irony, that Jelani found himself best friends with a lycan just as Yako shared a friendship with Darren Lacey.

She thought back to their last encounter. Unlike the first time they were intimate, she'd felt in him a need for release. Release of the burdens he'd been carrying, and of the responsibilities of the events that had happened in his life and the lives of his friends. Responsibilities he should not have borne to begin with.

She'd given him that release, that affection that she knew he had desperately needed. She asked herself why, wanting to know the answer while at the same time wanting to deny that deep inside, she already knew.

CHAPTER 46

"How's the steak?" Jelani pulled up a chair across from his friend.

Daniel glanced up at him, then went back to cutting into the large hunk of raw meat. "Disgusting and delicious."

Jelani looked down at the bloody red plate. He didn't find the blood appealing at all. Maybe it was because such a sight would have made him nauseous as a human and he still had the leftover feelings. "I always found raw steak unappetizing."

Daniel shoved another bite in his mouth. "Yeah, well how about thinking it's gross and loving it at the same time? Part of me wants to throw up while the other part of me could eat this all day." He took another bite. "The worst part is that I have to order it extra rare so that it's socially acceptable. If I had my way, I would just order the uncooked steak and have them slap it on a plate as-is."

Jelani sniggered. "Yup. Not the best thing to do if you're trying to keep a low profile."

"It's much better raw, but extra rare is the next best thing." Daniel seemed to realize what he'd said and put his utensils down and held his head in his hands. "Dude, I'd be a liar if I didn't say this is still hard to accept."

"I can imagine how hard an adjustment it must be," Jelani said. "But there are some plus sides to it also, when you think about it."

"Oh really?" Daniel looked up. "What could those possibly be?"

"Think about it, man." Jelani leaned over the table and lowered his voice. "You can walk around in the sun no problem—"

"So can you," Daniel interrupted.

Jelani wrinkled his lips. "You know I'm a special case."

"Yeah, you are," came the sarcastic reply.

"Full of jokes today," Jelani said. "You should take your act on the road." He glared at Daniel for a moment longer, then continued. "Anyway, before a jackass interrupted me, I was saying that you can walk around in the sun, you don't have to drink blood. You can live a mostly normal human life."

"And the whole transforming into a monster thing?" Daniel asked.

"Didn't you tell me it gets easier after the first time?" Jelani replied. "And you're not forced to transform during a full moon either."

Daniel never blinked. "But I will have to, every so often."

"And you live in the perfect city for that. There is no shortage of wilderness in the greater Vancouver area. A fifteen minute drive puts you right at the mountains." Jelani leaned back in his chair. "I feel sorry for the bastards who live someplace like LA or New York. Plenty of jungle, but it's all concrete."

Daniel chuckled. "Fair enough. I guess if I had to choose, I'd probably take being what I am. At least we're not thought of as unholy lapdogs of satan or anything."

Jelani blinked at him. "Thanks, dude. Thanks a lot."

"Any time," Daniel said, smirking behind a cup of water. He looked into the cup, then at Jelani. "Funny thing also. I don't crave anything but water. I don't want juice, or soda, or anything else. Just water."

"Well I guess your full-time canine counterparts don't drink any of the stuff, so it makes sense."

"Funny," Daniel said.

"Any time," Jelani replied with a smirk. "So, how do you plan to find your pack?"

"Dude, I know it is what it is, but could you just not refer to them as *my* pack?" Daniel looked out the window. "I don't mean to snap, but there is an undercurrent of a lack of freedom that really bothers me with all this. I don't like being tied to an organization of any kind without having a choice in the matter."

"But you do have a choice," Jelani said.

Daniel looked toward the door, and Jelani turned in his seat to see a hulking man standing behind him. He was just over six feet tall and had at least two layers of muscle stacked on top of each other. Jelani swallowed. He could smell the wolf in this guy. Never mind him being strong as a fully transformed wolf; Jelani knew without a doubt that if this guy could get his hands on him, he could snap Jelani in half without having to make the change. Jelani didn't fear him, but it was good to know what another man was capable of. "How's it going?"

The guy smiled. Even his smile seemed to have muscles in it. *What does this guy do? Workout with boulders?*

"Darren Lacey," Daniel said. He moved to stand, but the walking stack of muscle named Darren held up his hand.

"Please. Do you mind if I sit with you?"

Daniel looked at him skeptically. "I appreciate your politeness, but it's not like I could deny you, anyway."

"Have I done something that would make you wish not to be in my presence?"

"I suppose not." When Daniel realized Darren was still standing, he indicated the third chair at their table. "Please, excuse my manners. Have a seat."

"You already know my name," Darren said after he pulled his

chair up to the table, "and of course I know yours. But I think your friend here has me at a disadvantage."

Jelani held out his hand and introduced himself. Darren shook his hand. It was like shaking hands with concrete.

The huge lycan looked back at Daniel, smiling. "You are off to a good start."

"How so?" Daniel asked.

"You have already made friends with one who walks the night."

"Why is that a good start?" Daniel asked. "Aren't they our enemies?"

Darren's expression said he'd expected that question. "No. They are not our enemies, nor are we theirs. The tensions between our respective species was planted there a long time ago by the arrogance of an Elder, over two thousand years ago."

"An Elder vampire?" Jelani said.

Darren nodded. "Unfortunately, yes. He felt that the lycan-thrope species was an inferior hybrid animal that should exist to serve what he considered the true immortals, though we, too, live outside the cycle of mortality."

"Why?" Jelani asked. "Why kick up dust if everything is cool?"

Darren chuckled and Jelani figured it was his west coast American slang to blame. "Again, fledgling. Arrogance. It is often the cause of conflict. But vampires were not wholly to blame. My lycan brethren could have simply walked away instead of pushing back with foolish pride. There were not many who agreed with Elder Devin's opinion of us, but his view gained traction when we became hostile to him."

"So all this is related to our friendship, how?" Daniel asked.

"It stands in the face of the foolishness of the tension between our two species," Darren answered. "The more of us that disprove the lack of wisdom of our forefathers' way of thinking, the easier our lives as well as the lives of humans will be."

"Interesting," Jelani said. "Didn't know things went that deep."

"They go a lot deeper than either of you can imagine," Daren replied, "but that is for another time."

"How did you find us?" Daniel said. Jelani looked at his friend. Surely he must know. Just as he and Saaya could find each other because of their connection, Darren would be able to find Daniel through similar means.

"That brings us back to the words I first spoke to you. Though you were brought over by Imron, you are a member of my pack and bound to me. I have a connection to every member of my pack."

"Sounds like that can get to be overwhelming," Jelani said. "You don't have a thousand voices or emotions bouncing around in your head?"

"That would be maddening," Darren agreed. "No. I am constantly aware of every member of my pack on a subconscious level, but they only come into focus when I will it so, or there is some urgent situation with them."

Daniel was silently staring at the bloody remains of his steak. His lips were pressed tightly together. Jelani glanced at Darren, who was focused on Daniel.

"You will find I am not what you think I am," Darren said.

"How so?" Daniel asked, still staring at the plate.

"Had you been brought over into any other pack, you would have been compelled to go to its alpha and pay obeisance. I have come to you." He placed his large thick hands on the table and intertwined his fingers. "Any major life change can be disruptive. A change such as this, much more so."

"I guess you would know what it's like." Daniel said.

"Not through personal experience," Darren admitted. "I am a lycanthrope by birth." He stared at the table but seemed to be looking someplace much farther away. "I remember when we were referred to in the latin term, lycanthropus, and the greek, lukanthropos. Then came the english term, lycanthrope. And as with most everything in the english language, the term went through changes in pronunciation, and was shortened. We became lycanthro. Then later, in this modern age, we are now lycans."

"I can't lie," Jelani said. "That last one is a little easier to manage."

Darren nodded. "Lazy is the english language."

"Prudish was that comment."

"By more than a millennia, I am older than you," Darren said, looking at Jelani with eyes that spoke of centuries of experiences he couldn't even begin to imagine. I've seen your hybridized language in perpetual change through the ages.

"How do you know what it's like if you've never experienced it?" Daniel asked.

"I did not say I've never experienced it," Darren said. "I said I've never experienced it personally. But I have had the experience through those who have been brought over into my pack. *Every* one of those who have been brought over into my pack."

Daniel frowned and looked up at him. "Every one? How could you stand it? My change was excruciating, bewildering, and terrifying all wrapped into one horrifying experience. How could you stand to go through that every time? Indirect or not, that would drive me crazy."

"It is one of the strengths an alpha must have," Darren answered. "A true alpha endures the pain of his new pack member and welcomes him. There are some, such as the Woodland Pack, who had an alpha leader who used the pain of *the first turning* to give him strength. But that had a mental side effect that burned away his empathy. He constantly inflicted his will upon his subordinates. His loyalty was gained through fear."

"You talk about him in the past tense," Jelani observed. "He dead, or something?"

Darren nodded. "We obliterated his pack."

Jelani resisted the urge to swallow again.

"I didn't realize werewolves could be so compassionate," Daniel said.

Darren chuckled. Instead of a comforting sound, it had an air of warning to it. Jelani looked at Daniel, who seemed to be trying to keep his body from shaking.

"Young one," Darren said. "Remember this. I care deeply for every member of my pack, and would do all within my power to see us thrive. But I never, ever, tolerate insubordination, cowardice, disloyalty, and actions that endanger the pack and the species. From these four qualities there is no redemption. A strong pack is composed of strength, loyalty, and intelligence. Any who lack this will be, rejected."

"Rejected," Daniel said. "Sounds lethal."

This time Darren's laugh was more friendly. "It seems you already have the quality of intelligence. And since you are here to aid your friend when you are not required to do so, you display loyalty as well."

"Guess I have to prove my strength then, huh?"

"That is something I can feel within you already. That first day you transformed, I felt the strength in you. You will be a welcome asset to the pack, if you would have us."

"If I would have you?" Daniel repeated, incredulous. "You're asking me?"

Daniel spread his hands. "Have I not already said you have a choice?"

"Yeah, but I hadn't ..."

Daniel looked at Jelani, who shrugged. "Don't look at me, man. This is on you. I do have to say I've seen much worse options."

Daniel looked back at Darren. "Will a handshake do, or do we have to bite each other or something? And I'm not sniffing your ass."

Again Darren laughed. "I believe a handshake will suffice."

The two men shook hands across the table and it looked to Jelani like a weight had been lifted off his friend's shoulders. He felt glad for Daniel. All that time he'd been worried about whether or not he would retain his free will.

"I'm sure you want to talk about the party happening tonight," Jelani said.

"An interesting way to put it," Darren replied. "We're coordinating with your Eldest Hunter." He looked at Daniel. "Our two sides will fight as one. Yako will lead a team of vampires and lycans, as well as I."

"You mean ... mixed together?" Jelani asked. "That's unexpected."

Darren nodded. "A brilliant idea conceived by Yako. We spoke of our intentions and I think he may wish to have you at his side."

"He knows I'm here?" Jelani glanced around as if expecting the Eldest Hunter to be sitting at a table watching him.

"You are indebted to him, are you not?"

"Yes, but I was also supposed to link up with him to come here together. I never showed. I figured he might be mad at me. I thought I might just show up during the hostilities and help out. You know, prove I'm good for my word."

Darren's responding smile made Jelani wonder if the man was about to pat him on the head. "The Eldest Hunter is an impeccable judge of character. If he thought you would not hold to your word, he would have terminated you."

I'm getting tired of feeling like the weak man in the room, Jelani thought. "I see," he said.

"A healthy thing for you if you do, fledgling. And his judgement extends to my own. I do not believe Yako would be insulted if you chose to fight beside me, at least until we have fully entered the coven."

"If you don't mind," Daniel said, "I think it might be good if we start this with Yako. There's some personal business going on with all this and I think the three of us might need to watch each other's backs."

"Fair enough," Darren said. "I entrust you to him." He stood.

"He sleeps under the foundation of Casino Sinaia under the watch of several of the Shadow Pack that I have sent under his command. When they rise tonight, go with them."

"Thanks," Daniel said.

After Darren left and Daniel paid the bill, they stepped out into the bright sunlight. Jelani shaded his eyes with his hand.

"Still getting used to sunlight, eh?" Daniel asked.

"Sure am, eh?" Jelani said, making fun of Daniel's slip of Canadian accent. Daniel shoved him and they laughed. "Really, though. It's like I've been living underground. The light is so bright after months of nothing but night, you know? It's good to feel the sun on me again. I'm realizing just how big a gift Saaya has given me."

Daniel nodded, looking around. "Yeah she saved you on that one."

"Yeah," Jelani said, his voice taking on an ominous tone. Daniel turned to look at him, then in the direction Jelani was looking. A very tall person in a long coat stared at them from across the street.

CHAPTER 47

Not both of them, Jelani realized. *He's staring at me.* The towering figure, over seven feet tall was dressed in his customary ankle-length trench coat.

"I don't think he's smiling at you," Daniel remarked.

"Actually, I think he's scowling at me," Jelani said. "But it's a deeper scowl than normal."

"Want me to hang around?" Daniel asked.

Jelani shook his head. "No. This is going to be one of those man to man things, you know what I mean?"

Daniel patted him on the shoulder. "Sucks to be you, bro. Can I have your computer? Always liked it."

"Real funny," Jelani said. "Don't start planning my funeral yet. He might actually approve."

"Would you approve of someone ... having relations with your sister?" Daniel asked.

"Not until after I had a talk with the guy and issued a not so thinly veiled threat or seven," Jelani answered.

Daniel patted him on the shoulder again. "Yup. Well then. I'll just keep an eye on that computer and hopefully see ya later."

Jelani laughed nervously. "Right. See you in a bit."

Daniel started away and Jelani just waited, watching the tall man stare at him over the heads of everyone who walked by. Most people made a wide arc around him, and Jelani didn't blame them. He may not be a typical vampire prone to just feeding on anyone, but he was still on the dark side of intimidating.

Jelani glanced down the street and saw Daniel disappear around the corner. He looked back at Kafeel and the man hadn't moved. *What is this? A standoff or something?*

He'd barely finished the thought when he was suddenly enveloped in a rush of darkness that was both disorienting and left him feeling disembodied.

The experience came and went in a flash of time, and Jelani tumbled back into the sunlight. He righted himself and got one of his feet under him, coming up to a kneeling position while sliding backward several more feet. His instincts shouted for him to grab his weapons, but sometimes instinct got you killed.

He remained where he was, looking up at the man who stood a dozen feet away, staring at him. Slowly, Jelani stood and looked around. It would have been a beautiful view of the city of Sinaia under better circumstances. Instead, he wondered how in the hell this man did whatever he'd done to get him on the roof of a building.

"I can assure you there's no need for hostility, sir—"

Kafeel's hand was suddenly at his throat and Jelani's feet left the ground. He looked down into Kafeel's glowing lavender eyes. "Well," he croaked, resisting the urge to grab at the man's hand. "At least I know what it's like to be nine feet tall." He looked down at his feet, which dangled at Kafeel's knees.

"Do you know why I have come to see you?" the man asked.

"Pretty sure I do," Jelani answered. "I'd like nothing more than to talk with you about it." He indicated the hand that still clutched his steadily constricting throat. "But I can't manage it like this."

He released Jelani and he dropped to the ground. Before his

feet touched down, his throat had already healed. "Thanks," he said.

"You've caused my sister no small amount of difficulty," he said.

"Man," Jelani shook his head. "Seriously, bruh. Do you really think I've set out for any of this? Who found who in this little situation? I didn't seek her out."

"You would be dead and in the ground had she not saved you."

Jelani nodded. "And for that I'm grateful. I think you know that. But grateful as I am, I didn't even know she existed before she and yourself helped me out. Up till recently I haven't exactly been in the driver's seat of this whole ordeal."

Kafeel's stare was stone personified. "You are a distraction she does not need."

"Maybe," Jelani said. "Or maybe I'm a distraction she does need." Kafeel's face darkened.

Jelani held up a hand. "Just hear me out. What I'm saying is that despite my best efforts to the contrary, your sister has constantly felt it necessary to remain tied to me in some way. Things seem to happen to draw us together in more ways than one."

Impossible as it seemed, Kafeel's face hardened further. "You venture into an area I do not wish to explore."

"Fair enough," Jelani said, redirecting. "All I'm saying is that I think there is a reason we met. Maybe all of us."

"Doubtful."

Jelani shrugged. "You never know."

"I have never met a fledgling *shaquora* that was anything more than an irritant best removed from the lives of all around them," Kafeel stated.

"First time for everything," Jelani countered.

The man's right eyebrow twitched. Coming from this guy, it was probably the equivalent of outright laughter.

"We are in the middle of a huge situation with that coven over there." Jelani pointed in the direction of Castle Peles. "If this all works out for the better—"

"It will mean nothing at all to me or Saaya," Kafeel finished for him.

"Perhaps," Jelani said. "But like it or not, we're all involved now."

"You have derailed the discussion," Kafeel warned.

"Okay, fair enough," Jelani said. "Let's just be direct, since that's the way you roll. Saaya is conflicted about her feelings for me. I'm conflicted about my feelings for her. Neither of us has it figured out, but I promise you this. I've got her back no matter what. Both of you."

"The protection of a *shaquora*," came the deadpan response.

"I didn't say anything about protection. You want to make sure I don't cause your sister any problems, and I get that. I can't promise that won't happen, but I promise I'll always do my best to do right by her no matter what happens.

"You know I'm telling the truth, big man," Jelani continued. "I know you can see it in me. And Saaya can sense it in me. You honestly think I could fool her?"

Silence.

Jelani waited. For several moments they stood there, staring at each other. "Why are we up here?" he finally asked. "I admit it was a cool trick, however you transported us up here, but I also gotta admit you've got me stumped. Are you concerned I'll treat her badly or lie to her or something?" He snorted. "I don't know how the two of you stack up to each other in terms of strength or power or anything, but I'm sure you know there's not much I could do to her. So what's this man-to-man about?"

"You are right," Kafeel finally said. "She is conflicted about you. Do you know why?"

"Not exactly."

"Children. Fool children, both of you." Kafeel narrowed his eyes. "My foolish sister is conflicted about you because she allowed herself to fall in love with a human, forcing her to protect you and insert herself in the middle of a conflict that is meaningless to us."

Jelani's mouth fell open. "You think all this is meaningless?"

"Few vampires, pureblood or *shaquora* know of the existence of the *Ancestors* beyond vampiric lore. We are thought of to be the forefathers long gone. *Dampeals* are virtually unheard of altogether. It would be much easier to step away from this foolishness. Instead, she hovers around you like a mother hen, ensuring your continued existence despite your constant stumbling into danger like a witless infant."

Jelani whistled through his teeth. "That's pretty harsh, man."

"My sister is conflicted because she fell in love with a human. You are an undecided irritant that is the cause of no small amount of frustration to her."

"I won't deny any of that," Jelani said. "I'm doing my best in what you can't deny is a pretty damn tough situation."

Silence.

"Okay. Straight to the point. What do you want from me?"

In an instant, Kafeel was suddenly towering over him again.

"Make up your mind."

A TEXT from Daniel asked whether or not Jelani was still alive and if so, he could be found across the street from Casino Sinaia.

"Glad to see you still in the world of the virtually living," Daniel greeted when Jelani arrived.

"Virtually living. Cute. My heart still beats like yours, wolfman."

"Barely," Daniel said. "So what did you two talk about?"

"You already know." Jelani nodded at the building across the street. "That the place?"

Daniel nodded. "Doesn't look much like a casino, does it?"

It took no more than a casual once-over to agree with his friend's assessment. The long two-story building had windows on each floor stretching from left to right. Between them were two sets of stairs ascending in a **U** shape, meeting in the center of a semicircular entryway with a set of smooth white pillars on each side.

The pillars held up a semicircular balcony with a large doorway with gold trim along the outer edges and windows. On either side and on top of the balcony stood what looked like watch posts, where guards might stand. It looked like a nice place to visit, were he not in the city to shed blood instead of take a guided tour.

"Guess we should go in and talk to the local wolves," Daniel said.

Jelani remembered a little detail that spurred his visit to the Northwest Coven. He squinted over his shoulder at the barely risen sun. "I think I have a better idea.

CHAPTER 48

"You sure about this?" From his position on the roof of Castle Peles, Daniel looked out at the forest stretching between the castle and Sinaia.

Jelani could hear the anxiety in his friend's voice. He couldn't blame Daniel. Being a *shaquora*, he himself wouldn't have been welcomed with open arms even under the best of circumstances. A lycan, much less so. Still. "What's the point of being able to walk the day if I don't use it to my advantage?"

"Just because it is an advantage doesn't mean you should push your luck using it," Daniel said.

"I guess so," Jelani replied. "Believe me, I don't relish the notion of uncreation any more than you do."

"Uncreation," Daniel said, looking at him. "There you go with the vampire speak, again."

Jelani waved him away. "The same thing will start to happen to you once you've been a lycan for a little longer. Trust me on that one." He leaned forward and looked down at the balcony below, where one of the sentries slept. Obviously there was no bed, and the window was shuttered tight, but he was there, Jelani knew it.

"Anyway, Remy and some sour old man named Massius have a

pretty sizable group behind them. It'll give us a huge advantage if you and I could trim their numbers back a bit. What better time to do it than before sundown?"

"Wasn't it you who told me it was dangerous to go creeping into a coven where powerful vampires were lurking?"

"That was before I remembered the little detail about Remy's memories. I know what he knows, for the most part. I know what wing in the coven he sleeps in and I know who's loyal to him and Massius."

"And Remy doesn't give me the impression of someone who inspires loyalty from subordinates or respect from his superiors," Daniel said. "It's what he doesn't know, and by extension what *you* don't know, that concerns me."

"We'll just have to be careful, then."

Daniel sighed. "You're solid on this idea, then?"

Jelani nodded. "You know I'm not asking you to—"

"Man, shut up and lead the way," Daniel snapped. "You know I've got your back. What am I gonna do, leave and go back to town? Get outta here with that!"

Jelani's lips wrinkled. "Wow. Lycanthropy has made you hostile."

Daniel snarled, grabbed Jelani by the shoulders, and spun him around. He shoved the giggling Jelani forward, and then stepped up to the rail.

He dropped to the balcony without a sound, and a second later Daniel dropped down behind him, though not as quietly. Jelani ran his hand along the shutters, then elongated his nails and slipped them into the seem between the side of the building and the wood. The cracking sound of wood splintering and tearing apart followed as he forced the shutter open. They pushed through a set of purple drapes into an elaborately decorated room with red walls and carpet with a matching red couch. An unlit fireplace sat a dozen paces to the side of the door.

"I think I'm going to throw up," Daniel whispered, taking in the stylistic nightmare. "Purple drapes, red carpet, and a blood red couch? Wen would have a heart attack." He looked around. "You sure all that noise with the shutters didn't wake him?"

"Not a fully sleeping vampire," Jelani whispered back, looking the room over.

"Cool. Let's handle this guy and keep moving."

Jelani nodded. "I'm looking."

"I thought you knew where they all were?"

"Yeah but I'm pretty sure Remy doesn't know the exact location each one of the coven members sleeps," Jelani responded. "Just give me a sec."

He closed his eyes and stood perfectly still, focusing. His sharp hearing picked up everything from the fluttering heartbeat of a bird sitting on the rail of the balcony, to Daniel's breathing and heartbeat as well. He blocked those things out and continued to focus; waiting. A few minutes later he heard it. A breath. He moved to one of the two closets across the room and carefully opened the door. The closet was nearly the size of his room back in Coal Harbour.

The corner of Jelani's upper lip curled as he moved into the closet. *I should kill this bastard just on general principle with all this space and clothes.* He looked at some of the wardrobe. Early renaissance clothing lined the right wall, while outfits from other various ages lined the left. He heard a snort and looked over his shoulder.

Daniel ran his fingers along a red suit jacket with lace ruffles on the collar and wrists. He looked at Jelani and mouthed the words, is *this for real?*

Jelani just shook his head and proceeded to the throw rug toward the back of the closet. He removed the rug to reveal a large door in the floor. *Guy must have a servant to place the rug over his door when he sleeps*, Jelani thought. It didn't make much sense to him, but no time to ponder the irrelevant. He grabbed the latch on the door and pulled. The door opened without much noise, and Jelani peered into the pitch darkness.

A male vampire dressed in green pants and a light blue shirt lay on his back on a cushioned pallet. His oily black hair was combed sideways with a part at the left corner of his head.

Jelani looked back at Daniel, who nodded, then he dropped down into the room. He landed soundlessly beside the sleeping vampire. Daniel wasn't so graceful, so he climbed down the creaking wooden steps. Jelani rested his hand on one of his silver daggers and moved around to place himself on the other side so that the vampire was between himself and Daniel. He would do this quickly.

In a flash, Jelani drew the weapon and brought it down hard. He slammed the blade into the sleeping vampire's chest. His pale red eyes snapped open and his back arched. He opened his mouth but Jelani slapped a hand over it, muffling the scream.

It didn't take long. The lethal silver did its job, and in less than a minute, all that remained of the vampire was rapidly decaying bone. Jelani let out a breath, then looked up at the perspiring Daniel and sniggered. "You're sweating like a human."

"Ya, and I've never seen you so pale," Daniel shot back.

Jelani nodded. "Touché."

They left the room and went to the next, similarly finding and dispatching the vampire sleeping within. They had worked their way through what seemed like an entire wing of the castle, and were making their way to the other side. They hadn't spoken much, and Jelani knew Daniel felt the same as him. Best to get this business done quickly and quietly.

They came to another room, this one larger than any of the others. The room was decorated in much better taste, with a large floor to ceiling painting of some extremely pale man in a tuxedo and tails, an equally pale woman with her arm entwined with his. Both figures seemed to look out of the painting and directly into the eyes of the viewer. It was one hundred percent creepy.

They made their way past a plush vanilla-colored couch and descended a set of spiraling stairs. There was no need to look for a trap door in any closet or under a piece of furniture, as their target was lying right in the open. This one must have a flair for extravagance, for he lay on a plush king size bed, flat on his back with hands resting on his stomach, just like all the others.

Jelani glanced back at the stairs and understood why there was no need for this vampire to sleep underneath the floor. No sunlight found its way down here. To have a room so large, this man must have some sort of status in the coven. He knew it wasn't an Elder, for Remy's memories were specific. This one was much lower ranking than an Elder, but had some degree of authority. Jelani sensed that he was more powerful than the others as well. Best to be fast.

Jelani positioned himself on the other side of the vampire like before, placing his target between himself and Daniel. Jelani rested his hand on the hilt of his dagger and looked up at his friend, who nodded.

In a flash, the dagger snapped out of its sheath and down. Just as quickly, the sleeping vampire's hand snapped up and grabbed Jelani's wrist. Jelani struggled to free his hand but the grip was incredibly strong.

"Why does the stench of a dog fill my room and the smell of silver hover above?" the vampire asked in a low voice. Slowly, lazily, he opened his eyes and glowered at Jelani. "Stinking *shaquora* scum," he said.

A growl from across the room drew their attention. Daniel was in a wide-legged stance, arms out at his sides, fingernails extending. His canine teeth had elongated and the muscles in his body were pulsing.

"You think you can complete the change in time to get over here before I kill your partner assassin, dog?" the man said. He looked back at Jelani. "Only a stinking *shaquora* would mingle with such company. For that, alone, you should die."

Jelani's eyes smoldered, and he smiled down at the other man. "If you're surprised by this, then you have no idea what your leaders are up to."

The vampire gave him a curious look that changed to agony when Jelani's other hand flashed between them in a silver blur. The hand that gripped Jelani's wrist was disconnected from its wrist, and blood spat from the stump. "Where there's one, there's two," Jelani said, revealing his second dagger.

The vampire was on his feet and backing away. Jelani winced when he saw a clawed hand punch through the man's chest. His vampire's eyes went wide, and when Daniel yanked his hand out, the man stumbled forward. Jelani darted past him in a flash and landed by Daniel's side.

The vampire turned back toward them and coughed a mouth full of blood. A thin red line opened in his throat, and he fell to his knees, coughing and wheezing.

Daniel turned to go, but Jelani stopped him with a hand on his arm. "Always finish the job," he said, glancing over his shoulder. Though silver wounds were slower to heal, this one was already willing the giant hole in his back to close, though with obvious effort.

Jelani walked over to the kneeling vampire, reached around, and drove one of his daggers into his throat.

"You can thank your boy Remy for all this trouble when you see him," Jelani said. "I'll be sending him your way very soon."

He yanked the blade free and shoved the dying vampire in the back with his foot. He fell to the floor in a heap and began to decay.

Jelani looked up to see Daniel staring at his bloody arm. He looked horrified.

"Give yourself a minute," Jelani said, knowing exactly what his friend was feeling. "Killing someone is the hardest part of the transition, but it's the one you have to get over the quickest." He stooped and picked up a piece of clothing from the dust that remained of the vampire and wiped off his daggers. "If it makes you feel any better, at least we're not killing humans." He pointed a dagger at the dusty clothes. "And, I can assure you that guy has fed on his fair share of humans."

"It doesn't make me feel better," Daniel said. "But it helps."

Jelani tossed the piece of clothing to Daniel. He caught it and started wiping off his arm. Jelani gave him a friendly slap on the side of the arm as he passed, then started up the stairs. Nothing he could say or do would ease his friend's violent transition into this world. All he could do was be there to help Daniel cope with the reality of what they had become.

Once back on the main floor, they exited the room and continued down the hall. There was only one more room in this hall, and it was halfway down. They stopped at a set of ten-foot-tall doors, trimmed in gold.

Jelani looked at Daniel, who nodded and opened the door. Their mouths dropped open at the sight before them. Not a single window adorned the walls of the dark room. Instead, recesses were built into the walls, top to bottom, row upon row.

"Looks like a freaky above ground catacomb," Daniel muttered under his breath.

There had to be at least forty or fifty vampires sleeping in this room. Even more disturbing was that Jelani knew they had about six or seven more rooms to go, and at least four of those six were this size. How high were the odds stacked against them? How many allies had Remy and Massius accumulated?

Daniel looked at Jelani, and he saw the question in his friend's eyes. *You want to try to take them all?*

Jelani looked the room over again. This wasn't a room full of Hunters. Warriors carried more status than to be stacked in the walls like this. These were the "civilians", so to speak. That didn't mean they weren't dangerous, and it didn't mean that they wouldn't have a hard time trying to kill fifty of them quietly enough not to wake the entire coven. But what would happen if they did? How easily could vampires move with daylight shining through the windows of the many halls of this castle? Would they be lethargic?

He thought back to their last encounter. That vampire might have been of some status, but he still came awake quickly enough to give Jelani pause. He shook his head at Daniel and they backed out of the room.

After he had quietly closed the door, they started down the hall. "Not worth it," Jelani said. "If we weren't trying to be discrete, I would say lets have fun, but we don't want to bring the whole coven down on our heads while any help we might get won't be here till night."

They turned a corner and came to yet another set of tall double doors. Jelani frowned, not recognizing this through Remy's memories. They opened one of the doors and stepped into an indoor courtyard with a stained glass ceiling.

Various small trees and plants, filled the courtyard, which sat awash in bright sunlight. Smooth, multicolored river rocks lined the bottom of a gently running stream that snaked its way through the foliage.

A winding gravel path led through the plant-life along the side of the room. The beauty and tranquility of the place made the hairs on the back of Jelani's neck stand on end.

"I have zero doubt in my mind that we should not be here," Daniel said.

"Yet, here you are," a voice said from behind.

CHAPTER 49

J elani would have turned around to face the sound of the voice if he could move, or even turn his head. He did manage to turn his eyes and look over at Daniel who also only moved his eyes.

"How strange," a woman's voice said from behind. "Here, in my midst is a newly turned vampire and a more freshly turned werewolf. The voice moved around behind Daniel. "What should I make of this? Or, more importantly to you two, what reason would I have for not simply dispatching you right here? Aside from wasting such handsomeness, that is."

From the corner of his vision, Jelani saw a hand with smooth skin and pink painted fingernails reach up to stroke Daniel's cheek. "Has anyone told you that you bear a rather delicious resemblance to a human actor named Russell Wong?"

Despite the situation, Jelani actually snorted. "And you," the silky voice said into Jelani's right ear. "You bear no resemblance to anyone I can think of, but I could still just devour you." Jelani felt a chill go down his back and into his stomach.

The woman laughed. "Oh yes, you are ,new to this existence, aren't you?" She stepped fully into view and stopped in front of him. She practically exuded regality, resplendent in a long flowing dark green gown with detailed hand woven blue embroidery that was subtle but just pronounced enough to draw the eye to her cleavage and down the sides of the waist to the hips.

As tall as Jelani, the woman stared into his eyes with glowing red orbs. A smile crept across a face that looked as if it had been sculpted and smoothed by a master. She winked at him.

"You two are beautiful." She looked at Daniel. "Handsome, brave, and quite stupid to seek the trouble you have found." She looked from Daniel to Jelani. "Have you nothing to say?"

"Can't think of anything," Jelani admitted. That drew soft laughter from those lips that were almost too thin, but not quite.

"Quite the candid one, aren't you?" She craned her head back and looked up at the sunlight flooding through the stained glass ceiling that enveloped the three of them.

"What I find curious is that you are not what could be considered remotely powerful yet you walk the day. I have seen a great many things in my centuries of life, but not once have I seen a *shaquora* daywalker."

"I've had a complicated year," Jelani said.

"Do tell."

"It's kind of a long story and this is a little uncomfortable," Jelani replied, looking down at himself with only his eyes." The invisible restraint was suddenly gone. Beside him, Daniel stumbled forward a step.

"Now you two be gentlemen and don't make me kill you right away. It's been a long life and a long time since I've heard a good story." She turned her back to them and moved across the courtyard. "Come."

"Would have thought that little command was an insult if you weren't here," Daniel muttered to Jelani.

"Turned vampires aren't thought more highly of than dogs, buddy," Jelani replied.

"No mumbling, boys," the woman said from farther ahead. "Your social statuses are meaningless to me."

They came to yet *another* tall set of double doors, this one with the depiction of three women facing and staring directly at the viewer. The one in the middle looked exactly like the woman they were following. The other two were obviously her sisters, given the resemblance.

They entered a room as large as a house, and beautifully furnished. It even had a second floor. Jelani looked around the room. *Must be nice*, he thought.

"I've almost forgotten my manners," the woman said, turning around. "I am Lemanda of the High Council of Elders."

An Elder? Jelani's blood went cold. An Elder of the High Council? How much worse could their luck possibly be?

When they didn't respond, she tapped her foot. "I'm sure you were raised to be more polite than this, boys. Must I ask your names?"

Beside him, Daniel seemed to come out of a trance. "Oh, sorry. I'm Daniel, of the … High House of Daniel."

"Jelani," Jelani said, casting his friend a "what the hell?" look.

The woman's eyebrows rose. "Jelani. So the catalyst actually found his way here?"

"Catalyst?" Jelani echoed. "What does that mean?"

Lemanda grinned at what must be some sort of private joke. "Who turned you from the light, child?"

I haven't been a child in over twenty years. "Remy," Jelani answered.

"I have a hard time with that answer," Lemanda replied. "Remy is, among other things, not powerful. A glimpse of the sun would see his lovely cremation."

That was interesting. Yet another person who seemed not to care for Remy. Given his experience with the Hunter, Jelani couldn't imagine that anyone liked him. "It's complicated," Jelani said. "You don't seem to be a friend to Remy."

"Oh? And why wouldn't I be?"

Careful, careful. "Your tone implies that he might have rubbed you the wrong way."

"You have supposedly been turned by him," Lemanda said, moving on. "You are bound to him in body and mind."

Jelani shrugged. "That's what everyone keeps telling me."

"And yet here you are, moving about in the day and walking in the sun while your re-creator sleeps." She still looked as if she would laugh. "This is deliciously humorous."

"Why's that?" Jelani asked.

"The mere fact that you have been moving about the coven of your own volition is proof enough that he has no hold over you," Lemanda explained. "The fact that you do not share his weakness to the sun says that there is more to this situation than his contribution to your immortality."

Jelani tried and failed to hold back his laughter. "Huh huh. Sounds kind of embarrassing for him."

"Indeed." She seemed to be enjoying this.

Ah, the hell with it. "You don't like that cat, do you?"

Lemanda tilted her head. "Cat?"

Jelani took a deep breath. "Sorry, slang. You aren't enamored of the gentleman named Remy, are you, milady?" Beside him, Daniel snorted.

Lemanda smiled at him. "Sarcasm despite your precarious situation. You possess an intrepidity that your re-creator lacks." She looked them over again. "Both of you have charm. I suspect you know this quality is what has preserved your lives to this point."

"Thank you," Jelani said.

"Thank you." Daniel said.

Lemanda did laugh this time; a soft, stately sound.

"You seem rather interested in my affiliation with Remy," Jelani ventured.

"You could say that." She arched an eyebrow at him, waiting.

"What my friend is trying to ask you," Daniel said, "is whether or not you like the man, because we want to kill him."

Jelani's eyes went wide and he looked over at Daniel, who continued to look at the woman.

Lemanda clapped her hands together. "You two are unusual indeed. Your reckless candor combined with your friend's animated response is lovely. Would that there was more time, I would be pleased to sit and talk." She moved closer to stand in front of Daniel, placing the tip of a finger under his chin.

"But the sun is soon to fall, and there is not much time." She slid the finger under his chin as she made her casual way to stand in front of Jelani. "No, I do not care for Remy. I assume you have entered the coven to remove him?"

"That would have been nice," Jelani said, "but he surrounds himself with protection we couldn't get through on our own, so we settled for taking out as many of his allies as we could before the real fun starts."

Lemanda's elegant lips parted. "Assassins, then." Her tone didn't sound particularly approving.

"Well," Jelani said, his mind racing. "The fewer people he has with him to cause trouble, the better. Am I wrong?"

"You have entered the coven of the High Council. No matter the circumstances, that is a deadly infraction."

"What better time to punish that infraction than now?" another woman's voice said from the doors behind them. "I cannot think of a worse crime than to …" the new arrival trailed off when she saw Jelani. Her composure slipped, but only for a fraction of a second.

"Now, this is a surprise," Alicia said, looking him over. "Imagine a fledgling that somehow survived a bath in the light of the sun now comes to my very coven." She stepped closer. "And you've brought a friend."

"*Your* coven," Lemanda said. "I wasn't unaware the coven rested under your solitary rule."

"You are unaware of a good many things, child," Alicia said dismissively. "We will address your shortcomings later."

"Perhaps you have forgotten yourself, *child*," Lemanda replied, "and mistakenly entered my domain when you sought another?"

Alicia eyed the other woman. Her smile dripped with venom. Jelani wished he could turn into mist and seep through the vents, like the fabled vampires. As things stood, however, he dared not move.

"Ah, Lemanda. You are one of the most powerful in the coven. Nearly as powerful as Vicken himself. I wonder how Stavros would react if he knew that you've been hiding your true potential all this time."

They watched as Lemanda studied the other Elder. She didn't seem like the type to be caught off guard, but there was no doubt that was what just happened.

"I find no reason to flaunt my attributes," Lemanda replied. "Perhaps there is a lesson in that for those who have years yet to live and learn."

"Oh, indeed," Alicia said. "But you have it in reverse. How many centuries have you played at immortality? Seven, eight?" Her patronising smile suggested an adult patting a young girl on the head. "Less than a thousand years of life and you think to speak on my level?"

"I was unaware you were given to nonsense, Alicia," Lemanda said. "You would think to tell me that you have lived so long?"

"So long and longer, girl," Alicia said. "You know nothing. Your precious High Council of children knows nothing. I am long past bored of watching the lot of you play at authority. Your foolishness mocks the immortals."

"Has some illness taken hold of your mind, Alicia?" Lemanda, whose arms were crossed, came down to her sides.

"Generations of purebloods and *shaquora*, and with each generation, the knowledge of your betters falls farther away."

"Perhaps we can speak again when you have tired of speaking

nonsense," Lemanda said. "What you imply borders on blasphemy."

"Spoken like a human who worships those who do great things."

Lemanda's red eyes smoldered with anger. "You offer insult in my own domain?"

"I offer uncreation in your own domain," Alicia said in a dangerously even tone."

"Such awful manners," a third woman's voice said.

Jelani's mouth fell open and he looked at Daniel, who looked equally dumbfounded. Saaya? Who was going to show up next, Dracula?

"And, the most infantile of us has arrived." Despite the other two obviously powerful women in the room, Alicia actually looked amused. "Not many have a second chance with me. I'd have thought you smarter."

"Alicia," Lemanda said. "Leave my room. Immediately."

Alicia slowly turned her head to regard the other Elder, practically ignoring Saaya. "What would you do, Lemanda? Challenge me? To what end?"

"I would no sooner tolerate this disrespect than you would were the circumstances reversed. Do not force me remove you myself—"

"Please, be silent."

The sound of a loud smack cracked the silence and Lemanda's head snapped sideways. She placed a hand to her cheek and turned an incredulous look on Alicia. No, not incredulous. Confused.

Jelani's hands itched to grab his weapons, but he remained perfectly still. He glanced at Daniel and saw his friend studying each of the women. He was trying to figure out who he should attack. His eyes kept settling on Alicia. Good choice. They might not know Lemanda's intentions, but their chances of survival with her were much higher.

"That line of thought will kill you, little boy," Alicia said, looking at Jelani.

Great! She can friggin read minds?

Alicia smiled at him and turned back to Lemanda, whose fangs were bared. "The High Council cannot protect you from me in here," she said. "I will end your delusions now."

A glimmer flashed across Lemanda's eyes, and Alicia's arms suddenly pressed tight to her sides. She approached, nails elongated, and drew her hand back. She whipped it at the other woman's face, or tried to. Her hand stopped before it came close to Alicia's smiling face. "Your obliviousness will kill you that much faster, Lemanda."

Lemanda's eyes went wide when Alicia's body relaxed.

"A shame. I actually disliked you the least. I had even considered taking you under my guidance once the others were set aside."

"Traitor to the coven," Lemanda growled.

"Save the theatrics. This is your final moment of life ..." Alicia trailed off and looked over her shoulder at Saaya. "Must you, too, persist with this nonsense?"

Jelani looked at the *dampeal*, who was concentrating on the Elder. After a few heartbeats, Saaya blinked in surprise. Whatever she had been trying to do had failed.

Alicia smiled at her. "You are strong, even for a *dampeal*." Suddenly, both Lemanda and Saaya's bodies went taut.

Behind her, Lemanda blinked in surprise, then glanced at Jelani as though she had puzzled something out.

Alicia walked over to Jelani. Did she know he was unrestrained?

"Do you think you could move fast enough?" she asked him.

Dammit! I wish she'd quit doing that!

Alicia laughed. "Then do not make it so easy. Your mind is untrained." She walked a circle around him, practically ignoring Daniel. "I send a newly turned vampire hurtling over the rail of a balcony into the sun, only to find him here in my own coven," she said again. "I admit that before our little exotic flower here arrived," she nodded toward Saaya, who glowered at her, "I would have thought you were fresh out of vampiric lore." When she saw no comprehension from Jelani, she continued.

"Of course you wouldn't know about that yet. You're too new." She patted him on the cheek and he managed not to flinch.

"Relax, boy. I'm not going to kill you yet. There is still time left before the rest of the coven awakens. You see, when a vampire dies by the removal of something vital, such as a head or heart, they die. If one is fast enough though, the effect can be reversed."

"But when a vampire dies by sunlight or silver, death is final. In our lore, however, the exception is when a vampire manages to return from final death. They are referred to as Revenants in your language, but in the Romanian language, which is a derivative of our own vampiric tongue, Revenire would be the appropriate word." She waved her hand out, likely indicating Sinaia, which lay in that direction.

"That entire little city of mortals thinks of every last one of us as Revenire, walking amongst them in unholy unlife. Ignorant cattle one and all, scurrying the streets kissing those worthless talismans hanging from their necks."

Jelani couldn't resist the urge to speak up. "You have to admit that it's an easy conclusion to come to. A person with white, or glow in the dark eyes and fangs, trying to kill you and who is vulnerable to the sun? I'd say that's fair."

"Spoken like a true *shaquora*—"

"That can relate to what it's like to encounter one of you," Jelani interrupted.

Alicia looked at Lemanda. "This one is quite willful."

From the other side of the room, Saaya shot Jelani a warning look. Through their bond came the clear feeling that he was treading dangerously.

The powerful Elder turned back toward Jelani. "Do you know what is ironic, fledgling? Mortals view us as demons, pets of their satan, yet in the world's history we have done far less damage. Human lore has depicted us from mindless blood drinking zombies to near-humans, who can only function amongst them until even the slightest smell of blood reaches our noses. The closest any of them have come to the truth is the semi modern depictions of Dracula, who was indeed real, I assure you."

She laughed at the disbelief on Jelani's face. "Oh yes, he was very real, and very powerful. His mistake was his desire to live harmoniously with humans, the very animals on which he must feed. Unfortunately there were no such things as blood banks as we have in this modern world." She wrinkled her nose. "Which still is not the most attractive substitute, I might add."

She turned away from him. "And that is a discussion that would take more time than any of your current lifespans."

Jelani cried out as he felt a powerful will closing in. It felt like the weight of a mountain gradually crushing him. Beside him, Daniel was suffering the same pain. Through the agony, Jelani felt a tiny sliver of Saaya in his mind, struggling to grab hold of him, like a beacon of light in darkness. He struggled to grab hold of it and the pain lessened a bit. It was enough relief for him to open his eyes.

He saw Saaya, rigid as stone, staring into the eyes of Alicia while Lemanda, off to the side, stood in a similar restrained stance. There was some unseen struggle happening between them.

Lemanda suddenly screamed and flew across the room. She hit the pillar under the spiraling stairs and landed in a heap on the floor.

"Your strength surprises me, little half-breed," Alicia said.

"You'll find me more formidable when you've not caught me off guard," Saaya replied.

Alicia's eyes narrowed, and Jelani felt the vice on his body slacken a little more. Beside him, Daniel gasped.

On the other side of the room, Lemanda lifted her head. She turned a baleful glare on Alicia.

The Elder smiled at the comment. "Your human blood blinds you."

The crushing force suddenly fell away, then an invisible force slammed into Jelani, throwing him, Daniel, and Saaya across the room. Jelani crashed into the wall next to Daniel.

"Who *is* that?" Daniel whispered. "How can she be that strong?"

"She is an Elder," Jelani answered, standing. He slipped his hands behind his back, waiting.

"Elder indeed," Alicia replied, not even bothering to look over her shoulder. Her tone was still amused. "I suppose I shouldn't be surprised at your ignorance. We find mingling with you children distasteful enough for us to recede into myth."

"Myth?" Jelani said. Then his eyes widened. "No friggin way!"

Alicia laughed. "I like you." She walked toward Saaya, who struggled to stand. "Perhaps when I eliminate your little companion here, I will make some use of you."

Perhaps not. Jelani's hands whipped out and two silver daggers went spinning across the room … and flew wide as soon as they were within a few feet of the woman.

"That was not an intelligent thing to do," Alicia hissed. The crushing power of her will brought Jelani to his knees just as two more silver daggers went spinning past him. The force dropped away as Alicia spun and swiped her hand across her body. The daggers flew safely aside.

Saaya came gliding from behind, clawed hand arched back for a killing stroke.

Alicia spun toward her, swinging her arm out wide. The *dampeal* flew aside. The Elder continued her turn, thrusting her hand forward in Jelani and Daniel's direction. They lifted up and crashed into the wall with such force, they went through it and into the courtyard.

Lemanda was back on her feet. "I'm going to kill you, Alicia."

"Sure you are," Alicia replied. Lemanda staggered back, but

snarled and took a step forward.

Now Alicia stumbled back when Lemanda hit her with her will. "Impressive." She smirked up at the second floor of the room. A large piece of the second floor cracked and fell over Lemanda's head. The Elder spun away from the falling debris and leaped across the room at Alicia.

With a casual wave of her hand, Alicia sent Lemanda flying aside to crash into the wall. As soon as she hit, Lemanda was back on her feet. Behind Alicia, Saaya stood.

Alicia's narrow-eyed smile seemed to cut right through the other Elder. She glanced over her shoulder at Saaya, her crimson smile deepening. "Come, then."

The Lemanda and the *dampeal* flew at Alicia, slashing and stabbing with elongated nails. Alicia laughed as she avoided every razor-like claw, every lunge, every slash. After several moments of the dizzying dance, Alicia threw her arms out wide, and Lemanda and Saaya were thrown away.

Jelani heard Saaya cry out, and through their connection, he felt her pain. Rage took him. His fingers curled as his nails elongated, and he let out an angry hiss as his fangs extended.

He didn't run back into the room, but ran along the side of the wall toward the front door nearest the Elder. A dozen feet from the doors, Jelani stopped and leaped forward, crashing through solid stone. Beside him was another explosion of rubble, as Daniel, transforming midair, flew past him.

Alicia swiped her arm to the side and knocked away the giant black wolf that was Daniel. Jelani swiped a clawed hand at Alicia but she stopped him short. Alicia sent him flying into another wall, then his body lifted into the air and was sent flying into yet another wall, then crashing into the ceiling where he remained.

From his overhead vantage, Jelani saw Saaya score a glancing blow on Alicia's face, but the woman shrugged it off and slapped her so hard she went spinning across the room.

Lemanda launched herself at Alicia. They appeared to be

fighting with their will as well as their hands, for both women stumbled back even though neither had scored a physical blow. Lemanda brought her hand around toward Alicia's face, but it stopped and started to tremble.

There was a loud crack, and Lemanda screamed when her forearm bent backward. She flew away from Alicia, who was then knocked across the room by the giant black wolf. Daniel didn't stop. He bounded after the flying Elder and bit down on the woman's shoulder.

The force binding him was suddenly gone, and the floor rushed up to meet Jelani. He righted himself and landed on his feet from the twenty-foot drop. He snapped two more daggers out of the sheathes on his legs and sent them spinning at the Elder, who had the lupine Daniel by the throat. She leaned away from one, but the other struck her in the arm.

Alicia gasped and hurled the black wolf—over twice her size— aside as though he were nothing. She met Jelani's eyes, and he felt her in his head, crushing his mind. It was worse than any physical attack. She would completely destroy him from the inside, and there was nothing he could do to fight it.

Saaya's presence was there, like a barrier erected between his mind and the impossibly powerful woman's. The mental assault was gone and he fell to his knees, gasping.

"Ah, love," Alicia said to Saaya. "I almost regret that you'll not live to know your folly in falling in love, particularly with a former human."

"How lucky am I, to receive such wisdom from yourself," Saaya replied.

Alicia shrugged. "As you wish." She knocked Saaya away with her mind, but the *dampeal* came back to her feet and similarly hit Alicia. The Elder stopped midair, inches from the wall, and her feet slowly touched the floor.

"Powerful little girl," Alicia said, all the amusement gone from her voice. "It's time you know what true power is."

CHAPTER 50

How long had they been fighting this woman? Half an hour? An hour? Jelani climbed back to his feet yet again. *I've had my fill of being knocked around this room.*

Jelani had felt Yako's power when the Eldest Hunter had rendered him helpless on more than one occasion. He'd felt Saaya's power more times than he could count, and it eclipsed Yako's exponentially. This woman was so far beyond anything he'd felt that he wasn't sure she couldn't kill all of them by herself.

Saaya's angry lavender eyes glowed as she squared off with Alicia. Jelani had never seen the *dampeal* look so beautiful and deadly at the same time. Several dozen feet across from her, Alicia, standing tall and regal, concentrated. Jelani could practically feel the invisible energy crackling between them.

A line of sweat trickled down Saaya's face. Jelani looked at Alicia, who was clearly exerting effort, but remained calm and relaxed. She was too powerful.

Jelani drew his last two daggers and let fly. To his surprise, two more daggers zipped across the room from the left. Daniel, now back in his human form, crouched low to the ground. He looked at Jelani and nodded.

The four daggers flew toward the Elder's back, and without looking, Alicia half turned and threw her arm out. Three of the four daggers flew wide. Saaya shouted, knocking Alicia in line with the fourth dagger. The Elder screamed when the silver blade sank into the middle of her back.

Jelani let out a relieved breath. A knife right there would take the silver only seconds to burn the woman from the inside out.

Saaya leaped across the thirty-foot distance and slammed into the woman. She slashed Alicia across the face and drove her knee into the Elder's face.

Jelani winced. It seemed like overkill, since the woman was already dying, but Saaya drew back her hands, aimed her elongated claws, and stabbed repeatedly, driving them into Alicia's stomach and chest.

Daniel and Lemanda were closing in on the two women, and Jelani trotted over as well. Just as he reached them, a force so powerful he could feel the anger in it launched everyone in the room away. They crashed into the walls in opposite sides of the room.

Alicia, who had been kneeling, rose to her feet. She glared murderously at Jelani, then at Saaya. Her fangs slid down between her lips, her eyes glowed like flames dancing in their sockets. The woman pointed at Saaya, then turned her hand, palm facing upward. Saaya's body lifted into the air.

The angry Elder turned her hand out and pushed, launching Saaya into the wall. Alicia pulled her hand in, then pushed out again, and Saaya floated forward, then slammed back into the wall.

Over and over, the Elder pounded Saaya into the wall, and the force that held Jelani in place ensured there was nothing he could do about it.

Alicia looked to the side at the scattered silver daggers on the floor and one by one, four of them lifted into the air and turned toward the helpless *dampeal*. Jelani yelled, struggling against the invisible force. He couldn't move, no matter how much he struggled, no matter how tightly his muscles strained. He was helpless.

The Elder slammed Saaya against the wall again, then swung her other arm in the direction of the *dampeal*. The four silver daggers raced through the air and punched into Saaya's body. Her deafening scream shattered every mirror and glass in the room.

Her scream was answered.

A tall figure fell through the shattered glass in the ceiling, sword sliding from the sheath on his back. He brought the sword down and it stopped, inches from Alicia's face.

Alicia moved away. "This keeps getting more interesting," she hissed. "But I've no time to play, any longer."

The instant Kafeel broke Alicia's invisible bindings, she leaped away. Gliding backwards and leaning away from the intimidating man, she looked over at Lemanda who had managed to break her hold. Alicia gently waved a hand in her direction. Lemanda burst into flames.

Jelani gritted his teeth at the sight of the burning woman, her screams were almost as loud as Saaya's. How could anyone be this powerful?

Alicia's feet touched the ground and she leaped backward again, this time high into the air. Kafeel was right there, leaping after her. He brought his sword around and Alicia stopped it, not with the force of her will this time, but with what looked to be a forearm made of granite. She thrust her hand out and sent Kafeel flying away.

He landed on his feet and leaped forward, closing the distance just as Alicia touched the ground. Even with his enhanced vision, Jelani had trouble following the speed that the two moved. Kafeel's sword was a silver extension of his arms, and both were blur of movement equalled only by the woman he sought to cut down.

Kafeel managed to score a knick on the side of Alicia's cheek. She hissed and threw her arm out wide. Kafeel's sword tore from his grasp, and Alicia thrust her hand out. She launched the towering man across the room to slam into the pillar holding up the second floor. The sound of groaning wood and cracking stone was the only warning before a large piece of the second floor came crashing down.

Alicia pulled her left arm back toward her body just as she reached her right hand out. Kafeel's body burst out of the rubble and flew forward to meet his sword, midair, in a deadly embrace.

Jelani's mouth dropped. For several seconds everything stopped and all that could be heard was the crackling sounds of what was certainly a burned to death Lemanda. Kafeel hung limply over the floor, the hilt of his sword pressed against his chest, the length of the blade protruding from the center of his upper back. Finally, Alicia let her hand drop, and he fell to the floor.

On his feet.

Kafeel ripped the sword from his chest as he leaped across the room. He scored a cut alongside the retreating Alicia's arm, then kicked out, connecting with her midsection. The woman hissed, but it was cut short when Kafeel's sword found her abdomen.

The long silver blade dove deep into her stomach and came out her lower back. Then Kafeel ripped the sword free and swiped his arm wide, sending the woman flying across the room. As soon as Alicia's back hit the wall, Kafeel was there, driving his sword through her chest.

Kafeel growled, pushing the blade deeper, through flesh, bone, and cold stone.

Alicia gasped, then screamed again and pushed forward with both her hands.

Kafeel was thrown back but he held on to his sword. It ripped from her chest in a splash of blood. He hit the wall and hung suspended several feet from the ground.

"Your death will come only after I have completed your evisceration," the woman hissed.

Kafeel squinted his eyes closed, then suddenly dropped to the floor.

Alicia gasped in surprise, then whipped both her arms to the side, diverting the towering man as he sped toward her, sword angled for her heart.

He skidded to the side and flew across the room, and Alicia leaped backward, fading from view.

As soon as his feet touched the ground Kafeel sprang back toward the woman and he too, faded from view.

The force that bound Jelani dissipated, and he was across the room in a second, gingerly pulling the silver daggers free from Saaya's body. To his surprise and relief, she was alive, but groaned in pain with each blade he pulled out of her body.

Daniel was at his side. "I can't believe she survived that."

"I'm a little more durable than you would believe, love," Saaya groaned, climbing to her knees.

They heard shuffling from across the room, and everyone looked up to see what looked like a charred corpse rising out of the rubble.

"Damn," Daniel said, frowning in disbelief. "I guess it's true what they say. Women really do have a high tolerance for pain." And then he bounded across the room, carefully taking Lemanda by the arm and helping her rise.

"I imagine we've woken the entire coven with all that noise," Jelani said, looking up at the waning light.

"The sun retreats," Saaya confirmed. "All will awaken soon."

"I appreciate your concern," they heard Lemanda saying from across the room. "But it is less painful if you are not touching me."

"Oh, yes ma'am," Daniel released her.

""You have surprising etiquette, for a lycan," the woman croaked. Charred black flakes of skin fell from her body to reveal fresh pink skin underneath. She squinted through what must have been a great deal of agony as her body regenerated.

"It's the way I was raised," Daniel said, stepping back.

"You're a good boy," Lemanda groaned, managing a bit of humor in her voice. Ten minutes later, she looked no worse for wear than before the fight had started, aside from the wisps of charred clothing falling from her body.

Daniel and Jelani quickly averted their eyes, and Lemanda laughed. "Boys, either I should be amused at your chivalry, or insulted that you find me so repulsive. When Daniel's face colored, she laughed again. "I will take that as a sign of the former. I thank you for respecting the modesty, of a woman many centuries your senior."

Centuries or not, Jelani thought, *the woman's got a bangin' body.* He felt the mental equivalent of the question "is that so?" in his mind, and looked down to see Saaya's eyebrow arched. He shrugged helplessly. "I'd be lying if I said it wasn't true. It's not like I'm going to run over and tackle her into a bed or anything."

"That would be interesting," Lemanda's voice said into his ear, causing him to jump. Both the Elder and Saaya tittered.

Jelani looked in confusion from one woman to the other. *Guess I need a few hundred more years behind me to understand this.* The feeling he received through his bond with Saaya said that that was exactly the case.

"So, if we're done laughing at Jelani," Jelani said, "can either of you brief myself and my friend here," he indicated Daniel, "about what all that was?"

"*That* was Alicia," Lemanda said. "She is also a member of the High Council of Elders, and many times more powerful than I could have imagined. The things she did in this room are known to few of us and are considered fictitious to most. She also has sided with Massius in his foolish insurrection."

"Maybe not so foolish, considering what that woman almost did to us," Daniel said.

Lemanda nodded in agreement then looked at Saaya. "It seems your savior was a match for her. I cannot deny my surprise that one as young as yourself and he could so effectively battle such a powerful Elder."

Saaya frowned, her thoughts seeming far away. "This is unusual," she said. "I cannot recall ever hearing about such an encounter."

"Of course not," Lemanda said. "*Dampeal* or not, you are little older than a century, probably half that."

"Yes," Saaya agreed, "but my savior, my brother, is more experienced."

"He is little older than you," Lemanda said. "No more than a century or two."

"But he is the same as her," Saaya replied.

Lemanda looked disbelievingly at her. "That is impossible. He cannot be an Elder at such a young age."

Saaya climbed to her feet and looked up at Lemanda, the top of her head barely reaching the taller woman's shoulders. "Like her, he is not an Elder," she said, and her next words seemed to darken the room. "Kafeel is an *Ancestor.*"

CHAPTER 51

With the suddenness of the blink of an eye, Yako came awake. He opened his eyes and looked over the edge of the narrow protrusion of the wall upon which he'd slept.

Below, his unit of Hunters were still asleep. All but Mariska, though she lie on her back as if she were asleep. The Second Hunter opened her eyes and immediately found his. He nodded and she rose and moved to the locked door at the end of the room. Yako watched her and experienced a feeling he had never felt before. Pride.

The Second Hunter remained by the door, waiting patiently. He slipped over the edge of the protrusion and dropped nearly forty feet to the floor, then moved to the other side of the door. Mariska looked at him for one last confirmation, then unlocked the door and opened it just enough for Yako to see outside.

He remained where he was and listened. He heard the breathing and heartbeats of the lycans Darren had sent. He nodded at Mariska again, and the woman pulled the door open a little more for Yako to slip out. The Eldest Hunter moved through the rooms silently, knowing that his Second was making her way around the opposite side of each room.

Though the sun had not yet fully descended below the western horizon, the rooms and halls the two vampires navigated had windows that faced east, and they were able to safely make their way through the darkened halls. Still, they were careful.

Before entering every room or hallway they scanned the area with their eyes, remaining perfectly still. Unlike any other vampire or lycan, or human, Denari and Tannis were impossible to detect. Though vampires did not breathe as often as a mortal, and had infrequently beating hearts, the two Reapers seemed to do so even less. Or perhaps they didn't breathe at all. Perhaps their hearts rested still in their chests.

Yako had considered the possibilities before lying down to sleep the previous night, and now those thoughts were in the back of his mind as he focused on the task before him.

As silent as the night itself, the Eldest and Second Hunter passed through every east-facing room, scanning for the presence of The Wraiths. After last night's encounter, Yako had to agree with the nickname placed on the two Reapers. They seemed not at all alive, and very dangerous.

He glanced down at the hole in the lower right side of his black, fitted top. The hole left by the pure silver blade of Denari's scythe that had nearly ended Yako's existence. The wound still hurt, but it was almost healed.

Room after room they checked until they were reasonably certain the area was secure. They came to the front doors of the casino-turned-political-meetingplace, and waited the final half hour for the sun to dip safely below the horizon.

Yako looked to a dark recess across the room. "You are sure Marcos De La Vega is awake?"

"He is awake and in his concealed location, guarding the others," Tara replied, stepping out of the darkness. "Meilana has informed me from her position that he guards the others with her, each hidden on either side."

"We must leave quickly," Yako said, impatience clear in his voice.

"I understand your frustration, Eldest Hunter," Tara said. "I too would have liked nothing more than to creep into the coven just before sundown and exterminate every one of those traitors before they awaken, but the wounds we've all suffered from those two monstrosities are slow to heal."

Yako still felt the burning truth of that statement in his lower right side. "We will gather our lycan allies and depart immediately. I would not have those two find us here and discover our secret."

"I could not agree more," Tara said. "I can't think of a worse situation than passing through the underground tunnels with those freaks tailing us."

"The sun flees," Mariska said.

"Bring them," Yako replied, and the Second Hunter opened one of the doors and slipped out.

"All things considered, we were lucky," Tara said as they waited. "We lost two good Hunters, but only two."

"Yes."

"So chipper," Tara remarked.

Silence.

Tara studied him. "Sometimes I wonder if your heart is as still as The Wraiths' seem to be."

Yako looked questioningly at her.

"You seem not to feel at all," she continued. "We may not be prone to the extremities of the emotional spectrum that humans are, but we still feel. Were you born with a deficiency in this, Eldest?"

"If ever the luxury is available to me," Yako responded, glancing out the window, "perhaps I may indulge."

Tara snorted. "Don't try that with me, Yako. Feelings and emotions are not a luxury, they are a part of life, mortal or immortal. Some, typically the warrior type, often consider them to be weaknesses or a hindrance." She looked pointedly at him.

"They're coming," Yako said, turning to leave.

Tara smiled. "Very well, Eldest. But remember the definition of life and whether or not you are living it more than existing around it."

ॐ

TARA LED them to a room at the back of the casino and stopped at what looked to be just another part of the wall. The Reaper touched the corner seam where the front and side walls met. She ran her hand down the seam and pressed her finger into a tiny indentation. It slid inward less than an inch, and a thin section of the wall separated.

"Here we go," she said, and slipped through the opening.

Mariska went in next, followed by one of their lycan allies, who was then followed by Lydia. The stocky woman had a bit of trouble slipping through, but managed, and was followed by Marcos De La Vega, another lycan right behind him. One after another, vampire and lycan slipped through the opening until only Yako remained. He scanned the room one last time, then finally backed in and slid the wall shut behind him.

He turned to face the pitch-black corridor when two flashlights came on. Two of Darren's men held them shining into the darkness beyond.

"Are lycans unable to see in the dark?" Yako asked.

"We see just as fine as you," one of them replied, a gruff and burly male with a shock of dusty blond hair that hung just below his shoulders. "Just thought it might be good to walk through all this with some light. Make things easier."

Yako looked at Tara. The Reaper nodded back, an indication that she passed command to him.

"Extinguish it," Yako ordered. "We move in darkness."

"Damn ghoul," the man grumbled, but he and his companion switched the flashlights off.

Yako pointed at the grumbling werewolf. "I will have you at

point, with me. He pointed at Lydia and two of the other eight lycans Darren had sent. The numbers would have been even, had Tannis and Denari not trimmed his ranks. "You three are behind us, and I want four of you at the rear with the Reaper and Second Hunter." He looked at Reed. "You are in the middle." He pointed at the last two lycans. "You two as well."

"Please, if I may speak, Eldest?" Reed asked.

Yako nodded.

"I would be best put to use in the rear with the others. I have a sense for danger."

"You mean a sense for avoiding it," Marcos said, earning a chorus of chuckling from several others.

Reed ignored them. "Eldest Hunter, I know where I can be the most effective. I'm smaller than almost everyone here with the exception of our honorable Reaper Tara." He bowed to the woman. "In the middle of the group I can do nothing. In the back, I can be of greater use if danger follows."

"No one knows about this passage, young Hunter," Tara said, but she looked at Yako and shrugged.

"Very well, Reed." Yako took a step forward so that he was inches in front of the young man. "Earn it," he said, and the look on Reed's face said that he understood those two words. He nodded and moved to the back of the group. Yako watched him go. The boy showed promise, and the Eldest Hunter hoped the boy would earn his rank, and his life. He turned to face the dark tunnels ahead. "We move."

HIGH ABOVE THE floor of the hall where the group had passed, two sets of glowing red slits split the darkness.

CHAPTER 52

The tunnels stretching underneath the city of Sinaia were dank, and dark as pitch. The motley group passed silently from passage to passage with Yako, two lycans—Yako having changed his mind and thought it better to put the burly leader of the wolf group to the back—and Tara at the front, the latter of which had taken the lead again and guided their path.

"The boy keeps close to the big one," Tara whispered to Yako.

He nodded. Tara and her sister were invaluable with the connection they shared. If Reed proved to be a coward or treacherous, Meilana would deal with him.

"I didn't know you bloods had so many inside problems," one of the lycans beside Tara remarked. "The way you all give off the impression of being so perfect, I would never have guessed."

"Then, you would be naive, lycan," Tara said. "No civilization is immune to such things."

The man snorted. "Lycans stick together. The pack always looks out for itself."

"Hence the necessity for the extermination of the Woodland Pack and the occasional challenge by an upstart male against the alpha?" Tara replied.

"That's different. If the alpha isn't strong enough to lead, he isn't fit to do so. And that Woodland Pack was a bunch of traitors to our species."

"Much like the traitors we will exterminate," Yako said, his quiet voice laying a chilling pall over the conversation. He glanced at the one who had spoken. "What is the name of the one who leads your group with us?"

"Rickland," the lycan answered. "Why?"

Yako didn't bother to answer. "Reaper," he addressed Tara, "we should curtail conversation."

"Knowledge of these tunnels is not widespread, Eldest Hunter," Tara replied.

"That brings me little comfort," the lycan closest to Yako said.

They came to a junction and Tara stepped forward, paused for a moment, then took the right passage. "This will travel uphill a bit, then bend back toward the castle."

The group went silent after that, and Yako kept his senses sharp. He didn't know what lay before or behind them, but experience told him this would not be a simple path to their destination.

REED HUNG to the back of the group. The rough and unkept blond lycanthrope walking next to him kept grumbling to himself about elitist bloods, but he ignored him and focused on the path behind. A few steps in front of him was the twin of that Reaper. Reed had no illusions about his status in the group. He had managed to survive The Wraiths' attack despite being the weakest of the group, finally appearing after the action was done. He was just a survivor. He had always been that way.

He fell a few steps back, concentrating on the darkness. When he turned back, he saw Meilana just ahead. "Making sure I don't take off?" he asked her.

"What do you think?" she asked.

"That you'll try to kill me if I try to take off."

"No. I'm not going to try to kill you if you run. I *will* kill you if you run."

Reed chuckled. "Guess I can't really argue with that."

"You don't seem unnerved about it," she observed.

"That's because I'm not planning to run away," Reed said. "Just because I haven't proven myself yet doesn't mean I don't intend to."

"With all respect, Hunters," Rickland said, "you two mind keeping a lid on it? Even whispering, whatever's down here will hear us."

Meilana scowled at the lycan, but went quiet. Reed wasn't bothered. The man was right.

The group moved silently through the darkness of the underground tunnels, and with each minute that passed, Reed's sense of dread deepened. Vampires didn't typically fear anything, and he was sure lycans were the same. But those two things they'd fought the night before had put fear into him. They didn't move right, and they had an "off" presence.

"Something's wrong," Rickland said.

"Your nose is better than ours, lycan," Meilana replied. "What do you smell?"

"Other than the general smell of these tunnels, nothing," he replied. "That's the problem. I don't smell anything, but I can feel it." As if to punctuate the point, the hairs on the back of his neck stood on end. "Something's down here with us and we ain't getting much farther without meeting it."

Meilana and Reed shared a look. When Darren's wolves had joined with them at the Casino, Yako had only told them that they were being pursued by dangerous enemies. Reapers. He had spoken nothing of their nature. That Rickland felt a danger he could not smell put Reed on edge.

"Should we tighten the group or fall back?" Reed asked.

"Don't be a fool," Meilana said. "Your determination to show your worth will only get you needlessly killed."

"I could hide and wait for them to pass—"

"And do what, exactly?" Meilana asked.

The memory of Yako nursing the wounds he'd suffered from his fight with just one of those Reapers killed any scenario Reed might have thought up.

"They're getting closer," Rickland whispered.

"Are you sure?" Meilana said. "You still smell nothing?"

The lycan nodded, still focused on the darkness behind. Meilana frowned, but continued forward.

"Darren said to do what your Eldest Hunter says," Rickland said after a few minutes. "Do we run or fight?"

"Someone will have to ask him," she replied, but made no move to do so. "Reed," she said. "Come."

I'm not the dog, here, he thought, but kept it to himself. He reached her just as they came to yet another junction. She nodded in the direction of the tunnel beside the one the group was passing through, and he nodded back. She then moved right up beside Rickland and placed a hand on his shoulder. He visibly tensed at the contact.

She leaned up to his ear and whispered so softly Reed wouldn't have heard if he wasn't listening. After a moment, the gruff lycan gave a curt nod and continued on.

Meilana and Reed fell back and took the tunnel on the right. Luck was with them, for there was actually a ladder against the wall, and a drain almost right beneath it. She pointed at the drain and then climbed the ladder. *Of course I have to take the low one*, Reed thought, slipping down.

Minutes passed, and Reed glanced up at Meilana, who looked back down at him from her hidden position. She shrugged but remained where she was. Several more minutes passed and just when Reed was beginning to think nothing was there, a feeling of dread settled over him. His head snapped up at Meilana, but her questioning look said that she hadn't felt anything.

Maybe I am *a coward,* Reed thought just as a cloaked figure rounded the bend. Reed ducked a little lower, barely peeking over the top. Just as before, the only thing visible was the cloak that the Reaper wore, and the double-bladed scythe he carried. After pausing only a moment at the split, he continued on in the direction the others had gone. Reed frowned, watching that almost drifting gait. It was like watching the Grim Reaper itself slithering on two feet and barely touching the ground with each step. However unnatural vampires might seem to humans, that Reaper seemed equally unnatural to Reed.

They waited a while longer, expecting to see the other one, but he didn't appear. *Took a roundabout path, I bet!* Reed looked back up at Meilana and saw the same realization dawning on the other Hunter's face when her mouth tightened. For a moment her face took on a distant look, eyes seeming to go out of focus. Then she looked back down at Reed and nodded. She dropped from the ladder just as Reed leaped out of the drain. They touched down and sped after their pursuer.

YAKO KNEW by the look on Tara's face what she was about to say before she said it. The woman had obviously received contact from her sister. The short Reaper grabbed his elbow and pulled him down so that she could whisper in his ear. "We are followed by one."

Yako looked at her, then looked ahead. "We are not alone," he said quietly to the group. The Hunters visibly stiffened, but the lycans in the group seemed not at all surprised. They had been on their guard for a while now, no doubt sensing the danger some time ago.

"How could they have found us?" Lydia asked, drawing her axes.

"Have you forgotten our first encounter?" came the sarcastic reply from Marcos. "I don't expect we could have eluded them for long."

"Then, they can die and be forgotten down here," Lydia replied.

Marcos just grunted in response.

Yako hoped the woman wouldn't be so foolish as to try to challenge one of the Wraiths on her own. She would most certainly die.

"Move," he said, quickening his pace. "You two." He pointed at the lycans at his and Tara's sides. "Stay with us."

"We can't smell them," the one closest to Yako said. "I don't understand it."

Yako had his own suspicions why the lycans couldn't smell these particular vampires. "You can sense them, while we can't."

"So, we're running from our enemy, then?" one of the werewolves in the middle of the group asked, a hint of displeasure in his voice.

"No," his comrade said. "We're running toward it."

"Toward—"

"Be silent," Tara said. "They know we're here but there's no need to broadcast it."

The lycans grumbled but complied.

"How could one of them have gotten around us so fast?" Tara whispered to Yako. "We've been moving quickly down here."

"To get around us they would have to know which paths we've taken," Yako replied.

"Do you suggest they knew about these tunnels?" she asked.

"If they did, we would have encountered them shortly after our entrance," Yako replied.

"They followed us in?" Tara frowned. "Again, how did one of them get around us? I know of no immortal that could do such a thing."

"They are no immortals," Yako said.

"They are as much a part of our history as you or I," Tara said. "How can they not be immortals?"

"The definition requires one to actually live," Yako said.

"It's about to get ugly," one of the lycans said. "I can feel whatever it is ahead of us getting closer." He glanced over his shoulder at Yako. "You sure all of us should be worried about only one or two of—"

The sound of a blade slicing through the air cut off his last sentence. A loud thud echoed down the circular tunnels when his head hit the ground.

"Holy shit!" the other lycan yelled, leaping back.

Yako drew his sword just in time to knock the scythe aside as it came for the middle of his face. He fell back a step and came into a defensive stance. Beside him, Tara swore, taking a low stance, twin scythes spinning in her hands.

The cloaked figure lay against the ceiling of the tunnel, though there was nothing to hold onto. It dropped from the ceiling and came upright, gliding to the floor.

"I'm sure that is quite impossible," Tara said, moving a little to the side.

"Eeeldeeest," the Reaper hissed. Denari.

Yako stared at the cloaked figure. "I have no quarrel with you, Reaper."

Tara glanced at him. "You don't suffer from over politeness or anything, do you?"

Yako ignored the sarcasm, but Denari answered her.

"He dooooes. And he'll suffer moooore at the haaands, of Denari."

"Yeah, okay," the lycan to Tara's right said. "Whatever that is, it's creeping me the hell out."

The Reaper took a step toward them. The others retreated a step, but Yako remained where he was.

Denari pointed at him. *"You will not elude your uncreatiooon Eeeeeeldeeest."*

Yako's eyes smoldered.

The Reaper's red eyes narrowed into glowing slits. *"You know what I come fooor, Eeeldeeest."*

Yako's eyes narrowed further as he stepped forward to meet his foe. He spoke a word. "Messatsu."

REED AND MEILANA followed as closely as they dared. There was definitely something off about that Reaper. The way he moved, the very presence about him was just wrong. Not wrong, Reed decided. Unnatural.

Beside him, Meilana's eyes widened.

Reed cast her a questioning look, but she just shook her head and waved for him to speed up. They crept through the tunnels, keeping the cloaked Reaper just in view. Not much time passed, however, when they heard the sounds of metal clashing with metal. The fighting had already started. Reed drew his silenced 9mm and aimed at the center of the Reaper's exposed back.

When the rest of the group came into view he fired a single shot, not wanting to chance hitting the others.

The Reaper swung his scythe at the nearest lycan who was barely fast enough to duck the attack. He continued the motion but flipped the head of the weapon around and knocked the speeding bullet out of the air. Before Reed could register what had happened, the Reaper was in front of him. What was more claw than hand snapped around his neck and lifted him from the ground.

Meilana was there, swiping with her elongated nails. The Reaper dodged her attacks, still holding Reed aloft.

He turned aside when she snatched free her gun and fired a round. The Reaper easily dodged the missile, then kicked her in the face. The blow knocked her into a backward somersault that sent her crashing upside down into the opposite wall.

Reed saw that terrible scythe coming around in the Reaper's other hand, heading straight for his back. He lifted his gun and fired. The shot missed, but the Reaper released him.

He dropped to the ground and rolled backward. When he came back to his feet, he saw two fully transformed lycans leap on top of the Reaper, and they died just as quickly. Reed's mouth dropped open at the sight, but he took aim and fired again.

The Reaper kicked a lycan in the stomach mid transformation. He brought his scythe around behind his back to swat aside three of the five bullets Reed had fired, then swayed his body left and right, avoiding the last two. One of the bullets hit the wall, lighting the dark tunnel with a spark. The other bullet hit Rickland, who fell to the ground groaning.

"Son of a bitch, kid!" he growled. "Don't point that thing at the rest of us or you'll be fighting that monster on your own!"

The Reaper spun at the sound of his voice, but another of the remaining male lycans leapt on his back and scored a quick slash and retreated. The Reaper hissed and spun, bringing his scythe around with the motion. This lycan was more experienced than his dead pack members. He was already ducking and transforming as the blade passed over his head.

As soon as the weapon was safely aside, the werewolf lunged and bit the cloaked vampire on the arm. Reed saw the scythe coming back and thought it the end of the big wolf, but the beast whipped its muscled neck and sent the Reaper flying away.

Reed readied his gun. As soon as the Reaper touched the wall —instead of crashing into it—he fired. The bullets sparked off of the wall where the Reaper had been an instant before, and Reed could only watch as the cloaked monster flew back at the wolf and brought his scythe around and down on his head.

But the blade never tasted the wolf's flesh. Rickland was there, halfway transformed into his lupine form, and exuding rage. As the

Reaper passed over him, he leaped straight up, slamming into the vampire's midsection. They crashed into the ceiling just as Rickland finished his transformation. The wolf bit the Reaper's weapon arm and slung him aside, more to get the dangerous vampire away from him than to do any real damage.

The black werewolf landed on the floor of the tunnel, glaring murderously at the vampire with glowing yellow eyes. Behind him, two more lycans stalked forward, transforming with every step.

The Reaper glided to the floor, and stalked toward the three wolves. Reed had heard stories of Braggus Rayne taking down three fully transformed werewolves at once, but there was nothing in the stories about him walking into their midst without a care.

Behind the growling wolves, Lydia appeared, twin axes gripped tightly in her hands. The uncreation of Barakus had stoked a raging fire in that one.

Reed ejected the clip in his gun and reloaded. He lowered himself and moved forward, keeping pace with the stalking Reaper, but maintaining his distance. He just had to be patient.

❧

YAKO HEARD the fighting behind him but that was as far as he dared allow his awareness to drift. Everyone who had ever been to or spent any time in Peles Coven knew the stories about Denari and Tannis. The Wraiths, they were called.

Yako knew them better than most. They were different from any other vampire he'd ever known. Both seemed to exist outside of life and death. Both were deadly.

Yako ducked a swipe at his head and countered with a horizontal swipe that would have disemboweled a lesser foe. His sword missed the mark by inches.

Yako dropped into a crouch and spun away just as that terrible scythe came down, splitting the ground where his head had been. Yako leaned in and stabbed straight. His speed was enough to

384

score a hit in the instant it took the Reaper to dislodge his weapon.

Denari hissed and yanked his scythe free, bringing it upward in an arc that had Yako hopping to the side to avoid the keen silver edge. They circled each other, Yako's steps light and measured while his enemy seemed to glide over the ground. Yako studied him. Tannis was formidable, but Denari was the more dangerous of the two.

Yako kept the Reaper circling until his back was to Tara. She darted, her hand scythes a whirling blur of death. Denari never diverted his glowing narrow gaze away from Yako. He spun his long-shafted weapon behind his back, parrying Tara's attacks and forcing the other Reaper to retreat or be cut in half. In that same instant Yako attacked.

Denari leaned to the side and then back, avoiding Yako's sword even as he brought his scythe back around his body.

Yako leaped up and away as the blade came around. This creature was the most formidable enemy he had ever fought. "Help the others," he called out to Tara.

"So that you can be cut down and we have to deal with these two without you?" Tara said. "Don't be a fool."

Yako parried the scythe and kicked out. Denari flowed back, then back came in. Yako drew his foot back, then dropped to the ground in a spin, sweeping his leg out. Denari left the ground and glided aside, landing beside Yako. The Eldest Hunter swiped his sword out and forced the Reaper away before he could swing his scythe down on his back.

"All we can do is get in each other's way, here," he said. "Destroy the other and continue with our objective."

Tara grunted but called for the others to follow her.

Down the tunnel, he heard Tannis hissing as an entire group of Hunters and fully transformed lycans came upon him.

"You will faaail, Eeeldeeest," Denari hissed.

Yako answered with a forward stab of his black-coated silver sword. Denari easily sidestepped the attack, then moved away. Yako paced him but didn't attack. That the Reaper hadn't counter-attacked showed he was likely wondering why Yako would battle him alone.

The sounds of fighting further down the tunnel retreated as Tannis was being forced back. There was more than one tunnel that led to the castle, and The Reaper was probably leading them in that direction.

"Your allies leave you with deeeath, Huuunteeer."

Yako circled, the Reaper circling with him. From his vantage point he saw past the cloaked figure, the last of his allies disap-pearing around a bend. He was now truly alone with Denari. Yako went lower in his stance and they continued to circle. Excellent. Now he could move uninhibited.

"Embraaace deeeath," Denari hissed. His scythe spun before his cloaked body, vertically, horizontally, around his back and over his head. The scythe didn't stop spinning even as he came forward.

Yako ducked, then turned sideways, hopped over a low pass, then leaped in a sideways flip. He kept his body straight and tall as he passed upside down, his head only inches above the blade that passed under him.

When his feet touched the ground, the Eldest Hunter leaped backwards then dropped to the ground, this time sliding under another horizontal swipe. He came back to his feet, ducked, and spun sideways, again avoiding the incredibly fast Reaper.

Denari was relentless, his scythe never stopped spinning, his cloaked form never stopped moving. When Yako leaped backward, the Reaper leaped with him. Midair, their clashing weapons lit the tunnel in sparks.

When his feet touched the ground, Yako kicked forward, scoring a mild hit to Denari's shoulder. The Reaper made a sound that could have been laughter as he brought his weapon around. Yako ducked, then rolled backward as Denari stopped his attack and changed direction.

Yako was faster. When he came back to his feet, he brought his sword up and parried the blade, then spun toward the Reaper, bringing his sword around and down. Denari's ghost-like voice made a surprised sound as he dropped into a low crouch and skittered away, bringing his still spinning scythe in front of him defensively.

Yako didn't stop. He came in with a barrage of attacks that had the Reaper on the defensive. Every time Denari tried to counter, Yako was in too close and he was forced to defend. Yako leaped forward and brought his sword up diagonally for Denari's head.

Denari leaned aside but Yako had expected the evasion. He twisted his body midair and brought the sword back down, slicing the Reaper down the right side of the back of his shoulder.

The Reaper hissed and lunged in, scythe spinning. Yako jumped straight up, tucking his knees in against his chest, and kicked out. His feet connected with the side of Denari's head and sent him into a sideways stumble.

Denari recovered so quickly, he slammed his shoulder into Yako's chest before the Eldest Hunter's feet touched the ground.

Yako tumbled across the tunnel and slammed into the opposite wall. He'd barely touched the arched concrete when Denari was there, scythe spinning.

The Eldest Hunter brought his sword to bear, dodging and parrying, ducking and blocking. Every time he tried to sidestep or move away, the angry Reaper paced him. Yako took a cut to the arm, but he shrugged off the burning pain, bringing his sword up.

Denari swatted the blade aside and brought his scythe around his back and up, slicing Yako across the front of the chest. Then he brought the scythe back around and up the other side of his body.

Yako parried the blade but it was moving too fast, and came around and down, slicing him across his left leg before he could react.

Denari hissed again and pressed the attack. It took all of Yako's considerable skill to keep the whirling scythe from cutting him apart. The Reaper never slowed, never faltered, and never left an opening for a counter. But Yako didn't need to counter attack. He only needed to distract. And there, continuing to press his prey against the wall and into certain death, Denari was blind to the woman behind him, passing through the air in a downward arc.

So silent was Mariska's attack that Denari only registered her presence the instant before her sword would have run him through. He turned, bringing his scythe around in an attempt to knock the sword away. The parry wasn't strong enough and the Reaper was not fast enough. The Second Hunter's sword ran him through the arm. Mariska pulled the blade free and retreated, weapon ready.

Yako stalked in sideways until they had Denari between them. Both circled the Reaper, who stood in place, not bothering to look at either of them.

Now he had a chance. Mariska was the only Hunter who knew Yako well enough to compliment his actions. Three, or even four other allies would not have been as effective as only himself and his Second. He now had within his means the chance to kill this creature, and judging by his hesitation, Denari knew it, too.

The Reaper lunged to his left, scythe spinning, and forced Mariska into a sideways roll. Before Yako could attack, Denari came back to the right, bringing the scythe down. Left and right, Denari moved, darting in at each of them before they could coordinate against him.

Despite the desperation of the situation, Yako couldn't help but marvel at the speed and precision of his adversary. He couldn't think of moving so fast, yet this Reaper, this *thing*, effectively kept them on the defense. Denari darted back and forth again, double-bladed scythe flashing violently at the two Hunters.

After one last attack at both enemies, Denari leaped backwards, and retreated further down the tunnel. Yako and Mariska gave chase but the Reaper faded into the darkness and was gone.

"Keep moving," Yako said, "and be prepared."

"He flees for the coven?" Mariska asked.

"While seeking advantage," Yako replied. "Be aware."

Mariska didn't reply, but Yako knew she understood him when she dropped to her knees and leaned backward, her back almost touching the ground. The long blade of a scythe passed inches above her face.

Yako leaped over her and whipped his sword around. The darkness was pierced by the sparks from his sword skipping across the stone wall. He scanned the tunnel but there was nothing there aside from the two of them.

"What is this creature?" Mariska asked, standing back-to-back with him.

"A vampire that should not exist," Yako answered.

"I've never seen their like," the Second replied. "They seem unnatural."

"Because they exist outside of life and death," Yako said.

He continued down the tunnel, Mariska at his side. They increased their pace to a run, eyes forward but slightly out of focus. Yako sharpened his awareness, not relying on smell or sound, but intuition. It saved him.

He leaped into a forward flip as the scythe passed under his feet, then turned and darted back, stabbing at where his enemy should have been. Nothing.

Behind him, Mariska grunted. He turned to see her ducking and flipping sideways. Yako saw the cloaked menace for only an instant and then he was gone again.

Yako dropped to the ground and the scythe cut the air above him. He spun his legs, attempting to trip up the Reaper, but struck nothing.

He came to his feet to see Mariska leaping backward, sword arcing down to knock Denari's blade safely beneath her. Yako came in with a downward chop as she glided back, and cut nothing but darkness. "Move," he said, taking off as soon as he touched the ground.

The two Hunters sprinted down the tunnel, guessing which path to take since they didn't have Tara to guide them.

Out of the darkness Denari appeared before them in a flicker, slashing his scythe. Yako ducked and slashed horizontally while Mariska leaped forward and slashed downward. Neither of them scored a hit, and both continued to run, making their way quickly to what they hoped was the end of this cursed underground passage. Inside the spacious walls of the coven they would find better odds, for down here, in the cramped dark space of the underground tunnels, the Wraith held advantage.

CHAPTER 53

Neither Jelani nor Daniel could fully grasp the implications of Saaya's words, but the stricken look on Lemanda's face was enough for him to believe they had a big problem. Hopefully big brothaman could deal with the woman, but Jelani had never considered himself lucky.

The halls of Peles Castle were nothing like what he'd expected. After they'd arrived in Bucharest, Jelani and Daniel had looked online for photos of the interior of the castle to get an idea of what they were in for. Although Jelani had somewhat of a working knowledge of the castle through Remy's memories, he still wanted to be as familiar as possible.

All of the photos were of brightly lit halls and rooms with rows of chairs; beautifully furnished, decorated and colorful. The halls and rooms they passed through now were as dark as the night itself. No lights shone, no rows of chairs where tourists would sit for presentations. While tours of the castle were still given, they only happened in certain parts of the castle. The other parts, the parts that were "restricted for preservation" were where the coven's residents lived.

They turned another hallway, following Lemanda's lead. She

had suggested they find and dispatch Massius as quickly as possible, and no one had argued the point. Although Jelani wanted nothing more than to put an end to Remy for all that he had done to him and his friends, the bigger threat was anyone closely tied to that lethal woman Kafeel was hopefully killing at the moment.

As if on cue, Alicia crashed through the wall ahead of them, touched the floor, then leaped backward. Right behind her, Kafeel's sword flashed in a downward arc, cutting a long scar into the floor. As with Alicia, he was in the air as soon as his feet touched the floor, leaping after her. Both faded from view as the group skidded to a stop.

"What the hell?" Daniel said, mouth hanging open. "How the hell do they do that? It's impossible." He looked at Lemanda, but the Elder seemed at as much a loss as he was.

"I know nothing of it," she said. "What I have seen tonight is out of legend."

"Because you have forgotten," Saaya replied. "Or have been willed to forget."

"Let's talk about it later," Jelani said as they entered another open room. "I'll feel a little better when ole man Massius is dust under my feet."

The response that came could have been from none other than Massius himself. "Why do I hear such harsh words from one I have never met?"

Jelani turned in the direction of the voice and saw a man who looked to be in his sixties, white hair and semi-wrinkled skin. His eyes shone with pale red malice above a poisonous smile.

Massius turned his smile on the Elder beside Jelani. "My dearest Lemanda. May I ask after the source of such hostility?"

"Dispense with your mockery of politeness," Lemanda responded in a voice of controlled, frozen anger. We've already encountered your handler, and she is too occupied at the moment to help you."

That tore the smile from his face. "I would have sent her away even if she was here. I need no help to deal with such a ragtag group."

"Oh," Lemanda replied, taking a step toward him. "And you truly believe you are more powerful than I?

Jelani glanced through the hole in the wall where Kafeel and Alicia had passed. Through the window in the adjacent room Jelani saw the last of the failing light dip below the horizon. The night had come, and with it, a fully awakened coven of vampires that bore no allegiance to him, Daniel, or Saaya. He glanced at the other two. Daniel watched the confrontation between the two Elders while Saaya scanned the hall.

"You are truly the fool, Massius, if you believe you are in control of Alicia." Lemanda looked at the other Elder in clear disgust. "That woman is far beyond you."

"Beyond you, perhaps," Massius shot back.

"Enough of this," Lemanda said. "After tonight's attack I am finally within my rights to kill you."

"You believe you can?" Massius said.

Jelani suddenly felt an invasion in his mind, a compulsion to attack the female Elder. To his side, Daniel grunted and pressed his palm to his forehead. He looked questioningly at Jelani, then at Massius. On Jelani's other side, Saaya frowned, then took on an amused expression.

Lemanda glanced over her shoulder, then smiled at Massius. "I see. I'd almost forgotten your *talent*. For what you lack in physical strength and courage, you compensate with compulsion. But your problem is not solved …"

Jelani felt Saaya's connection with him strengthen, and Massius's clamp on his mind shattered. He blinked and looked at Saaya, who winked at him, then turned a grave look on the Elder.

"Hey! Old man!" Daniel shook his head. "Get the hell outta my head before I rip you apart. Actually I think I'll just rip you apart anyway!"

Jelani thought he was shocked at the explosive rage and

aggression in his friend's voice, until he saw Daniel's fiery golden eyes flare.

"It looks as though you cannot compel this lycan," Lemanda said. "Nor can you compel a *dampeal*. And judging by the fact that even this fledgling is resistant to you, I wager he was turned by our little half-breed as well."

"What?" Massius snapped. "Impossible ..." he trailed off as the trio stepped closer.

"No," Lemanda said, and the others stopped. Even Saaya looked surprised that she'd done so. "Leave this cravenly old crow to me. The coven is about to tear itself apart, and you will be needed."

They turned to leave but Lemanda's voice called out to them again. "After this is done, I would have a word with you."

Jelani turned back to see the woman actually smirking over her shoulder at all of them. "Go."

They went.

§

LEMANDA WATCHED the treacherous old man carefully. She had no doubts about overpowering him, but with Massius, nothing was straightforward.

"Why the hesitance, Lemanda?" he taunted. "You seemed so confident about killing me in front of those children you've herded together."

"As usual," she said, "you do not have the whole of it." They began to circle each other. "And I would be more concerned with myself, were I you."

Massius sneered at her. "You think me a fool. The entire High Council thinks me a fool. You've always thought me a fool!"

Lemanda shook her head at him. "Is that what this is about? All this trouble? The scheming of this grand insurrection of yours is little more than to soothe your tender ego? Come, Massius. You must have more depth than that." She tapped a finger to her cheek. "Although, your choice in "lead lackey" says otherwise."

Massius made a disgusted sound. "Bah! That fool boy will live or die by his own hand. If he is clever enough to survive, I will see him rewarded appropriately. In the more probable event that he perishes, he will be replaced. But, no more about others. You and I have business, do we not?"

Lemanda's eyebrows raised. "You surprise me. I wouldn't have taken you for one eager for conflict." Massius smiled at her, and then she felt the mental assault. It was like a knife attempting to pierce her brain.

Lemanda gasped and dropped to her knees. She clamped her eyes shut at the surprisingly powerful attack and pushed him away from her mind. Then she heard the unsheathing of a sword. She opened her eyes and leaped backward just as Massius's longsword stabbed the marbled floor where she'd knelt.

"Impressive," he purred. "I wouldn't have thought you could recover so quickly."

Lemanda stared at him. "Impressive," she echoed. "I wouldn't have thought a simple *shaquora*, no matter how old, could be possessed of such strength."

Massius's lips curled back to reveal his fangs, and Lemanda laughed at him. "Oh, Massius. Do you truly believe your little condition has escaped notice?" She felt the attack again but she was prepared this time. With a wave of her hand, Lemanda shattered the mental attack. "Your little trick can only work once, *Elder*."

Massius roared at her mocking tone and lunged, sword flashing in a downward arc. Lemanda sidestepped the blade just as another mental barrage assaulted her. She knocked it away, but another came just as Massius's sword leveled for her heart.

Lemanda hissed, her fangs elongating. She leaned away from the sword, shrugging away another mental attack, and throwing her will against him.

Massius stumbled back and she was instantly in front of him, nails elongated as she launched a dizzying assault of slashing and stabbing claws. Massius tried to bring his sword to bear, but she grabbed his wrist and snapped it. The Elder let out a primal growl and whipped him around in a circle and released him.

The old man crashed through the wall and into the next room, and Lemanda was already at the hole in the wall as Massius picked himself up from the floor. The sound of popping bone and cartilage told of his repairing wrist.

"You heal quick enough," she hissed, "but did you know that were you a true pureblood, I would not have been able to so easily snap your bone?" She laughed again when she saw the anger in his eyes. "Old fool. Who turned you to the night? And why?"

He came at her again, predictably leading with his mental assault. Lemanda knocked the attack on her mind aside like one would swat away a gnat, then stepped out of reach of the descending blade. She moved back in and slapped him across the face. He went spinning to the ground but was up in an instant, sword slashing and stabbing.

"Did a vampire come to you on your deathbed?" she taunted, her tone on the edge of more laughter. "Did you make a deal with the *devil*, Massius?" she hissed in a mock evil tone at the word "devil", and Massius roared again.

Lemanda's lips tightened at the raging attack. With every swing of that sword came a mental assault. She had to admit to herself that the old man was quite clever in the use of his *talent*. One slip and he could overwhelm his opponent.

"Not bad at all, *shaquora*," she said, dodging the sword and blocking out the mental attacks. "But you'll have to do better."

She fell into perfect calm and erected an impenetrable wall between her mind and Massius's. In that same instant she slammed her will upon him and threw her arm out wide. Massius's eyes widened in surprise an instant before he doubled over in the air and crashed onto the floor.

"I don't know how you got into High Elder Vicken's mind," Lemanda said, bearing down on him. "Your *talent* for subtlety must be legendary for you to so carefully infiltrate the mind of one so far above you. You must have known you couldn't subvert his mind through pure force of will, so you turned to guile instead. Smart."

He tried to rise but her will slammed him back to the ground. "How you managed to align yourself with Alicia, an *Ancestor*, is beyond my comprehension, but I suppose anyone can benefit from dumb luck." Lemanda was instantly beside him. She grabbed the hand holding the sword and crushed the fingers as she wrenched the sword from his grasp.

Massius's confused expression came and went as he tightened his mouth to keep from crying out. Lemanda was back in front of him, watching him cradle his hand as the fingers popped back into place.

"You truly didn't know," she said. "You had no idea you had aligned yourself with something out of legend. Do you even know what the *Ancestors* are?" When he didn't answer, she continued. "I do not know why one of them would so disdain us as to wish the death of the coven, but that is her goal."

Lemanda turned the sword in a reverse grip, aiming it at Massius's heart. "And without a little luck of our own, she would have succeeded. But you didn't know that either, did you? You believed she was your partner in this, following your lead."

"You always have the answers, don't you, Lemanda?" Massius said, and she was surprised at his unconcerned attitude. "Having the answers," he continued, "is only one side of the coin. How well do you prepare?"

"Stop burbling, old fool, and speak your last words."

"Hardly my last words, Lemanda." Massius stared into her eyes and smiled. "You believe your Eldest Hunter comes with allies to help you. He alone will lead a force to repel my own. A good answer to my challenge, but I prepared for that, and The Wraiths would have finished him by now."

Lemanda froze. Impossible. "Don't game with me, Massius. Those abominations were dealt with ages ago."

"Do you think I would have let such valuable assets be wasted, Lemanda?" Now Massius grinned at her. "Do you really think I would have let all of you destroy such powerful tools?"

Lemanda's infrequently beating heart sped up. "You have no idea what they are—"

"I know exactly what they are. You are the fool, Lemanda. Wraiths, you call them. Not wraiths at all, my lovely. They are death returned, death personified, and death at my command. You are idiots to think that I was so dull-witted that I would believe you would have ever accepted me as your equal, so I planned otherwise. What power you would see me unfit to wield, I created for myself."

He glanced at the hole in the wall where she had thrown him and smiled again. "And speaking of death, It is time for yours."

Lemanda stepped back and eyed the massive form of Braggus Rayne as he hunched and climbed through the hole. He stopped before Massius, who had come back to his feet.

"Your timing is less than impeccable, Eldest Reaper," Massius snapped.

"My apologies, Elder," Braggus's baritone voice boomed. "But the fighting has already begun."

"I suppose that is forgivable," Massius replied.

Lemanda watched the two. Should she attack now, or wait? A fight with both of them would be much more difficult. Though not an Elder, Braggus's prowess was legendary, as was his mystery-shrouded lineage.

"I must see that our efforts at restoring the coven to glory move smoothly, Braggus," Massius continued. "See to this woman in my stead. I won't have her interfere further. The High Council has gotten weak and decadent. It's time to start anew and reforge the coven into the symbol of strength our species has known since the beginning of time."

Braggus bowed, and Massius moved to the doors behind. He stopped and favored Lemanda with a mocking smile. "Goodbye Lemanda." He disappeared through the doors.

Several tense moments passed as Braggus straightened and moved to the double doors and closed them, then turned and stalked toward Lemanda.

"You have had a place of honor with the High Council of Elders for more years than I can remember, Eldest Reaper," Lemanda said. "Would you throw that away for a traitorous craven?" The giant continued to close the distance between them, drawing his massive scythe from behind his back.

Lemanda stood her ground. It would be a shame to destroy the magnificent warrior, but she would not die here. To be honest, she wasn't completely sure how the fight would end.

She held the sword aloft in her right hand, ready to strike quickly, when Braggus dropped to one knee, placing his weapon on the ground at her feet and bowing his head in submission.

"Lady Lemanda of the High Council of Elders. For years I have bent my mind into the belief that you, Lord Stavros, and Lord Vicken are weak and in need of replacement. Without such sincere belief, Massius would have seen the deceit in my mind and I would not have gained his trust. I have withheld the truth from the High Council and betrayed your trust, and I ask only that you allow me the time to detail Massius's plans to remake the coven before you lay your judgement upon this unworthy servant."

With an effort, Lemanda kept her mouth from falling open. She lowered the sword to her side and with her free hand placed her fingers under his chin and lifted his head. "Rise, Eldest Reaper."

The man straightened and was near to her height before he came fully erect. "Your efforts are recognized and commended by the coven and the High Council of Elders." She lifted his scythe and proffered it.

With hands double the size of her own, he accepted the weapon with reverence, bowing as he did so. "On the honor you have given me, and the honor I retain, I serve and only serve the true High Council of Elders."

"The High Council of Elders accepts you, warrior," Lemanda replied. "Go, Eldest Reaper Braggus Rayne. Destroy our enemies. Go in the name of the High Council."

The giant man bowed once more and departed through the door where Massius had left.

Lemanda stood alone in the room, wondering what had just happened. Her first thought was that it would have been better had the man simply killed Massius where he'd stood. The opportunity was certainly ripe enough. But then she thought of the many who served Massius covertly, and how the old man never revealed everything. Braggus had earned a measure of his trust, but not all of it.

"Clever, Massius," Lemanda whispered under her breath. "But not clever enough." She smiled. Braggus was waiting until Massius inevitably placed him in command of his forces. Together with Yako, and Lemanda with the Elders, they would obliterate him.

Her smile fell away at the thought of the Eldest Hunter. Massius had to have been lying about Tannis and Denari. No. She had seen no deception in his face. She looked at the sword in her hand, golden handle attached to a blade of pure silver. Gaudy and perfectly suited to Massius's tastes.

She turned in the direction of the sounds of blades clashing and suppressed gunfire. The fighting had begun. She hoped Yako had not encountered Tannis or Denari. Despite his skill, she was unsure the Eldest Hunter could survive such a confrontation.

CHAPTER 54

I n the midst of silenced gunfire and swordplay the trio managed to navigate the castle relatively unnoticed. Jelani had to hand it to Yako. The man was coordinated. In the back of his mind he felt Remy come awake, but there was nothing to indicate he had seen or encountered the Eldest Hunter. That meant that the attack had probably started before the Eldest Hunter had even arrived.

"This is like something out of a movie," Daniel said. "Bullets flying around and swords clashing?"

"A little different when swords are unsheathed outside a class-room isn't it?" Jelani remarked.

"You don't seem too bothered by it," Daniel said.

"I've had a little time to adjust," Jelani replied. "You'll get used to it."

"I recommend getting accustomed quickly, lovely boy," Saaya said. She indicated six vampires who came running around a corner and spotted them.

"Well, now. What's this?" one of them said, stepping from behind the group. "We've got one freshly turned fledgling, hanging out with a filthy *skiek*, and a dog."

Jelani's expression darkened. He didn't know what angered

him more, them calling his friend a dog, or Saaya a *skiek*. "I bet this freshly turned vampire will knock the shit out of you before sending you to hell in a pile of ashes, homeboy. How 'bout that?"

"Oh! A willful one," the man said. His friends laughed, all but one, who was looking into Jelani's simmering lavender eyes. Jelani figured he was the smartest of the group.

"I suppose you believe the three of you can take us," the vampire continued, flashing a half smile, the tip of a fang dipping below the corner of his upper lip.

"I don't need to take them," Jelani said, his anger rising. "I only need to take *you*."

The man responded with a bored look. "Then bring it on, stupid—"

Jelani closed the distance and took the man's head from his shoulders. He landed in a crouch, not even bothering to turn around. He didn't need to, because Daniel and Saaya had dispatched the others, all but one. Good. They must have seen the look in the eyes of that other guy as well. The fight lasted less than five seconds, leaving the last vampire backing away.

"Hold, I ask."

Jelani straightened and faced him. "You ask?"

The man's mouth worked a few times before he found more words. "To beg is to be unworthy of life."

"Fair enough," Jelani said. He walked over and grabbed the guy by the neck and lifted him into the air. "But you better speak up."

"You are Remy's enemy," came the strangled reply. "I am no enemy of yours."

"Yet you were hanging around with them," Jelani said, nodding toward his decaying friends.

"Opportunities are not always readily apparent. I would fight with you if you will have me."

Jelani dropped him. "You can fight with us without fighting beside us."

The vampire nodded his head, which was covered with curly black locks. "You'll find Remy in the—"

"I know where to find him," Jelani interrupted. "And watch who you attack. There's lycans on our side as well. Don't get yourself in trouble with Yako."

At the mention of the Eldest Hunter's name, the man looked like he would turn to ash right there. "Of course."

Daniel watched as the vampire took off down the hall behind them. "Was that wise?"

Jelani stared down the hall at the retreating man's back. "He'll help out or die. Either way, I don't think he'll be a problem."

"Pretty cold, man."

"But true," Jelani replied. He noticed Saaya watching him. "What?"

"Humans still exist because vampires retain a measure of compassion, *jaan*." She continued down the hall.

"What the hell was that?" Jelani asked Daniel as the beautiful woman made her way in front of them.

Daniel's only answer was a squeeze on Jelani's shoulder before he followed behind the *dampeal*.

The fighting was starting to heat up, the sounds of hissing and gunfire, swords slicing through air, skin, and bone. Jelani was starting to wonder just how many vampires lived here. He wouldn't have believed there could be so many in the world, much less in one place, castle or not.

"He's here," Daniel said, just as they came to a huge open room filled with fighting vampires.

"Who …" Jelani started to ask, but then part of the stone wall across the room burst as though a bomb had exploded. Through the thick cloud of dust and rubble came at least a dozen massive lycans. Their fur was so black it shimmered in contrast with a mix of golden, yellow, and orange eyes.

Even more astounding was the group of glowing red eyes right in the middle of them. Vampires.

"I know the histories of our respective species, but never would I have thought to see this," Saaya said.

Indeed it was a sight to behold; vampires and werewolves in interwoven ranks, leaping into the fray.

In less than two minutes of efficient brutality, the room was cleared of anything resembling an ally of Massius.

Jelani fought against the natural tension in his body at being in the presence of so many werewolves; fully transformed at that. He remained where he was as Daniel moved to the front of the group. In front of him, vampires and werewolves alike moved aside to admit what was absolutely the biggest and most intimidating werewolf Jelani could have imagined possible. The thing was easily closing in on nine to ten feet tall, and was muscle stacked on top of muscle.

Before their eyes, the giant wolf dropped to all fours and began to shift back to human form. Jelani just shook his head. "Damn," was all he could say. Darren Lacey, standing before Daniel, was not much unlike his lupine form.

"Ran into a little trouble, did you?" the man said to Daniel.

"More than you know," Daniel answered. "You know what an *Ancestor* is, among the bloods?"

While the other vampires in his group seemed to know nothing about what Daniel said, Darren's face darkened. "What did you say?"

"*Ancestor*," Daniel repeated. "A woman who almost killed us all. Apparently she's an *Ancestor*."

"You are lucky to be alive," Darren said.

"We had some pretty tough help," Daniel replied, looking over his shoulder at Saaya.

"Yes," Darren replied. "And your manners are lacking, Daniel."

"Oh, yeah, right." Daniel half turned. "This is our ... pack-leader, Darren Lacey."

Jelani felt for his friend. It was still difficult to come to terms with being part of something like this, having to adhere to the rules of an organization. Whether it was a club, or a pack of giant wolves, it wasn't in Daniel's personality to be a part of any kind of group like this any more than it was Jelani's.

"You've already met Jelani," Daniel continued, "and this is Saaya."

Darren smiled at her. "A pleasure."

Saaya's eyes flicked down and up and she smiled back. "Yes it is."

Jelani frowned and looked at her, then, after glancing around Daniel to see the very naked Darren Lacey, closed his eyes and leaned his head back. "Man, damn! I really didn't need to see that."

Behind Darren, the members of his pack—a mixture of larger black wolves, and several different colored wolves that weren't as large—began to grow restless. The vampires in their midst also looked to be on the edge of their patience. Through the walls they heard more sounds of fighting. The group looked around anxiously, eager to join in.

"It's time for warriors to test their mettle," Darren said. "We stand at a point in history that will be long remembered. We fight with honor." He took a step back and bared his teeth, which were quickly elongating. It looked like the man had a mouth full of serrated knives!

In seconds, Darren Lacey was a massive black wolf once more. He stood to his full height, heaved his huge furred chest, and let out a roar that shook the walls. The other wolves in the room roared with him. Daniel let out a roar of his own that wasn't nearly as powerful, given his human form, but still added to the call of the pack.

The giant wolf that was Darren looked down at Daniel and there seemed to be a silent discussion going on between them. Then the wolf turned aside and bounded around the trio, vampires and wolves in his wake.

"I don't believe I've ever heard of a lycan speaking of honor before," Saaya said, watching the unusual group depart.

"Not your typical alpha," Daniel replied, then frowned as if he didn't know why he'd said that.

"Let's move," Jelani said. "Remy's awake and probably trying to find a way to avoid the action while controlling it from a safe place."

"Coward," Daniel spat.

"Smart," Jelani replied.

"A smart coward," Saaya said. "Watch those the closest."

It didn't take the trio long to encounter another skirmish. The beautiful castle was quickly becoming a war zone, immortals of vampiric and lycanthropic heritage tangled in deadly conflict. Sticking to the halls, they made their way mostly undetected as Jelani led them closer to Remy. Lemanda had probably—hopefully—killed that old man, and Kafeel was either still dealing with that lethal *Ancestor* or had killed her. Again, hopefully. Jelani found he was doing a lot of hoping lately.

He couldn't help feeling a little concerned about Kafeel. Massius might have gotten the jump on them, but that Alicia woman made him seem like a mouse standing next to a mastodon, which in turn made Jelani feel like a flea standing next to them both. Would Kafeel be able to best someone that powerful? It was an unsettling thought and he pushed it from his mind to concentrate on the current business. The closer he got to Remy, however, the less important his own personal business with the Hunter seemed. Jelani planned to deal with Remy for the grief he'd caused himself and his friends, but seeing what was happening to this coven showed him that there was more at stake here than his desire for revenge.

They came to a group of burly men—and women—as they turned down another hall. The two groups stopped and looked at each other. "Hey guys," Jelani said. "You looking for ..." He cut the question short when a blur rushed past him and tackled the nearest man.

Daniel snapped his neck and slung him into the nearest woman. There was a sickening tearing sound, and when the man flew free, Daniel was holding a bloody piece of his throat.

The other four lycans began to transform. "Oh, hell no you don't!" Jelani said, rushing forward. He whipped out two silver daggers and sent them spinning through the air. One caught a male in the eye and one of the other women in the throat. Though he had killed more than a few female immortals since his turning, Jelani still winced when he did. That wince would have cost him if Saaya hadn't been there.

The *dampeal* pummeled the remaining three lycans in short order. She lifted a hand to move a stray lock of hair from her face, saw the blood, and made a disgusted face. At her feet, her victims lay twitching in death. Her elongated nails retracted and she wiped her hands off on the nearest male's shirt.

"You two are messy," Jelani said, mouth turned down.

"Some of us get in and get our hands dirty," Daniel replied, "instead of hanging back and throwing rocks."

"Rocks?" Jelani said, frowning.

Daniel shrugged. "You know what I mean."

"Boys?"

They both looked at Saaya who was tapping her foot. Jelani was absolutely certain not to pay attention to her hips as she shifted her weight from her right foot to her left. She arched an eyebrow at him and he looked away.

"Right. Well, um." He pointed further down the hall. "Yeah um, he's not far around that corner. Feels like he's still in his room, or wherever he's holed up."

They continued forward until they came to the end of the hall, then turned right. Finally, they came to one of the few normal sized doors in the castle. Jelani glanced at his two companions before turning the handle. The handle didn't move.

Jelani laughed. "At least he has a sense of humor."

He snatched the door off its hinges and tossed it aside. When they stepped through, they found Remy sitting in a cushioned chair with two men standing at either side of it.

"Well. I can't say I'm surprised to see you here, but I am surprised at how you found me." Remy still didn't bother to stand.

"I'm a little tougher than you think," Jelani said, "and I found you because I have your memories in my head." Jelani made a gesture, sliding his hand through the air and making a waving motion. "It's like a slimy trail that a slug would leave, except it's in my head and not on the ground. I was hoping I could get rid of it by killing you, but you keep running away."

That wiped the smugness from his face. Remy glanced at the two men at either side of him. Their faces were neutral, but when Remy looked away, the twitch at the corner of one of their mouths betrayed repressed laughter.

"Kill them," Remy said.

"You think two Hunters are gonna take us out?" Jelani asked as the men moved forward.

"No," Remy said. "But two Reapers will."

That changed everything. "You just can't do your own fighting, can you?" Jelani asked. "You just can't fight like a man."

"I'll consider your words as I'm languishing in my newfound power while your ashes are fertilizing my grounds."

The pale blond men stepped forward, each brandishing a scythe in front of them. Saaya let out a huff, hardly concerned. Daniel went into a crouch, circling out wide while Jelani circled in the opposite direction.

"You take care of your business with him," Daniel said. "Leave this to me."

"You're sure?" Jelani asked. He ducked as the scythe came for his head. Daniel sprang forward and drove his elongated nails into the Reaper's shoulder then leapt safely away as the blade came whipping back.

"Yeah. I've got this." A golden glow flickered in his eyes.

"All right man. Get it done." Jelani saw the muscles underneath Daniel's clothes shifting. "I really wish I could strap a backpack on you," he said. "Now I've gotta see you naked."

Daniel let out the most guttural sound Jelani had ever heard from him, and he leaped high above the swinging scythe, then came back down and drove both his feet into the vampire's face.

The Reaper staggered back, then came back in, trying to prevent Daniel's transformation. Impossible as it seemed, Daniel continued to dodge and counterattack while transforming, bit by bit. He leaned sideways to avoid the top of the sharp blade, and his teeth elongated. He ducked, just as his front arms popped and the joints dislocated and reattached.

When he doubled over in transformation, the Reaper jumped forward and brought his scythe down, aiming for Daniel's back.

Weapon over his back and coming down, the Reaper was helpless to stop Daniel as he leaped from the ground and met the Reaper in the air, uppercutting the vampire under the chin with a fist double its normal size and covered in black fur.

The Reaper's head snapped back and the sound of breaking neck bones echoed through the room. Daniel landed on his feet at the same time the vampire landed on his back, coughing and gurgling as his neck healed.

By the time the Reaper regained his feet, he stood before a fully formed black wolf standing over seven feet tall.

SAAYA HADN'T SEEN this much excitement in many years. A miniature war in the seat of vampiric power, and its leaders in the middle of it. And an *Ancestor*! As she avoided the blade of her Reaper adversary, Saaya wondered what could bring an *Ancestor* to this place.

The Reaper growled and darted forward, thrusting out with the top of the curved blade. Saaya swatted the weapon aside, slipped in close, and slapped him across the face. After being thrown into a sideways tumble, the Reaper came back to his feet, shock clear on his face. "You are strong and fast for a *skiek*," he said.

"You're not bad, yourself," Saaya replied. "But sadly, I don't have time to indulge you."

He came at her again, sweeping his scythe low, and when she hopped over the blade, continued his turn and brought it around high.

"It will be painless," Saaya said, stopping his two-handed swing cold, with one hand. "I will kill you quickly." The Reaper looked from his white-knuckled, double-handed grip, to the little hand holding the shaft of his weapon. He looked back to her in disbelief. Slowly the *dampeal* pulled the weapon down despite the larger man's efforts. "Jelani?" she said, looking in his direction.

"Yeah?" he answered from farther in the room.

"I must leave you for now. I trust you can deal with him?"

"I got this," he called back. How she loved the way he talked. She looked back at the Reaper who was pulling and twisting at the shaft of his weapon. No matter what he tried, he could not break the woman's iron grip.

"It is your time, warrior," she said. With a flick of her wrist she snapped the shaft of the weapon. Before the Reaper could register what had happened, she broke his wrist with a chop of her hand.

She snatched the scythe blade free as it fell from his weakened grasp, and planted it square in his chest. The blade punched through his body and came of out his upper back. The blond man staggered back a few steps, coughing blood.

Once Saaya saw the life leave his eyes, she turned toward the opening where the door had been just minutes earlier. She stopped one last time to see Jelani standing before Remy, who was just now rising from his chair. This wouldn't be a straightforward fight. That one wouldn't fight unless he was certain the odds were in his favor. She hoped Jelani understood this. She glanced at Daniel, who was now in his lupine form. Despite being a newly changed werewolf, he was more than a match for his adversary.

Her smile was for both of them. Two men, brought into this alien world and both seemed so quickly adjusted and capable of surviving in the midst of a conflict that was halting the lives of many immortals who had seen centuries of life before the human ancestors of these two men had been born.

She left the room. This was Jelani's fight. He would live or die by his own skill and intelligence. Through their bond, she felt confidence, but also wariness. Good. He would not rush foolishly to his death.

As she moved down the hall, she willed the light to bend around her body, rendering her virtually invisible. The last thing she felt in a corner of her mind was the equivalent of a mental slap on her backside.

"Fool boy," she whispered to herself with a smile.

⚓

THE BEAST that was Daniel circled his prey, who held the long-shafted weapon before him like a talisman. Through his innate connection with the pack and the alpha, Daniel knew that Hunters were specifically trained to track and kill his kind, and Reapers were more dangerous.

His flank quivered as the flesh knitted itself back together. A wound inflicted by silver was slower to heal, but luckily his species of lycan were the most resistant, other than the *First Ones.*

The Reaper came forward and brought the silver weapon around and down, attempting to drive it through the top of Daniel's head. With but a twitch of his muscular legs, the wolf hopped away, then lunged back in. With a snap of his jaws, he caught the blood on the arm, ripping away a chunk of flesh.

He spat it aside. Vampire flesh was unappealing except under the most dire circumstances. A werewolf would have to be near starvation to willingly consume the bitter and dry flesh of a blood.

The Reaper hissed and came at him again, spinning his scythe over his head and bringing it around to the right. The wolf ducked under the blade, swiping his huge claw out and nearly disemboweling the vampire in the same motion. The Reaper bared his fangs and leaped backward.

Daniel leaped forward, his powerful legs propelling him faster and farther to plow into the Reaper's midsection. The vampire hissed angrily when the two crashed into the wall. He flipped his curved silver blade around and stabbed Daniel in the shoulder.

It burned like acid and lit Daniel's rage. He clamped his jaws around the vampire's throat and squeezed, crunching through bone. The pressure of that awful weapon ceased, and the vampire went limp. Daniel started to release the Reaper, thinking him dead. As soon as he loosened the pressure, he felt the bones starting to heal.

Daniel released him, then swiped his claw across the Reaper's neck, snatching out his throat. He watched as the vampire slumped to the floor and started to decay. It was always that way with a blood. They shared a lycan's vulnerability to silver, but a grievous wound inflicted by his kind was also fatal.

The wolf threw his head back and howled in triumph. He turned toward the center of the room where another blood, his friend, faced the one he hated. The blood that was his friend could handle that Hunter, he was sure. But then two more vampires entered the room.

The one Daniel hated smiled. The wolf that was Daniel snarled.

FROM THE CORNER of his eye, Jelani saw his monstrous friend tear out the throat of the Reaper he fought. He smirked as he approached Remy, who seemed not at all concerned.

"You can put up that confident front all you want," he said.

"It's just you and me Remington."

A flash of anger lit Remy's expression, but he blinked it away. "You really aren't too smart are you?" He snapped his fingers, and two more men stepped into the room from the balcony. They snarled, baring mouths full of serrated teeth, and dropped to the floor. The sound of snapping bone and popping cartilage broke the silence as the lycans transformed. Seconds later two large brown wolves stood on either side of Remy. Across the room, a door Jelani hadn't noticed before opened to admit yet two more men.

"Damn," Jelani said. "Are you really that afraid of a fight?"

"I fight to win. That's why I survive, and you will perish beside your pet."

Jelani eyed the two men and kept his distance, retreating for every step they took toward him. He knew these two. One was slender and six feet tall, the other halfway past six feet tall and bulkier.

The slender man in the leather trench coat held his hands out wide, revealing a silver blade attached to each of his spread fingers and thumbs. The big one reached over his back and drew an intimidating sword Jelani had come to know more intimately than he preferred. Marcus and Berius.

"You two got here quick," Jelani said as they moved about the room. The two lycans had moved from Remy's side, attempting to position Jelani and Daniel between them.

"It's a long way here from North America, but not that long," Marcus said.

"Can I ask you a question before we get on with this?" Jelani asked.

Marcus looked at Berius, who shrugged. "I think we can put off your funeral for a couple seconds," the slender Reaper replied.

"Yeah, right," Jelani jerked his chin at Remy, who stood off to the side. "How the hell can you swallow taking orders from this guy? Doesn't it piss you off having to do what a coward says?" He sniggered when he saw Berius's mouth turn down, not in anger, but in an attempt to keep from laughing. "I mean, surely it's got to be obvious to you he's scared to fight," Jelani continued. He glanced at Remy, who was failing to hide the outrage on his face.

"Don't you dare try to stand there and deny it," Jelani prodded, and Remy's face went beet red.

"I admit you have a point," Marcus said. "But unfortunately we have to protect him per the orders of an Elder, which sadly supersedes any personal preference we may have."

Jelani waved his dagger nonchalantly in Remy's direction. "You could just let me kill him and be on your way. It's not like I'm gonna tell anyone."

"Have you met Elder Massius," Berius asked, and Jelani nodded. "Then you know there is no hiding things from him," the big man continued. "I'll admit it's a shame to kill you. I actually kinda like you, even though you're a *shaquora*." He hoisted the claymore over his shoulder and pounded his chest. "This may not make you feel any better, but we will give you a warrior's uncreation."

"Not planning to die today," Jelani replied.

"None do," Berius countered.

"Some do," Jelani shot back. "But I ain't either one of them. Let's get this over with so I can gut that son of a bitch and be out of here."

Marcus's shoulders bounced as he chuckled. "As you wish."

As the men circled and closed the distance, Jelani took note of the location of the two werewolves. They hadn't attacked yet, but were assessing the threat of the much bigger wolf that was his best friend. Jelani didn't think he could beat these two in a straight up fight, but he would need to find a way.

His daggers spun in his hands as he thought about how he wished Saaya had remained a few minutes longer. Another thought occurred to him just before Marcus leaped in at him with a flash of silver-tipped claws.

Where was Yako?

CHAPTER 55

W ithout the benefit of Tara's knowledge of the tunnels, Yako and Mariska had been forced to guess which way to go. Over half a dozen cuts burned all over his body from the bite of Denari's double-bladed scythe. How the Reaper was able to constantly get in front of them to attack was a mystery they hadn't the time to figure out.

"He is keeping us distracted," Mariska finally said.

Yako kept his eyes forward. "He keeps us from catching up with the others," he replied.

Several times they had heard fighting in the tunnels, but the way sound bounced off the walls, the others could be anywhere.

Mariska frowned. "The night is on in full."

Against his very nature, Yako made a decision. "Do not stop," he said. "When Denari attacks, avoid him, defend if need be, but press on. He'll tangle us in a fight down here alone if we let him. For now, we will reach the coven, and then we will deal with him."

The words had barely left Yako's mouth when the curved blade flashed out of the darkness, coming straight at his face.

Yako dropped to his knees and bent backward, sliding forward and passing under the seemingly disembodied weapon. He came back to his feet just as Mariska was landing in front of him. As instructed, the Second Hunter continued her flight, Yako close behind.

Through the dark tunnels below the city of Sinaia, the sound of Denari's voice slithered through the air.

"You walk the niiight. I am the niiight, Eeeldeeest. Faaace meeee."

Yako didn't respond. Despite being able to see perfectly in the dark, Yako was not able to see Denari until the Reaper was right on top of him. He didn't know if it was a *talent* or something about the odd vampire's nature, but what was certain was that down here in these pitch-dark tunnels, the Wraith held the advantage. That still wouldn't have deterred the Eldest Hunter from fighting, but his obligations bore more weight than a standoff with this creature. When the time came, he would finish this business with Denari.

They heard the roar of a werewolf and turned down the tunnel they suspected the sound came from. Again, Denari attacked from the shadows but Yako and Mariska simply dodged and pressed on. The Reaper's angry hiss reverberated through the tunnels.

Around a corner they saw the flickering light of gunfire and quickened their pace. They came around the bend to see the final corridor leading to a metal ladder built into the wall. Tara and a werewolf were embroiled in a fight with Tannis, who deftly handled them both.

Yako lowered his torso and sprinted, only his legs moving. He reached each hand over a forearm and gripped a silver throwing blade.

Tara glanced at him from the corner of her eye, then shouted at the lycan, who stood on its hind legs and leaped up through the opening in the ceiling of the tunnel. She glanced at Yako, nodded, then fired off a few more rounds down the tunnel to the right and leaped up and out of sight.

They were nearing the end of the tunnel when one of the cloaked Reapers stepped in front of the ladder. The whispering hiss of Denari chased them straight to the ladder, and the waiting Tannis.

Mariska came up beside him and drew her modified Glocks.

Tannis lazily lifted his long scythe and held it in an angle in front of himself. Yako let fly, and Tannis deflected both missiles. Mariska fired and the Reaper ducked low and twisted away.

Yako jumped forward, turned in midair while reaching over his shoulders, and snapped out two more throwing blades, sending them flying at the pursuing Denari.

The Reaper dodged the weapons but was then forced to dive aside as Mariska fired back at him as well. Tannis came rushing in, but Mariska was there. She leaped forward, held one Glock out in front of her and one behind, and fired at Tannis and Denari at the same time. There was an angry but pained hiss from behind, and Denari disappeared from view.

Tannis managed to avoid the barrage and continued forward. Yako drew his sword. It would come to a fight, then. He didn't know if he and Mariska could deal with these two on their own, but there was nothing for it.

He and the Reaper raced for each other, but then Tannis lurched and stumbled to the side. Yako darted forward and glided by him, slicing the Reaper across the arm as he passed.

At the foot of the ladder they saw Reed take aim and fire again. This time, Tannis was ready, and he dodged the silver bullets and came at them. Reed continued to fire, which managed to slow Tannis enough for Yako and Mariska to reach him.

"Go," Yako said to the young Hunter, and Reed leapt from view.

Mariska turned and fired both guns at the angry Reapers, forcing them to dodge and dive aside. She looked at Yako, who nodded, and she was gone up through the hatch. Yako leapt up after her, and as soon as he came up the thirty-foot assent, they closed and locked the iron hatch.

CHAPTER 56

Something had happened, but Vicken wasn't sure what, at first, so subtle, was it. Then he felt it. Like a haze lifting from his mind. A haze he hadn't known was there. A haze, he now realized, that had coated his mind for more years than he could count; slowly, patiently creeping through his thoughts, his intellect. His judgement.

Vicken looked at the screens in front of him. The screens linked to the many cameras along the halls and public rooms throughout the castle. Fighting everywhere. Lycans and vampires fighting side by side for and against the coven. He could hardly believe what he was seeing, and found it harder still to believe he had not prevented it.

Massius.

Just the thought of that name was enough to turn his blood to lava. Vicken would take his time with that one once he got his hands on him. And then, there was Alicia.

"High Elder," a powerful voice said from behind.

Vicken never looked up from the screens. "Yes Stavros."

"We have a particularly thick infestation moving in this direction."

"Of course we do," Vicken replied. "The idiot thinks to eliminate us and thereby sever the head of the snake. How many?"

"Thirty-three."

"How many of them are Reapers?"

"Three Reapers, seven Hunters, thirteen lycans."

Vicken huffed, running his tongue across the back of his teeth. Massius would have to wait.

He went to one of the two statues standing at the side of his large room and gripped the sword in the stone warrior's hands.

He lifted his greatsword in front of his face and admired the polished steel. "How long has it been since last we fought together, Stavros?"

"Longer than I care to recall, old friend," came the baritone reply.

Vicken turned to face his ancient comrade. Stavros was the embodiment of a warrior, his broadsword strapped to his right hip and a scimitar on his left. The contrast in weapons was glaring, but Vicken had seen his friend put the combination to deadly use on many occasions over the centuries.

They were from the old world, Vicken and Stavros. They had no use for the modern toys some of the younger vampires used. Let them play with their guns loaded with silver bullets. Theirs were the weapons of the ancient warrior.

Vicken looked at the second statue and grabbed the handle of the large double-sided axe. It was like holding two parts of himself that had been missing for too long. He turned back to Stavros, the other Elder's eyes smoldering, spoiling for a fight.

He crossed the room and gripped forearms with his closest friend, and side-by-side they left the room to meet their enemy.

As she crushed a male vampire's windpipe, Lemanda had to admit to herself that Alicia had planned well. Gone from her mind was any thought that Massius was the true architect of this insurrection. There were too many enemies swarming through Peles Castle for Massius's uninspiring presence to organize.

Lemanda aimed Massius's sword just above the man's abdomen. She saw the fear when he turned his pleading eyes on her. Lemanda sighed and ran the pure silver blade upward into his heart, then tossed him aside. "Disgraceful," she said, a sour note to her tone. "Rodents. Our species has been infiltrated by rodents."

In all her thousand years, Lemanda couldn't recall ever seeing so many cowards. These were not immortals, but rats that lived on until someone put them down.

Three more vampires came for her, two women and a man. Lemanda never broke her stride as she beheaded the male that leaped for her, ran her sword through the abdomen of one of the females, then sidestepped the other as she lashed out with elongated claws. Still moving down the hallway, Lemanda snatched a handful of the woman's hair and dragged her along. The other woman kicked and hissed, and Lemanda rolled her eyes, turning mid step and running the sword through her back.

The Elder completed her turn and continued down the hallway as the woman fell to the floor, death rushing to claim her. Lemanda's mood turned dark. Judging from the number of vampires she had already dispatched, and the level of fighting she could hear throughout the coven, not only was this a mix of pureblood and *shaquora*, but they were not all from this coven. And apparently Massius had found some lycan allies to side with his cause.

As soon as the thought entered her mind, one of the giant dogs crashed through a wall, a vampire clenched in its maw. It clamped its jaws around the man's neck with a sickening "snap", and tossed him aside. The giant wolf rose to its full height and turned to face her. This werewolf was larger than most, with a shimmering black coat.

Lemanda narrowed her eyes and raised her sword, but something odd happened. The giant wolf looked at her with eyes that seemed to retain rational thought, and crouched.

She thought it was about to spring at her, but instead it backed away a few steps, then turned and loped away. Lemanda lowered her sword and tilted her head. "Odd," she thought aloud. If she hadn't known any better she would have thought the movement a gesture of respect. Lycan allies?

The unexpected moment flew from her mind when she heard a sound that made her smile. The sound of a war cry, followed by another had Lemanda giggling like a young girl. She quickened her step, forcing herself not to break into a run. A lady must hold to decorum, after all.

When she opened the door and stepped into one of the largest rooms in the castle, she saw two men surrounded by a host of lycans in their lupine bodies, and perhaps two dozen vampires. One of the men held a two-handed broadsword in his right hand, and a scimitar in his left. The other held a greatsword in his right hand and a double-headed war axe in his left. Stavros and Vicken.

Lemanda felt her infrequently beating heart leap in her chest. Her glowing red eyes flared above and open-mouthed smile that revealed a set of elongated fangs.

Without hesitation, the female Elder was over the rail of the balcony, descending on an unsuspecting wolf. The beast rounded and looked up at her, jaws agape. She brought her sword before her, reversed her grip, and drove it into the monster's mouth. She rode it to the ground as it crumbled, coming gracefully to her feet as it convulsed behind her.

Two nearby vampires leaped at her and fell to her sword. In short order she made her way to Vicken and Stavros, and they formed a back-to-back triangle.

"It is good to see you, my Lady Lemanda," Stavros boomed over his shoulder.

"You see me all the time, my Lord Stavros," Lemanda replied, smiling.

"But not under such invigorating circumstances."

"I presume it is too much to hope that you've found Massius," Vicken said, disemboweling a silver werewolf. It fell to the floor, reverting to its human form in death. "I would have words with him."

"He has eluded me," Lemanda said, impaling a vampire with her sword and lifting him into the air. With a single hand, she swiped the sword sideways, dislodging the dying man and sending him flying into one of his comrades.

"Just as well," Vicken replied. "I want to skewer the wretch myself.

Stavros ran a vampire through with his sword, reaching so far that he impaled a second enemy behind him. He brought his scimitar around and lopped off both their heads. "We waste time here," he said. "Let's find the little bottom feeder and deal with him now."

"*I* … will deal with him," Vicken declared, and his tone brooked no argument.

Lemanda glanced at the man, as he brutally cut down three more vampires. He followed up with a chop of his axe across the torso of a werewolf. She was relieved to see the anger there. It meant that he was aware of what Massius had done to him; what Massius had been doing to him for years. She had to admit that the old buzzard was good. To spend decades creeping into such a strong mind as Vicken's must have required an unlimited amount of patience and control. And none, not even Lemanda, had been aware of it.

"As shall it be," she responded. "But if it shall be, then we need to move quickly. I wager you aren't the only one who sees Massius's throat in need of being cut."

"Those bastards think to wait this out and study our tactics," Stavros said, nodding at the second floor where four men and three women were crouched on the railings like crows, watching.

"I recognize three of them as Reapers," Lemanda said. "Disappointing."

"The rest are Hunters," Stavros confirmed.

"Are any of our elite guard loyal to us still?" Vicken asked, dispatching two more enemies.

"At least two," Lemanda replied.

"Please tell me that one of them is Braggus," Stavros said. "I've always had a liking for that one. A true warrior. It would be a shame to have to kill him."

Despite the truth of his words, Lemanda couldn't help thinking what a grand sight it would be to see those two clash. "The Eldest Reaper stands with us," she answered. "As does Tara."

"And by default, her sister," Vicken added. "That is good."

Their enemies began to back off, seeing their numbers being so easily decimated. On the second floor, the watching warriors sprang from the rail. They glided over the bottom floor, one Reaper and one Hunter landing before each of the Elders, and the extra Hunter landing with his two comrades before Vicken.

"If I didn't know any better, I would say they are more concerned with killing you," Lemanda said to the High Elder. "Such a horrible blow to a lady's ego."

The Reapers went into a low stance, holding their scythes before them defensively. The Hunters took position just behind, waiting.

"A shame you fail to realize that you were our elite guard more to save us the trouble of a fight than actual protection," Stavros said to the one facing him. "A leader cannot fight every battle. You've forgotten your place."

As one, the Reapers lunged in for a feint, then retracted, and the Hunters leaped in for a more decisive attack. The Elders dodged and counterattacked, but the Hunters were fast and coordinated.

"The more time we waste with this trash," Stavros said, "the more time Massius has to either make more trouble or escape if things do not go his way."

"I know of a certain Eldest Hunter that would find him," Lemanda said.

"All the same," Vicken replied. "Let's be done with this."

Several times the Elders sought to fight their way through, but the team in front of them were cunning. They knew they could not overwhelm the Elders by force, so they remained cautious and coordinated, one holding the attack only long enough for the other to spring in to take their place before retreating again. Were they holding for reinforcements?

"Enough!" Stavros bellowed. The fiery Elder went into a flurry, sweeping that massive broadsword for powerful strikes while darting in with his scimitar for more speed and precision. Lemanda and Vicken each launched their own offensive, and the trio had their enemies back on their heels.

The Reapers held off the onslaught at first, then leaped to the retreat, leaving their Hunter subordinates in the face of the raging Elders. All four Hunters were cut down in short order, leaving the remaining three Reapers.

The six warriors circled each other for several moments when the giant figure of Eldest Reaper Braggus Rayne stepped through the broken doors of the hall.

The normally calm and even-tempered Eldest Reaper looked at each of his subordinates in turn, leveling an icy glare on them that gave the warriors pause. To Lemanda's eyes, the Reapers seemed more afraid of their Eldest than they were of her and the other Elders.

"My Lords and Lady Elders," he said, his voice like a glacier, both cold and powerful. "If you wish to pursue Massius and Alicia, I will see to the punishment of my Reapers, here."

"See it done, Eldest," Vicken commanded, yet there was a subtle affection to his tone. "And be quick with it. I would have you at our side to see this through."

"It is my honor," the giant said.

The three Reapers looked almost undecided throughout the exchange. Lemanda felt a tinge of irritation that these Reapers so willingly challenged them with equal odds while they balked at the idea of attacking the solitary Braggus.

"Your battered ego can wait, Lemanda," Vicken chuckled, placing a hand on her shoulder. "There is more to that one than you know. Come."

The last thing Lemanda saw when she left the room was the towering Braggus Rayne stalking toward his enemies.

BRAGGUS MIGHT HAVE ENJOYED this if he were fighting enemies from outside the coven. That these three were from his own coven and his own ranks lit his blood on fire.

"Would that I could follow you into death and kill you again, you would die a hundred times more," he said, reaching behind his back to draw his seven-foot-long scythe. As one, the Reapers eyed that weapon. They knew what it meant. Whenever the Eldest Reaper drew his weapon, it meant you were dead.

His scythe gripped in one massive hand, Braggus stepped forward, and eyed them, wavy black hair hanging to his shoulders. His black eyebrows lowered, casting a shadow over his smoldering blue grey eyes.

"Come and die with honor. Do not force me to kill you as cowards." Two would fight, he knew, but when he looked into the eyes of the one on the right, Max, he knew that one would run. He fixed Max with his icy glare, and the man actually started to tremble. The other two Reapers knew what was happening and backed away from him.

Braggus released the terrified Reaper, but just as he turned to flee, the Eldest had closed the distance between them. With a one-handed upward sweep of his scythe, he impaled the coward.

The other two Reapers came in at his back, and Braggus continued the sweep, lifting the dying Max from the ground and turning to launch him at the other two.

They leaped over the body and flew at Braggus. The Eldest Reaper dropped his scythe and launched himself from the floor. With each of his powerful hands he reached forward. The two Reapers brought the shafts of their weapons before them defensively, but the mighty Eldest Reaper thrust his palms forward and snapped the shafts, gripped each of them by their throats.

Not only was their descent halted, but so much power had he used in his leap, that Braggus carried them thirty feet into the air and slammed them into the ceiling. As they began to fall, Braggus still held them by the throat, and twisted around during their descent to slam them to the ground. He snapped their necks on impact, and while they lay there twitching in pain as their crushed windpipes repaired themselves, he stood, grabbed up his scythe, and waited.

Their necks healed, the two shaken Reapers came back to their feet and Braggus dashed forward, sweeping his mighty weapon. He skidded to a stop behind the frozen warriors, then walked toward the door, not bothering to look back. He needn't have bothered, for the two former Reapers fell in half to death's welcoming embrace.

CHAPTER 57

With every minute that passed, the fighting seemed to escalate towards a full battle. Vampire and lycan bodies —both humanoid and lupine—crashed through walls and flew through the air. Biting, slashing, shooting, howling, screaming, hissing. The human side of Saaya's nature recognized it as something out of the worst of a human's nightmares. The vampiric side, the *Ancestor* side of her nature, felt both thrill and disappointment.

As she made her way through the halls, searching for her brother, she came to understand firsthand why the *Ancestors* avoided contact with the rest of the world. The infighting in this beautiful coven was shameful. It was inexcusable for immortals to fight each other in such a way. Scheming ambitions were a trait of short-lived humans. Did the endless years afforded an immortal not bring wisdom?

She encountered a lone pureblood who looked as though he had seen quite a bit of fighting, judging from his tattered clothes. When he noticed her, he sniffed the air and smiled, his pale red eyes hungry.

"I smell a *skiek*," he said. "I never thought to see half a vampire in our midst, especially when I'm so in need of replenishing." His fangs elongated as he approached her. "I guess it's true that there is such a thing as free lunch—"

Saaya was instantly in front of him. She rammed her hand into his chest, and in one motion, crushed his heart and ripped her hand free.

The other vampire looked down at her in shock for only a moment before dropping to his knees to decay on the floor.

Saaya tossed the destroyed organ down the hall behind her and ripped his shirt off his body. She continued down the hallway wiping off her bloody hand. Perhaps she should listen to her brother and find a weapon. She disliked getting her hands dirty.

The floor started to vibrate, then the pictures on the walls shook, some of them falling to shatter on the floor. Saaya stopped and glanced around, listening. Then she heard the growling and barking sounds of giant wolves. Two of them.

The floor vibrated again, and she looked down just as a huge claw burst through the floor and gripped her ankle. Before she could react, the werewolf pulled her through the floor.

Broken mortar and tile, and splintered wood cut her skin as she traveled through the floor. The wolf pulled her free and slung her away. Saaya landed on her back, immediately rolled to her feet, and launched herself back up at the werewolf clinging to the ceiling.

Another wolf tackled her midair of her descent. Both Saaya and the new attacker crashed into a thick pillar, cracking it. Saaya kept her eyes open through it all, knowing how fast a lycan attack could happen.

Her instincts saved her, for as soon as they hit the pillar, serrated teeth in a huge gaping maw rushed toward her face.

Her tiny hands snapped up, one under the monster's chin, and when she lifted its head, she grabbed its neck with her other hand. Pinned to the pillar by a wolf three times her size, feet dangling four feet from the floor, Saaya held the wolf at bay. Then, with strength beyond anything the surprised lycan could understand, she tucked her legs in and kicked it in the chest. It flew back a distance, but righted itself as soon as it hit the floor and raced in again.

Lavender eyes aflame, the *dampeal* ran toward the beast and jumped over its head just as it snapped at her. Upside down in a forward flip, she reached down and grabbed the sides of its head. She kicked her feet out to create more momentum and brought the wolf over her in a upward arc, sending it flying into the ceiling.

As the brown wolf fell, two more werewolves came at her from both sides, one of them the one that pulled her through the floor. She leaped backward as the third lycan climbed back to its feet, and the three wolves charged her.

The *dampeal* ran toward, then up the side of the wall. Just as they reached her, she kicked off the wall in a sideways flip, driving her elongated nails through the top of the nearest beast's hard skull.

She landed on the back of the second lycan as the first collapsed to the floor. Her hands were a blur as she drove her nails through the back of the wolf's neck with one-two jabs, sending blood spattering everywhere.

Again, she was away before the beast fell, charging then dropping to the floor. She slid under the legs of the third wolf as it slashed at her with a claw larger than her head. Saaya gripped the ankle of one of its hind legs and pulled, throwing it off balance.

The *dampeal* was up again and hopped on its back. She had to work fast. There was a little secret the *Ancestors* knew that even few Elders were privy to. If one didn't have silver, the only other way to kill a lycan was to remove the heart or brain, and destroy it. Any organ, no matter how damaged, would repair itself, just as in a vampire. But unlike a vampire, if the wolf's heart or brain was replaced in its chest, the body would recognize it and re-assimilate it.

The second wolf leaped at her, and Saaya ducked behind the wolf's back on which she still clung. With a quick jab, she drove her nails in and out of its neck as it sailed overhead. Blood spurted from the wound as its limp body crashed into the floor and slid into the wall. That would buy her perhaps half a minute. More than enough.

Saaya repeatedly drove her nails into the wolf's back. The beast grunted and howled, and she held on as it spun about, trying to dislodge her. When it stumbled, she drove her right hand into the back of its neck. When it arched its back she swung her legs around and dropped down in front of it, then hopped forward and drove her hand into its chest as she did with the vampire just minutes before.

The thickness from the lycan's much tougher bones required more force, but her hand found the pumping organ. With a brutal squeeze, she crushed the heart and ripped it free, then on instinct, threw it behind her.

The lycan that was coming from behind to bite her in half suddenly found its mouth full of its pack-mate's heart. It spat the thing out, but that brief moment of distraction was enough. Again, the *dampeal* was there, and drove her hand through its chest, to similar fatal result.

She looked over her shoulder to see that she must have cut that third wolf deeper than she'd thought, for it was barely struggling to its feet. In short order she went across the room and the number of dead lycans numbered three.

She looked around at the broken and crumbling walls. A giant hole in the ceiling showed a glimpse in the room above, where she'd just been.

Saaya looked down at herself and shook her head. She had expected to fight, of course, so she hadn't worn one of her many elaborately hand woven saris or other valuable clothes. Still, her simple blue formfitting top and bottom—for ease of motion of course—were ruined. "I liked this color," she lamented, still looking at herself.

A man's agonized voice echoed through the halls just before Kafeel crashed through the ceiling and slammed into the cracked pillar behind her. She turned, eyes going wide at the sight of her injured brother. Not once in her life had she seen him so pained.

In the hole above, Alicia grinned down at them. "You should be proud, little half-breed. There was an instant when I believed he might gain the upper hand." Saaya's lips curled away from her elongated fangs, and the Countess laughed at her. "Oh the flaming anger of retribution," the *Ancestor* said dramatically. "Save it for later, little girl." She stomped her foot down on the floor, which was also the weakened ceiling of the room where Saaya stood over the still struggling Kafeel. It sounded like the entire room groaned.

"I shall have to leave you here while I attend to the rest of this nonsense."

Saaya leaped, ascending more than thirty feet toward the woman, but an invisible force slammed into her and sent her racing back to the floor. So hard was her impact that it sent a spiderweb of cracks slithering away.

Alicia smiled, and the already damaged pillar crumbled. Behind the *dampeal*, two more pillars started to break apart.

"Bye, now," the woman said, then disappeared from view just as the final pillar burst. The ceiling fell in huge chunks, crashing around them. Saaya braced herself and rammed her shoulder into a large piece of the ceiling. Despite knocking the chunk away, the effort was futile. The rest of the ceiling crashed down on them and Saaya and Kafeel were buried under a ton of darkness.

CHAPTER 58

M ore than once Jelani stole glances at Remy, who leaned against his chair, smirking back at him.

"Careful, young man," Marcus joked. "Never take your eyes off your opponent."

"Less opponent and more enemy," Jelani quipped.

Marcus and Berius looked at each other as though their feelings were hurt. "Not at all," Marcus said, grinning. He lowered his stance, creeping closer as they circled. "We are no more your enemy than you are ours."

"What?" Jelani ducked and dove aside as that damned claymore came rushing at his head. He came to his feet and brought both his daggers in an upward counterclockwise arc, knocking the huge blade aside. The parry took a considerable amount of strength. He reminded himself to be wary of the stronger Berius.

"We aren't enemies," Marcus said, leaping forward and slashing at Jelani's face with his silver-tipped claws. "It's business, buddy. A guy has to follow orders or everything goes to shit."

This had to be the strangest fight Jelani had ever been involved in. Granted, as a human, he had never been forced to use his skills in a real life or death fight, but even sparring, he had never actually been engaged in conversation, let alone of this nature.

"You can't take these types of things personally," Marcus continued, sidestepping to allow Berius in for a forward thrust, which Jelani also sidestepped to the opposite direction of Marcus. Marcus then hopped over Berius's sword, having anticipated Jelani's dodge.

Jelani was familiar with this duo's tactics from their last encounter, so he was ready. He snapped his foot up into a sideways kick to Marcus's abdomen, stopping the man's descent. Jelani snapped his foot back, then out again into the other man's face. He followed up with a sideways swipe of his dagger.

Marcus's head snapped back, but then he continued backward, bending all the way back to lie on the floor, his legs bent backward. Once Jelani's weapon passed safely over him, Marcus came upright again and grinned at Jelani, who hopped away.

"C'mon, mate," the Hunter said. "You're gonna have to do better'n that if you plan to survive this."

"Stop playing and get this done!" Remy shouted from across the room. "There's no time for this!"

"Why not deal with your more important business and leave this to us, yes?" Marcus replied.

Jelani came in fast, jabbing and kicking. Marcus deftly avoided every attack, then when Jelani stabbed forward, the Hunter leaned aside and grabbed his wrist. "When our business is done here, we'll be at your side ... Eldest Hunter."

That seemed to placate the irritated Remy. "Fine. Be done with him and join me. By now Elder Massius is securing his place and I want to be right there."

"Of course," Marcus said, slinging Jelani around in line for Berius's wicked sword.

Jelani ducked and felt a rush of air above his head from where the claymore just missed him. He slashed out at Marcus's stomach, forcing the Hunter to release him, then leaped backward inside the reach of that silver girder that Berius called a sword.

He turned and drove the butt of his dagger into the larger man's nose, then brought his other dagger in line with Berius's ribcage.

The big man was fast enough to avoid the killing blow, but still felt the bite of the silver blade as it dealt a glancing cut through his skin and struck one of his ribs. Berius growled and limped aside.

The small victory cost Jelani, and he felt four lines of fire rake down his back. In pure reaction to the pain, Jelani's back arched, and then Marcus's hand clamped around his throat.

Jelani saw the second silver tipped claws coming for his chest, and he dropped the dagger in his right hand and grabbed Marcus's wrist. He twisted it to the left, forcing Marcus to go with the motion and overextend his body, then spun the dagger in his left hand into a forward grip and stabbed over his chest. The maneuver had little power, as Jelani was reaching across his body, but he managed a shallow stab to the other vampire's shoulder.

Marcus hissed and leaped into a handless cartwheel, relieving the twisting pressure on his wrist, then turned his hand and grabbed hold of Jelani's wrist, reversing the hold. He suddenly let go, but in doing so, raked his claws down Jelani's hand.

The searing pain of the silver forced Jelani to drop his remaining dagger. He snatched his hand back and on instinct, dropped to a crouching spin that brought him underneath Berius's stabbing sword. Jelani scooped up his dropped dagger as he turned, and stabbed it up into the big man's leg.

Berius growled, reversed the grip on his claymore, and drove it straight down. Jelani let go of the dagger and dropped and rolled away. He came to his feet just as Berius dislodged the blade from his smoking leg and launched it at him. Jelani snatched the weapon out of the air and skipped backward as Marcus came in again.

"You know it needn't be like this," Marcus said, slashing those silver claws.

"This coming from someone who says things like 'needn't',"

Jelani replied, leaning away and ducking under the other man's swiping and stabbing claws. From over Marcus's shoulder, he saw Berius gritting his teeth as he held his leg, the smoking wound slowly knitting closed. He had to find a way to injure one of them enough to buy him time to deal with the other.

Marcus apparently read the thought in his face. "Patience, now," he soothed. "Patience wins the race."

"I'll keep that in mind."

From somewhere else in the room, Jelani heard his best friend, in lupine form, battling the brown werewolves. It stabbed at him to hear the biting, tearing, and pained howls and not know if Daniel was winning the fight or dying a horrible death.

"A question," Marcus said just before kicking Jelani in the abdomen. He followed up with an uppercut that knocked Jelani off his feet.

Jelani hit the floor on his back and he rolled aside, narrowly avoiding the silver claws stabbing for his chest. "I suppose you'll ask me, whether I respond or not," Jelani said, springing back at the Hunter. His path was altered when Berius's thick shoulder smashed into him from the side and sent Jelani tumbling through the air and then rolling on the floor.

He righted himself just as that claymore came down for his head. He leaned aside and the blade drove into the floor so close, it cut the side of his head. The burn of that silver felt like it would fry his brain. Jelani grunted through it and swept his feet out in a scissor motion, throwing the big man off balance.

"What would you do," Marcus continued, passing over his stumbling partner. His knees crashed into Jelani's chest and bore him to the ground. "… if you did manage to get your hands on Remy?"

Jelani reversed the grip on his remaining dagger, but before he could drive it into Marcus's side, the tip of Berius's claymore appeared directly over his forehead.

A glimmer passed over Marcus's red eyes as he smiled down at Jelani. "Hmm?"

Helpless, Jelani looked from Marcus to that sword. He had to think fast. Where was Daniel? Was he still alive? He heard the sound of fighting, but it was no longer in the room. That brought hope that his friend still lived and fought, but little hope for Jelani to get out of this situation. Perhaps if he could knock Marcus over him …"

"You're making this harder than it has to be, mate?" Marcus continued. He leaned down until his face was right over Jelani's. "What is it with you Americans and your 'never say die' shit?" He winked at Jelani, then sat up again, knees still pressed on his chest. "But, one question at a time, right?"

"I'd like to say that I'd take my time gutting him in front of all his followers," Jelani answered, "but that's a little too macabre for me. I'd just kill him, but I'd still do it in front of all his buddies."

Marcus leaned back a bit, nodded, then stood. Berius moved his sword.

As soon as that sword was away from his head, Jelani was on his feet and backpedalling from the two Hunters. To his confusion, though, he saw Berius sheathing his claymore across his back.

"Relax," Marcus said with a lazy smile. They approached Jelani, who paced them, moving away.

Marcus scooped up Jelani's other weapon and inspected it. "Nice dagger," he remarked, turning it this way and that. "Bugger's got a nasty bite, but all silver does, doesn't it?" He tossed the weapon to the disbelieving Jelani, who grabbed it out of the air.

"Close your mouth or flies'll get in there," Marcus said, then laughed when Jelani's teeth clicked when he shut it. "Look, mate." He glanced to his left and right as though making sure no one was listening. "I'll admit that if the real Eldest Hunter or one of the Elders ordered it, you'd be dust right now. But they ain't given us the orders, just some craven upstart who got the position handed to him."

Jelani didn't know how to react. "So … what? You're just gonna let me go kill him?"

Marcus shrugged. "Whether you do it or not, I don't think Remy is gonna survive tonight. He's made a few enemies, not least of which is a ninja-like fellow who's probably searching for him now. If I were you, I'd get moving before you miss your chance."

"Why didn't you just kill him?" Jelani said. "There's nothing that could make me believe you couldn't have done it a long time ago."

The mostly silent Berius laughed, and Marcus joined in.

"I say something funny?" Jelani asked, glancing from one to the other.

"Indirectly," Marcus said. "Trust me …" he saw the responding expression on Jelani's face, then amended, "well, trust in the fact that it would be more satisfying to watch Remy's uncreation at the hands of a fledgling *shaquora*. That would make my day." He gave Berius a playful backhand to the stomach and the pair shared another round of laughter.

"So, we fighting together, then?" Jelani asked, not sure whether or not he liked that idea. These two, especially Marcus, struck him as a lighter shade of psychotic.

Marcus snorted and turned away. "Don't push your luck. Normally I'd say you could find him where the least bit of fighting is going on. But if Yako lives, he'll be on Remy's trail, so he won't take any chances. He'll be somewhere in the middle of the action."

"Why wouldn't Yako be alive?" Jelani asked just before the Hunters were out of the room.

"I don't know of anybody who's survived a run-in with The Wraiths, mate" Marcus replied. "But then, Yako ain't just anybody."

The Wraiths? Whatever that was, it didn't sound good. Jelani needed to get this done and be away from this place.

The sound of fighting and dying brought him out of his thoughts and he remembered Daniel. He hated himself for thinking it, but he would have to hope that Daniel could survive this on his own. His friend could be anywhere now, and Jelani couldn't just roam the castle looking for him. And what of Saaya and Kafeel?

He shook his head and headed in the direction he'd last seen Remy go. He'd have to worry about them all later. They each had their part to play in this, as did he.

CHAPTER 59

From his vantage point near the ceiling, Yako scanned the chaos below, noting every individual who fought against the coven, and thus, him. He looked up and confirmed Mariska's similar position across the open audience hall.

Peles Coven was in shambles. Beautiful architecture and art had been shredded and broken, the polished marble floors stained with blood. It didn't matter.

Yako never much concerned himself with details like this. That was for the coven's leaders to deal with. His province was vampiric law, and the death of those who stepped outside of it.

Below, several brown werewolves and a traitorous silver attacked and killed three Silver Pack wolves. Yako narrowed his eyes. Darren thought he'd obliterated the Woodland Pack, but this scene spoke a different truth.

He moved on, leaping from balcony to balcony, railing to railing. The Eldest Hunter only touched the floor when it was unavoidable, preferring to remain above the conflict. He needed to reach Massius and Remy as quickly as possible and fighting would only slow him.

He took note of Mariska's position. The Second Hunter had

been forced to drop to ground level to make her way to the next room. A Woodland Lycan took notice of her, but with a well aimed silver bullet into the eye, it dropped dead as she passed.

Yako made his way across the room and came to the second floor walkway. He jumped the remaining distance and landed on the walkway, making his way for the door.

Just on the other side of the door were two vampires watching the action below. They turned and saw the Eldest Hunter approaching them, and their eyes widened in fear.

He continued his steady pace even as they leveled their guns at him. Yako's hand snapped over his shoulder and he drew his sword. The vampires fired, and he deflected and dodged the bullets, closing the distance.

The vampires swore and fired again, to the same result. When he was within a dozen feet of his enemies, Yako dashed forward with a horizontal swipe of his black sword. He continued on as two heads fell from their decaying bodies.

He found Mariska in the next room, perched high above the floor. She was tucked so tightly between the side protrusion of a pillar and the ceiling that he almost missed her. A heartbeat later he saw the reason for her concealment.

He quietly lowered himself to the floor and looked down at the cloaked forms of Tannis and Denari stalking about the room, scythes in hand searching the area. The corpses of werewolves and the ashes of vampires littered the floor around them. These two would have to be destroyed, but Yako and Mariska alone would be sorely pressed to deal with both of The Wraiths fighting together. They would either need to separate the pair, or increase their numbers.

That still posed the problem of delaying his confrontation with Remy and Massius, and that didn't account for whatever Elder Alicia was capable of. Yako would have to figure out how to deal with her.

With seemingly not a care at all, the Reapers left the room in the direction Yako had just come. He waited a minute longer, then looked up at Mariska, who was watching him. He nodded at the woman, then came to his feet and sprinted silent as a shadow across the walkway.

He stopped at the door and listened. There was conversation on the other side. Massius's voice. Yako continued to listen until he heard what he had hoped for. Remy's answering voice.

Yako signaled for Mariska to join him, and the Second dropped from the top of another pillar and raced across the room. She leaped the forty-foot height to grab hold of the rail and hoisted herself over and onto the walkway behind him.

Yako eased the door open and crept in. Close behind, Mariska carefully closed the door and took up a position beside him.

"This is not going as smoothly as I might have hoped," Remy was saying.

The old vampire regarded him with irritation. "You really thought this would go perfectly, Remy? When has anything in life ever gone exactly to plan?" He turned his back. "Don't be so impatient, boy. Things are well in hand. I left Braggus to deal with Lemanda, who is surely dead by now, and I sent The Wraiths to deal with Yako. Whatever his skills, they are no match for Tannis and Denari."

Remy looked like he might have actually trembled at the mention of the Reapers. "A good plan, Elder, but I would feel better to look upon the ashes of the aforementioned with my own eyes."

"Easy enough," Massius said with a grin. "Go and seek out Braggus and The Wraiths and ask that they supply you with the proof you desire."

"There isn't time for that," Remy said.

Massius sniggered. "Of course there isn't."

"How fairs what is left of the Woodland Pack?" Remy asked.

"Not many of them left," Massius answered, his voice going sour. "Although this Darren Lacey was incorrect in his assumption to have killed them off, he did succeed in severely reducing their numbers. Still, with their help and our allies from my own contacts in Russia, we will win the day."

Russia. Now it made sense. Yako's already narrowed eyes smoldered. That was where the augmented numbers of Massius's force had come from.

"And Vicken and Stavros?" Remy asked.

Massius clasped his hands behind his back. "When Braggus returns to me, and your reckless duo returns to you, we will combine our efforts to finish them. With Alicia's help it should be no problem. Once the High Elder and his war brother are dust at my feet, the rest will be simple enough.

"Simple does not denote difficulty," Remy replied.

Yako arched an eyebrow and glanced at Mariska, who also looked amused. It was the wittiest remark either of them had heard from the irritating Hunter.

He signaled for Mariska to hold her position, and he crept closer until he was nearly above them. Fortunately, the more powerful Massius was closer, so Yako would take him first.

The muscles in his legs tightened, then he sprang up and over the rail, gliding down on his prey. His mind was suddenly assaulted as if struck by a hammer, and his head snapped back, causing him to fall awkwardly the rest of the distance to crash into the floor.

"What the hell?" Remy said, looking up toward the walkway above, then back down at Yako, who was struggling to his feet.

"I imagine that were I not here, you would be a pile of nothingness, Remy," Massius said.

"I thought you said The Wraiths took care of him! Did he kill them both?"

"More probably, he ran from them," Massius replied, standing over Yako.

Remy's wide eyes darted this way and that. "Then let's kill him now and be done with it."

"You would not engage him in a fair fight?" Massius teased.

"Was it fair that he sought to kill you from above and behind?"

Massius waved a hand at him. "This one is a ninja first and always. With them, it is about efficiency. His forefathers were the same, though it is arguable as to whether or not they were as skilled this one."

Massius took his time approaching Yako, whose head felt like it was in the grip of a vice. "But you are right. We dare not trifle with him—"

A silver bullet slammed into the back of his shoulder and passed through the front. Massius growled and fell to his knees.

Remy drew his gun and fired. "Dammit! We should have known he would bring his little toy along."

Mariska had bought Yako the relief he needed, and the Eldest Hunter—still gripping his sword—swiped it outward at the distracted Massius, severing his foot.

The old vampire wailed and tumbled to the floor, then sent a mental attack so powerful, it took all of Yako's will to keep his mind from being destroyed.

Mariska and Remy continued to fire at one another. Though her gun was silenced, Remy's was not, and the sound of gunfire shattered the quiet of the room. The blade of a giant axe split one of the doors to the side of the room, and the two pieces flew apart to admit an enraged Vicken and Stavros, a smirking Lemanda in tow.

"Finally, the rats have been cornered," Vicken boomed.

"Another step," Massius threatened, "and your precious Eldest Hunter will be reduced to a babbling idiot for the duration of his miserable existence."

Vicken didn't hesitate. "My precious Eldest Hunter would never allow himself to be held hostage, least of all by one such as yourself, Massius."

Massius's confidence wavered just a little, but it was enough for Yako to push him farther away from his mind.

"Kill him now, you idiot," Massius hissed at Remy, but Mariska had reloaded and was firing again.

Remy dove aside, firing back, and Massius was forced to release his attack on Yako and hobble away.

Stavros shook his head. "Disgraceful. This is what you are reduced to, Massius? A crippled old fool about to die in dishonor?"

Yako looked past the three Elders to see what looked like a room reduced to rubble. The ceiling had fallen and now lay broken and splintered on the floor.

"I think I'm hardly about to die, here," Massius replied, and suddenly Mariska cried out and dropped her gun. She collapsed beside it and pressed her hands agains the sides of her head.

Yako hopped to his feet and charged the Elder. He brought his sword up and forward, the tip lined perfectly with the old vampire's side. Massius attacked his mind again, and Yako dropped to the floor.

"I've seen enough!" Vicken bellowed. "See how well your mind tricks work on me, craven!"

The enraged High Elder stalked toward Massius, and Yako's mind was once again released. From the corner of his eye, he saw Vicken's step falter just a bit before he continued toward Massius, who was still hobbling away.

Mariska was back on her feet, taking aim at Remy, who was hiding behind one of the pillars, taking aim at Lemanda and Stavros.

The door behind Massius opened to admit Tannis and Denari. The two Reapers entered side by side, then parted to reveal a widely smiling woman. Alicia.

She clapped her hands together. "I couldn't have wished for a better conclusion. I was certain I would have to hunt you all down individually, but you've so conveniently bundled yourselves together for me."

"Have your wits left you, Alicia?" Vicken said. "Have you—"

"Be SILENT!" the woman commanded. Vicken's eyes widened in shock as he suddenly lifted into the air and flew across the room. He crashed into the wall and was held there, surprise and outrage clear on his face. Alicia looked back at the other two Elders. Stavros looked as equally dumbfounded as the High Elder, while Lemanda looked resolved.

"You're tougher than I thought, Lemanda," Alicia said. "It never crossed my mind that you could recover from such a burning. Your sisters would be proud."

"What do you know of my sisters?" Lemanda demanded.

"More than you could imagine," Alicia replied evenly. "They were much more than you will ever be." Her tone was almost regretful.

"And you." She looked at Yako, who had backed away to keep her and The Wraiths in his field of vision. "You are also more resilient than I had anticipated. I find myself at a loss that I could so misjudge you."

On the walkway above, Mariska shifted her aim to Alicia.

The Countess closed her eyes as a half smile crept across her face. "Oh, little Second. If you pull that trigger I will torture you in ways you cannot imagine. I actually quite like you, which is why I suggest you reconsider. Mariska looked to Yako. He locked eyes with her and gave a subtle shake of his head.

Tannis and Denari started toward Yako.

"Not yet," Alicia said. "There may be hope for him." The Wraiths halted instantly, as if they'd never moved in the first place.

"No!" Massius commanded. "He is a disgrace to my Order of Hunters! He must be executed—"

His last words choked off with a grunt, and Massius fell to his knees, clutching at his chest.

"This is why you shouldn't talk, Massius," Alicia said in a gentle tone that belied her viciousness. "I'd actually forgotten about you, which is surprising, given our little adventure here. But, you really are quite forgettable … if supremely annoying."

An invisible force lifted the wide-eyed Massius into the air, and all he could do was watch as Yako's own sword was ripped from the Eldest Hunter's grasp. The blade hung in the air, turned, and flew past the smiling woman to sheath itself into the old vampire's chest.

Blood spurted from Massius's mouth, and steam seeped from the wound. He looked down at his chest, then back at Alicia, disbelief clear on his face.

"Aw. Don't look at me so," Alicia said. "Had you no idea of the true nature of our arrangement, you old badger? How could you not know ..." She trailed off as Massius began to decay, death greedily claiming him. Alicia shrugged. "Ah, well, I suppose I should have spoken more quickly, shouldn't I?" She looked at the others in the room, none of whom spoke. "Not a one of you are much fun at all."

"What the hell are you, woman?" Stavros demanded.

Alicia laughed. "I must admit that one of the things I most like about you, Stavros, is your mettle. Here you are, helpless and about to die, and still you season your question with the spice of a demand."

Yako's sword, now hovering over the remains of Massius, turned to face Vicken. The Elder watched the sword with steely-eyed resolve. No coward was Vicken.

"In answer to your question, Lord Stavros, I am what came before you." She looked at everyone. "All of you. I am Countess Alicia Magnus Lerae."

Stavros gaped at her. "Countess? You would have us believe you are one of the illustrious *Ancestors* from history?"

"She speaks the truth, old friend," Lemanda said.

"What do you know of this?" Stavros demanded of her.

"I have recently felt her power," Lemanda said. "It's true."

Stavros stared into her eyes. "You don't think we can stop her, do you?"

In response, Lemanda held his gaze, but said nothing.

Stavros turned back to face Alicia. "I have lived too many years to bend my knee before an unfit ruler. You fancy yourself an

Ancestor, but what I know of them speaks of honor, nobility, and respect."

"You know nothing of us," Alicia spat, and Stavros flew into the far wall, then lifted to slam into the ceiling. The big man dropped heavily to the floor, then was lifted again and thrown in every direction around the spacious room.

Yako eyed his sword, which was positioned behind and to the side of the woman. He glanced at Tannis and Denari. Their unwavering attention was fixed on him. They would be on Yako before he made it halfway to his sword.

"Despite having more fun in just a single day than I've had in many, many decades," Alicia declared. "It's time we bring this night to its conclusion, shall we?"

Behind her, Tannis moved to her side, placing himself between Yako and his sword. "A shame the lot of you could not be swayed to my cause." There seemed a genuine tinge of regret in the *Ancestor's* tone at that. "I see you as the only assets of value in this rather … sordid organization you call a coven. Our entire species has fallen into a horrible state of decadence and degradation." She looked at Stavros. "If you wonder why we disappeared from the world, it is because of our desire not to mingle with members of a declining species. I for one, could stand aside no longer."

Stavros lifted from the ground again and slammed into the wall next to Vicken. "I will see to the uncreation of your mighty icon first," the Countess said, "after which, the rest of you will join him. I give you time to rethink your position, or attack in futility and expedite your demise. Your choice is your own."

Yako glanced up to see Mariska taking aim at Alicia, but then several things happened at once.

A spinning silver dagger flew from the walkway to Mariska's right and buried itself in Tannis's shoulder. When the screeching Reaper lurched forward, Yako burst into action. He leaped over the bending Reaper and snatched his sword out of the air. He landed in a kneeling position and at the same time, swiped his sword out, staring directly into the eyes of the surprised Countess.

Tannis stumbled back a few steps, then fell away, his torso separating from the lower half of his body. Denari hissed in rage, but even he was not fast enough, for Yako spun on his heels, coming up, then down again, driving his sword through Tannis's chest and into the marble floor. The dismembered Reaper screeched again, clawing at Yako, but the Eldest Hunter held on.

Denari was nearly upon him, but he trusted his Second. Bullets rained down on Denari, forcing him back.

In that moment, everything turned to chaos. The doors from where Alicia had come shattered under the weight of a werewolf. More poured through the opening, vampires in their midst.

Alicia half turned to regard the new force. "Kill them."

Her words were lost in the explosion of the wall on the other side of the room. Through the door, Yako saw the rubble explode upward, stone, mortar, and wood flying everywhere. A baritone voice bellowed as though cursing heaven and hell alike. Two figures materialized in the cloud of dust and debris, lavender eyes aflame.

CHAPTER 60

J elani realized it was a risk to creep into the room, but he
hadn't imagined how close to death he would come when he
slipped through the door and found himself next to the very
woman who had hunted him what felt like a lifetime ago.

As soon as he'd opened the door and slipped in, he was facing
the barrel of a Glock. Apparently Yako must have passed on the
memo of their little alliance, for he saw recognition in her eyes,
and she returned her attention to the action below as though he
mattered not at all.

Jelani looked over the rail to see Yako in a difficult situation.
His sword was hovering behind the woman who had nearly killed
Jelani and the others earlier, and two grim reaper-looking things
were watching him.

He considered the scene below him. It was pointless to even try
something with that woman. For all Jelani knew, she might bring
the whole castle down on their heads. A flicker of movement
caught his eye, and he looked farther across the room to see Remy
struggling to get a good shot at Lemanda from around a pillar he
was hiding behind.

Jelani wanted badly to take him out, but he had to be patient.

He did a quick scan of the room, seeing two dangerous-looking men—well, they would have looked dangerous if they weren't pinned against the wall—Alicia in the center, and the two grim reapers watching Yako. There was a pile of ash indicating that someone had recently bit the dust, and then there was Remy and Lemanda.

He looked back down at Yako and the two ghost things. They were the closest and the clearer shot.

Jelani slid a silver dagger from its sheath strapped to his leg, and took aim. He glanced at Mariska who was now watching him. The threat in her cold eyes was clear. Whatever he was planning to do, he'd better get it right.

He looked from one of the cloaked figures to the other, unable to make up his mind. The decision was made for him when one of the grim reapers moved away and stood next to Yako's sword. Perfect.

Jelani let fly. His aim was true, and the spinning dagger buried itself into the back of the cloaked thing's shoulder. Its screech was deafening, but the result was what Jelani had hoped for.

When it lurched forward, the Eldest Hunter dashed toward his sword and executed the most amazing maneuver Jelani had ever seen. Yako leaped in a straight-bodied flip, grabbed his sword while upside down, and cut that thing in half at the same time he landed in a kneeling position.

Jelani's mouth fell open, but then the action started and hell unleashed. Mariska was up and firing at the second grim reaper thing while Yako finished off the first. Remy started firing at Lemanda, who simply waved the bullets aside and thrust her hand out, knocking him away.

The two rough-looking men were still pinned to the wall, and Jelani was wondering if he should try to help them, since they were obviously enemies of Alicia. Again, events happened that made the decision unnecessary.

The door behind Alicia crashed open and werewolves and

vampires poured through. Jelani was trying to decide whether to watch the fight or join in when an angry voice roared, and rubble burst through the doorway.

To Jelani's astonishment, Kafeel stalked through the cloud of dirt and dust, his tiny sister next to him. Both siblings looked positively incensed, and despite their distance, Jelani felt immense power radiating from them.

He spotted Remy trying to use the distraction to leave the room. "I don't think so, buddy," Jelani muttered, sprinting past Mariska.

Remy had circled behind the others and was almost to the door. Jelani knew he wouldn't reach him in time, so he leaped over the rail, drew the last two daggers he had strapped to his hips, and let fly.

One of the daggers struck Remy in the leg, causing him to bend sideways and accidentally avoid the second blade. *Dumb luck*, Jelani thought as he descended.

He hit the ground in a roll and sprinted toward the Hunter, snatching up one of his daggers mid stride. He sprang forward, gliding the last dozen feet toward Remy when the wall burst apart in several places, sending him spinning head over heals to crash and roll on the floor.

"Ah damn," he groaned. "What now?"

A roar that shook the room answered him. Jelani looked back and saw a massive fully formed black werewolf that could only have been Darren Lacey stalking through the destruction on two legs, his pack behind him. It was like watching seven giant two-legged wolves behind an even bigger one, come marching straight out of a nightmare.

The two men pinned to the wall dropped to the floor, and immediately took up their weapons. Alicia paid them no heed and instead, focused her attention on this pack of huge werewolves.

"After so long, the descendants of the Wargkhull show themselves," the Countess said. "I would never have thought your noble race would stoop to this."

In response, the giant wolf that was Darren barked, and even that sound made Jelani's chest vibrate.

The wolves on the opposite side of the room charged, and the great black lycan roared again, and his pack surged forward.

All around Alicia, Saaya, and Kafeel, was a medley of raking claws, snapping jaws and flying fur. Wolves growled, howled, and died. Vampires entered the fray, darting this way and that, firing guns equipped with deadly silver bullets, or wielding silver bladed weapons.

Kafeel circled around until he was in front of Alicia, Saaya still beside him.

"You and your baby sister look as though you wish for a fight," Alicia said brightly. "Are you certain you want me to oblige?"

The siblings said nothing.

From the corner of his eye, Jelani saw Mariska leap from her perch above the action. She landed in the thick of the chaos and went to work. At the side of the conflict, Remy held back, picking his shots but staying mostly unnoticed.

"I got something for you," Jelani said, taking aim. He was just about to throw one of his daggers when he saw that remaining cloaked grim reaper-thing coming in his direction.

"Son of a bitch," Jelani muttered under his breath, turning and backing away. His gut told him he didn't want any part of a fight with that one. He glanced back at Remy, who was still creeping on the outskirts of the fighting. "Does that guy have nine lives or something?"

"*Shaquoooraaaa*," the thing hissed.

Ever since he had been turned, Jelani had only retained a fraction of his human warmth. Now it seemed like every bit of that warmth fled him at the sound of that ghostly voice. "What the hell are you, man?"

"*Youuuur uncreatiooon.*"

The thing was nearly on him, and Jelani backpedaled, trying to buy time. To his disbelief, it was holding a scythe … a scythe! And, a blade at each end! *I guess now I know why they call you Reapers*, Jelani thought. He wanted to laugh at what should have been ridiculous, but that curved blade looked as if it was itching to cleave him in half.

"Plenty of folks here for you to uncreate," Jelani replied, "but it's not gonna be me."

The Reaper launched into the most furious attack Jelani had ever encountered, and in the span of a few seconds he was cut in several places and fighting for his life. The daggers in his hands spun, blocking and parrying. His hands moved of their own accord as he worked to keep up with the whirling curved blades. His enemy had the advantage with that long shaft and blades on either end, but Jelani would eventually find an opening.

The Reaper moved back a few steps and Jelani took that opportunity to glance about his person, taking note of how many daggers he had left. Two in his hands and three that he'd recovered.

The Reaper came back in, this time leading with the top of the blade thrusting forward. Jelani dodged to the side and chopped down, forcing the blade low. He was about to throw his free dagger into the thing's face, but it moved forward and gripped him by the neck. Before Jelani could react, it threw him back.

As soon as one of his feet touched the marbled floor, Jelani leaped backward again, keeping his distance from the pursuing Reaper. His arms whipped out left and right, launching two daggers at his enemy. Not waiting to see if they hit the mark, he spun around and landed just behind a vampire that rounded on him, gun leveled at his face. Jelani's hand was at his side, and he launched his third dagger into the man's eye.

Jelani had already retrieved the weapon and was gone even as the male vampire screamed and began to decay. He found his other two daggers, but unfortunately they were still embedded in the cloaked Reaper. Smoke seeped from the wounds, but the creature came on.

"Damn," Jelani said. "How am I supposed to kill this?"

SAAYA FELT the rage radiating from her brother mingle with her own. She also felt the power emanating from the Countess, who grinned at them. She was powerful. Very powerful, and cared not at all that Saaya and Kafeel were the children of another *Ancestor.* She'd tried to reason out why an *Ancestor* would deign to involve herself in the affairs of outsiders like this, but now all she cared about was killing this woman.

"Do you plan to do something?" Alicia inquired, "or will this be a simple staring contest—"

Kafeel was in front of her in an instant, bringing his sword down on her head.

Alicia's grin widened, and she easily moved aside, but Saaya was there. She punched out and the Countess grabbed her hand and began to crush it.

Kafeel came in with another vertical swipe at the woman's head, but she moved away and hurled Saaya toward the blade. So perfect was her brother's control, that Kafeel stopped the sword a hair's breadth from Saaya's face.

The *dampeal* jumped backwards and turned in midair with a barrage of clawed swipes and stabs at the Countess.

The grin never left Alicia's face as she dodged every stab and swipe, every punch and slash of Saaya's elongated nails. Kafeel joined her, stabbing and spinning his long slightly curved sword with such skill and speed, it would have been a marvel to watch, had she not been so engaged.

"Not bad at all," Alicia remarked, ducking underneath another swipe of Kafeel's sword, then leaning away from Saaya's claws. "But you'll have to do a little better, children."

Saaya was suddenly unable to move. Only able to turn her eyes, she looked up to see Kafeel, frozen in a downward stroke.

"Tsk tsk," Alicia said. The two siblings were launched away, crashing into opposite walls of the room.

Kafeel was back in front of the woman, and it seemed this time, Alicia was caught by surprise at his quick recovery. He stabbed toward her abdomen, which she narrowly avoided, then he swiped down and diagonal, scoring a cut to her leg. The distraction freed Saaya, and she came to her brother's aid in an instant.

The *dampeal* delivered a left to right backhand and forehand slap, followed by another lefthand slap, then followed again by a punch to the face.

The Countess staggered back a few steps from the barrage, then looked at Saaya with murderous crimson eyes. Kafeel came in, but the Countess lifted a hand and stopped him dead, then threw him back.

She then came in front of Saaya, assaulting the *dampeal* with punches, slaps, and thrusting claws that slipped through every defense. The endless rain of blows left her disoriented and falling.

Before Saaya hit the floor, however, Alicia grabbed hold of her wrist and yanked her upright. "Let me help you up," the woman said, her voice a whispering rasp in Saaya's ear. The Countess hurled her into the air.

The *dampeal* crashed through the ceiling and into the hall on the second floor, then crashed into the ceiling above that hall. The invisible force wrenched her from the ceiling, and the floor rushed to meet her.

WHITE-HOT RAGE FILLED Kafeel at the sight of his younger sister being thrown through the ceiling and out of sight. *Ancestor* or not, this woman would die. He led with a stabbing feint, then following up with a sideways cut. He turned in the same direction as the dodging woman for another swipe at her head.

Alicia avoided his every attack, grinning that evil red-eyed grin. He was fast but she was faster, always one step ahead. Kafeel moved back, then came forward again, stabbing for her heart. The maneuver worked, for the Countess was caught by surprise when she moved back in.

"Oh my! Not bad!" she said, looking down at his sword, which was now beside her. So fast, was she! Alicia looked down at his hand, which she now held in her unbreakable grip. "You nearly had me, child."

Kafeel dropped to one knee, but braced himself as her arm tensed. He felt the pressure increase, but he fought against it. If she snapped his wrist, the sword would drop from his hand, and likely rise and turn against him. Never, would that happen.

Alicia didn't hide her surprise. "You are a strong one, aren't you?" She tightened her grip, but Kafeel held on, willing the bones in his wrist not to give under the tremendous pressure. "You've aroused my curiosity of your lineage," the Countess remarked.

"They are both well beyond you," Kafeel growled. He struggled back to his feet and grabbed hold of her neck. As her grip tightened on his wrist, so too did he tighten his on her neck. Seconds passed, then a minute, until Alicia's other hand snapped up to grab hold of his other wrist. Slowly, steadily, she forced his grip to loosen, then forced his hand away from her neck.

"So powerful, young *Ancestor*," She said, looking up into his eyes. "I lament that I must destroy such potential."

"Reserve your lamentation for your own uncreation, Countess." Kafeel pulled her close and drove his knee into her chin. The blow snapped her head back and her grip loosened just enough for him to free his sword hand. Kafeel flipped the blade around beside his face, aimed at her chest. He stabbed for her heart.

Alicia hissed and swatted her hand outward. An invisible force slammed into the side of Kafeel's head and sent him flying away, but the woman wasn't done with him yet. His body stopped, then collided into the marble floor, then he was lifted again and held in the air.

"I have exercised with you long enough. I send you to whatever lies beyond death's veil."

Kafeel felt his sword struggling to wrench itself free of his grasp, but he held on to it. He heard Alicia's frustrated hiss, and the struggle intensified. Then the sword began to turn his hand so that the cutting edge was facing his throat. Slowly, it forced its way toward his neck.

"You think I will die by my own sword?" Kafeel growled, and he clamped his eyes shut, willing the blade back.

"Very well," Alicia rasped.

The force that held him aloft now slammed him into the floor again. The beautiful polished marble cracked and broke apart under the weight of the force pressing down on him. At that moment, it was as though the Countess had dropped a mountain on his back.

THE LARGE BLACK wolf struggled to rise. Blood flowed from dozens of cuts and bite marks that covered his battered form. He waited, snapping his jaws at the pain. As the heartbeats passed, his injuries closed and healed until there was nothing left of his battle but the soreness to his body, and even that rapidly faded.

His golden eyes fell upon the two lycans at his feet, reverted back to their human forms in death. Both were female, and both had nearly killed him. They had been faster and almost as strong as he. His primal instincts told him their superior strength was due to age, and their superior speed due to a combination of being smaller and more experienced.

They were two remnants of the Woodland pack, he knew. Every pack had a distinct smell. Feeling the need to return to his human sensibilities, the wolf began the painful process of shifting back to his human form. In less than a minute, he was standing naked in a destroyed ballroom.

"That was faster than last time," Daniel muttered to himself, remembering how long and agonizing that first transformation had been.

He looked around the room and spotted several piles of clothes covered in the ashen remains of dead bloods. They had vampire stink all over them, but it was better than trotting through the place naked.

Properly clothed again, he made his way down the halls, following his ears and his nose. His nose proved the better guide, and soon he found himself entering a room with a hole in the floor. "Place is going to be no more than a pile of rubble when this is done." He remained in the doorway, scanning the room. He thought he smelled Saaya, but there was no sign of her. He continued to sniff, but then he saw a pile of plaster and wood shift.

He ran across the room and lifted a wooden beam with one hand, digging through the rubble with the other. The diminutive *dampeal*, still beautiful despite being covered in dirt and debris, shook her head, dazed. When he thought back to the times he'd felt a tiny bit of her strength, Daniel didn't want to think about what it took to do this to her. "Hold on. I'll get you outta here."

With strength many times his former human body, Daniel moved the beam aside and started on the rest of the debris. She had to have been buried under six or seven hundred pounds of ceiling, at least.

A low, threatening moan seeped from her lips, and her eyes flared. When she turned those glowing orbs on him, Daniel hesitated. "Whoa whoa! Saaya it's me, Daniel. Take it easy—"

Saaya clamped her eyes shut and screamed. Every window in the big open room shattered and Daniel—along with millions of shards of glass—was blown away.

He hit the slick marble floor and slid until he crashed into the wall. The tiny *dampeal* stood in the middle of what looked like rubble exploding away from her. The shards of glass that had been blown through the windows slowed in the air and reversed direction, then went speeding back into the room and streamed through the hole in the floor.

He heard another woman's scream from below. Saaya looked over at him, and whether there was recognition in her frightening lavender gaze or not, he couldn't tell. She stepped to the hole and dropped through.

CHAPTER 61

Jelani spotted Remy still off to the side of the action. Despite all of the carnage around him, he was actually on his phone. As ridiculous as it looked, that sight made him nervous. With Jelani's luck the bastard was probably calling in an airstrike or something.

The Reaper whirled its scythe and brought it around at Jelani's head. When he ducked, the Reaper reversed, bringing the butt of the blade back and smacking him in the side of the head.

Jelani went spinning to the floor, but he was quick to his feet, daggers working furiously. The sudden counterattack caught his enemy off guard, and Jelani scored a few glancing cuts here and there, though it seemed only to anger the Reaper.

Jelani pressed the attack, forcing the Reaper back. But then it did something impossible. The tall cloaked figure began to flow, more than step, away from every one of his attacks. It was like the thing became just a little less substantial as it avoided his offensive. *What the hell* is *this thing*, Jelani wondered.

"Tryyyyy shaquoooraaaa. Tryyyyy to defend against deeeath. Tryyyyy to defend against Denaaaari."

Finally, a name for the grim reaper. "Seriously, man," Jelani said, ignoring a painful cut across his left cheek. "You've got to get some bass in your voice and stop dragging your words. You kinda sound like a drunken ghost."

Denari slammed his shoulder into Jelani's face. Then the Reaper spun and smashed the butt of his weapon into his forehead, and came back around. Long, icy-cold fingers wrapped around his neck and lifted him from the floor. Jelani blinked away the stars and glanced down at the hood that covered nothing but darkness and two red slits glaring up at him. He looked down at his feet, which must be dangling three feet off the floor.

Denari tossed him away, and he rolled back to his feet as soon as he hit the floor, ready. Someone interrupted the fight. A man stepped into the room from where the enemy vampires and were-wolves had come. If there was a such thing as a barbarian, this guy would have fit the bill. Well past seven feet tall, the man was a mountain of muscle not unlike the humanoid Darren Lacey, but much taller. Strapped across his back was absolutely the biggest scythe Jelani had ever seen. Even Denari's double-bladed scythe looked small by comparison.

The huge man—Jelani guessed he was yet another Reaper judging by his choice of weapon—stepped in between Jelani and Denari, but turned toward the other Reaper, apparently not noticing or caring that Jelani was crouched behind him and armed with two silver daggers.

"Once, I sent you into death, Denari," the huge man said. "It seems you welcomed its embrace." He looked around the chaotic room with more calm than Jelani figured anyone should have. Werewolves were bounding all over the place, snarling and growl-ing, biting and slashing, and the vampires weren't much less savage, hissing and slashing with swords, claws, or firing guns.

"I don't see your brother Tannis, so I might be allowed to hope he has met his final uncreation."

He reached behind his back and drew that massive scythe. Denari hissed warily, hunching low, his own scythe held defensively before him. The mountain of a man nodded. "As will you, revenire."

Jelani frowned. There was that word again. *I thought vampires being undead was nonsense.*

Denari hesitated, which Jelani found understandable, given his own relief not to be the object of this man's aggression. The giant Reaper stepped toward the cloaked Reaper, who stepped back.

"Denari. You, who have no fear, wish not to engage me? I knew you in life to have been born deficient of fear. Has death actually given it to you?"

The cloaked Reaper hissed angrily and charged in, scythe whirling. Despite the onslaught that would have had Jelani back on his heels, the giant never retreated a step. Denari changed directions, attacking from the left, then the right.

The big man, whoever he was, merely turned with Denari, fending off every swing, every jab. Denari hissed again, coming in low, then high, then low again. Then he did that thing where he flowed on the air, and came up and over the big man's weapon, scoring a knick on his shoulder.

As soon as the cut happened, the giant knocked Denari's scythe aside with such force, it sent the Reaper into a circle as he tried to hold on to his weapon. Then he reached out and grabbed the cloaked vampire by the neck, lifted him from the ground, and brought his scythe around and down on Denari's head.

Or he would have.

Ten vampires streamed through the door from where he'd come, all brandishing scythes and all coming directly for the huge man.

In that moment several things happened. The big Reaper hurled Denari toward the hole in the ceiling where Saaya had been thrown. At the same time, a shower of jagged-edged glass rained down through the hole and fell upon Alicia.

Then he saw Saaya descending from the hole, Denari hurtling toward her. The beautiful *dampeal*, face stony in anger, leaned away and swept her arm out wide. Denari was sent crashing through another part of the ceiling and disappeared from sight.

Jelani saw the new vampires—all brandishing scythes—form a circle around the big one. Where the hell had they come from? He looked over his shoulder and spotted Remy taking aim at him.

⚜

KAFEEL WAS PARALYZED in the center of a spiderweb of cracks, bent under the powerful will of Countess Alicia. The woman was like a mountain compressed into the petite form of the woman smiling down at him from a dozen paces away.

"So stubborn," Alicia remarked, and the pressure pounded down on him again. "This is getting so interesting I'm tempted to see just how much you can endure before death claims you."

Kafeel clenched his teeth and pushed back. Never had he felt such power, and he wasn't sure how much effort the woman exerted. He threw all of his focus into pitting his will against the older *Ancestor*. Slowly, inch by inch he pushed her back, then rose and put one foot on the floor. The pressure hammered down on him again, and this time he felt a bit of trepidation through the contact.

On shaky legs he forced himself upright, then gathered himself and pushed back harder.

"Surprising," Alicia said. "Unfortunately for you, I do not like surprises."

She inhaled, then exhaled, and what must have been the full force of her will slammed down on Kafeel's back again. The marble floor crumbled beneath him, and Kafeel sank below floor level until he was kneeling in the middle of a tiny crater.

It wasn't enough. She would not best him. The fledgling *Ancestor* struggled to his feet and leveled his wrathful gaze on her. He inhaled, then exhaled, and a glimmer passed across the inferno raging in his lavender eyes. The pressure against him shattered.

Alicia fell back in shock. "Impossible. You are a fledgling, an infant. You have not the age—"

"Then, perhaps the lineage," Kafeel replied just as a shower of glass shards rained down on the Countess. Her scream shook the room.

❧

SAAYA WAITED as the screaming Countess gathered herself. Of course the glass wouldn't kill her, but it still hurt all the same, and the woman was covered in it.

Alicia's eyes glowed in crimson rage, and the glass exploded from her body. She whirled and threw her will at Saaya, but the *dampeal* was ready for her. She braced herself against the full force of the Countess's will, an ant pushing against an elephant. But the ant was smaller in size only.

Alicia's eyes widened as Saaya pitted the full force of her will against the other woman and held her. She could not dominate the older *Ancestor*, but nor would she be dominated by the woman.

"This is impossible," Alicia breathed.

"Contemplate the impossibility in death," Saaya replied.

"Fool girl—"

Alicia cut the statement short and leaned aside as Kafeel's sword came for her back. In the same instant Saaya reached elongated claws at Alicia's face, but the Countess slapped her hand aside and struck back. Saaya leaned away and countered.

The two women spun in a circle, slashing and stabbing at each other until Saaya scored a blow to the side of the woman's face. Then Kafeel's sword came through the back of her shoulder. The strength of the attack forced the Countess forward. Alicia's mouth fell open in a silent cry of pain. Her head fell back, arching her neck enough for Saaya's claws to find her throat.

With a blinding swipe, Saaya opened the woman's throat while Kafeel retracted his sword.

Alicia clamped her hand to her neck and slammed her will into both siblings. The effort was considerably weaker this time, and they were only knocked back a few steps. It was enough for her neck to heal, while they recovered, however.

Kafeel came in again, and Alicia batted his sword aside and dealt him a backhanded slap that sent him crashing into a nearby pillar. Saaya was there with another slash of her claws. The other woman leaned left, then ducked, then grabbed Saaya's wrist.

The *dampeal* stabbed low with her other hand, but the woman caught that wrist as well. Seconds passed as the two women struggled to gain an advantage. Slowly Saaya was being forced down. She redoubled her efforts, but only managed to hold the woman at bay.

A crash from above along with the sound of a roaring lycan briefly drew the Countess's attention. The split second of distraction was enough, and Saaya snatched her wrists free and kicked the woman in the chest.

Alicia slid backwards a couple dozen feet before she stopped. When she looked up, it was just in time to see a great black claw slash her from the left side of her face to the right side of her hip.

The large black wolf never stopped its stride as it bounded away and leaped onto the back of a brown wolf and tore out the back of its neck.

More vampires came streaming into the room, some of them Saaya recognized as allies of the Eldest Hunter. She cared nothing for them or the battle surrounding her, for the *dampeal* needed every bit of her focus for the *Ancestor* in front of her, straining to close those deep wounds.

Saaya attacked hard and fast, stabbing her claws into the woman's abdomen, then slashing her across the face.

Kafeel lunged in, sword leading, and ran Alicia through the chest. He pulled the sword free, then whipped it across. The silver sword passed through her neck, but this was an *Ancestor*. What would have resulted in a beheading if it were a normal vampire, was no more than a painful injury that almost instantly healed.

The Countess coughed a bit of blood, but her neck closed. That second of time might as well been an hour, for the two siblings were a blur of stabbing and slashing claws and sword. They came from all sides, raining stab after slice on the stunned Countess.

Saaya rushed in with a one-two slash with her left and right claws, once again opening the woman's throat.

She retreated and Kafeel swiped his sword across her neck. Then he bent his arm and ran the sword straight through Alicia's chest. The fledgling *Ancestor* threw the full force of his will into the motion and sent the woman flying away to crash into the wall, pinned aloft by the five foot long blade.

The Countess gripped the hilt and pulled, but the strength seeped from her body along with her lifeblood. When she looked up at Saaya and Kafeel, the *dampeal* saw no anger or resentment, or even fear. She only saw resignation and something else. Regret?

Finally, after moments of struggle her body went limp, and Countess Alicia Magnus Lerae began her descent into death.

Saaya, too, felt regret at the death of an *Ancestor.* A death she and her brother had brought about. She looked up at her stone-faced brother, but Kafeel simply stared at the rapidly decaying woman.

"It was an honorable death for one whose actions were without honor," he said, feeling her emotion through their familial bond.

She nodded and looked around at the carnage that filled the ballroom. The two men she came to know as Elders, one of them the High Elder of the Council, practically butchered any enemy that approached them.

The Eldest Hunter, Yako, was similarly decimating the enemy ranks alongside his Second. Although a new force had arrived to bolster the enemy ranks, a Reaper no bigger than Saaya herself had arrived with a woman who looked like her mirror image. Together with their small force of allies—vampire and lycan alike—they chopped through their enemies with coordinated efficiency.

To the side of the room, a giant of a man singlehandedly battled a group of Reapers, and the Elder Lemanda—a woman Saaya believed she could come to like—dealt death with the sword she had claimed from Massius.

"There," Kafeel said, pointing to the left.

Saaya looked in the direction her brother pointed to see Remy take aim at Jelani. Before Saaya could move, the Hunter fired.

REMY FIRED the gun just as Jelani noticed him. In that moment his thoughts fell away and instinct took over.

Jelani threw his right shoulder back as though falling away. As the silver missile passed over his chest, he spun around and came down to one knee. Before his knee touched the floor, he whipped his hand out and launched one of his daggers in an underhand throw across the room. As soon as the weapon left his hand, he snatch the other two free and let fly.

Remy dodged the first, but that dodge put him perfectly in line for the second dagger, which took him in the arm and turned him just enough for the third to take him in the leg. The Hunter grunted and hurriedly snatched the daggers free.

By the time Remy tossed the daggers to the floor, Jelani had closed the distance between them and dealt Remy a sold punch to the face. The impact shattered the Hunter's nose and knocked him off his feet. Remy lifted his gun as he fell, but Jelani snapped his foot up. Remy's wrist broke with a resounding "pop", and the gun went skidding away.

The Hunter climbed back to his feet, shaking the hand of his already healed wrist.He smirked at Jelani. "So, the fledgling wants a fight, does he?"

Jelani's face tightened. "I've got something for you."

"Save it," Remy said, and he rushed in with an elbow to Jelani's face, then spun around and kicked his feet out from under him. Remy made a gesture with his right hand, and when Jelani stood, a brown werewolf plowed into him and pinned him to the wall.

$\mathcal{f}$

AS UNBELIEVABLE AS IT SEEMED, Alicia, Countess Alicia, was dead. And without the threat of the ancient vampire, Yako was able to fully focus on the task of slaughtering the enemy.

He saw ten Reapers converging on Braggus, but the Eldest Reaper was not at all concerned. As the battled raged on, however, he saw that the giant Reaper had not given quarter, but had not gained advantage either. Then the Reapers leapt away and four of the remaining enemy lycans fell upon Braggus.

Even with his immense size, the Eldest Reaper was buried under a mass of snapping jaws and racking claws, and Yako thought it the end of the one he had hesitantly come to call friend.

An enemy Hunter fired a gun, and Yako ducked and reached to his side, launching two throwing knives. The bullet passed over his back and struck another enemy that had come up from behind, just as his blades struck the shooter. Both enemies died at the same time while Yako sprinted away to recover his weapons.

The booming voice of Braggus Rayne shook the room, and the pile of wolves flew apart to collide with enemy and ally alike. Braggus's massive shoulders heaved as he took up his scythe. In that moment, the Reapers fell upon him again.

"Second!" Yako called.

"Eldest," came Mariska's reply.

"You have command, second only to Reaper Tara."

"Yes, Eldest." And the Second Hunter moved away, taking up coordination of the assault with the twins. The three worked well together.

473

Yako sprinted toward the group of fighters and leaped the last dozen feet, taking one of the Reapers in the back of the neck with his sword, and skidding to a crouching stop just as Braggus's massive scythe passed over his head to send a blocking Reaper stumbling away.

"HA! The big man barked. "And so, finally, we fight!"

"As so it has always been destined to be, mighty Braggus," Yako replied, his voice as quiet as a ghost.

"Mighty!" Braggus Rayne laughed, parrying a stab from the butt of another scythe while angling his own weapon upward to deter the stab of one from behind. "I didn't know I was regarded as mighty!"

"Then, you know nothing of your reputation, Eldest Reaper," Yako replied.

"Perhaps I should learn from the Eldest Hunter, then," Braggus said. "Enough ego stroking! Side by side—"

"We will deliver them into oblivion," Yako finished. He parried a scythe and spun inside the reach of the weapon, bringing his leg around for a kick to the side of his enemy's face. He retreated as another Reaper lunged in.

Back-to-back, the Eldest Reaper and Eldest Hunter fought the now nine Reapers who surrounded them. With Yako standing not much above the Eldest Reaper's elbow, it was a perfect duo. Braggus could swing his weapon freely, oftentimes passing clean over the crouched Yako, who delivered his blows fast and sure.

Nine Reapers became eight, then seven. The fight was not without difficulty, for Yako had earned more than a few burning injuries in what was the fight of his life against the elite of their warrior class.

Braggus impaled another enemy with his wicked scythe, lifted him from the floor, and slung him at a nearby lycan. The Reaper knocked the wolf to the ground just before he began to decay, and the impact gave a nearby ally the chance she needed to deal a killing stab through the neck of the wolf.

Yako rolled under the sweeping shaft of his giant ally and stabbed out, taking a Reaper in the abdomen. The instant the sword entered the man's body, Yako pulled it free and struck again to the chest. He retracted and brought the sword around to block the heavy stroke of another enemy. He rolled with it to absorb the impact, which gave Braggus the opportunity to stab out over his head with the butt of his scythe.

Struck in the face, the Reaper stumbled back, and Braggus brought the scythe around in a horizontal sweep, taking his enemy through the torso. Braggus continued around as the dead vampire fell in half, and struck another blocking Reaper. The weapon cleaved through the blade of the surprised warrior and decapitated him.

In that short span of time, Yako had sidestepped an attack by another enemy while at the same time severing the arm of his first opponent. Before the limb hit the stone floor, he simply snapped his black-coated silver sword back up. The finely honed blade sliced cleanly through the vampire's disbelieving face.

The Reaper fell back a step, and Yako, sword still raised high, altered the angle of his sword, and swept across to the left. He was already on the move as the Reaper's head fell free of his shoulders.

Time passed immeasurably as Yako and Braggus decimated the force that stood against them. When the last of the enemy Reapers fell, three Woodland wolves came for them.

With a thunderous battle cry, Braggus swept his scythe around and up, the curved blade impaling the wolf and lifting it into the air.

At the same time, Yako leaped over the Eldest Reaper's head, then atop the impaled lycan as it passed over Braggus. He then leaped forward again, descending on another charging monster. He drove his sword down into its skull, then pulled it free and was gone.

One final wolf remained, but another would deal with it. A giant wolf with fur black as pitch and nearly twice the size of the enemy lycan, came forward. The clearly intimidated smaller wolf crouched low and backed away.

Its ears pinned to the side of its head and it barked and snapped its jaws at the air. It was the last sound the wolf made, for the giant black lycan that could be none but Darren Lacey, punched out, his claw coming out the back of the other wolf. He lifted the dying beast into the air and slung it aside as though it were a toy. Held in his giant claw was the other wolf's heart. The great werewolf crushed the heart and dropped it.

DANIEL WAS a whirlwind of black fur, slashing claws and snapping jaws. After he'd killed one of the remaining two Woodland wolves, what was left of the enemy bloods fell over him. Silver swords and short blades dug into his skin, slashing nails raked his body, and the combined strength of the seven vampires weakened him.

The wolf that was Daniel surrendered more of himself to the rage within; the primal rage of the wolf who now held sway.

A silver sword came in for his midsection. Daniel snarled and recoiled, then lunged forward and bit down on the blade, shattering it. The acidic burn in his maw stung, but the black wolf held onto his senses and disemboweled the surprised blood.

Daniel turned and slashed his claws across the face of another vampire, then rammed his giant shoulder into another. As soon as the vampire hit the floor Daniel fell over him and ripped out his throat.

The other bloods pursued, but Daniel met their charge and ripped them apart. His rage still not sated, Daniel loped off in the direction of the stench of the last remaining Woodland wolf. It had a blood pinned to the wall, snapping at his head. Jelani. Daniel roared from deep in his belly and launched himself at the other lycan.

He tackled the brown wolf aside and they tumbled to the

floor in a jumble of furry muscled limbs, claws, and teeth. It bit down on Daniel's leg, sinking its fangs through the flesh to crush bone.

Daniel howled and clamped his jaws down on the back of the brown wolf's neck. It squealed and released him. His leg already on the mend, Daniel rose and slung the wolf into a nearby pillar.

As soon as the wolf hit the pillar, Daniel crashed into it, and the thick round column shattered under the force of the impact. Daniel clamped one of his claws around the neck of the smaller wolf and with his other claw, stabbed it repeatedly in the abdomen, then lifted it again and threw it into the wall.

The enraged black lycan rammed himself into the over-whelmed wolf once more, and again they crashed through stone and mortar. Daniel bit down on its rear leg and crushed it. The wolf's pained howl choked off when Daniel hurled it back into the audience room where it tumbled end over end.

Daniel charged into the room and leaped high into the air, falling upon the wolf with such force the already ruined marble floor burst into chunks of flying debris. The black wolf bit and clawed, savaging the enemy wolf.

The Woodland wolf fought back, but any damage it did to Daniel only made his rage burn hotter. He bit down on the lycan's foreleg, shook violently from side to side, then hurled it into the air. With only a twitch of his muscled legs, Daniel launched himself after the wolf. He tackled the wolf midair and they fell in a savage tumble as gravity claimed them once more. Daniel snarled and rent the other beast as they fell, the enemy lycan's only response in the form of pained barks.

Daniel curled his body and shoved his giant hind claws into its shredded chest. The Woodland wolf hit the hard stone floor quite hard and quite dead. Daniel landed in a four-legged crouch, then rose up on two legs to his full height, heaving as his golden eyes scanned the room for more prey. He saw two large male bloods watching him with hands gripping large silver weapons. But then the Elder blood, the female he'd fought beside, went to stand with them.

Daniel looked away, and saw another group of bloods, but they stood with the Eldest Hunter. Then Daniel's eyes fell upon a female blood with bright red hair and matching eyes. His golden eyes simmered with a mixture of recognition and renewed rage.

He charged the redheaded blood that had nearly killed him; the one that had hurt his mate and taken her away from him.

The redheaded blood pointed the weapon that could shoot silver at him, and he darted left, then right. The others around her readied other shooting weapons and silver blades, but Daniel would not be deterred. He would die, but he would take this blood into oblivion with him.

He leaped, but his course was altered when something knocked him away. The wolf was immediately on his feet, growling deep in his throat. It was the female half-blood that had attacked him. The friend.

Daniel circled her, watching her movements. The tiny female circled with him. She still smelled friendly, but also unhappy. Sad. Daniel growled again, and she spoke. Her voice penetrated his rage, the friendly familiarity dissolving it.

"Be at ease, silly boy," she said, "Come back to us. It is done."

Daniel eyed the red-haired blood again. She was watching him, too. She smelled not of fear at all, but challenge. Daniel barked, then growled again, muscles tensing.

"Daniel," the half-blood cooed. "Come back to me, that you might understand. The wolf would bite and tear; the man would listen and think."

The wolf that was Daniel wanted to rip the female blood with the red hair apart, but the whisper within, the man inside, became louder. The whisper became more insistent, growing louder until it subdued the wolf. After a bitter struggle, the man prevailed and once again held sway.

Daniel rose to his full height, and willed his body to shift. He would not give any of these bloods the satisfaction of seeing him hurt while on all fours. He stood on hind legs, enduring the pain of shifting cartilage, joints dislocating and popping back into place, bone breaking and re-knitting.

In seconds he stood as a man once more. With the full return of his human intellect, came the rapid defeat of his primal anger. The last remnants of his animal rage winked out when he noticed the salacious grin on Saaya's face.

Daniel turned away, ignoring the rising heat in his cheeks, and found a nearby patch of clothes covered in the ash of a dead vampire. Luckily the pants fit, but the shirt was too small.

"And all the animalistic savagery melts away in one cute moment of modesty," the *dampeal* teased. "Such a curious duo, are you two."

Daniel glanced past her at the redhead again, but Saaya held up a hand. "All will be understood in time." She glanced over his shoulder and he followed her gaze to see Remy aiming a gun at Jelani's chest.

Remy cast his nervous gaze around the suddenly calm chamber. "If anyone doesn't want to see this peasant die right here, you'll clear the way and I'll be gone."

Jelani rolled his eyes. "Bruh. You can't be this dumb." Across the room, Jelani heard Daniel snicker. "Most of the people in this room don't even know who I am," he continued. "And I doubt they care one way or another. And even if they did, you think I'd let myself be victimized by *you*, Remington?"

Across the room, a barritone snort indicated Braggus Rayne's repressed laughter.

Remy looked on the verge of an explosion. "One more word and I'll end you and take my chances."

Jelani watched him, took note of his finger, which pressed

lightly to the trigger, ready to squeeze. If he was just fast enough, he could spring forward and maybe dodge to the side when Remy fired—

His thoughts were interrupted by a blur that passed between them. Remy's gun skidded away in two pieces. The surprised Hunter hopped back, or tried to. Kafeel caught him by the neck, turned, and tossed him back toward Jelani.

Remy landed easily enough, and looked around the room for an escape route. Jelani took that moment to have a glance around as well.

Vicken and Stavros stood near one of the doors while Lemanda —arms crossed over her chest—leaned against what was left of a pillar not far away. On the other end of the room, Darren Lacey, now in human form and also wearing some "borrowed" clothes, stood by the other doorway. Tara and her force were under the second floor walkway, and Saaya and Daniel were not far from them.

"You're making this very unsatisfying," Jelani said. "I came all the way across the damn ocean for you. Can't you at least *act* like you want a fight and aren't the biggest coward on the planet?"

Remy snarled at him. "I'm not afraid of *you*, you idiot. I'm surrounded. I kill you, they'll kill me."

Before Jelani could respond, Lemanda tossed Remy the sword she'd claimed from Massius. A second later, two silver daggers went spinning past the surprised Hunter.

Jelani snatched them out of the air and nodded in thanks to Kafeel, who merely stared back at him. "I'm not well versed in vampiric tradition just yet," he said, spinning his daggers in his hands. "But I think that means nobody is going to give you a problem if you," he snorted, "manage to kill me."

"You think you're capable of killing a pureblood? You? A grimy lowlife *shaquora*?"

"I'm getting real tired of that word, homeboy," Jelani said, his lavender eyes flaring. "I kinda want to just beat the hell out of you and let you live with the shame of it."

"You really are delusional enough to believe you can kill me?" Remy said. "A Hunter?"

Jelani noted the other man's eyes, and how they darted up and down, left and right. He was trying to pick out any visible weakness, or maybe devising a tactic in his mind. "I've trained my whole life," Jelani said. "That's not many years to you, but in proportion, I think I could probably lick you one." He grinned. "Don't you think?"

Remy sprang forward, stabbing for Jelani's heart. He leaned out of the way and brought the dagger in his right hand up, scoring a nick on the other man's wrist.

Remy recoiled, stung by the burn of the silver. The wound began to heal, but slowly.

"Personally," Jelani continued as Remy came at him again. "I think it would be much worse to let you live in shame than to just kill you …" he parried a downward chop of the sword, then spun away. "I mean, you turned me, and all. That's *bad*, right? Being beaten by the human you turned less than half a year ago?"

Remy grunted and came in with a flurry of stabs and swipes, scoring a few cuts to Jelani's arms, then another across his chest.

It felt like tiny fires had been lit on every part of his body, but Jelani ignored them. "Not bad," he said. "But if you're gonna bring pain, you better be ready to get it back."

Jelani attacked. He came in high, and when Remy brought the sword up to defend, he tapped it with his left dagger while spinning to the right and low, scoring a cut across the front of the Hunter's leg. He came back up as Remy reflexively bent in the direction of the injury, and brought his left dagger back around. He cut Remy deep across the right arm, then spun the dagger in his hand.

"A fledgling," Jelani taunted. "Let that sink in, man. You're going to be killed by a *fledgling* that *you* created."

"Shut up!" Remy stabbed forward, then quickly retracted.

Jelani recognized the feint for what it was, and stepped in at the same time the tip of the blade retreated. Remy tried to stab out again, but he had already committed to the backward movement, so there was no force behind it.

Jelani slapped the sword aside with his right hand dagger, then delivered a downward cut to Remy's right arm. At the same time he brought his right dagger in for another swipe.

Remy choked off a cry of pain, likely trying to hold on to whatever dignity he had left. Jelani could see in his eyes that the man recognized he was not winning this fight. He heard Yako's voice from across the room.

"His shame is more complete than the failure of the legacy he sought to create. End it now, or I will intervene."

"Hear that?" Jelani said, circling the Hunter. "I'm not gonna lie, bro. I'm getting some kind of sadistic pleasure out of this, but I think I'm entitled, don't you?" Remy spat a curse, and Jelani chuckled. "I guess this is it. I'd say goodbye, but I don't much like you."

Remy shouted and attacked in a relentless barrage with his sword. To his credit, the Hunter did have skill. He forced Jelani back on his heels before he was able to settle into a comfortable defense. Jelani just held his position, watching Remy's movements, his rhythm and body postures. He would do this quickly, but efficiently. For some reason he couldn't understand, he wanted Yako to see what he could do.

Remy lunged forward and delivered a horizontal chop at Jelani's head, and when he ducked, the Hunter angled the sword toward the side of his head and stabbed.

Jelani turned away from the attack and swatted the blade away. He stepped in close and launched a barrage of well-placed stabs and slices, scoring cuts to the Hunter's wrists, his throat, the side of his neck, a stab under the arm.

He kicked Remy in the abdomen, and as he doubled over, Jelani rammed his dagger into the other vampire's chin. He pulled the weapon free and turned his back, walking away and sheathing his weapons at his sides.

He walked up to Daniel who stood with his arms crossed, a slanted smile on his face. Jelani put his hand out and Daniel slapped it.

When he turned back, Remy was still stumbling, bleeding out. The injuries individually were not grievous, but together, they were just enough to kill, but also just enough for the Hunter to struggle to heal.

Finally, the hated Remy, who had caused so much pain, so much fear and death in their lives, surrendered to death. He dropped to his hands and knees, and was there claimed by death.

"Dude, I have to say that was a little disturbing," Daniel said, as the Hunter decayed. "Rather unlike you, don't you think?"

Jelani nodded. "Yeah, I know. I think life as a vampire changes you in some ways."

"Changes that are permanent only if you allow them to be," Saaya said.

Jelani considered the comment, then nodded. Whatever he had become, he wouldn't allow himself to be the sort of thing he'd always imagined vampires were.

Seconds passed, and finally Remy was no more than a loose pile of dust coating the broken marble floor.

Jelani looked around to see all that remained of the fighting. It was over, but there were still questions to be answered, not the least of which was what Jelani and Daniel's futures were. Beside him, Daniel heaved a great sigh. He followed his best friend's gaze to see the mountain of muscle named Darren Lacey staring back at him.

As much as he wondered what was in store for Daniel, Jelani had his own issues to deal with. He looked over his shoulder to see the giant Reaper studying him. If Darren was a mountain, that man was Everest.

Next to the towering Reaper stood Yako, who also studied

Jelani. The top of the Eldest Hunter's head might not quite reach the other man's elbow, but his presence loomed equally large. He saw approval in those icy brown eyes, but whatever else was there, Jelani couldn't tell.

"Immortals!" Across the room a man with a huge greatsword strapped to his back crossed his arms. Jelani noticed a double-bladed axe strapped on his left hip, and wondered if the man actually wielded both at the same time. "We gather in the audience hall at once."

All vampires in the room bowed in deference. Saaya inclined her head, while Kafeel simply did his usual statue-thing. Darren Lacey also bowed, the members of his pack following suit. Jelani and Daniel offered hurried bows, straightening to see the lycans beginning their departure.

"I address all of the immortals in this room," he boomed again. "All who are not of Peles, but are allies to the coven, vampire and lycanthrope alike, are invited to convene in the audience hall."

Everyone glanced at each other and began filing out. Daniel and Jelani looked at each other, then at Saaya, who winked at them.

"Shall we?" the *dampeal* asked.

"I have no intention of offending anybody in here," Daniel said. Jelani couldn't have agreed more.

CHAPTER 62

The audience hall lay in much the same condition as the rest of the castle. Ruined marble columns and torn tapestries, ripped curtains and paintings, and broken furniture. The big man Jelani and Daniel had come to know as Vicken, had sent the majority of the coven's residents to assess the damage and begin an immediate cleanup.

There wouldn't be nearly enough time to get everything fixed up before dawn, or several dawns, for that matter. The major damages would be tallied the following night. Jelani wondered how or even if they could hide or explain this to the local human population. Plenty of people had to have heard what went on tonight.

After most of the assembled left to complete their assigned tasks, Jelani, Daniel, Saaya, and Kafeel remained. To their side stood Yako and his Second, Mariska, along with a short woman with two miniature versions of scythes strapped to both hips. The woman beside her—obviously her twin—stood at ease, a gun strapped to her right hip and a short sword on her left.

Saaya watched everyone. The *dampeal* seemed to find all this quite interesting. As usual, Kafeel towered behind her like a guardian angel. Jelani shook his head. As if she needed one.

Muscle Man, Darren, spoke to Mr. Gigantic, the guy Jelani came to learn was named Braggus Rayne. Both seemed to be enjoying some sort of humor. Little experience as he had as a vampire, Jelani found the scene to be quite strange.

Vicken's voice quieted the room. Sitting in the foremost seat of a **V** formation of seats, the High Elder's commanding tone echoed through the hall.

"There is no intelligent civilization that has existed without experiencing some form of inner conflict, but what has happened today is a disgrace to the central coven and our species. It is the intention of the High Council of Elders that this never again come to pass."

The High Elder looked over the assembled until his eyes rested on Darren. "As with any darkness, however, light follows."

Jelani thought that an odd metaphor, given vampires' aversion to sunlight.

"We have forged anew an alliance," Vicken continued, "indeed, a friendship, with Darren Lacey, and thus the Shadow Pack." He nodded his head to the big man, who bowed.

"And, by extension, every pack under my leadership, High Elder," the alpha replied.

Vicken nodded again with a conservative smile. "It does not escape the attention of the High Council that Eldest Hunter Yako Shimamoto was instrumental in the reforging of this relationship." He settled his heavy gaze on the Eldest Hunter.

"Once again, the High Council of Elders offer you ascension to the rank of Reaper."

Yako bowed. "High Council of Elders. I have come to know that the Order of Hunters was created in disloyalty, and is thus a fractured force. It must be destroyed and rebuilt. At your sufferance I would see this done by my own hand."

"Noble words, Eldest Hunter," Stavros said. "But the High

Council has suffered your continued insistence of remaining Eldest Hunter only because there have been none equal to the task of succeeding you." He and Lemanda and Vicken shared a glance.

"The High Council of Elders allows you to see this task done," Stavros continued. "Upon its completion, you will return and stand before us once more." He nodded at Braggus Rayne, who bowed in respect.

"The High Council is aware that I have been in need of a Second Reaper for too long," the Eldest Reaper began.

"It is," Stavros replied.

Braggus turned to Yako. "Your leadership is second to none, Eldest Hunter, and I understand what it means to see your Order strong and whole. See to the restoration of the Order of Hunters. Finish this task and return to the High Council. Then, we will speak again."

Yako bowed. "It is the wish of the High Council of Elders and the Eldest Reaper, so shall it be done."

Soft laughter drew everyone's attention to Lemanda, who favored Yako with half a smile. "Don't sound so grim, Eldest Hunter. You are a man with skills that would be wasted if not further challenged. Just as there is another with talents that would be wasted if not challenged." She turned her attention to Mariska, standing behind Yako.

"Step forward, Second Hunter." Mariska complied, then bowed and looked to the three remaining Elders.

"Through years of service and training beside Eldest Hunter Yako, you have proven yourself competent, with a cunning equalled only by your own Eldest. Second Hunter Mariska, it is the intention of the High Council of Elders that you assist in the restoration of the Order of Hunters. You are then to return with the Eldest Hunter to submit yourself before the High Council to begin your ascension to the rank of Eldest Hunter. What say you?"

"The High Council lays upon me an honor I hold high. Should the Council wish it, and Eldest Hunter approves it, so shall it be"

Lemanda smirked at Stavros, who chuckled. "Spoken with a cold precision that we're sure makes your Eldest proud. But forget not that it is the world of the High Council that speaks the final word on your ascension, not your Eldest."

"With all respect, High Council," Mariska replied. "Should you honor me with such rank, I would sooner walk into the sun than accept it without the approval of Eldest Hunter."

Vicken and Stavros's eyebrows raised at that, while Lemanda gave a subtle nod of her head. "You are two of a kind," the latter said.

Attention turned to Jelani and Daniel. Jelani felt the weight of those three stares settle over him like a cloak.

"And, what are we to do with you?" Lemanda said, tapping a finger to her cheek. "In all my years I have never witnessed such a thing. A fledgling vampire and newly turned lycan, thrust into a civil war. So recently turned from the light, most vampires see at least a year or two of immortality before attaining such ... ability. And though I cannot speak personally of the experience of a lycan, I assume it is a similar situation." She glanced at Darren, who nodded. "I suppose desperate situations force one to rise to the challenge, Lemanda said."

"Or buckle beneath its weight, Stavros added."

"Your name?" Lemanda asked, looking at Daniel.

"Daniel Ng."

"The High Council of Elders names you friend and honorary member of Peles Coven. Our halls are forever open to you in friendship."

"Thank you for the honor, High Council of Elders," Daniel said.

"And you," Lemanda said, speaking to Jelani. "You have proven yourself to be as much an asset to the Coven as an anomaly. It is the intention of the High Council of Elders that you assist in the restoration of the Order of Hunters. Upon your return with the

Eldest Hunter, you will come before us once more and begin your training to become a Hunter. What say you?"

Jelani had never felt more trapped in his life. He hadn't any intention of even remaining here this long. He just wanted to kill Remy and go back home to try to reclaim any normalcy he had left of his life. Now they wanted him not only to do more fighting— beside the one who'd been a part of the mess his life had become— but then come back and join in what seemed like vampire law enforcement? The idea was horrifying!

"I ..." he coughed. "I thank the High Council of Elders for this honor." With every word, it seemed he was surrendering just a little more of his freedom.

Lemanda laughed. "Try to retain some of the blood in your face. Your body no longer produces it in abundance. Be assured that your freedom has not been taken."

Reading my mind again, Jelani thought. She arched an eyebrow at him. He swallowed.

Finally, attention turned to the siblings standing inconspicuously to the side of the assembled.

"The High Council of Elders asks that you approach."

When Saaya and Kafeel were standing before them, the three remaining Elders surprised everyone by standing. As one, they bowed in deference. Everyone else shared a quick glance and bowed with the Elders.

When Jelani straightened, there was nothing resembling surprise on either of the siblings' faces.

"It grieves the High Council and the coven to see the uncreation of an *Ancestor*," Vicken said. "Our surprise is complete to learn of the presence of a Countess in our midst for these many centuries, and it grieves us further that we have so disgraced the ancient ones that one of their own would seek our destruction.

"The *Ancestors* are not in agreement with the sentiments expressed by Countess Alicia," Kafeel said. "It would be the wish of the ancient ones that this matter remain in the confidence of those assembled."

"Of course," Vicken replied. "So it is and shall be done, on our honor. It is also the wish of the High Council of Elders that the son and daughter of Count Omari be welcomed as friends of Peles Coven. We are ever at yours and your sire's service."

Saaya raised an eyebrow. "Curious that you know whom our father is."

Vicken smiled. "I've had the honor of meeting many of the *Ancestors*, and I assure you the presence of the mighty Count Omari is obvious in his descendants. I expect nothing less than what I've seen of you this night."

"We and Count Omari extend our gratitude, High Elder," Saaya replied.

Vicken inclined his head. "I would like a word with you in private if I may."

Both siblings inclined their heads.

Vicken looked over the assembled group, and in his hard, infinitely experienced eyes was a flicker of pride. "Life and death, destruction and creation. Two sides of one coin. The coven will be long in recovery, externally and internally. But never have I seen strength as I have this night. Peles will resurrect itself from the ashes, bigger and stronger than ever it was before. With its cancer purged, the coven will stand tall."

With those final words, the meeting adjourned.

"YOU LOOK like you just received a life sentence," Daniel commented, elbowing Jelani in the ribs.

"Pretty accurate way to put it," Jelani replied dryly.

Now Daniel slapped him on the back. "Quit sulking. You heard what Lemanda said."

"You gonna assault me any more times, bro?" Jelani asked.

And, yeah, I heard what she said. Do you really think I had a choice? How do you think things would have gone if I'd said, 'Oh sorry, Milady. I don't think I'd like to do that.'"

"That would not have gone well," answered the booming voice of Braggus Rayne.

They stopped and turned to see the Reaper towering over them. It felt like standing at the base of a mountain. He seemed amused.

"Well," Jelani lifted his hands and let them fall to his sides. "There you go. Like I said."

"Immortality comes with a degree of responsibility, young vampire," Braggus continued. "You have qualities that are valuable and set you apart."

"I'm not trying to sound ungrateful for this 'gift' of immortality," Jelani responded, "but it's one I didn't ask for."

"You wish it revoked?" the big man asked, his eyebrows twitching.

Funny guy. "Is there a non-fatal procedure available?" Jelani asked.

"No."

"Well, there we are. I'm sure I had at least four or five, maybe even six or seven decades left to me, but if I ended it all now, I'd be shortchanging myself."

"Then, perhaps live out your life for the next seventy or eighty years and have someone deliver your end at that time," Braggus offered.

Jelani made a show of thinking it over, then shook his head. "That option doesn't sound too appealing, either."

"As you said, there we are." Braggus glanced over his shoulder at the approaching Yako, then turned back and bent toward Jelani, who instinctively leaned away. "You are the first of your kind, *shaquora*," he said in a low voice.

"There's that word again," Jelani said sourly.

Braggus chuckled. The sound vibrated in Jelani's chest. "It is not a slur toward your status, but a definition of your existence.

Shaquora is simply the vampiric term for one who was turned to the night and not born of it."

"I've had it thrown at me like it's a bad thing," Jelani replied.

"The same as one might use the term human," the Reaper said. "One could twist the term into an insult, no?"

Jelani shrugged. "Fair enough."

Braggus looked over his shoulder again. "You have a place in Yako's Order. That is no small thing."

"I guess I can say I'm grateful," Jelani said. "I can't say it brings me comfort, though."

Braggus straightened and laughed aloud. "Then you will do just fine, my friend." He started away. "Fine indeed."

"What now?" Jelani asked as they watched Yako and Mariska approach.

"I'm thinking we'll have to spend some time getting this all figured out," Daniel said. "Seems like our freedom is tied to a leash."

"How much freedom does a person really ever have?" Jelani asked. "In some places people may have more freedom than others, but at the end of the day, you're on some sort of leash."

Daniel shrugged. "True enough, and I guess this could be a lot worse, you know?"

"No denying that," Jelani said.

Yako and Mariska arrived, along with one other who'd been walking behind them. The red-haired woman from back in Vancouver. Daniel's nostrils flared, and a golden glimmer passed across his eyes.

"Hold up, man," Jelani said, placing a hand on Daniel's chest.

"You should know all the facts before you seek my uncreation, lycan," the woman said. "Though, whether you could actually carry it out is questionable."

"Wanna step outside and find out?" Daniel asked.

"Enough." Yako's quiet voice was absolute. "I won't have

quarrels between us." He looked at the woman, who took it as a cue to speak.

"I was ordered by Remy to kill you, your girlfriend, and his girlfriend." She nodded her fiery red head at Jelani. "Instead I spared the two women and wiped their memories. You weren't as lucky because you'd already had too much experience with us. I could sense it in your mind."

"I'd been telling you from the beginning I wasn't going to go running and shouting your existence to the rooftops," Daniel said.

"Our law cares nothing for your intentions or lack thereof," came the reply. "I am not known for solicitousness, especially for a human. Your two female friends received what little I have of it."

Daniel crossed his muscular arms. "You tried to kill me."

"They live," Yako interrupted. "And so do you. This conflict is passed, and you still exist. Leave your past where it belongs." He looked at Jelani. "We will meet tomorrow night to discuss matters of the Northwest Coven."

They watched Yako and the two women depart down the hall. "After a conversation with that one," Daniel said, "I don't feel so bad."

"Yeah right," Jelani replied. He nodded in the direction of Darren Lacey, who was watching them. "Looks like you'd better get a move on. I think big man is ready to go."

"Yeah I can feel it," Daniel said in a strangled voice.

"What's that like, anyway?" Jelani asked.

"Think of your bond with Saaya. I imagine it's kind of like that, but more one way. I can't really sense anything about him, but he gives me what he wants me to get. I don't like it."

"Understandable." Jelani said. They clasped hands and gave each other a half hug and pat on the back, then leaned away and bumped fists. "You take care of yourself, bro."

"You too, bud," Daniel said. "I'll catch up with you back in Vancouver."

Vancouver. So much had happened in the short time they were away that it felt like they'd been gone for years.

"Yeah. Catch you then." Jelani called out again as Daniel started away. "Hey." Daniel half turned. "You all right? With everything, I mean."

Daniel smiled, his trademark Russell Wong dimple showing. "Yeah I'm good."

YAKO RETURNED with Mariska to find the Northwest Coven in better condition than he would have figured. Apparently his fortune hadn't ended with the victory in Sinaia. The restoration of the coven had already begun with the efforts of Remy's creation, the woman named Melinda. Apparently she'd been working with Jamir, the Reaper that had been under the dead Hunter's employ.

Although there were still some traitors to find, quite a bit of the work had already begun. Scarlene laughed at the irony of yet another of Remy's re-creations working against him.

Ever pragmatic, Mariska asked that she be allowed to test the young vampire's competency. *Shaquora*, she may be, but the fact that she had somehow managed to align herself with a Reaper and hold affairs in order at the coven spoke volumes of the woman's cunning and adaptability. Perhaps she may even be capable enough as a Hunter. Time would tell.

With free rein to remake the Order of Hunters into what his ancestors envisioned them to be, Yako would purge the weak of will and loyalty, and forge the sword that would hold strong beside the scythe, both held in the iron grasp of the High Council.

JELANI LOOKED across the rooftops and into the apartment of his former girlfriend. So much had happened and, blessedly, she had no knowledge of any of it. That Hunter, Scarlene, may have tried to kill Daniel, but she had spared the girls, and that was no small comfort. With Remy and his loyalists gone, Jelani no longer had to worry about Alisha.

He felt Saaya's presence near, long before she spoke. "I see a new life begging to be explored."

Jelani's smile was both sad and exhilarated. He took one last look across the quarter mile distance from the rooftop where he stood, and the beautiful woman he had fallen in love with. He knew it wasn't to be. Vampiric law prevented it, and his was an existence that would be impossible to hide from her. Though it pained him, it was for the best. If he loved her, he would let her go.

Jelani turned to Saaya, who stood waiting patiently behind him. Through their link, he knew that she understood him. "Yeah, a new life."

Saaya's smile was hypnotic. Despite all that had happened, the fighting and the conflicts, the chaos his life had become, and the love that he had lost, she'd been there. What wrong she'd caused, the once apathetic *dampeal* had done her best to set right. He and his friends were alive even now because of it.

He walked over and set his hand on her tiny waist, feeling the warm skin. He felt the muscles in the side of her chiseled stomach twitch as she leaned to the side to look around him. "You're sure?" she asked.

Jelani nodded, and she stepped closer and wrapped her arms around his waist, resting the side of her head against his chest.

"Silly boy," she said, pulling back just enough to look up at him.

"Why am I silly now?" he asked.

"You wouldn't be Jelani if you weren't," came the reply.

They started away. A part of Jelani wanted to look back one last time; see Alisha once more. But he didn't. A part of him would always love her, but he had to let her go. She was lost to him, but she was alive.

He looked down at Saaya, and felt a surge of warmth through their bond. "Over the months, he had grown feelings for her that had gotten stronger, though he had denied it to himself. His smile turned smug when he thought of how she had done the same with herself."

"So certain, are you?" she said, blinking those long eyelashes up at him.

"Am I wrong?" Jelani asked

"Perhaps. Perhaps not."

"You know you luurve me, gurl," he said, making his voice deep and raspy.

Saaya giggled. It sounded funny coming from the woman, given what he'd seen of her back in Sinaia, weeks ago.

"I'm guessing it's not going to be much longer before I have to go back to the High Council and do this Hunter thing," he said.

"And then, you will come back to me," the *dampeal* said.

"You could come with me?" Jelani offered.

"I would stay here," she replied.

He shrugged. "Suit yourself."

"You will not be forced into servitude, *jaan*," she said.

That word, "my love", in the language of her mother, sent flitters of electricity through him. "That's what they tell me."

"You will make a fine Hunter," Saaya said. "A suitable protector for me."

Jelani snorted. "First, you don't need protecting. Second, I doubt there's any protecting I could do that's half of what stone-face brotha over there is capable of." He nodded toward Kafeel, who stood not far away. The statuesque *Ancestor* looked from him to Saaya, then at their joined hands, then back at Jelani.

"I think he wants me to let go of your hand," Jelani whispered.

"He will grow accustomed, in time," she said.

Jelani stole a quick glance at Kafeel. "Be sure to let him know that."

They stopped and Saaya turned to give him another slow

blink of those eyelashes. Jelani leaned forward and kissed her. Her lips were full and soft as always, and he wouldn't have minded if the kiss lasted forever. The baritone rumble of what sounded like Kafeel growling broke the moment, and Jelani pulled away.

"You will be tested," she said.

"Hopefully the test won't involve that ghoul, Denari," Jelani said. He felt cold just speaking the name. "I don't know what that thing was."

"There may come a day when you will learn, love," Saaya replied. "He still stalks the night in unlife."

Jelani didn't like the sound of that. "He's beyond me, Saaya."

"But you are strong and smart," she replied. "Pass their tests, become a Hunter and return to me. I will wait for you."

He smiled down at her. "You can't say it, can you?"

"Say what?" Saaya asked.

Jelani stared at her. "Just say it, woman. I'll even start it off." He clasped his hands together behind her lower back and pulled her close. In his peripheral vision, he saw Kafeel's sword hand twitch, then he turned and stalked away to wait at the edge of the roof.

Jelani waited till Kafeel was a discrete distance away, then leaned in and kissed her again, longer this time. "I love you, Saaya." He leaned back, waiting.

"I ... love the way you say those words to me," Saaya replied, turning away.

Jelani tightened his grip and pulled her back to him. "And?"

She let her head drop with a dramatic sigh, looking up at him through her eyelashes. She blinked at him again, her beautiful brown lips stretching into a shy smile. "I love you, Jelani." The words floated in the air, passed through his ears, caressing his mind, his skin, his heart.

Such power vibrated from the statement, and Jelani knew beyond any doubt that she meant it. Intensely. A part of her was in those words, which he now understood was why she had been so slow to speak them.

She searched his eyes, and he smiled down at her. "I love you," he said again, and he let as much of himself flow through the words as he could. He hadn't the power she did, not even a fraction of it, but he let it flow through their bond. A glimmer passed over her eyes, and her smile widened.

"I knew it," she said. "You're totally smitten."

Jelani laughed, but it was short-lived when his mind went to Daniel and Wen. Any happiness he found was colored by the loss of his friend's fiancée. Whatever he had felt in losing Alisha, surely Daniel felt the same.

Saaya released him, and moved toward her brother. Her beautiful raven hair in one long braid down the center of her back bent partially over her shoulder as she looked back and smiled at him. "Lycan society is not the same as that of vampires. He will be fine, *jaan*. As will you. Find me when you return."

"You could find me," Jelani said.

"That is not the way of a lady," Saaya replied. She stopped and stood in front of Kafeel, who turned toward Jelani. With a wink, she moved toward the edge of the roof and stepped off. Kafeel stared at Jelani for several more uncomfortable seconds. The man gave a barely perceptible nod, which Jelani returned.

The towering *Ancestor* turned and stepped off the roof.

Jelani walked to the other side of the building and looked down at the street below, watching passersby as they milled about, shopping, running errands, talking, laughing. He almost envied them their obliviousness; their naiveté.

He was about to turn away when he saw an extremely attractive Chinese woman walk around a corner and stop at an ice cream shop. She went to open the door, but a man came from inside and opened it for her. Wen smiled up at him and he stepped aside. After she moved past him, Daniel turned and looked back over his shoulder. He looked right up at Jelani and winked, that damned pretty boy Russell Wong dimple creasing his cheek.

Jelani laughed and jerked his head in an upward nod. His friend went inside to sit at a small round table, and share a cup of ice cream with the woman of his dreams.

Thus ends the Hunter's Moon Series. I extend my heartfelt thanks for reading, and if you enjoyed the book, please, tell a friend, and a review on amazon would be greatly appreciated.

RAMÓN TERRELL

Thus ends the Hunter's Moon Series. I extend my heartfelt thanks for reading. If you enjoyed the book and series, please tell a friend and leave a review. It helps more than you know.

Ramón Terrell

ALSO BY RAMÓN TERRELL

Legend of Takashaniel

Echoes of a Shattered Age

Legends of a Shattered Age

Heroes of a Broken Age (coming soon)

Saga of Ruination

Unleashed

Emergence (coming soon)

The Fairies

Out of Ordure

ABOUT THE AUTHOR

Ramón Terrell is an author and actor who instantly fell in love with fantasy the day he opened R. A. Salvatore's: The Crystal Shard. Years (and many devoured books) later he decided to put pen to paper for his first novel. After a bout with aching carpals, he decided to try the keyboard instead, and the words began to flow.

As an actor, he has appeared in hit television shows such as Supernatural, izombie, Arrow, and Minority Report, as well as the hit comedy web series Single and Dating in Vancouver. He also appears as one of Robin Hood's Merry Men in Once Upon a Time, as well as an Ark Guard on the hit TV show The 100. When not writing, or acting, he enjoys reading, video games, and hiking with his wife in Vancouver BC.

www.ingramcontent.com/pod-product-compliance
Lightning Source LLC
Chambersburg PA
CBHW020626020726
47494CB00001B/73